MATHEMATICS OF MURDER

MATHEMATICS OF MURDER

NORTHAMPTON'S DEADLY CALCULUS

PETER S. HALL

YOUCAXTON PUBLICATIONS
OXFORD & SHREWSBURY

ISBN 978-1-911175-56-8
Printed and bound in Great Britain.
Published by YouCaxton Publications 2017

YouCaxton Publications
enquiries@youcaxton.co.uk

Contents

The Crossley Family Tree

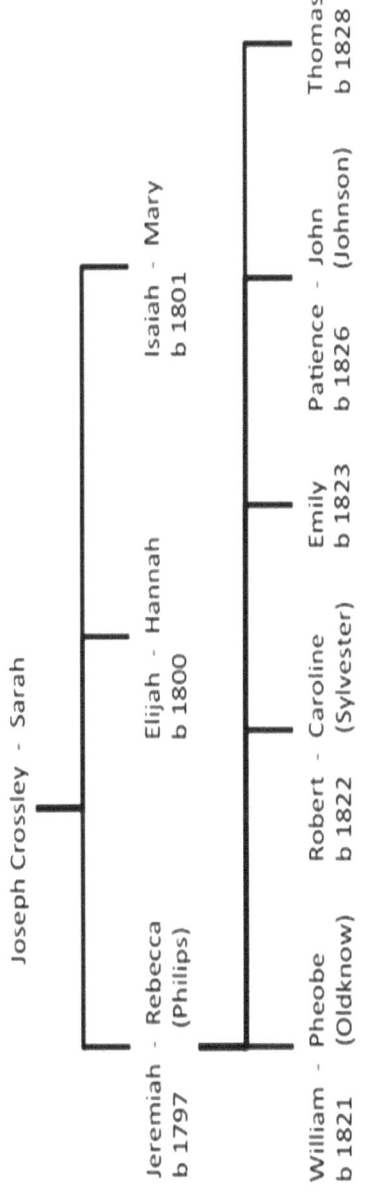

Joseph Crossley - Sarah

Jeremiah - Rebecca
b 1797   (Philips)

Elijah - Hannah
b 1800

Isaiah - Mary
b 1801

William - Pheobe
b 1821   (Oldknow)

Robert - Caroline
b 1822   (Sylvester)

Emily
b 1823

Patience - John
b 1826   (Johnson)

Thomas
b 1828

PART 1

NORTHAMPTON

CHAPTER 1

The Investigators

Despite banners that declare their independence, all newspapers pander to the perversions and prurience of their readers. The well-dressed gentleman, sitting in a First Class compartment of the 2:15 train from Bletchley, travelling the Rugby loop to Northampton, was thumbing the pages of the Morning Chronicle for an appropriate piece of nonsense to entertain the lady sitting opposite. He found something, and said: "Ah, here it is: The Ear at the Door. His column is turning what was a perfectly respectable Whig newspaper into a scandal sheet. Oh, it is about Tommy, poor old thing; I quote:"

'Sixteenth of March 1859. Late yesterday afternoon, Lord Clapper...'

"Ah, they call him Clapper because of his speed when leaving the homes of his mistresses. Everyone knows that the name refers to Lord Clapton."

'Late yesterday afternoon Lord Clapper was seen leaving the house of a prominent member of the Opposition. Upon being interviewed by the Ear, Bert Hansom, a cab driver stationed opposite, reported that he had seen the wife of the said member, waving farewell from a first floor window. A cab

driver, parked just behind Bert, contradicted him, saying that it was the gentleman's daughter waving from a second floor window. The mist of confusion was clarified by a third cabby, who clearly saw both the gentleman's wife and daughter waving from different windows.'

The lady's face showed disapproval, so the gentleman scanned the pages for a more appropriate story. "Here is something that might interest you."

'The Strange Case of the Doctor of Death
Judges recently presided over the strange case of a London doctor who had killed his patient. Dr James Bartholomew was accused of killing Mrs Violet Carter, a wealthy widow, by means of administering an overdose of the medicine that he was treating her with. The widow's son, who had some knowledge of medicines and appropriate doses, took his suspicions to the police. Upon being questioned, the doctor admitted the crime and added that he was responsible for the death of seven other patients. When he was asked what the motive for his crimes was, the doctor remained silent. A police detective who had investigated the affair said that nothing of value seemed to have been taken from the widow, although a notebook that the son recollected seeing his mother using could not subsequently be found. Bartholomew was found guilty and was hanged on the 27th'

Edward Pennington, the distinguished mathematician, put down the newspaper and gazed hopefully at Clara Cox. Clara was equally distinguished, She was a practising doctor and also one of the first women members of the

British Medical Association. The two were travelling to Northampton to gather information on Robert Crossley. Crossley was being considered for the award of a prestigious medal by the Royal Society, for a paper on infinitesimal calculus which had revolutionised several fields of scientific enquiry. However, quiet questions had been asked concerning Crossley's authorship of the paper. The search for evidence of plagiarism on his part formed Edward and Clara's secret agenda for the visit.

"Clara, What do you make of that?" asked Edward.

"It is a very sad case. Doctors depend on their reputation for compassion." Clara replied.

"Indeed, eight murders mark the doctor down as a very special case of the criminal class. What would you say it was that drives a person, of any profession, to that extreme?"

"It is hard to say," Clara said, shaking her head. "Disease of the mind is not one of my specialties"

Edward said, "I was surprised that the detective did not look for similar small thefts: notebooks, or papers perhaps, in the other alleged murders; he probably checked the family silver. It is extremely unusual for murder to be committed without a motive, and all the more so when multiple murders occur. Without a motive, it is usual for a doctor to be asked to examine the mental attitude of the accused."

"Edward, you seem to have a particular interest in crime." Clara responded.

Edward smiled. "Ah, I have a particular interest, as you call it, in many things." Edward enjoyed the pretense of mystery.

"We are going to Northampton to investigate a case of plagiarism. This is not a criminal matter, or the President would have called on the police," said Clara.

"You are right, Clara but, nevertheless, it can be a rather serious matter, which in this case it is. It is stealing another's work and publishing it as your own. In some cases the world is not changed by it, as in the case of the Bernoullis. The father stole some mathematics from his son and included it in his own book. Both father and son were respected for their other work and the world moved on. However, in the case we have to investigate, Robert Crossley built his whole career on the piece of work he is accused of stealing. If he is found guilty, it could destroy him."

"But it was the murder that brought Dr Bartholomew down, not the stealing of a notebook, even if the theft could have been proved," replied Clara.

"Of course, Clara, of course." Edward waved his hand. "But, I wonder? What was in the notebook that was so interesting to him? Perhaps the widow was a mathematician?" Edward burst into laughter and the lady smiled. He was glad that he had managed to bring levity into their rather tedious journey.

Edward was tall, but not unreasonably so. There were, amongst his friends, those who believed that his height must give him an advantage, but he never felt that himself. He stretched his legs. At the beginning of their journey, he had been uncertain about what would be a proper subject for conversation between him and Clara. There had been long periods of silence, when both of them had been reading. He considered sharing with her his mathematical preoccupation with the number *pi*, but was afraid of boring her. The case of Dr Bartholomew had resulted in a companionable conversation and he now felt satisfied.

The train slowed. "This looks like Northampton now," said Clara. Edward pulled out his watch, saying, "indeed and we are on time!" A few moments later, they were in the station. The gentleman stepped down from the compartment and offered his hand to the lady. A porter, seeing a potential tip, raced over to them, pushing a trolley. Edward was struck by the bustling view before him, for he had expected the town to be all smoke and dirt. The station building was a well-proportioned brick edifice with Dutch gables and tall chimneys. There was a crowd of well-dressed people outside in the road, which resulted in some delay before they found a cab. Ten minutes later they arrived at the calm of The George Hotel, opposite All Saint's Church.

"Look, Clara, our lodging has a view of the church, whose portico is pretending to look like St Paul's," said Edward.

They settled in to their rooms: Clara in the Queen Anne Suite and Edward in the Presidential Suite. They met again in the lounge to discuss business over tea. Clara suggested that it was time to get down to work. She had a sheaf of papers she had accumulated, including the reply from the family to the President's letter asking for information.

"As the President warned us emphatically not to reveal our real mission, we must tread carefully," began Clara. "Apparently, Robert's brother, William, is a partner in Crossley and Dyke, Clock & Watchmakers, in the Market Square. I will send a note round to the shop in a moment; there is a messenger at the hotel reception. I will propose a meeting tomorrow evening at William's home. But, before that, I think we should walk around the town tomorrow morning, and do some sightseeing. What do you say, Edward?"

Edward was staring out of the window in a rather distracted way. Rain clouds had gathered ominously. "I am not sure that I have brought the best clothes for walking."

Clara said, "Oh, it will be just a stroll to view the shop, the churches and the houses. I think it will help to see the places we might be discussing in the next few days. Of *course* you have appropriate clothes for walking."

Edward stared at his companion with an earnest sigh and nodded. She was a little older than he, but the travel had put a bloom into her cheek that he found attractive. He had first met her at an evening lecture at the Royal Society, on the arm of her husband, Percival Cox. He was struck, not only by her poise, but also by her mouth, which had a marked resemblance to his mother's, especially when she smiled. He became further attracted to her, when at another such meeting, this time with her husband conveniently on the other side of the room, he talked to her alone. Her wit and her remarkable *curriculum vitae* demonstrated to him that she was a woman of comparable energy and intelligence to his own. Of course, he knew that this deduction was based on his lack of modesty with women, just as his attraction to a woman with a similarity to his own mother was based on his own self-doubt. Clara was yet to discover these tendencies; Edward was aware of them, but chose to forget them.

She smiled indulgently at him. "Have you read Robert's paper yet?" she asked.

"Clara, I read it the day after we were briefed by the President. It is rather good, actually. I wish I had written it myself. It has helped to advance so many fields: magnetism, astronomy, hydraulics and so on. It is really quite an important piece of work."

"I tried to read it, but I have to admit that I could not get past the third page."

"Really, Clara, you must try harder."

"Now, Edward, do not treat me like a schoolgirl. I outrank you."

"How?"

"I am a member of the BMA."

"And that outranks the Mathematics Board of the Royal Society?"

"Of course. What is mathematics without medicine to cure those who over indulge in it?"

Edward was momentarily nonplussed and, luckily, the gong for dinner interrupted their game of nonsense. Clara swept past him towards the dining room. Edward shrugged his shoulders and followed her in.

The dinner disappointed them both, but the wine was passable and they were relatively content. Afterwards, as they were strolling to their rooms, Edward said, "Do not to expect me for breakfast, but I might join you for lunch and we can stroll afterwards. No protests, please. After all, I am the senior officer in this investigation."

§

The following day, after an early dinner, they took a cab from The George to the Crossley house. Clara had told Edward to wear a plain grey business suit, to put the Crossleys at their ease. She wore a similarly subdued dress and jacket, without her customary hat. The house was in an elegant terrace of three story brick and stone dwellings, located in a quiet road just off a busy thoroughfare leading from the Market Square. On the ground floor, the front door was flanked by a large window, which lit the drawing room. Above were two windows on each floor. Edward rang the bell. A well-built man, who looked a little older than Clara, opened it.

"William Crossley, I presume? I am Edward Pennington. This is Doctor Clara Cox."

"Of course," William bowed his head to Clara. "We have been expecting you. Please come in."

He led the two visitors into the drawing room. Edward found it small and rather cluttered. William introduced them to his wife.

"This is Phoebe."

"Ah, it is charming to meet you."

"Shall we sit down?" said William. "Louise will bring us some tea in due course."

When they were settled, Edward took the lead. "Perhaps I should begin by explaining why we are here. I know that the President has written to you about this, but I will explain again to discover whether you have any questions. The Royal Society periodically awards a medal to a person of extreme distinction. Your brother, Robert, is being considered. This award is taken very seriously by the Society and it is important for us to know as much as we can about the recipient. And, who knows, if Robert continues to impress, then someone might be asked to write a biography. Now, if a biography were to be agreed, I would be honoured to write it, or at least to contribute what I know of Robert and what I hope to learn whilst I am here in Northampton. We know much about Robert in his professional capacity, that is to say, his life after his lecture to the Royal Society and his degree at Cambridge. His life before that is as yet a blank page to us. I have a personal interest in the lives of great men and have found that in many cases, events in their childhood can throw a light on their subsequent achievements. Great men never work in a vacuum, but those close to them shape their actions in their early years. I am sure, William, that you have a deep understanding of your brother and, to some extent, you may have contributed to his great work. I could also say the same about the whole of his family."

Edward looked about him. He saw interest in William's eyes and awe in Phoebe's. "Of course, how events fit together is not always obvious at the outset, but I hope that we can begin to piece together the story of Robert's early life."

Clara was impressed by Edward's methods. She had wondered how he would open the family to reveal its secrets. And, as William and Phoebe would pass on Edward's message to the rest of the family, she now had every confidence that they would learn the truth.

William nodded. "We are both very flattered that Robert is being considered. We understand that his work has been well received by many people, although we are not sure what the work is about. I myself have some knowledge of mathematics, but I fear that his work is well beyond my understanding."

They all smiled and Clara replied. "I am a physician, Mr. Crossley, with a university degree, but the details are also beyond my grasp."

"Indeed," said Edward pleasantly. "But fortunately, understanding it is not needed for what the President has asked us to do. What we want is to get a sense of Robert as a person, to inform the decision to be made by the Awards Committee and help them frame their citation if the award is agreed upon. Would you try to describe him, William? Perhaps you might bring to mind any stories of growing up that might help us understand him."

William became serious. "Yes, yes, of course," he said. "I understood from Professor Hyde's letter that you would ask that question. I thought that I should give a short description of our early life and then we can give you any details after that."

"Excellent, please begin."

"Robert and I were brought up in this house. When we were old enough we went to the Grammar School. We both worked hard because ours was an ordered and disciplined house. Because of Robert's overwhelming curiosity he was sent to work in our Uncle's clock shop on Saturdays. Well, that and the incident of the clock, in which he opened our grandfather clock and stopped it through his ignorance, causing chaos in the house. I soon asked to go to the shop, when I found out from him how interesting it was. I ended up working there full time after I left school. When Robert finished, a year after me, father got him a job at the school, helping with the scientific demonstrations. Because father wanted him to go to university, as he himself had done, he tutored him. But under his care he did not progress in his studies. In despair, father and uncle found him another tutor. After several years with this new man, the mathematical miracle happened." William paused. "Robert and I grew up in a family in which discipline came before love."

Edward, Clara and even Phoebe stared at him in astonishment.

"That may surprise you, for our mother, Rebecca, loved us as a mother should. But Jeremiah, our father,..." William hesitated, as if holding back his emotions. "Well, our father's love was concealed beneath a rigid demeanour that placed obedience before all else. You should understand that Robert and I were close in our early years; Robert was born a year after me and we grew up experiencing the same things. Father expected us to follow him in our lives and he watched us closely to ensure that we did as he bid us. I broke away from him through a single act of defiance. It took Robert a long time to do the same."

William tilted his head back to exhale noisily and started his recollection.

"The first time that I began to understand this trait in my father, was when the two of us, Robert and I, had gone to the river to collect some coot's eggs. As usual, Robert won the race to the Cattle Market Road from home and ran on, across the cow meadow, past the oak and down to the willows that grew on the bank. He stepped carefully amongst the mud and clumps of grass and reached into the nest hidden from my view by the reed bed. 'Will, there are four' he said. 'I will take two, in case I damage one on the way home, and leave two, so the mother does not desert the nest.' I nodded my head in agreement. 'It is good that she is not here' he called. Robert picked up the eggs, and wrapped each carefully in the pieces of cloth that he had brought with him and placed them in his jacket pockets. We doubled back through the meadow and, after pushing through the hedge, ran across the road. There was a dray, pulled by an enormous shire horse, carrying beer barrels from the Albion Steam Brewery, and the name conjured up visions in my imagination. I had a fascination with all things mechanical and Robert and I had read about steam engines in our father's newspapers. At that time, the railways had not reached the town, and steam power was a novelty to many."

"I told him that I was going to invent a steam powered canal bridge. Robert laughed at this, for he had seen the dray as well. He said, 'I bet there won't be as much steam as comes out of Reverend Tate's mouth.' We ran on together. I was sorting out, in my head, the arrangement of pistons, valves and counterweights to enable the bridge to tilt at the touch of a lever. I had a strong imagination and it enabled me to weather the storms that the world threw at me. I could turn quickly from my difficulties, to my world of imagination, peopled not by imaginary friends and comrades, but by invention and the understanding of the things about me. To many this seemed a strange and lifeless occupation, but for me it had its own beauty and excitement. I would come across some natural phenomena, such as how an insect could walk on water, and ponder it for hours. For it was not just that the mere phenomena was wonderful to me, but the search for an explanation was, in my boyish thinking, a holy quest, and the answering gave me joy and meaning beyond compare."

William hesitated. Edward prompted him. "And Robert?"

"I know what Robert was thinking, because he told me afterwards. He had no such comfort as I had, even though his understanding of what our mother called modern things was as sharp as mine. Robert was remembering the Reverend's words from Church, the previous Sunday, with a mixture of horror and disbelief. Reverend Tate had preached the parable of sheep and goats. Was Robert to be a goat forever, he asked me? To be separated in the final judgment from me, his brother, the sheep. For, he knew that, when he blew the eggs, the chicks would die. When the Reverend spoke of sin, was he talking about killing chicks? How could the search for knowledge and truth not result in pain and suffering to some? Collecting was a natural thing for a man to do. Robert collected eggs because he loved their shape and colour, but more, because it was what the great scientists had done. Those, like Darwin, who had collected endless species in their search to understand how they were all related to each other. And had Robert not already discovered that the coot was a cousin of the moorhen, a fact that he was sure that not many of his classmates knew? I think that his ridiculing of the Reverend helped to dissipate his unease. He could utter such comments to me; but he knew that he must guard his speech with everyone else, especially father."

William hesitated again, for he had become heated in defence of his brother. Edward did not prompt him this time, but waited patiently. William continued. "After jogging up the streets, we came to our house. We ran along the path between the church and the back of the terrace, through our gate, up the long garden and in the back door. Mother and father were both in the kitchen, awaiting our return. Father had his pocket watch out as we entered.

'My word, wonders will never cease', he said. 'You are five minutes early. I trust you had an invigorating walk?' He looked us up and down. 'You need not tell me where you have been.' He had a sly smile on his face, which alerted us to an impending problem."

The recollection brought much emotion back to William. He sighed and shook his head.

"For father had seen mud on Robert's left boot, whilst the other one was perfectly clean, apart from the dust that might be gathered during any innocent walk. He said that the mud was of the sort that makes up the banks of the river. Mother looked at him with wonder and apprehension. Robert's eyes were cast down and his face was rigid."

"Father went on. 'Robert, I wonder what you have been doing on the banks of the river?' Then he said quietly. 'Would you please empty your pockets?' Robert walked reluctantly up to the kitchen table and emptied his pockets of their innocent belongings. A handkerchief and a piece of string lay on the table. Then, the cloth bundles were placed gently down; one fell open to reveal an egg. Robert dared not raise his eyes. 'Tell me what these are', father demanded. Robert replied, 'Coot's eggs, sir.'

'I see', father said. 'Robert, I do not believe that collecting eggs is good for a young boy. The eggs are nothing but God's bounty to the animal kingdom and are not intended for boys. Collecting such things will encourage mere ownership for its own sake; and that will form a root for envy and lust.'"

William looked into Edward's eye and said, "I offer no judgment on this, but merely recount it as it happened. The words that father spoke are burned into my mind as surely as they are in Robert's. Of course, I thought Robert was too young to understand our father, and he did not question him. He merely hung his head, for he knew that worse was to come."

"Father's overwhelming need was to reinforce his discipline. He simply said that he must administer two strokes upon Robert's palm. A heavy silence hung over the kitchen, until father returned with a twelve-inch ruler in his hand. Robert held out his open hand. The first blow stung and made him jump; the second stung and made him cry. Mother had turned away her head. I was silent, but felt the blows."

"Father's final words to Robert that evening were that he should thank his father for seeing this tendency in him and rooting it out before it became fixed in his mind. He directed Robert to leave the eggs where they were and go to his bedroom to begin his Bible reading for the day, to calm his mind and fill it with pure thoughts."

Phoebe took out a handkerchief from her sleeve. The visitors were silent.

"I joined Robert a few minutes later in our bedroom. He lay on his bed with his knees pulled up to his chest and his fists clenched. When the pain in his palm eased, and the anger in his heart subsided, he began to talk softly. He said that his father had never before suggested that collecting was wrong, but it was not this injustice that held his thoughts or drove his convoluted logic. Nor was it the wretched exhortation to thank him for the punishment, for he had heard that doctrine preached in the pulpit of the Gold Street Methodist Church many times. What fascinated him was that he had committed a sin, and this undoubted sin had not occurred to his father. The sin was that his collection involved the killing of the chick before it had had a chance to see the sun. His father had punished him for the collection, rather than the unnecessary killing. He concluded that this was just a mark of his father's slow wittedness. The thought came to him that his father's omission might just be his own good luck. Good luck for him, for the punishment could have been worse. But no, that was nonsense, he said. It was not luck. I could see that he was realising that our father was fallible, and if he was fallible, it must be possible to outwit him."

"I knew that these thoughts appeased his injured psyche. The following day, I went with him to the coot's nest and, to my surprise, he smashed the eggs that he had left for the mother. It was not until I saw the look on his face, that I knew that he had found a temporary peace within himself."

CHAPTER 2

The Adelaide Works

E dward and Clara stood in the Presidential Suite in The George Hotel, gazing from the window on the traffic passing by. Clara was musing on how she had come to be with Edward in this country town.

"Oh, Edward, I meant to ask you."

"What?"

"Did you say that the President asked specifically that I should accompany you on this investigation?"

She noticed a hesitation in Edward's reply. "I did, yes," he said

"Then you were lying, Edward, were you not?"

This was the second time that she had caught him out, trying to be chivalrous to her. She wondered whether his chivalry was a screen for the baser motives common to all men.

"Yes, you are right," replied Edward. "I admit that I asked him if you could come with me. He then asked me why I should not choose another mathematician. I replied that two mathematicians might not get along so well in the same railway compartment. However, a physician would not question my theorems."

Clara bore his humour, for she knew something intelligent might follow. She soon realised that she was mistaken. Edward continued unabashed.

"Although he did know you or, at least, he knew your husband, Sir Percival. I said that a medical person would be a first rate assistant, because there might be medical matters associated with our work."

Clara became tired of his obfuscation and wanted to be plain with him about his bigotry. But something held her back from reprimanding him, for she knew that she had some feelings of gratitude for being brought into the fold of the Royal Society on an investigation with this dashing young mathematician.

"I suppose he said," she replied with a hint of weariness, "that I might be useful at interviewing servants and tradesmen, whose evidence might be needed, due to my experience in running a large household."

"How did you know that?" asked Edmund.

"Because most men believe that it is the only thing that women are good for. The fact that I have a medical degree from the Sorbonne and am a member of the British Medical Association, one of the first women members, in fact, has nothing to do with the matter. Did you tell him this?"

"Well, no. No, I did not. Did you tell me?"

"Yes, when my husband introduced me to you at that Royal Society evening."

"Ah."

Clara decided that they had talked enough about such things. She turned away and sat in an armchair. Her papers were on a small table beside her. "Edward, let us discuss our mission. During our briefing, the President referred to accusations against Crossley from well respected members, accusations that include plagiarising the paper he presented at the Royal Society."

She now had Edward's attention. "Yes, he did," he replied. "He did not say what the other accusations might be."

"Yes, I was also struck by that omission. I felt like challenging him, but I held back because I thought he might be in a difficult position and would not want to disclose them. Plagiarism is a very serious misdemeanour in the scientific society. It is sufficient in itself to launch an enquiry."

"What would happen to Robert Crossley," she said, "if we found evidence that he had stolen the paper?"

"That depends on the President."

"Yes, I suppose so. I heard of a physician who had used imaginary findings in a paper in a medical journal. He was expelled from the BMA and was later discovered by the police to be practicing without a licence. He was sent to prison."

Edmund replied, "I do not think that this is as serious as that. Patients' lives are not at stake here, just the reputations of both Robert and the President. The work seems to be genuinely useful and is benefiting scientists throughout the country and on the continent, too. It might be corrected simply by printing an erratum in the journal."

"But Robert's reputation would be ruined."

"Yes, of course. However, the President might prefer that we do not find any evidence. He might be using us to silence those malicious voices whispering in his ear. The use of Commissions to investigate problems that one would rather forget is a time-honoured device in politics."

Clara was surprised by Edward's cynicism. "Edward, how are we to find evidence of this crime?" she asked.

"Well, first of all, by considering how it might have been committed and when. The President did not suggest who might have done the work that was stolen by Robert. However, we know when the President received the manuscript. Robert read it to the Royal Society in February of 1846. It would take a couple of months for the President to have it read by his experts, so Robert must have sent it late the previous year. The paper refers to the work of others done ten or so years before. Therefore we can assume that the work must have been done between 1835 and 1845. It is clear that we must establish what Robert was doing during this period."

"And who he stole it from," added Clara.

"Indeed. First of all, we must look for that person close to Robert. Crimes of passion are often committed by those close to the victim."

"Crimes of passion?"

"Yes, this case has some resemblance to that type of crime. It was done out of vanity, or a desire to advance at the expense of a family member. I mentioned Johann Bernoulli to you on the train: the man who stole some mathematics from his son. I would imagine that the father could not bear his son being cleverer than he was. So we must consider Robert's father or brothers as the original author of the work."

"Or his mother or sisters," Clara corrected him.

"That is true, but there is less precedence for that. If and when close family members are eliminated, we should investigate uncles or cousins. And aunts, of course."

Clara had grasped the method. "Then," she said, "When these are eliminated we could assume that the work might have been done by another, unrelated to Robert. A teacher, or someone in Northampton who Robert might have come across in his everyday occupation."

"Yes, and then further afield. Because, who could imagine that Northampton contained two people who understood infinitesimal calculus? There are hardly any in England who do. Then, of course, the author might have lived on the continent. Remember that Newton, who laid the foundations for the subject in England, had his rival, Leibnitz, in Germany."

"But how could Robert have established contact with a person outside his family?" replied Clara.

"We might never know. Even if we found such a person, but then could not explain how the connection happened, the President would have strong grounds to suppress the whole matter. He needs to look to his own position in this matter, as well as the reputation of the Society."

"It will be an awkward investigation," said Clara. "We will have to appear to be gathering background information for the award of a medal. Our real motives must be well covered."

Edward laughed. "We will have to listen to many a long story about domestic matters, no doubt."

"Which is exactly why you invited me, was it not, Edward?"

He tried not to react. "Would you like me to tell you what I have discovered so far about Robert?"

Clara nodded.

"I have obtained a list of the attendees at Robert's lecture to the Royal Society." Edward handed Clara a page.

"There are two different hands here?" she said.

"Ah, yes. The names are in the hand of the person I obtained the list from. The comments beside each are in my own hand."

Clara began to study the styles, for she had an interest in the interpretation of handwriting. The names were written in a cramped but legible style, whilst the comments were in broad strokes with flourishes that often rendered them illegible. "The source was an assistant in the President's office. I assume," she said whilst reading.

"Naturally," replied Edward.

"Three of the names have War Ministry Committee beside them. What is that?"

"It is a committee tasked to bring the findings of modern science to the assistance of our soldiers. Robert is now a member."

"Is that so?"

"Knowledge of the existence of the committee is secret. Please do not divulge what I have just told you."

"Of course not." Clara felt simultaneous emotions of pride that she was now privy to secrets and horror at the thought of science being used to kill. She returned to the document. "Other names have words, which I assume describe the sort of mathematics that they were doing?"

Edward nodded.

"What does this mean? 'Feeling – chase'"

"That means that I have a feeling that that person might be significant, and that I should get more information about any possible links to our investigation."

Clara continued to read. "Ah, Mister Steyn was there; he was the mysterious man who was at the President's shoulder when he briefed us about this mission."

"That man puzzles me still. I have seen him before, but I cannot remember where."

Clara handed the sheet back. Edward picked up another sheet. "Robert is living in Bedford Square in London," he said, "in a house that is owned by an Arab gentleman who is married to the cousin of James Joseph Sylvester, a mathematician well known for his work in the field of optics."

"How very curious?"

"No, optics is a well respected field."

"No, I meant it was curious for Robert to be living at the home of an Arab married to an English woman."

"Ah, yes. It does bear some more investigation." Edward glanced at the paper and began reading again. "Robert has an office on Howland Street, which he attends three times a week on average. When he is not there he is usually visiting other businessmen." Edward looked up from his reading. "It is not always possible to know who he visits. When he enters a building, one cannot know what he is doing inside. Sometimes the concierge might know, but sometimes not. Once a week, he is visited by a detective."

"How do you know all this?"

"I have a man. I call him my bloodhound. He is experienced at sniffing information out."

Clara took this in her stride. "Does your bloodhound know Robert's bloodhound?"

"Of course. The bloodhounds of London are a small and intimate community."

"Can you not ask Robert's bloodhound where he goes?"

"Oh, no. It is an unwritten rule that information stays between the client and the hound, unless lives depend on it."

"Oh."

"I went with my hound one day, to learn his methods. Sometimes, he said, he poses as a cabbie."

Clara's mind went back to Bert Hansom and The Ear at the Door.

"You see, it is easy to sit outside someone's house. It looks like you have been summoned by the butler, and are waiting for the fare to come out. Additionally, if you are behind a cab at a suspect's home, when he drives off, you can follow him without attracting notice. I was very impressed by my man's expertise."

"And I am impressed by the breadth of your acquaintances."

"There is more. I also have a bloodhound here in Northampton, one Henry Grieves. He is an unpaid archivist to Northampton Town Council. I found him through Robert Vernon Smith, who was the Member of Parliament for Northampton. Vernon Smith was recently elevated, as the first Baron Lyvedon, to the Upper House, which is where I met him. Henry has been finding me pieces from the newspapers of the time. Apparently, Robert's father was an usher at the Grammar school and had a particular skill in mathematics. We should therefore visit Henry and the Master, as well as going back to William; I have the Master's address here. William and Robert both attended the school."

"Do you know anything else about Robert?"

"Yes. I told you he sits on the Ministry Committee. I have a list of the members and agendas for some of the meetings that Robert attended." Edward handed her some papers. "I got them from an assistant to Mister Henry Boyd, who is the Secretary to the committee. It cost me a considerable sum of money. However, the assistant, whose wife had just given birth to twins, is now finding it easier to make ends meet.

We will have to make do with the agendas, as the minutes are much harder to get. Minutes are highly confidential because they bear on our military capability. There are intriguing items on the agendas, related to arithmometers or mechanical calculating machines. The Artillery Regiment is considering them to improve the accuracy of their big guns. Although, I must say, that it all sounds a bit too technical for the sort of soldiers that I know; cutlasses are their preferred weapons."

Edward lay back in his armchair with a satisfied look on his face. Clara was impressed. "My dear, you have been busy."

Suddenly a cloud obscured his sunny moment. He leaned forward and said, "There is something else."

"What is it?"

"There is something dark under all of this. I was out with my bloodhound, one evening, following Robert. We were parked in Bedford Square, near Robert's house. He came out and took a cab to the Ministry building just up from the Embankment. We followed at a respectable distance. He went in and came out about half an hour later. Rather than get a cab, he looked around and then set off on foot towards the river. There are some steps down to the road that runs along towards St Paul's. I decided to try some hounding, so, telling my man to stay put, I took off after Robert. A moment later, I was at the top of the stairs. Suddenly I heard voices and a scuffle. Looking over the balustrade I could see Robert and a man dressed in working clothes, pushing each other. The man had a flat cap pulled down over his face, so from above I could not see his face. The man stood back and pulled a knife. The blade glinted in the moonlight. He spoke clearly to make sure Robert heard and then lunged at him. Robert reacted well and parried the thrust with his arm. The man steadied himself to make another lunge at him, when a whistle blew. I could see a policeman running from the other side of the road. The man darted up the stairs. He turned the corner at the top and my presence surprised him. For a moment, we look into each other's eyes and then he ran off. I went down to Robert, who was nursing a small wound to his arm. The policeman was demanding to know what had happened, but Robert declined to be helped by anyone, neither me, nor the policeman. Robert went back up the stairs to get a cab outside the Ministry and I walked off down the Embankment, meaning to double back, after a suitable time, to my bloodhound in his cab. The amusing thing was when I got back to the Ministry my bloodhound was nowhere to be seen. It seems that Robert had used him to get back to Bedford Square. I had to walk."

"How extraordinary. So Robert has been engaged in affairs that have driven ordinary people to want to kill him."

"Indeed," replied Edward.

"Did you hear what the man said when he tried to stab Robert."

"He said 'this is for all them at Adelaide Works who got thrown off 'cause o' you.'"

"Do you know what that meant?"

"My bloodhound found five factories bearing the name *Adelaide Works*, all of which have had workers thrown off in the last few years. It might be a coincidence, but Arthur Blackham, who is a member of the Ministry Committee, owns one of them."

§

Henry Grieves, Edward's bloodhound, peered over his spectacles.

"Hmm..." he said. "I expected someone older. Nevertheless, it is good to meet the man that I have been serving in this small way for the last two months."

"Henry, let me introduce Doctor Clara Cox."

The old man had jumped up from his chair with an energy that belied his sixty-odd years. He took Clara's hand and, to her surprise, kissed it. "My dear doctor, you must be the assistant that Edward has referred to in several of his letters. However, I would expect, that due to his youth, you are more like an equal partner."

Clara laughed at this disarming speech. "How very perceptive of you, Mister Grieves. We have had a discussion about leadership and I believe that I came out on top."

"I am sure that you did. And please call me Henry, now that we have done with the formalities. Clara, it is rather unusual to find a lady doctor. I know of none in this town. But I can see that you are a rather unusual woman. Both in looks and intellect."

Edward intervened before the archivist could woo his assistant further. He looked around. Henry's room was small and its shelves were half empty. "Is this where the town archives are kept?" he asked.

"Goodness me, Edward. From your letters, I expected a more perceptive eye. This is my little office, where I do my fishing. You see, Clara, I retrieve a bundle of documents from the vaults and bring them here, where the light is better for reading. Then, if I am lucky, I will hook something and reel it in."

"And are you also responsible for ordering the archives,

Henry," replied Clara. "That is something of a challenge, is it not?"

"An excellent question, my dear," replied Henry. "I have a dual system. First of all, I classify the documents by year. Then I match their content to a codified list that I have created. See, on the wall. A is for Agriculture; B is for Boots and Shoes; and so on. Of course, I could just order them alphabetically by any word that might come into my head at the moment..."

"But that would mean you would have to thumb through all the documents of that year until you found what you wanted."

Henry clapped his hand. "Your have understood already! Now what I propose to do, my dear, is to give you a guided tour of the vaults." He opened the door and before Edward knew what was happening, Henry was leading Clara down the stairs by the hand, as if she was a small child. Clara did not seem to mind, as she was conversing animatedly with the old man on the age of the Town Hall. In the vestibule, he lit an oil lamp, opened a narrow door and disappeared. Clara and Edward followed down some steep steps to a corridor with several openings. Henry turned into one and stood in front of a wall of dusty wooden shelves. He put the lamp on a table behind them.

"Here are the records for 1830," he said. He pulled a thick book down, placed it on the table beside the lamp and opened it. "You can see the expenditure of the Council on the celebrations after the Coronation of King William IV."

Edward and Clara peered at the book. "This is fascinating, Henry. My word, that is a lot of small beer," said Clara, pointing at an entry. "And how many bottles of spirit is that?" She pointed again and when Henry told her, she gasped. "They must have been drunk for a week."

"Oh, longer, I would estimate. Correlating the number of bottles with the population of active men at that time..."

"Henry, that is most interesting," interrupted Edward, "and I thank you for all your help in our investigation."

"That is kind of you to say so. But what you have paid me is far more than the Council pay me, and I am most grateful. In fact, anything would be more than they pay. But, I get by."

"Can we move on?" Edward had become impatient. "Do you have anything for us?"

He pulled another volume for the same year, laid it on the table and opened it at the page indicated by a slip of paper protruding from the top.

"This is the record of the Council meetings," he said. "Late in September of 1830, there is an item concerning derogatory statements about the town made by a Professor at a meeting of mathematicians in Cambridge. The President of the Royal Society, Davies Gilbert, made the following remark. *All mathematicians should freely open their work for inspection by others. It is necessary for the true functioning of our noble Society. However, there remain some, such as the mathematician from Northampton, who will reveal nothing for fear of criticism.* The rest of the Council discussion related to whether this mathematician should be found and forced to open his work or whether the Council should publish a rebuttal of Gilbert's argument in a London newspaper."

Henry turned over several pages, until he found another slip of paper. "There is an entry in the report of the next meeting, regarding the cost of an entry in the London newspaper. Obviously the indignation that the comment had generated in the good councillors of the town had died down and there are no further references to the matter. Does that interest you, Edward?"

"It does indeed. For it tells us that there was another mathematician in Northampton at the time who could have done this work."

"Well, ten years before," added Clara. "Of course, that person could have died before the period we are interested in. It may thus be coincidental."

"She has a point, Edward," said Henry, bowing his head at Clara. "She has a point."

Edward's brow furrowed and he said, "I think we are finished here. Clara, shall we go?"

CHAPTER 3

The Grammar School

Rain was threatening. Edward and Clara were on their way to the home of Samuel Nettleby, the Master of the Grammar School, but had left their intended route to see the school itself. The streets were alive with traffic, both human and animal. The pavements were crowded and the two had to frequently give way. Straying onto the road way was ill advised as the variety of horse drawn carriages and carts meant that one might step in the manure and worse be trampled by a horse. They made their way to the end of Gold Street and crossed the junction. The school stood on the corner opposite. It was a dour brick building devoid of the ornament that decorated other privately owned schools and academies. The door of the school was open and Clara led Edward inside. They stood in a vestibule adjacent to the Master's study and a wide staircase. Clara looked about and then pointed to a board, fixed high on the wall, listing the donor's names in gold paint. The first name was Thomas Chipsey, who endowed the school in the fifteenth century.

"I see that many an aspiring town statesman has been proud to see his name below that of the founder," said Clara. Edward smiled as she continued, "I doubt whether either of us attended such a school. It might be hard to imagine how these children felt, thrown into education with little behind them but the aspirations of their working class parents. The donors gave money, but the library would be sparse and the classrooms bare and uninspiring. And the children would be taught their Latin and Greek by rote, with little knowledge of where the classics might get them."

"Be careful not to say that when we meet him." Edward guided her out. A drizzle had started and the overcast skies reflected Clara's mood. What they had heard from Robert's family had dampened her spirit, and the little joy that Henry Grieves had given her had been but temporary.

§

In ten minutes or so, they found the Nettleby's dingy cottage. The front room was dark and the odour of the invalid hung in the air. The beams were stained with the pipe smoke of a lifetime and Clara noticed that the windows had not been washed for some time. A grey haired woman bid them sit on a settle by the parlour fire. Samuel Nettleby, or what was left of him, sat in a wicker chair on the other side, with a blanket over his legs and one around his shoulders. As their eyes became accustomed to the gloom, they saw that the man's eyes were watching them intently. But it was the woman who spoke first.

"If you've come to talk to him about the past, you'll get nothing out of father that makes any sense." The woman cast a careless glance at the old man in the chair. "Particularly, if you want to rake over old troubles."

"Ha." The body in the chair uttered its first word.

Clara pitied him. She could not believe that such a venerable character was reduced to the state that she saw before her.

"I am Doctor Cox and this is Mister Pennington. I wrote to your father some little time ago. I understand that he was the Master of the Northampton Town and County Grammar School. We are here seeking knowledge of Robert Crossley."

"That's as may be," the daughter replied grudgingly. "He was Master for over forty years. And what did the town give him? Nothing but this leaky old hovel."

"No, you are wrong, Lily!" Samuel's high-pitched cry made Clara start. "The Corporation had given the site of St Gregory's Church for the school to be built on. We lived in the school house." Samuel's voice had an urgency about it, but in his eagerness, he strained and coughed, as he fought to catch his breath.

"I meant this house, not that house," said Lily, shaking her head. "Although that one wasn't much better."

Samuel's memory was clear, as was the antagonism between father and daughter. The woman carried the remains of their breakfast from the room. The old man relaxed.

"Master," said Edward, "Was Jeremiah Crossley a pupil at the school?"

"Jeremiah Crossley?" Samuel thought for a moment. "No, he had a tutor. I first met him in 1817. He had just got his degree from Cambridge. Upon his return we interviewed him and offered him a post as an Usher." He smiled benignly at the memory. "He was nervous on his first day. He was a lot like I was at his age: learned, conscientious, keen to do things properly. Before we got down to business, I took him for a walk around the school. Walking and talking is much better for getting people to say things that they would not say in other circumstances, do you not think?" The old man winked at Clara, who did not react.

Edward reacted. "And what did he tell you?"

"Nothing. He was tongue tied."

"So what did you talk about?"

"I asked him to recite his family history, despite the fact that I knew it from his interview before the Board of Trustees. Jeremiah was the eldest of the three children of Joseph and Sarah Crossley, and the three were brought up on the family farm, 200 hundred acres of prime land, leased from Lord Wilbraham."

"Ah, he was a gentle country lad," said Edward.

"Gentle?" replied Samuel. Clara wondered if his tone revealed, for a moment, his real feelings about Jeremiah? His geniality quickly reasserted itself. "He was an important member of the staff, for he was in charge of the upper forms. He was molding the minds of the pupils just before they left us to become useful members of society. Many of our old boys have achieved great things in the town and beyond. Why, I remember..."

Edward cut short his reminiscences. "Did Jeremiah enjoy the task of teaching?"

"He was a good teacher. He knew the classics well and natural sciences..."

"Did he enjoy it?"

Samuel's face hardened. "Ha! Jeremiah was never content in the job. He was continually asking me to change the way things were done. When I met his father, Joseph, some time later, I asked him what sort of child he had been. His reply did not surprise me. His father had always expected his children to take their fair share of work around the farm, but Jeremiah showed early on that he had a preference for the dogmatic direction of the labourers, rather than the labour itself. Joseph recognized this divisive behaviour, before rule by a six year old had poisoned the amicable spirit of his farm. He knew that he had to keep Jeremiah away from the barns and the fields. Jeremiah's father was a knowledgeable farmer, the land was well drained, and his sheep and barley earned him enough to employ a daily tutor for Jeremiah. The farm prospered and so did Jeremiah. He won a scholarship for Cambridge when he was fifteen."

"He was a bright boy, then."

"Yes, indeed. Jeremiah's excellence in Euclid and Newtonian mechanics, and his emphasis on discipline so impressed the School Appointments Board that they recommended that he be given the title of Head of Mathematics."

"Excellent. Might I ask whether you yourself have a mathematical disposition? Do you solve algebraic equations to get yourself to sleep?" Edward smiled at his wit, but Samuel was unmoved.

"My expertise lies in the classics, sir. That was the reason that we employed Jeremiah."

"Of course. And when he was appointed did he have an office? Was a place provided where he could prepare his lessons quietly and in private?"

Samuel eyed Edward suspiciously. "Yes, I found him a small room in the school buildings."

"And would he have had enough time to study other things. For instance, would he have worked on any mathematical theorems?"

"Whether he was doing mathematics or plotting my downfall, I cannot tell. It was his son that has done the mathematics."

"Yes, of course." Edward smiled benignly. "I ask because I am a mathematician myself and so I take an interest in who has done what. Are there others in the town famous for their mathematics?"

"I know of none."

There was a silence. Clara then took over. "Can you tell us anything about Jeremiah's home life and his family?"

Samuel resigned himself to continue. "Three years after taking up his position at the School, he met Rebecca," he said. "She was the second daughter of Arthur Philips, the largest brewer in the town. Her ordinary looks and timid character meant that Philips, ever the hardheaded businessman, was concerned that she would grow old as a spinster and consequently be a drain on his resources. He searched high and low for a prospect and even offered a fine family house, close to St Giles Church, as part of the dowry. Rebecca was impressed by Jeremiah's serious nature and his learnedness. She must have felt, deep down, that to be associated with a man of learning would elevate her to a position that she could never attain using her own modest powers. I assume that Jeremiah was attracted to her quietness and the attention that she gave him."

"And they married?" Clara asked.

"Yes. These dubious attractions brought them together and they married in All Saints, in the centre of town, with all the pomp that went with the town brewer, moderated by his cautiousness with money and the couple's serious demeanor. Jeremiah and Rebecca moved into the house, which had been the abode of Philips's spinster aunt. They hired a maid who lived in the attic and set up the well-ordered household that William and Robert, Emily, Patience and Thomas grew up in. Jeremiah and Rebecca had planned a large family; it would have been larger but for two girls, between Emily and Patience, who died in their early months."

"How awful for them."

Samuel nodded, but there was little sympathy in his voice. "After the birth of Thomas, who was born a cripple, Jeremiah must have taken pity on Rebecca and slept apart from her."

Clara was disturbed by the hint of coarseness. An unpleasant silence hung in the air, mixing with the smoke from the unswept chimney.

Edward affected ignorance and said. "I understand that Jeremiah and his wife attended All Saint's Church."

"Yes, until they all moved to Gold Street Church."

"How did that come about?" asked Edward.

Samuel seemed eager to relate this story. "I sensed that Jeremiah had become a little disappointed with All Saints and its conservative ways."

"That was perceptive of you, Samuel."

"Indeed. Jeremiah was also surprised at my understanding of him. I suggested that he investigate Methodist theology. I knew something of it, as one of my many cousins was a Minister, down near Salisbury. We had talked. I had much sympathy for what they were doing amongst the working classes. I also understood that the chapel in Gold Street had recently sent a petition to the House of Lords calling for the abolition of slavery throughout the British Dominions. It occurred to me that Jeremiah's sympathies might also lie in that direction."

"How did Jeremiah react?"

"I talked to Jeremiah again about it, a couple of weeks later. The germ had grown. He told me that he had read as many books as the School Library contained on Methodism and the lives of the Wesleys and George Whitefield. He could not contain his admiration for the clarity of their Gospel and the call for holiness, both on the inside and in a man's behaviour. Methodism, he told me, also had a heart for the working class. There was zeal in his voice that I had heard before in others and detested, because it put emotion above reason. It was clear to Jeremiah that he should change his religious affiliation."

"Samuel," said Edward, "your actions were those of a most understanding and solicitous Master. I am certain that he was very grateful for your advice."

"I like to think so, sir." There was a momentary hesitation in his voice. "But he had deeper motives than theological belief and where he should take his family on a Sunday morning. He combined his joining of the Methodist Movement with an appeal to them on another matter, that appeared to be rather dear to his heart."

Clara noticed that Edward was nodding his head, as if he knew what was to come.

"He told me," continued Samuel, "that his idea for a Society for Scientific Experiment and Mathematics had come about through newspaper articles of the efforts that were being made around the country to educate people in science and mathematics. In some of the bigger towns and cities, energetic proponents were forming Societies to demonstrate scientific experiments and thus show the value to mankind of progress in the natural sciences and engineering. And it was clear that where this form of outreach to the people was backed by Christian charity, it was being shown more by the non-conformist than the established churches."

"Yes, that is true," agreed Edward.

"He had written to the Methodist District Supervisor. The Supervisor had thence written immediately to me for a reference to Jeremiah's good name and intentions. I, of course, supported him."

§

In the moment of silence that followed, Clara asked, "Master, did you observe Jeremiah in his lessons?"

Samuel turned to her with narrowed eyes. "Yes, of course I did. Like all of us, Jeremiah began his teaching career with diligence and settled into the daily battle with the stubbornness and ignorance of his pupils." Then he smiled at the memory. "He had a sharp nose, thin lips and a pallid skin, and his hawk-like face became forever the embodiment of learning and pain for his pupils. There was normally a sharp questioning look in his eye, so that when he frowned, the boys doubly feared him." Samuel leaned back as the memory brought a laugh from him.

Edward adopted an innocent tone, as he asked, "Did he discipline his pupils?"

Samuel abruptly became serious. "Of course. He exercised unbending discipline in his classes. Time was kept and all was in order; when this was tested by a pupil's disobedience, he was not slow to apply the ruler to the palm."

"And did you approve?"

"Of course, discipline is a necessary element of good teaching, so I approved of his methods at first. But I came to see that he applied discipline without any compassion for the boys."

"Was there ever any case of pederasty?"

"How dare you suggest such a thing!"

"It is my duty to suggest it. Teachers have been known to abuse their pupils, just as fathers abuse their children."

"No there was never a possibility. His punishments were applied in the class or with me present, in the more extreme cases."

"Very well. Did you respect Jeremiah, as a colleague?"

Samuel hesitated and then the admission burst forth. "He wanted to introduce some elementary arithmetic into the syllabus of the First Form. At that time, we taught mathematics only in the top classes. I had to say no. I could see that Jeremiah was growing exasperated with me. He told me that he was disappointed to discover that the post of Head of Mathematics meant nothing."

"What did he do?"

"Whilst I accept disagreement as part of my job as Master, I could not approve of what he did then. He requested a meeting with the Board of Trustees to express his concerns. Of course, Jeremiah, not being well versed in the political arts, was far too bold in his condemnation of my behaviour and this had the effect of losing any sympathy that the Board might have had towards him. His mention of Bentham was met with silence." Samuel laughed, as if both he and his visitors would know that the notion was preposterous.

"Ah. Not Jeremy Bentham's chrestomathic scheme?" asked Edward.

"Yes, yes, of course."

"Why, I remember meeting Bentham last year, when I was preparing a question to ask in the House."

Samuel's eye narrowed at mention of the House, but he said nothing.

"I am not surprised that its mention silenced them. Bentham is an enterprising and energetic proponent of progressive education. And his scheme is based on the philosophy of Aristotle. I am sure the Board had no answer to the scheme."

Clara recognized that Edward was goading the Master. Samuel reacted as Edward had intended. "Sir! Bentham's theories are nonsense. The Board knew that Jeremiah had gone too far."

"The scheme presumes that art and science are intertwined and thus should both be taught, side by side."

"The presumption is false! The arts represented by the classics are the pinnacle of learning and should be taught first to show a boy what is noble and good."

"Even if the boy will then go to work in a steam brewery or enter a factory building locomotives for the railway? Jeremiah knew the future better than the Board did."

"Fie on you, sir! Jeremiah Crossley had no compassion for his pupils and very little humanity. He complained continually and went over my head to the Board. I despised him, as a teacher, as a colleague and as a man."

Samuel sighed heavily after his defeat in hiding his feelings about Jeremiah and began to stare at the fire, lost in his recollections.

"Thank you, Master," said Edward pleasantly. "You have been most helpful. It is time for us to go."

Before the invalid could call for his daughter to show them out, Edward strode over to the door and said, "We can find our own way out. Good day, sir."

§

Edward followed Clara out of the small parlour and when they were in the hall, he steered her down the corridor, towards the back of the cottage. They found Lily sitting in a tiny kitchen. She leapt up and glared at them. Edward was unperturbed.

"You do sterling work for your father. Yet, I fear that he does not give you the appreciation that you deserve."

Lily's face softened. "That's very true, sir."

She was dressed in a skirt and jacket that had seen better days. She snatched off her pinny, filthy from the smoke of the fire and from splashes from the broth bubbling on the range. She pointed to the table and they sat down.

"Your father has been telling us about Jeremiah," continued Edward.

"Jeremiah!" The sarcasm in her voice was withering. "He thought he was better than father. But I knew that he was still just an Usher, whilst father was the Master. Little good it did us, living in the slum of a schoolhouse. Crossley had that big house, obtained by the exploitation of the poor alcoholics of the town by his wife's father. Jeremiah was living a lie. He had no care for the poor and unfortunate. The Society for Science that he set up was not about improving the people, it was about increasing his own importance." Lily was almost shouting. "I had to live there and see him every day. He treated me as if I was a servant, ordered me about, get this, get that. He whipped the boys, but he wasn't going to whip me. No, I stood up to him. But it just provoked him the more and he took it out on the boys. As Diogenes the cynic said, 'Why not whip the teacher when the pupil misbehaves?' My father was too lenient on him, the old fool. Crossley could have done with a whipping himself."

Edward slapped the table and a laugh exploded from him. "Lily, you have put it perfectly. Your father took an hour to say what you have said in a sentence; and put into the words of a philosopher. Did your father teach you the classics?"

"Ha! No. I learned when I could. I picked up father's books or the pupil's exercises when father had gone to bed. He was too much in love with his school to remember to educate me. My mother died in giving birth to me; father managed to engage a housekeeper with a small allowance that the School Board gave him. I hated the woman. She tried to snare father into marriage and, when he rejected her, she walked out on us. I convinced father that I could take over her duties."

Clara remembered the President's hypocrisy about her interviewing servants and quickly directed the woman to tell them what they really wanted to know. "What can you tell us about Robert?"

Lily shrugged her shoulders, as if what she would say was of no value. "I watched the boys. I listened to them and I talked to them. For much of the time, I would be invisible to them, like a slave. But when I wanted to know more, I would smile at them and win their confidence and sometimes their adoration. William was upright, attractive, but of little interest to me. Robert was quieter and I saw deviousness in his eyes, which seemed to have developed out of fear; he intrigued me."

"You saw more of them than the other boys?"

"Yes, I watched them. Due to their father's position at the School, they got free places, even though the Crossley's were richer than some of the fee paying boys' families"

"They were well educated, then?"

"Jeremiah had little control of the standard of their education in their early days, for father had assigned him exclusively to the top forms. But Jeremiah knew they would get a reasonable grounding in the Classics at the School. He wanted more, though. He recognized the bright look in his sons' eyes and, like his own father, arranged for a tutor, one of his recent Grammar School graduates, to coach them in mathematics every weekday evening. Their time was full. School occupied them from Monday to Saturday, excepting Wednesday and Saturday afternoons, and Sunday morning was Church and afternoon was Bible study at home. William told me that his father had worked hard as a boy and won a place at Cambridge. He believed that there was no reason why the boys should not do likewise." Lily paused and anger suffused her face. "He never questioned that the girls and the cripple, Thomas, would have to find another way through life."

After a pause, Clara asked, "So they were successful in their studies?"

"Despite the stern atmosphere between the boys and their father, it was clear that William and Robert had an aptitude for mathematics. On another occasion, William told me that arithmetic had come to them almost without instruction. Algebra was a delight, once they had been told the fundamental rules of manipulation of equations and they treated geometry as a pastime, each devising problems for the other to solve. Robert was less poetic. He said that their father would look over their work and thank the tutor, but would not congratulate them. He scowled as he told me that Jeremiah had said that it was expected of them, so congratulations were unnecessary."

To Clara, this last report seemed to be perfectly in character with what they had heard at the Crossley's house the previous evening. Lily continued.

"But the Classics were a problem for Robert and where there is a problem there is a profit. After it happened, I came to realize that Robert was a quiet boy, not out of nature, but because of the severe discipline that his father exercised at home. He had learned that speaking often led to disapproval or worse still to punishment. He used words out of necessity rather than out of pleasure. And access to the Classics was through words and, what was worse for him, through Latin and Greek words. Although, I am sure that being a vigorous young boy, he would have been pleased to consider the excitement of Homer's Odyssey or Virgil's Aeneid. But, the barrier of languages was too much for him. A worried look was perpetually on his face. I approached him, for I knew how many of his predecessors had overcome the same difficulty. There was a currency of cheating abroad in the school, which relied on the passing of exercise books from one pupil to another."

Lily hesitated.

"Please go on," said Edward.

"It was a long time ago. Robert is a famous man now and I do not want to embarrass him."

"Oh, you can rely on the discretion of myself and Doctor Cox." Edward paused, watching Samuel's daughter closely. "And the President of the Royal Society would be very grateful for the information."

She was not so sure. "Robert got a book off of Ben Edge."

It was clear that she would say no more. "Lily, I must congratulate you, for that was an excellent piece of detective work. How did you ever persuade Robert to tell you that?"

The woman laughed nervously, but then to Edward's surprise, she opened up one last time. "Ah, you're a man of the world, aren't you? Of course, I suggested to him that his father would be interested to know what had happened. He was so frightened that he agreed immediately to tell me how he had got it. I wouldn't have taken his money either, but he did offer it. What else could I do?"

Edward mused that proud learning and low cunning are but different doors on the same corridor. He suddenly felt the need for fresh air.

"I completely understand," he said. "No more need to be said. We will let ourselves out."

CHAPTER 4

The Society for Scientific Experiment and Mathematics

The first light woke Phoebe. She lay half on William and let her mind drift. She remembered the moon and the night, and the pleasure that they had exchanged during it. And she thought of their two sons, now asserting themselves in the nursery upstairs. Would their next child be a boy or a girl? She longed for a girl, but suddenly realised that was what William's parents had had, and an unknown doubt came over her.

She moved her hand from William's chest. He stirred, but his waking was troubled. He cried in his sleep and his body shook. He opened his eyes.

"What is it, my love?"

"It is a dream," whispered William. "Nothing but a dream."

"Do you want to tell me?"

"Faces from the past. My father and Robert were standing over me. No, just one of them, but I cannot remember which. It was dark. There was a pool of black water nearby, as still as the grave. I felt that someone would drown, perhaps me, perhaps Robert." He sat up and Phoebe laid her hand on his back.

William shook his head. "This storytelling to the two from London has unsettled me. Or perhaps it was the preparation for the telling, the remembering of it all, whether good or bad. And I fear that it will have a dark end that I cannot see. Whilst they are friendly, I cannot understand why it is needed for the presentation of a medal. It is as if they are searching for something deeper, something darker."

"I am afraid, because I felt the same. But such dreams and feelings are not for us to understand. Soon, they will be gone. Who knows, the medal might come and go with nothing but joy. We must just carry on, my love."

William turned back to her and kissed her. "You are right," he said.

"And perhaps, in a month or so, there will be another Crossley on the way; for the bull has had his way."

They smiled and kissed again.

Later that evening William and Phoebe were seated in their drawing room with William's mother, Rebecca. Emily, William's sister, sat at her side, holding her hand. Opposite them sat the two from London.

Rebecca was a frail woman with a drawn, pale face to match. She had thin lips and gaunt eyes that spoke of irresolution. There was a hesitant sadness that hung about her, as if she never expected things to go well, as though her heart had endured too many disappointments. Jeremiah had died five years earlier and after he passed on, she had mourned for an appropriate time. Then she put her black dress and veil in the bottom of her trunk and for the first time in her life considered herself. She was not shocked at what she saw. Such emotions had been suppressed for too long to enable her to perform the role as wife and mother.

But she could remember only one or two times when she had disagreed with her husband, and only then by whatever stealth she had left. Little by little she re-evaluated her marriage and realised what a one sided affair it had been. Word by word, she found the language to tell the truth about her husband, who in the past she had automatically defended in whatever he did.

She had asked William, Phoebe and Emily to be present to support her. Despite her pain, her storytelling was clear and direct. She began slowly and in a flat, deliberate tone.

"A month after sending his letter to the Methodist District Superintendent requesting support for his Society, Jeremiah received a reply. The Committee said they were happy with his proposal, and that he could have free use of the assembly room in the church and twenty pounds a year for materials and labour for the construction of experiments. They suggested that he bring details of his proposals to the committee, and then he should begin building a set of..."

Rebecca hesitated and shook her head. Her brave attempt at storytelling had proved too much for her. She bowed her head and whispered something to William. He took her hand and whispered some words of comfort to her, for she turned her head and smiled weakly at him. William turned to the visitors.

"Mother wanted to tell you herself, but it is still too hard for her. I will carry on."

Clara's heart went out to the woman who had obviously suffered much. Then William began.

"Jeremiah made his presentation on the new Society to the committee. Their only modification to his plans was to suggest that he hired an usher who would operate the experiments, whilst he took the primary role as Master. Charles Laverty answered Jeremiah's advertisement and he seemed ideal. He had studied at one of the independent academies, but had not succeeded in gaining a place at university. However, he wished to continue his interest in science and considered Jeremiah's Society to be a chance for him to pursue it in the educational sphere. He was respectful and neatly dressed, and thus immediately gained Jeremiah's favour. Jeremiah had ordered a glass prism from a supplier in London, with funds from the Methodist Superintendent. Jeremiah and Charles spent one Saturday afternoon in the dining room in our house with the curtains drawn in an effort to split the light from an oil lamp into its constituent colours. They placed the lamp behind a card in which Charles had carefully cut a thin slit. The resulting beam of light was arranged to hit the prism, and another card, blackened beforehand by the smoke from the lamp, was placed on the other side to view the diffracted beam. When they had successfully demonstrated the colours, Jeremiah invited us all into the dining room to view it."

"All our family attended the first meeting of the Society. The room at the Methodist Church was full. At the front was a table, upon which stood the apparatus and Jeremiah's oil lamp. Next to it was a blackboard. Jeremiah's audience was mainly male, of whom the majority were middle class, self-made men, most of whom had never been to university, but who had succeeded nevertheless. There were one or two working class men who I recognised from the church congregation. There were a small number of influential town men, no doubt watching this interesting development in education. To both my mother's and Emily's disappointment, there were only a few women."

Clara nodded her head in support of Rebecca's feminist leanings.

"At the beginning, Jeremiah stood up to talk and nervously referred to a sheet of paper held in his shaking hand. It was as if his years of teaching had not prepared him for public speaking. 'My name is Jeremiah Crossley,' he began, 'and I am the Master of this *Society for Scientific Experiment and Mathematics.* The Society is supported by the Gold Street Methodist Church,' he glanced at his paper, 'which I acknowledge. Mister Charles Laverty is my usher and will help me with the demonstration. It is my plan to hold meetings of the Society regularly and to explain the science that is changing our world, with the assistance of a variety of practical demonstrations. It is my dream that these meetings will awaken in the hearts and minds of the men and women of this noble town of Northampton, a thirst – nay, a deep hunger, for the future life that science and mathematics will create for us.'"

Rebecca frowned and interrupted her son. Her voice trembled as she spoke. "It was the first time I had ever heard him say what his dream was."

William took her hand, squeezed it and whispered something in her ear. Clara saw that Rebecca was crying. William continued.

"Father turned to the blackboard and wrote the words, 'Sir Isaac Newton, 1666', on the blackboard. He then lifted the prism from the wooden box in which it had been delivered and held it up. 'This prism,' he announced, 'is a window into a new and enchanting world for the inhabitants of this town. It is the world of science.' There was a laugh from one in the audience. Charles, his assistant, frowned as he took the prism from his Master and polished it with his gloved hands to remove the fingermarks. He placed it on the table in the beam of light."

"A hush came over the room. 'Charles, I cannot see the colours,' father whispered, although he was audible to the whole room. 'Sir,' replied Charles, 'your jacket is blocking the beam from the lamp.' 'Ah, yes.' Father moved to one side, but still the colours were invisible."

Edward, with an understanding look on his face, said, "Jeremiah had made the mistake, common to many, of not practicing the experiment in the place in which it was to be performed."

"Indeed," replied William. "Whilst Charles had been as careful as he could with the curtains, to exclude as much light from outside as possible, the large room was not as dark as our dining room. Charles calmly considered for a moment and then turned to the audience. 'Ladies and gentlemen, please accept my apologies for this slight delay. Mister Crossley and I witnessed the colours last week in the Crossley dining room. Unfortunately tonight, the wonders of modern science are not so easily coaxed to appear, for if they were, we would all be scientists in our own dining rooms. Please let me make some rearrangements to the apparatus.' With this, he had gained the confidence of the audience. Some smiled, and all watched him quickly remove the apparatus from the table and gather up the dark cloth that had been laid upon it. He then placed his and Jeremiah's chairs on their side on the table and threw the cloth over them, thus creating a small dark box. He put the lamp, the prism, the slit and the viewing card under the cloth, and emerged a moment later with a triumphant smile on his face."

Edward laughed. "Such mistakes have even been made at the Royal Society," he said. William smiled with him and continued.

"Charles explained in a confident voice what had happened and invited any to step forward. Several brave and curious men came up and one by one viewed the colours beneath the tablecloth. The first withdrew his head and exclaimed, 'It is indeed a wonder', whilst the next rubbed his chin in consternation and said that he had never imagined such a thing. This drew others from the audience, including one lady, and the viewing lasted for more than thirty minutes, during which time Charles regularly lifted the cloth to allow the smoke from the lamp to escape. The noise of comment and conversation prevented father from making any explanation about the wonder. When no more waited to go beneath the cloth, he took his chance."

William hesitated, seemingly embarrassed by what he was to say next. "Father wrote an equation on the blackboard, relating the wavelength of the various colours to the velocity of light and the frequency of their source. Although he attempted to explain the equation, it meant nothing to those present, although Robert and I had read about it to prepare us for the meeting. He then related the origins of the crepuscular theory and the to-ing and fro-ing of the battle with the wave theory. It was clear that his head was full of the excitement of the science, the way in which it had become to be understood, and the nobility of man's struggle with the mysteries of God's creation. However, he had completely overlooked how much his listeners were able or willing to follow. As the clock on the wall ticked on, the audience became restless. Eventually someone whispered an apology to those around him and slipped quietly from the room. Jeremiah only noticed when a second, a third and then more people left but, still seeing faces looking at him, he ploughed on until the end."

Clara had her head bowed and her eyes shut, because her heart was saddened. Edward asked, "How did Robert feel about his father's performance?"

"He was not disappointed, as I was," William replied. "We were walking home together. I suppose that in the street he felt free to say what he thought. He laughed, a cruel and unkind laugh. We were still young, I was thirteen and he twelve, and his laugh unsettled me, because I began to see how much he hated father. When he saw my consternation, he explained himself. 'Father is incompetent,' he said, 'incompetent in practical things. Charles made a fool of him. And when he tried to explain the experiment and draw conclusions from it, why, you saw the people walk out.'"

Rebecca drew herself up with some effort and said, "Jeremiah told me later, that when the audience began to leave the room he was not offended. Rather, he was uplifted, for he believed that, at that moment he was Aristotle. 'Aristotle,' he said, 'had suffered persecution for his work as a bringer of science and was forced to leave Athens. But, unlike Aristotle, I will not retreat. No!' he exclaimed in that ridiculous and pompous way of his, 'he would remain resolutely on the course that fate had mapped out for him, of bringing science and mathematics to the unlearned.'"

Rebecca shook her head slowly, absorbed by the telling of the story. Then she breathed deeply and looking first at Edward and then Clara, said, "That was the way he was."

"Mrs Crossley," said Edward, "may I ask whether Jeremiah spent time working on mathematical problems? His son clearly had a special gift. Perhaps it was handed down from father to son?"

Rebecca looked at him blankly, as if the question had never entered her head. William answered for her. "As far as I am aware, he did not. His mathematics was confined to what he taught at school. I remember a certain moment when I consulted him on a geometrical problem that Robert had set me. I should say that Robert and I enjoyed testing each other on mathematics. We were brothers in..." He hesitated, as if correcting himself. "It is the sort of thing that brothers do. When my father saw the problem, he studied it for a moment or two and then excused himself. I knew that it was beyond him."

Edward smiled to himself, for he had had the same experience with his own father. "Thank you," he said. "Another question, if I might. Do you think that Robert took after his father in other ways?"

Rebecca seemed to shrink further into herself. Emily's arm went around her shoulders. Suddenly she drew herself up and said, "He was my beloved son. He was not like my husband, except in the way he treated Emily."

§

Emily's eyes opened wide with surprise. She was the very opposite of her brother William. She was short, and her hair, pinned tight about her head and her way of holding her arms close to her sides seemed to diminish her further. She reminded Clara of a wren, hopping from branch to branch.

There was a silence.

"I had not wanted to talk of that matter," Emily said, "but as my mother wishes it to be known, so be it." Her speech had a sincerity about it that Clara responded to immediately, perhaps sensing a young woman with noble ambitions for a career outside the home.

"Despite being formed as Grammar School for boys," Emily began, "by the time I was seven, in 1830, they had begun to admit a handful of girls. So, I spent four years learning ancient languages and deciphering the initials that my brothers and their friends had scratched on the desks. I had also attended Sunday School, until I felt that I had learned all I could from them. Thereafter, William, my elder brother, had tutored me further in Greek, Latin, the Classics, and in science and mathematics."

Clara nodded in approval.

"I applied to an advertisement for a position at the Cartwright Academy for Girls. Despite losing my temper with a member of the Appointments Board, who goaded me on the topic of the education of women, I was offered the position."

Being reminded about the success of the daughter, Rebecca had taken heart and wished to continue the narrative.

"Later in the evening of that day, as was our custom, Jeremiah and I sat together in this very drawing room. Jeremiah was in an expansive mood. The children seemed to be happy that evening. 'It is pleasing to a husband for his wife and children to be content and looking to what is right in their household.'

I wondered what had caused this sentiment. I mused to myself that he must have thrashed several of his pupils that day and it had caused him to compare his own children to those he had to teach.

'Indeed they are happy as I am,' I responded. 'For their sister Emily has shown her qualities by becoming a schoolteacher.'

I waited for Jeremiah to react. It took him a few moments to realise what I had said.

'Did you say that she has become a schoolteacher?'

'Yes, my dear.'

'What! Is this a joke?'

'No. She has applied to a small academy in the town and been accepted to teach some lessons to the children.'

'But do you not mean the Methodist Church School? Of course, ladies teach there. But only as support to the male teachers.'

'No, I do not think so, Jeremiah. She specifically said an academy. I seem to remember her say, Miss Cartwright's Academy for Girls. I understand that Miss Cartwright only employs female teachers.'

'But whilst I know that she has some talent in mathematics, and has attended Sunday School, how can she have got to a standard where she can become a teacher?'

'In your wisdom, my dear, you have established a household where learning is normal. It floats in the aether and has been absorbed by the very walls.'

This last sentence was too much for Jeremiah.

'Do not trifle with me, Rebecca! Why, what she is

doing is contrary to the very nature of man. And as a consequence, no good will come of it. The Lord has instituted different bodies for the two sexes. It is clear that the man's role is outside the household in the political sphere, where the woman's is inside, in the domestic sphere. There are two sexes and they each inhabit separate spheres. Why, this has been clear from antiquity. Aristotle made it clear in his *Politics*, that this is the best way to order our life. He names the two spheres as home, *oikos*, and the city, *polis*. This philosophy has been understood and explained time and time again through the ages. Rebecca, it is also perfectly clear in what modern science knows about the human body. The differentiation is for all to see. All the denominations of the churches also understand it. Why, the Reverend...'

'Stop it, Jeremiah! Stop it! You have no need to lecture me.'

He did not miss my criticism of his very way of life. His mouth remained open as his eyes looked at me questioningly. I continued.

'Your daughter is twenty years old. When do you propose to stop running her life for her? When is your stiff-necked fathering going to stop? This is what Emily wants. She will make a very good teacher. Let her go.'

I was shocked at what I had said. So shocked that I had to stand up and leave the room. I left Jeremiah to ponder his philosophy and his life."

Emily patted her mother's hand and took the story from her mother again.

"It was Monday morning. I was ready for my first day at the Academy. I was standing at the bottom of the stairs, ensuring for the final time that I had everything that I needed. Robert came down the stairs behind me.

'Emily, may I have a word with you before you leave?'

'Oh, Robert, of course you may.'

'I understand from William that you have gone behind father's back in the matter of educating yourself and of applying and obtaining a job as a teacher at an academy. And now I see that you are determined to carry through this madness. Sister, the ways that the world has determined for us are not to be turned lightly aside. You know what you are doing is wrong and will bring shame on this family.'

I stared at him with mounting apprehension.

'For my part,' Robert continued, 'I know that father is right and your action is wrong. If you mean to continue on this course, you will no longer be my sister. Our relationship will change and I will no longer consider you to be part of this family.'

He opened the front door and calmly walked out. I breathed deeply and, with anguish in my heart, made my way to the Academy."

All in the room that were not familiar with the story were astonished. Clara looked at Emily and shook her head. Edward was rapidly trying to fit what he had learnt into his analysis of Robert. Phoebe comforted William. After a long moment, Edward rose. William and Rebecca followed him to the front door. As they were parting, Edward took Rebecca's offered hand in his and begged to ask one further question. His voice was quiet and even.

"Did Jeremiah have a hatred of the Jews?"

Rebecca closed her eyes and sighed deeply. "Goodbye, sir," she said and turned back into the house.

CHAPTER 5

The Grandfather Clock

When the blood boils with impetuous imaginings, men with no fixed employment are often driven to violent exercise early in the morning. Edward was no exception. At school he had excelled at sports, and when he was in London maintained his muscular frame by regular bouts of running in Hyde Park. The door swung open with alarming force and Edward flew in on the breeze. He collapsed into the armchair opposite Clara.

She had been sitting quietly in a private part of the George Hotel's lounge reserved for residents. It was an hour after breakfast, and the lounge was empty except for her. She had noticed Edward looking at her on the train and it had disquieted her. Although she knew that she had a not unpleasing face and a well-shaped figure for a woman in her late thirties, for the first time in her life she was contemplating the attentions of a man who appeared to appreciate her as a woman. From this idyll, her mind moved to the meetings that she and Edward had had the previous day. With Edward's arrival, her indignation due his anti-Semitic remark to Rebecca came back with a force she could not contain.

"What was the meaning of your question concerning Jeremiah's view on the Jews?"

"Ah, Clara, it is good to see you. I had a presentiment."

"A presentiment? Edward, do you realise how insensitive

it is to ask such a question without evidence. Furthermore, it is grossly unprofessional and risks alienating our witnesses."

"Unprofessional? Let me remind you that we are not being paid for this work. And, furthermore, neither of us have had any previous experience of how to conduct such an investigation. Professional does not come into it."

"Oh, Edward, you are infuriating."

"I did get an answer to my question."

"You got no answer. Rebecca turned away with distain."

"She turned away without answering, because I was correct in my presentiment."

There was an awkward silence. "Well, perhaps you are right," Clara finally said, conceding that she should not try to control Edward until she knew him better. "What else have we learned, so far?"

Edward put his hand to his chin and considered. "Samuel clearly wasn't the author of the disputed paper, nor was there any other obvious candidate in the town. Nor was Jeremiah. He had no time for it, because he spent his time considering himself and his own importance. In a town like this where education is thinly spread, having a little more than most was sufficient to lift him above the many. Both Samuel and Jeremiah had that in common. I do not yet know how we can eliminate William. It appears that he was as clever as his brother at mathematics. But by going into the clock shop, he chose not to exploit it. I hope that we will hear more of that decision soon. That leaves those outside the town, in the rest of England, and many on the continent."

Clara agreed with all of this.

"Robert's psyche," Edward continued, "has been cruelly distorted by his father. I do not believe his mother's statement in his defence that he is not like his father. Some of his father's tendencies might have been inherited. Inheritance is the fear that stalks us all." Edward paused to think of his own father's drinking problem, which he felt he had inherited, but had so far kept in check. After a moment, he continued. "Through the same paranoia as his father, Robert's small deceit over his classics classes might now be magnified into deceits that are resulting in factory workers in the Adelaide Works being arbitrarily thrown out of the jobs. And in between the two, a simple case of plagiarism might have changed Robert's life for the better, enabling him to finally get his revenge on his father, a father who goaded him mercilessly to succeed."

Clara nodded; Edward was at last making sense, she thought. He continued.

"Let us consider Emily. Her position is interesting. The following is a possibility that I had not considered. That Robert is the author of the work and yet someone has made the suggestion that he is not, simply to ruin his reputation. There must be many that we are not yet aware of, beyond Arthur Blackham, who might have a motive. Emily certainly has. It is sometimes the case that the loyalty between brothers is strong, which is the case here, yet the relationship between a brother and a sister reacts to it and is twisted into other directions. Is it possible that she has influenced someone else in a higher position to betray her brother? Remember Robert removed her from the family in his eyes. To a person like Emily, the family must have loomed large as a consolation to her frustrated position as a woman fighting for her rights.

These last words quietened Clara's vehemence somewhat, but she was still quick to Emily's defence. "No, she is not responsible."

Edward shook his head.

"You think I take her side because we are of the own sex and face the same challenges," replied Clara. "If you do, you see what is not there, like most of the men that have put themselves against me. Do not underestimate me, Edward. If she had any show of guilt I would say so. No, I too have a presentiment. Like her father, she is too wrapped up in herself and her tribulations to have either the means or the inclination to seek revenge."

Edward considered this. "Very well," he said, "you might be right. However, we must still question the possibility. If we find no other evidence to indict Robert, we shall consider Emily further."

Edward had fallen back insouciantly into his armchair, staring fondly at Clara. She was perturbed by his look, but said nothing. "I found Master Samuel," he went on, "a resolute and energetic believer in the Conservative policy of doing nothing. He is no worse than I have encountered in Westminster and I enjoyed jousting with him. Samuel uses his education to paint over the cracks in society and has an overweening view of his own importance. He had two or three teachers under him and eighty pupils. Several of the independent academies in the town have many more than that."

"However, Samuel's daughter is to be pitied," Clara said. "Her mother died when she was young and her father was absent in any meaningful way as a parent. She has spent her life, since the age of eleven, caring for him; in other words, she gave her life for him. Does that excuse her behaviour?"

Edward pushed himself up in his armchair and became earnest. "You are right to ask that question, Clara. But it is Jeremiah that interests me more and Robert's reaction to him. Remember that Rebecca told us that Jeremiah thought he was Aristotle. What is your medical opinion on delusions?"

"It is a well know symptom of mental disturbance, but its precise cause cannot yet be fathomed. Research in the area is still at the stage of classifying and codifying various mental symptoms with the aim of understanding through insights at the group level. In their extreme form, delusions usually lead to incarceration in an asylum."

"Yes, I see," he replied. "But I assume that Jeremiah was never diagnosed."

"I assume that he told no one but Rebecca. And of course, she would never divulge it."

"If Jeremiah had insane tendencies," Edward continued, "it is hard to imagine Rebecca's plight, and the pain of being a woman in a marriage like that."

Clara's mind went to her own marriage. She considered herself lucky, for Percival made few demands on her, beyond requiring that they ate dinner together, when they were both at home. "It must have been difficult," she said.

Clara then listened attentively, as Edward began to talk with earnestness. Beneath his sometimes careless exterior, she knew that he had a heart for the disorder that was human society.

"My dear," he began, "have you read Christina Rossetti's poem called *A Triad*? It is full of emotion and darkness concerning the predicament of women. It speaks of one woman who shames herself by becoming a mistress, of another who becomes an old spinster, and of a third, who is trapped in a loveless marriage. Rebecca reminded me of this last woman."

"Yes, Edward, I know the poem." It was new and exciting for her to have a conversation on such matters with a man. "It is very moving indeed. Its drama comes from the highlighting of these three conditions. But these conditions are not all there is to being a woman. I know many elder women who have had a full life without marrying. And for some couples, marriage can be a most fulfilling occupation, provided they find the right partner before they commit themselves. I think that William and Phoebe are like that."

"And which are you, Clara?"

She hesitated. She was discovering that Edward had a habit of asking the most forward and disarming questions.

"Before, I answer you, let me tell you something of my life. I am of the middle classes. My father was a self made man, who became rich by investing in the railways. He was wealthy enough to enable me to be trained, first as a nurse, then as an apothecary and then finally as a doctor. He was also sensible enough to allow me to do it, without trying to marry me off to some upper class incoherent."

Edward grinned at her, for he knew several.

"I had a governess at home, whom I despised and tried to outwit in our classroom. I therefore have some sympathy for Robert's violent reaction to his father. I also had scant regard for my teachers in school, for they knew almost nothing of science and mathematics. My life has always been hard, because I had to fight to get where I am. I became a nurse at a hospital in London. I employed a tutor to teach me anatomy and physiology in the evenings and became a licensed apothecary. I then studied for a university degree in medicine. None of the English universities admitted women, so I went to Paris..."

"You studied in French?"

"Of course."

"Oh, c'est merveilleux."

Clara wondered how much knowledge of the French language Edward had. She was to find out some time later.

"I opened a clinic in London," she went on, "with some money from my husband and gained admission to the British Medical Association, which allows me to practice as a doctor. Directly after that the Association voted against the admission of further women."

"Well, I never..."

"So, Edward, which of the Triad am I?"

"Ah, that depends on what sort of marriage you have."

Clara looked into his eyes for a long moment, before deciding that she could trust him.

"We are married only in name. We have never been through a ceremony."

"And has the marriage been consummated?"

Clara was about to speak, when the door to the lounge opened and William walked in.

§

"Edward, Clara! I am a few minutes late. I do apologize."

"For a man who has just come from a watch and clock shop, that is a little surprising," said Edward with a sly smile on his lips.

William had the look of a man that you could trust. He

had had a handsome face that over the years had softened and spread, just as his waist had.

"You asked how my brother and I came to be at the shop with Elijah," he said.

"Before you begin," said Edward, "can you tell me where Ben Edge is now?"

William remembered his dream and his face hardened. "He works in Isaac Campbell's shoe factory," he said grudgingly. "He won't talk to me now. I cannot understand why."

"Thank you. Please begin."

"I told you that it was the incident of the clock that got Robert into the shop. It took place on a warm Wednesday afternoon on June. Robert had grown tired of his Greek exercises and was walking around the house before returning to his books. Our father was at School and would not return until dinner time. Our mother was engaged in the kitchen. Robert sauntered from room to room, taking a young man's interest in whatever took his fancy. In the drawing room was a long clock standing next to the sideboard. We knew it well, for it was the main means of telling the time in the house, apart from our father's pocket watch. It had a plain face and a rather naive polished case. On the face was the maker's name, Crossley and Dyke.

Robert looked at the clock and watched the minute hand move slowly, but inexorably around the face. He could hear the tick-tock of the mechanism and, having just learned about different types of energy, wondered how the potential energy of the weight was converted into the kinetic energy of the hands. For that was what the energies were and so a conversion of energy must take place. He saw a small door on the side of the box in which the mechanism sat, and opened it. He pulled up a chair and stood on it to peer in. Inside was a confusion of wheels and strings. He stared at it for some time. 'William would understand it' he mused. But he can be rather boring at times.' Robert was determined to work it out for himself. He looked around the box housing the mechanism and realised that it could be pulled off from the front. He removed the hands from the clock face and pulled. Yes. He placed it on the table and climbed back up to the mechanism. 'Ah', he said to himself, 'the weight turns that wheel, which turns that one.' This was straightforward, he believed.

But when he got to the escapement, he was baffled. He touched the small swinging arm attached to the pendulum and to his horror after two or three more ticks it stopped. A cold thrill went through him. He bent his head and closed his eyes. He imagined the reaction of our father. He breathed deeply and tried swinging the pendulum. Nothing happened. He tried again, and still the motion would not sustain. Three ticks and it stopped. He could feel his heart thumping inside his chest.

He ran upstairs. I was lying on my bed, reading.

'William, help me.'

'What is it, Robert? You look white as a sheet.'

'The clock! I have stopped it. And I don't know how to make it go again. Father will kill me.'

I jumped off the bed and raced downstairs to help my brother in his time of mortal danger. I climbed onto the chair and looking in at the mechanism, pushed the pendulum. It went for five or more strokes and then stopped. Robert had breathed a sigh of relief at the third and fourth tick and then his heart sank after the fifth. I scratched my head.

'No. There is nothing to be done. We had just better put the box back.' I slid it slowly into place. 'Here, Robert, put the hands back on. There. Now we will just have to brazen it out.'

Robert was not so sure that he could brazen it out, for his silence to our father that he had now adopted, meant that he had lost the ability to look innocent.

Our father discovered that the clock had stopped just before dinner. He immediately suspected that it had been tampered with. The clock's reliability had been guaranteed by his brother and attested by him, as it had gone continuously for the last seven years with only small adjustments.

As Robert suspected, he was unable to silently plead innocence and at our father's exhortation for him to tell the truth or suffer eternal damnation, he admitted what he had done. I also admitted to my part in the crime, because I neither feared my father's anger or his punishment. The punishment was six strokes of his slipper upon our backsides, which he administered with the gusto of the righteous.

Mother complimented father on his discipline and seeded the idea that Robert needed more mental exercise of a scientific manner, perhaps related to clocks and their workings. Of course, she pretended that she did not know what the exercise should be, and waited until father had the idea of sending Robert to help at the clock shop."

§

"Robert pushed open the door of the shop and a bell tinkled. Ahead of him was a narrow flight of stairs, flanked by a corridor. To his right, the door into the shop was open. The converted drawing room had glass fronted display cases on two walls and a counter in the middle. Mister Dyke introduced himself. He told Robert that his Uncle had had to go out unexpectedly to attend to the church clock and would be back presently. Crossley and Dyke were the best-known watch and clockmakers in the town. Fifteen years ago they had built the famous gilded clock in All Saints Church and that resulted in them being awarded the contract of £15 a year for the upkeep of all the five clocks in the church and Vicarage.

Ten minutes later, the bell rang and his Uncle came in. Robert stood up.

'Robert, my dear man. It is good to see you in our humble shop.'

He took Robert's hand in the two of his and breathed deeply.

'Let me get my breath back. Well, when I came to maintain your long case clock, your father said that you have an interest in learning about clocks.'

'Yes, Uncle.'

Elijah smiled and the brown stains on his teeth puzzled Robert, until Elijah took out a tin of tobacco from one of his waistcoat pockets and a pipe from his other. He had seen the smokers totter out of the Wig and Pen on his way home from school; he hoped Uncle was not one of those.

'Follow me.' The old man waddled through the door at the back of the shop, into a rather scruffy room whose walls were lined with workbenches littered with lamps, magnifying glasses and the paraphernalia of clockmakers. In one corner sat a thin youth bent over a clock mechanism.

'Let me introduce you to Albert Hawley, our apprentice. Albert is putting together a clock to replace one we sold last week. We cannot have spaces in our display cabinets, can we Albert?'

The youth turned shyly and he shook hands with Robert. Elijah turned away and filled his pipe, lit it and began to emit smoke. Robert watched the curious performance.

'To get straight to the point: for watches, we buy movements and cases from London or Coventry and assemble them according to customer's orders. For clocks, we buy the parts from the same factories and assemble them. We make simple clocks in simple cases for the working class, or commission better cases from furniture makers for the wealthy. We repair everything. Do you have a question?'

'Why do you not buy clock movements, Uncle?'

Elijah's eyebrows moved slowly up. It was a good question.

'Because there are too many variations. Long case movements are much bigger and can have many functions that a smaller mantelpiece clock cannot easily contain. On the other hand, the pocket watch is generally the same size, so the movements have been standardised. And it is cheaper for us to assemble the clocks here. But the financial side of the business belongs to Mister Dyke. Now, what are we going to do with you, young man?'

Our Uncle knew the reason for Robert being at the shop. Our mother and his wife, Hannah, were close and she, being childless, was keen to hear whatever gossip our mother had concerning the children. They laughed long about the chaos that Robert had created when he stopped the clock, for father had over-reacted by calling out the time, every hour, on the hour, for the next few days, until Elijah had visited and restarted it.

Robert watched the old man struggle to bend down and reach a low drawer. When he had found what he was looking for, he laid out a number of parts on the workbench. Robert noticed the delicacy with which his Uncle handled the beautiful brass wheels.

'Pick one up.' He handed Robert a pair of tweezers. 'Look at it under this glass.' He pointed to a large lens supported in an elegant stand, which had thumbscrews to allow adjustment. A mirror was similarly supported and was used to throw additional light from the lamp onto the part being examined. Robert dropped the gearwheel at his first attempt, but quickly saw his way. He held it and peered at it with amazement, for he could see the tiny scratches in the surface of the metal made by the machine that had produced the part.

'The factory in Coventry has a room ten times the size of this, full of machines making these. They send them all over the world.'

This aroused no emotion in Robert, for despite his seeing maps of the world hung on his classroom wall, his world thus far had been the town. The family visit to our other Uncle's farm had seemed like journey into the wider world to him. Elijah noticed his blank look.

'Robert, I intend you to make a part like this. It is what I did when I was an apprentice to old man Clarke, who has a shop in Draper Street. I still have the machines that we used to use before the factories started up. We will get them out and have a rare old time getting them going again.'

He rubbed his smoke stained hands.

'But before that, I intend to explain how the clock works, so that when your father's long case stops again, you will amaze him by restarting it. The weight turns this wheel, very slowly. These wheels serve to make that rotation faster, so that this, the escape wheel, is rotating once a minute.' His chubby hands held a needle-like tool that he used to point out the part he was describing.

'You can see that the escape wheel has different shaped teeth to the others. See, just above it, that piece shaped like an upside down anchor, whose shaft is connected to the pendulum. The escape wheel gives one point of the anchor a little push to keep the pendulum going. And when the push is given, the other point of the anchor blocks the escape wheel from moving on more than one tooth.'

He held the pendulum gently in one hand and swung it so that Robert could see the escape wheel click round.

'The hands are then driven through these wheels....'

Robert interrupted him. 'And the ratio of the teeth in the wheels driving the hands must be exactly sixty.'

Elijah's head jerked upwards a fraction and his eyes opened wide at the boy. 'Indeed, they must. Indeed.'

Robert was in full flow now. 'And the length of the pendulum is such that its period is one second. Or the teeth ratios of the other wheels are such to make the minute hand rotate in sixty.'

Elijah's smile had widened. 'But there is one subtlety, which I think may have eluded you.'

Robert looked puzzled. Our Uncle pointed at the anchor. 'Push the anchor.'

Robert put some pressure on the lever. He felt a cold thrill run through him, for the pendulum swung no more than three times and then came to a halt. It was what he had done to his father's clock. So our Uncle knew all. Resentment grew in him that he fought to suppress. He looked coldly at Elijah, who pretended not to notice as he continued educating the boy.

'You see, Robert, the anchor is a friction fit to its axle. And your little push displaced it from its correct position.'

Robert immediately realised what he meant. He had read that a pendulum always swung about a line to the centre of the earth. The anchor could be adjusted, so that even if the floor on which the clock stood were not flat, the escapement would work successfully. His head throbbed for not realising this before and he did not hear our Uncle's explanation. He silently watched the old man take the pendulum in his hand and adjust the anchor until the clicks of the escapement were even and continuously sustained.

The rest of the afternoon was taken up with Elijah and Robert bringing down the parts of an ancient looking lathe from a dusty room in the attic. Our Uncle cleaned off each part carefully and set it up on an empty bench near the back of the workshop.

'I bought this from Coventry. Look, Robert, see the maker's name. Next week, Robert, I will show you how we cut the teeth in the wheel, and you will make something yourself.'"

CHAPTER 6

The Adding Machine

The evening was dry as Edward accompanied Clara out of the George Hotel. They were to interview the clockmaker, Elijah Crossley and his wife Hannah, with William, at the shop in the Market Square.

They were early, so Clara steered him in the other direction, down to the river. She had noticed that Edward had eaten heavily since his arrival at The George, and that factor, coupled with the richness of what was set before him, made her eager for him to get some exercise. However, his mind was on other things.

"My dear, what a perfect evening for love making," he whispered as they passed a young couple sitting on a bench and took Clara's arm in his.

Clara feigned annoyance and pushed his arm away. "Edward, you should keep your heart tightly buttoned up. Please tell me, in rational sentences and without sentiment, about your upbringing."

"Very well. I shall not begin at the beginning, for my family history is a long one, which would require a walk from here to London and back to relate. As you may know, I am the sixth Baron Cleat. The only advantage that gives me is that I can talk in the House and pursue mathematics. Having to earn my own living would make both of those much harder." He paused to consider. "It is strange, Clara, that I have not been asked to describe my upbringing before. I am loath to do it, for it might afford the questioner much to use against me. It might also sound as if I am justifying myself, and I most certainly do not want to do that."

"That you are loath to relate it, tells me something of you already, Edward. That you have something to hide, perhaps?"

"There you are. You have beaten me, before I begin. So, let me be honest. My father drank too much and as a consequence lost his sense, but not his fortune. I sometimes feel that I am like him, but not because of drink. For me it is women and gambling. For any woman that comes within five feet of me falls in love with me, due to my good looks and manly stature. And consequently, I must not disappoint them. My other problem is that most gamblers that come within five feet of me feel the need to wager with me because they see that I have no sense. But being a mathematician, I understand better than most the probabilities involved, and how those probabilities can be combined to one's advantage. Thus I fear that I must always disappoint them."

"You do not disappoint me, Edward, for that nonsense tells me nothing about you, yet it speaks much. What was her name?"

"Who?"

"The woman that broke your heart."

"She did not break my heart."

"But there was a woman."

"Yes, but more of a girl. She died. She was only eighteen, but she died."

"Ah." Clara was touched that he had trusted himself to her. She placed her hand gently on his arm. "I am sorry. And are you still in love with her?"

"Yes. Her name is,... was Alice," said Edward, almost inaudibly. Clara walked on beside him in silence, a companionable silence.

They walked along the riverbank, watching the swans feeding and the mallards escorting their chicks. Clara reflected that she had seen inside him for a fleeting moment, and felt his loneliness and the ache of lost love. But what he said then surprised her the more.

"There were times when a bout of melancholia would lay me low, sometimes for days on end. Only laudanum would bring me out of it, laudanum and whisky."

The doctor, Clara, stared at him with wide, alarmed eyes.

"Perhaps," he continued, "it was the loss of Alice that brought it on; I don't know. Perhaps I caught it from my few years at Rugby School, where a sensitive boy might suffer under the strict routine and the derision of his imbecilic fellow pupils. Or perhaps from breathing the air in certain parts of London, where the poetry of lament is regularly discussed."

She was holding him gently by the arm, listening intently.

"You know Matthew Arnold's father was Headmaster at Rugby School when I was there. He wrote stanzas in honour of Etienne Senancour, the author of Obermann, the chronicle of a fellow melancholic." He smiled at his recollection of Obermann, for the book was long and dark. "But now I am less afflicted. Work and charming company protect me."

§

They had reached the Market Square and walked across to the shop, as the sky began to darken. William opened the door and escorted them in. Elijah was waiting for them, with his hand ready to welcome them both. His enthusiasm engulfed them immediately.

"Welcome to Crossley and Dyke, high-class clock and watch makers," Elijah announced. "Let me show you around."

Clara stood back and observed Edward's interest in everything; by then she knew that this was Edward's method for finding out information. They passed into the workshop and William told them how much it had changed since he had first arrived. There were many more complicated machines for cutting and grinding the components for the calculating machines, which had pushed the clock and watch assembly into a small corner close to the shop door. They were overcrowded and soon would need more space if the tests that they were carrying out were successful.

Finally, Elijah led them upstairs to meet Hannah. Hannah was the mirror image of Elijah, being as short and plump as he was, with a perpetual smile on her face. Edward and Clara were ushered into comfortable armchairs, whilst the clockmaker and his wife squeezed into the small settee. William sat on a dining chair and, after brief introductions, began another tale of the Crossley family.

"Uncle," boomed William, for the old man was losing his hearing, "these are the two people I told you about. Edward Pennington," Edward nodded at Elijah, "and Doctor Clara Cox." Elijah's eyebrows went up at the conjunction of the words doctor and the woman sitting in front of him. "They want to know all about Robert. They are from the Royal Society, who are thinking of giving Robert a medal."

"Robert, eh. A medal? He was different to you, you know, William," replied Elijah.

"Yes, I suppose he was."

"He didn't have the practical skill that you had, but he could understand it all."

"William, your Uncle makes an interesting point," interrupted Edward. "But, I would like to take the opposite point of view to him about your relationship to Robert. From your stories of your early childhood, you seem to have as deep an understanding of him as I have ever known one person to have for another."

"Yes, it is strange, I will admit," William replied. "However, there was something we had in common: mathematics. We both grew up with it. We loved it and we played with it; we even called ourselves Brothers in Plato. So when it happened, his being invited to lecture at the Royal Society, I had to know everything about him that had led up to that point. I did not think that he was unworthy of the invitation, but I was so surprised. I had known nothing about what he was doing. I cannot express it more clearly; I am sorry."

Clara looked at him sympathetically and said, "Do you want to continue telling your story of how you got to the shop?"

"Yes, I do, thank you. One evening, I was lying on my bed reading. Robert called out, trying to catch my attention about his job in the shop. 'We are making a wheel, with teeth, on his clockmakers lathe', Robert said. He had my attention again. 'How does the lathe work?' I asked him. It took Robert less that a couple of minutes to explain it all. It struck me as too interesting to miss. I wondered if father would let me go. He did, and Uncle's welcome was as warm as it had been for Robert."

Elijah broke in. "Congenial we might have been, but Horace and I were watching Robert as closely as we watched Albert. Both of us had a strong desire to see the business continue and prosper, as it had since we formed our partnership. Horace was a keen businessman and saw in me an aptitude for clocks and watches. It was Horace's wife's money that was used to start the business, to purchase the shop in the square, and to fill it with the necessary parts and tools. So successful was our business that we rapidly paid back his wife who, on seeing her money thus increasing, was happy to let Horace take an interest in several other clock makers in the town. But Horace had a need for an activity other than watching his wife's money and chose to indulge his love of fine timepieces by standing behind the counter of Crossley and Dyke."

"How did Robert get on?" asked Edward.

"Robert did not develop a facility for machining small clock parts," replied Elijah, "but he knew the processes involved and was then fascinated to watch myself and Horace and our apprentice in running the business. William, though, had gifted hands and a brain for clocks. He and I struck up a close bond. We would talk for long periods about metals, about machining, and about mechanisms. Robert would, of course, listen to our discussions and I knew that he took it all in, for his mental capacity at that time seemed infinite. But Horace told me later that he also talked with him, when there were no customers in the shop, about the business and about money, and about the people in the town who were important to know."

"Tell them about Robert and the arithmometer, Uncle," interrupted William.

Elijah drew his breath in and scratched his head. "Indeed, that was remarkable, was it not? One afternoon, the boys were telling me about the mathematics that they were doing in the evenings with their tutor. Robert related how a tangent to a circle is always at so-many degrees to the radius. I put my palm up to stop him. 'Why goodness me' I said, 'do not try to explain about that to me. I can do arithmetic and simple geometry related to wheels and ratios, but nothing more. And Hannah, bless her, still has difficulty with arithmetic. Why, when she has to serve in the shop, if there is addition of amounts of money, she has to call me in'. Hannah beamed with pleasure at being mentioned in the story.

Edward was loath to interrupt Elijah's flow, but knew that he might not get the chance again to ask his question. "Elijah, it is clear that your skill is in the mechanisms of clocks and watches and not in the mathematics that so delights men like Robert."

"Indeed, sir."

"I understand that you have another brother, who runs a farm. Does he practice mathematics?"

Elijah laughed at the idea. "Why no, sir. He can count his cows and his sheep, and those numbers are large ones. But he knows nothing of algebra or equations."

"Thank you. I apologise for interrupting you. Please continue."

"Where was I?" He had genuinely forgotten.

"The boys were telling you about their mathematics," prompted Edward.

"Ah, yes. Robert spoke up. 'Excuse me, Uncle,' he said, 'but one evening, when father permitted us to attend his Society for Experimental Science and Mathematics, there was a man who told us about machines that could do arithmetic. He showed us pictures of them. They were called arithmometers, and were based on the Leibniz wheel. He showed us how they worked. If you have paper and a pencil, I could explain them to you.'"

"He then spent ten minutes, firstly explaining the basic operation of adding two single digit numbers together using several specially designed toothed wheels, and then how many such devices could be connected together for adding multiple digits. During this time, William encouraged him with, 'yes, yes...' and 'well done, yes...'. I was dumbfounded, but after a moment managed to ask, 'Robert, did the man say whether such machines were being manufactured?' He said that none were made in numbers, because the machines were too crude yet. Robert looked at the two of us, paused, and then said, 'I am certain that we could make one.'"

Elijah paused and nodding slowly, said, "I could literally feel the thrill that went through my body, for I realised that Robert had opened for us a window on a whole new line of business, which would surely become as important as clocks and watches as time went by. I breathed deeply and then regained my composure, but could not contain my excitement, which flowed over into the boys. Then we settled down and discussed the niceties of the design and how it should be improved to make it easier to manufacture and more robust to the wear of everyday life. Finally, I promised that the three of us would begin construction of the single digit adder as soon as we could. Before Robert and William left that day, all three of us made a solemn undertaking not tell Mister Dyke or Jeremiah."

"Why not," asked Edward?

"For I believed," replied Elijah, "that we needed to have made something before we should try to convince anybody that the arithmometer had a future."

Edward said, "You were right to be cautious, Elijah, for there were others in the country contemplating the same thing."

"So you see, Edward, that it was Robert that started us off on the project," said William. "I am not surprised that the Royal Society was impressed by him."

"Indeed. May I ask you a question, William?"

"Of course."

"Did you go to university?"

"No."

Edward detected defiance in his voice. "Did you have the opportunity?"

"Yes. But I wanted to stay in the town. I felt an allegiance. If I had gone to university, there was the chance that I would not have come back. But there was Phoebe and there was my family. And I knew that university was all book learning. I wanted to do practical things, to make things and, to tell the truth, I was enthralled with clocks and watches and the thought of changing the world with mechanical calculating machines."

"I see," replied Edward. "William, would you explain what happened when you made that decision?"

"Of course. My mother became agitated. 'William,' she said, 'have you told your father yet?' She was wringing her hands. She feared father's reaction to this news, more than she feared for my future. We heard the front door slam.

'Rebecca!' It was father. He pulled the door of the drawing room open dramatically and looked at us both accusingly.

'So, he has told you. When was he going to tell me that he refuses to sit the entrance examination?'

My mother cringed before him. He strode into the room and confronted me.

'Father, I intend...'

'I know what you intend. You intend to throw everything back into my face. All of the years of hard work, for nothing! All of our care, your mother's love! No, you will do what I say...'

He hesitated, for I was standing steadfastly in front of him. He continued. 'You... you chose to defy me?'

He lifted his hand to strike me, but I caught his wrist and held it firmly. I was now as tall as my father, and stronger. I spoke clearly and slowly.

'It is my decision to make, father. It is my life now. I thank you with all my heart for getting me thus far, but now I must make my own decisions and take the responsibility.'

Father's arm became limp and I released it. He looked at mother, but it seemed that he was looking through her to some distant place that he could not quite understand. He turned and walked out of the room. We heard him enter his bedroom above us and turn the key in the lock. Mother glanced at the resolute look on my face and hurried out to the kitchen.

Later that night, Robert and I were alone in our bedroom, lying on our beds. Our father had not joined us for dinner, which, despite his absence, had proceeded as usual. However, a feeling of oppression hung about us all. Mother had looked serious and the younger children caught her mood. Robert and I kept our own council. After dinner, in our bedroom, free to talk as we felt, Robert had asked me what had happened.

'He tried to strike me. I do not know what to think of him now.'

Robert knew, but said nothing.

'But he made it clear that I was making a mistake. He had my life planned out for me, in a mirror image of his.'

'Well, I shall go to university,' said Robert quietly 'It is my destiny.'

I turned to look at him to make sure of what I had heard. Robert was staring at the ceiling and he continued talking.

'Father is right in one thing: it is important to take whatever chances we get to make the most of our lives. He is wrong in many other things and wrong to try to strike you.'

My stand against father had given Robert much satisfaction. It was a signal that something had changed. A junction in the road of our lives had been reached, at which the influence of our father had been diminished and all of us, including our mother, could begin to stand on our own legs.

'Of course, you will be carrying on at Uncle Elijah's shop, when you finish school.' Robert continued.

'Well, yes,' I replied. Robert's intuition surprised me.

'You have an understanding with Elijah and Horace, do you not?' Robert knew more than I thought.

'Yes, we have discussed the future. Since Albert, the apprentice, left, things have been difficult for them. Even Horace has said so. He told me that there is a full-time place for me there, in some capacity or another.'

'You know I resented you joining me at the shop. I got on well with Uncle. Well, I still do.'

I was surprised again by Robert's willingness to discuss such close matters. We had grown up as friends, very close friends, but recently we had spent less time together and

I knew that we were moving apart. My defiance of father had momentarily brought us together. But I did not expect it to last. Robert continued.

'But, I wish you well in whatever you do at the shop. I hope you remember that.'

What did Robert mean by that? I wondered. Robert was thirteen and I just fourteen. Admittedly I was about to leave school and begin work in earnest, but I was not aware that young men had conversations such as this."

§

"Mother told me later of her conversation with father over my future. My disobedience had seemed to take the energy out of father. So, it was that when father appeared to be back to full strength, mother broached the matter of my employment. It was still two months until I finished, but some arrangement had to be made.

'He needs to do something,' mother said to father, 'whilst he forms in his mind what he really wants. And it is for you to make representations to prospective employers for him.'

Father was dismissive. 'I will talk to him tomorrow.'

'No, Jeremiah!' Mother said that she wanted to sound firm. The action must come from him. 'You must think and act. What would suit him? He has a nice way with people, but longs to make things, mechanical things.'

'Well, perhaps you are right. Perhaps I should talk to Elijah. He seems to know William's mind.'

'Ah, yes, I had not thought of that.' Mother had found that being duplicitous came naturally to her. 'Work at his shop full time. What a good idea.'

'No, I did not mean that. Something better... But, well, perhaps it would form an instructive preparation for him, towards a more important position.'

'Thank you, my dear.' "

§

The room was awash with emotion as William finished. Edward broke the silence.

"So, William, you joined Crossley and Dyke as a partner?"

"No. I was to be taken into the company as an assistant to the partners, at a salary to be decided by the partners. The position was neither as a partner nor an apprentice and had duties that were to be specified by the partners as needed. I would become a partner upon the decease of either of the current partners or when both partners felt that my contribution was of sufficient value to the company. The partners or partner would determine the percentage of my share of the company at that time. I was happy with this rather unspecific agreement, although it made me painfully conscious that business was not one of father's skills."

William's surprisingly frank explanation of his being taken on at the shop had brought the evening of genial reminiscence to a flat end.

CHAPTER 7

Abraham's Bank

Clara had on a thick jacket and skirt and her high boots. She had banged on Edward's door before breakfast and demanded that he joined her on a walk down to the river.

"I have not taken a holiday in years," she said as they crossed the same road that William and Robert had taken on the fateful egg-collecting expedition. "My clinic and my husband take all my time. I am beginning to realise what I have missed, for my mind has been refreshed and my body rejuvenated."

They found themselves in the meadow and paused to take in their surroundings. The insects hummed and the waist high grass sighed in the breeze. Suddenly the sun came out from behind a cloud and the meadow was riven with colour; the blue of the cornflowers, the yellow of the rattle and the cowslip and the peppering of red poppies.

"What do you think of William?" asked Edward. "He has a similar intellect to yours. He is of a similar age."

"William is the innocent in all of this. He has no notion of what Robert might have done."

"No," said Edward with a sly smile. "I was asking if you felt any attraction to him?"

"Don't talk nonsense. I am a married woman."

"That has not stopped many women in the past. Do you have any feelings for him?"

Clara thought for a moment. "Yes. I fear that he may be hurt."

They waded through the long grass towards the riverbank letting the grass caress their hands. Edward bent down to examine a cornflower, bowed by the overnight rain.

"Might he be hurt like this flower? If the wind and the rain is too strong, it might break the stalk and bring the flower down before it produces its seed."

She stood beside him, watching his gentle fingers hold the flower. "William has Phoebe, he has his children and he has a flourishing clock shop. And he was strong enough to stand up to his father. He seems well placed to weather any storms."

Edward stood up and looked at her. "I hope so. Come on. I will race you to the river." Edward bolted and Clara ran as best she could in her boots and caught him at the bank.

"Look." Edward was pointing. "Just under that tree, on the opposite bank. A family of coots."

"Yes, they must be common around here."

Edward looked around, for he sensed a movement behind them. He saw nothing and began walking along the bank, all the time glancing back at the coots. Further up river they came to the canal that went northwards into the town. There was a sign on the other side of the river for the boats coming down from the quay with their load of boots and shoes. It pointed west, down river, to the Grand Union canal that linked Northampton to London.

"Yes, the railway and the canal are signs of the new times that the town is facing." He glanced back along the way they had come. "You know that the hedge we passed through above the meadow marked the place where the walls of this modest old county town once stood." He glanced again. "Northampton used to be one of the most important places in middle England. The King had once brought his Parliament here."

Clara could see that his mind was not concentrating on what he was saying, for a furtive look had entered his eyes as if he was a huntsman with a quarry in his sights. They were standing beside a lock keepers' cottage. Edward pulled Clara around the corner of the wall and placed his finger on her mouth. He mouthed the words, 'stay here', and ran up the canal side and disappeared around the further side of the cottage.

Edward had seen the figure of a man, dressed in dark jacket and trousers with a flat cap pulled down over his face. He had been taking cover behind the trees along the bank, whilst maintaining a steady distance from the couple. Edward stood behind the cottage looking for the man. He needed to be patient, because there was no movement for at least five minutes. And then he saw him, darting from behind a broad trunk to another, but in the direction of the road. Was he following them, Edward asked himself? Did the man want to rob them; no, he was much too furtive for a common thief.

Another few minutes passed by and then the man left his cover and began to walk to the canal side, further up from the junction. Edward realised that because the man had lost sight of them, it was vital for him to regain the trail as soon as possible. The man stood more than fifty yards from him up the canal. When the man turned his gaze up the canal, Edward took his chance and ran from the cottage to the cover of some bushes that would allow him to turn the tables and approach the fellow.

When he was within ten yards of him and still hidden, he rushed headlong at him. He hit the man's side at full speed and felled him. The surprise was sufficient to allow Edward to get the better of him, with the man's arm pushed painfully up his back. He allowed him to get up and then walked the man down the canal to where Clara was waiting.

"Here is our fellow," called Edward. "A fine catch, do you not think?"

"Was he following us?" asked Clara.

"He was, indeed."

"Why?"

"That is what I hope he is going to tell us." Edward had reached Clara. The man was still silent and had a rueful look on his face. "Talk," said Edward, forcing the man's hand further up his back.

The man went up on his toes in pain and spoke. "All right, all right, sir. I didn't mean you no 'arm. It's just my master; he wanted to know what you were up to and where you were going."

"Who is your master?"

The man did not answer, until Edward wrenched his arm again.

"It's Mister Abraham. Jacob Abraham. He lives up on Cheyne Walk, number five."

"And you are?" Edward threatened him again.

"I'm 'is stableman. I look after 'is 'orses."

"Very well. Perhaps you could tell Mister Abraham that we will call on him tonight. Here's a shilling for your trouble."

Much to Clara's astonishment, Edward let the man go and fished out a coin from his waistcoat pocket. The man held out his hand, touched his cap and sauntered off.

"You paid him?" she asked.

"Indeed. He was a rather poor detective, so I do not think that I will employ him to do that for me. But he may well be a source of information. The stablemen and boys of the town always know more than you imagine."

"And do you really intend to visit this person Abraham tonight?"

"I do and I hope that you might accompany me. There will be no danger. Did you know that Abraham's Bank services the financial needs of the sizable Jewish community in this town? I assume that Mister Abraham simply likes to keep an eye on certain people, those who claim that they cannot repay their debts, for example. And newcomers like us, who have secret agendas, might also attract his interest."

"But how would he have found out about us."

"Well, we could ask him, although he will probably like to keep his sources secret. I would assume that someone in the Crossley household has let slip to a friend that the award of a medal is being considered. I did consider warning the Crossleys that our mission was secret, but I was loath to spoil the genial atmosphere that we generated. And I knew that a leak might happen whatever we said."

§

"Let us walk to the Market Square. There is something I wish to show you, before we head for Cheyne Walk."

The cuisine at The George was improving. Edward and Clara had dined well and were satisfied as they walked out of the front door. The evening was still light, without any prospect of rain. They reached the Square in a minute or two and approached the northwest corner. Above the door of a fine building was the name, 'Abraham's Bank'.

"Do you think this is the business of the man we are going to see," asked Clara.

"I do indeed. Henry Grieves sent me some information on the Jewish community in Northampton. Many of the men of influence are Jewish, boot manufacturers, owners of emporiums and banks. Amongst people with more strongly held Christian beliefs like the dissenters, there can be a tendency to associate the Jews with the death of Christ. And that is why I suspected that Jeremiah Crossley might be anti-Semitic."

"Do you think that Mister Abraham was interested in us because of Jeremiah's views."

"Clara, that is exactly where my thoughts were leading me. You see, it is a temptation for a schoolteacher to pass on their views to their pupils, even in an unintentional way. It is perfectly respectable for them to pass on their Christian views, but not their anti-Semitism."

"My word," replied Clara. "If that is the case, I am sure that would give Samuel Nettleby another reason for detesting Robert's father."

They had reached Cheyne Walk. From the Square to the Walk, there was an upward progression in the prosperity of the house owners and hence in the size and opulence of their houses. As they approached number five, Clara whispered, "Thank you for warning me to dress appropriately, Edward. I hope that I am smart enough."

"You look charming," replied Edward with a smile.

A manservant opened the door.

"Baron Cleat and Doctor Cox to see Mister Abraham,"

said Edward. They stepped inside and waited. The servant ushered them into a well-furnished study. A man with curly greying hair and a piercing gaze got up from an easy chair next to the fireplace. He approached. "My dear man, thank you for coming to see me. I was not aware that you were from the aristocracy."

"Indeed. My name is Edward Pennington and this is Doctor Clara Cox."

Abraham stared at Clara. "Doctor," he seemed to say to himself. He turned back to Edward without acknowledging Clara and said, "Please sit down, Baron. Can I offer you a drink? Brandy for yourself, perhaps, and sherry for Mrs Cox?"

Edward did not react to Abraham not using Clara's title, and merely nodded his head. A moment later the drinks arrived. They each sipped silently. Edward was content to wait for Abraham's apology, either for putting a man on their tails or for insulting Clara. As he expected, the apology did not include the Doctor.

"I am sorry for intruding on your walk in the park."

"Thank you."

"I am sure you know who I am?" asked the banker.

"Yes, we certainly know who you are."

"My family have been in the business for generations. We have served and supported the people of this town faithfully. Without us, the businesses that provide work for so many could not have got through their difficult moments. The war with the French tested us all and the Empire has had its dark moments. But, we too have our problems. There are those that tell lies about us."

Edward understood this sombre speech perfectly; he now knew why they were here. He had some sympathy for the man, but he could not excuse Abraham's views on women. He decided to move the conversation on.

"Perhaps I could help you by explaining what we are doing in your fine town."

Abraham nodded.

"The President of the Royal Society, Professor Bartholomew Hyde, personally asked myself and Doctor Cox to visit Northampton. The Society wishes to honour one of its notable citizens with the award of a medal for services to science. I am sure that you know who that person is."

"Robert Crossley." There was bitterness in Abraham's voice.

"Doctor Cox and I are merely servants of the President in this matter. We are gathering information about the man to help the committee write the citation and to help in the writing of a biography, if the committee deem it appropriate."

"I see."

There was another silence. It seemed that there was nothing more to be said at present on that subject.

"I should compliment you on your man," said Edward. Abraham was puzzled for a moment. Edward continued. "Yes, it was only by pure chance that I saw him. He was doing a fine job in following us unobserved, up to that point. Had he been on our tails from the beginning?"

Abraham appeared to decide that it was time to open himself a little. "You must understand my position, Edward. Abraham's Bank is like all other banks. It accepts our customer's money for safekeeping and also lends money to them. Occasionally they tell us that they cannot pay us back. Now, in most cases we are happy to extend our terms, if it is in our interests. But customers are only human and sometimes they try to deceive us. In such cases, the use of a man to find things out is useful."

"I understand entirely. How did you hear about us?"

"The news of Crossley's lecture to the Royal Society was everywhere at the time, as was his elevation to membership of that august body. Then there was a rumour, a small word floating on the breeze, that a gentleman and a lady were asking questions about him. It was my son, Michael, who picked it up. He has such an open face that people talk to him. As you can see, I am getting old and the time will come when I can no longer run the bank. He has a degree from Cambridge, but his wits have survived intact."

He let his joke float on the breeze between them.

"What college?"

"Gonville and Caius," replied Abraham.

"At the same time as Robert Crossley?"

"Not exactly. But he did hear rumours that Crossley had been solving mathematical problems for a Professor at London, while he was studying."

"Really?"

"Yes, it surprised us too. His degree classification was well down from the Wranglers. People used to say that the Wranglers were so clever that they were good enough for nothing but staying around the university and being clever."

"Yes, I can understand that."

"I have a friend in a London Bank, which handles Crossley's account. He is making enough to be comfortable. It is not clear what he does, but amounts are paid in on a regular basis from a Government Ministry and various businesses."

Edward nodded and wondered why Abraham was giving him this information.

"And the most peculiar thing is that he has secretly married the cousin of James Joseph Sylvester, who is a mathematician and also a Jew."

Edward let his eyebrows lift a little at this. Abraham saw that he had his interest.

"He also has some business interests that overlap with other Jews in London and the provinces. We say that such a thing makes Crossley a friend of the Jews. He is not one of us, but is a friend. His father is not our friend, but our enemy." There was an edge to Abraham's voice. "This is the reason that I am interested in what you are doing. Jeremiah Crossley was an anti-Semite. In the position of an usher at the Grammar School he poisoned the minds of many of his pupils, men who are now abroad in this town, longing to bring us down. Crossley's father was our enemy and by association, his son is also. The sins of the father..."

"Clearly, Sylvester's cousin did not think so."

"Of course not; she sees him as a friend. It is the way with women. But do not misunderstand me, Edward. A man may be our enemy, but we will still do business with him. However, I will get to the point. The memory of Jeremiah Crossley still rankles with many of my friends. I want you to do whatever you can to prevent the award of a medal to Crossley. It will cause all sorts of resentment in the town. The man has had enough success. Let him be."

"I understand. But as I said earlier, there is a committee at the Society, which I do not sit upon, that will decide the matter. However, I do promise to mention your feelings to the President. It is all I can do."

"Very well. Thank you," replied Abraham.

But Edward was not ready to depart yet. "I know James

Joseph Sylvester well," he said. "I have met him at several gathering of mathematicians in London and the provinces. You are right; he is well known for his irresistible personality, and by our community for his significant contributions to the theory of numbers and other such things. But I was not aware that he had a cousin; most interesting."

"Ah, I should have realised that the President would send a mathematician to investigate a mathematician."

"Yes." Both Edward and Abraham had relaxed a little now that their initial antagonism had passed.

"There is one thing I would like to ask you," continued Edward. "I am always interested to find men of our community. Is there another mathematician in Northampton?"

Abraham shook his head slowly. "No, not that I know of."

"Or a mathematician that might have died recently?"

"Ah, yes. There is. He owned a flourmill, would you believe? He was one of my customers at the bank. But he died in '35. I understood enough about milling when he had explained it to me, but I never understood his mathematics. But he was a nice old fellow. I could get the records checked for his name, if that would help you."

Edward nodded his head. He was conscious that Clara was still with them and probably still feeling upset. He rose. "Mister Abraham, it has been a most interesting visit. We must go."

§

They had only gone twenty yards down the road, when Clara turned to Edward and said, "That was the most poisonous man I have ever met!"

"Clara, I must apologise unreservedly for Mister Abraham and his unregenerate manners. I assume that he can be polite to his wife, but then he might have married her for her qualities of procreation and domestic management rather than her intellect. I apologise to you on his behalf, but I know that the man does not deserve my help."

Clara wanted to pass on to other matters and said, "We already knew from your bloodhound that Robert was living in a house owned by an Arab who was married to Sylvester's cousin. Abraham has now told us that Robert has now married that woman and that she is a Jew. What strikes me is that the Arabs and the Jews have a long-standing enmity. What sort of woman can this be?"

"Indeed. Of course, everyone knows that Sylvester is Jewish. I wonder what happened to the Arab. I will write to my hound and get him to investigate further."

Clara concealed her annoyance that Edward had not told her this at the time. "Do you think," she continued, "that Robert could have come across the miller's work and taken it? But to then present it at the Royal Society would require an understanding beyond his capability; how could that be? Either Robert has powers of comprehension that we cannot appreciate or it is a false trail of clues and our prognosis is built on sand."

Edward strode off down Cheyne Walk towards the river. When Clara questioned him on his route, he said, "I hope to meet another person of interest to us. I sent Abraham's stableman a note this morning, asking him to locate this person and ask him to meet us by the bridge tonight. We will see how well he has done."

Dusk was falling and they made their way carefully along the bank toward the bridge. Clara followed Edward and he peered intently all around him as they went. The man saw them first and stepped out from under the shadow on the bridge.

Edward called, "Charles?"

"What do you want with me, sir?"

"You are Charles Laverty?"

"Yes."

"My name is Pennington and this is Doctor Cox. We are seeking information about the Crossleys. I understand that you worked for Jeremiah for a short time."

"Crossley? Ah, he was a fool. He had no awareness of who he really was, just who he wanted to be. He poisoned those he taught about the Jews, as well as beating the life out of them. Jeremiah had many enemies in town."

"Why did you leave his Society?"

"I was working as an assistant in an ironmongers shop, when I helped him at that first meeting. There was a problem with the demonstration that he couldn't understand. I was sacked when the owner, a Jew, found out that I was also working for Jeremiah. They all knew him. So, I left the Society; thought it would make finding work easier. Then I got a job in a drapers shop. Getting on well, I was, until a customer recognised me from that meeting and told the owner. I even went back to the Crossley's house, whilst he was at school, and begged Mister Crossley to find me something in the brewery. But then a rearing horse kicked me and I was laid off. Now, I'm trying the boot factories. At least I can sit down there."

"How has the mathematics been progressing? Have you solved any theorems recently?"

"What are you talking about? I don't do mathematics. It was those boys that did mathematics and they did it better than anyone else I know."

"And what do you remember of them?"

"They were both clever. William was easy going. Robert was tighter and defensive; it was as if he hid behind his brother. But I could tell he was sharper than William. People thought they were the same. They were on the outside, but inside they were opposites, as far as the north is from the south. They will fight eventually. Robert will win, because William is too honest."

Edward had been watching his eyes. It was clear that he didn't want to be seen talking to these two strangers. Edward put his hand in his pocket. "Here is something. Thank you for your time."

A second later Charles had disappeared. Edward turned to Clara. "I am not sure that that was worth the money. But I think we can tick him off our list."

CHAPTER 8

The Boot Factory

L ate the following afternoon, Edward and Clara arrived at the gate of '*Isaac Campbell & Co., Boot and Shoe Maker*'. They faced an impressive two-storey building of stone and brick, with a front door and windows like any other large house. At one end was an entrance wide enough to drive a carriage through.

"So this is the place," said Edward to Clara. "Henry Grieves wrote the story down for me. It appears that the workers, who previously sewed the shoes by hand, in their own homes, or in small local workshops, recently went on strike, for they feared the machines would put them out of work. They formed the Northampton Boot and Shoe-makers Mutual Protection Society to look after their interests. It took the owners, who banded together as the Northampton Manufacturers' Association, some effort to explain that the new arrangement would not put them out of work, but simply require them to go to the factory where the machinery was housed. Since both sides agreed, such buildings as this will become common in the town. I will show you his report, if it interests you."

A notice beside the entrance told factory visitors to report to the gateman, whose door they saw just inside. They knocked and were admitted. The gateman looked at them. "Selling or buying?"

"Neither, my good man. We are here to talk to Benjamin Edge. I understand he works here," replied Edward.

"Well he can't see you, because he's workin'."

"And when will he finish working?"

The man twisted in his chair to look at the clock. "In ten minutes."

"Can you inform him that we wish to talk to him?"

"You're not from the police, are ye? Or the authorities?"

"Benjamin is not in any trouble, to be sure," said Edward with a smile.

The gateman nodded. "Lad!" he shouted.

"Edge is like a machine," he went on, "he runs his workers without a please or a thank you. No one likes him, which is how he likes it."

Edward said nothing.

"Lad!" cried the man again. A moment later a small boy appeared. "Go and tell Ben Edge that there is a gentleman and a lady to see him. Hurry now or you'll get caught in the rush of workers comin' out."

The boy ran off.

"When the hooter goes, it's like an army in retreat, sir," said the gatekeeper. "I suggest that you wait five or ten minutes and then the boy'll take you over."

The boy led them to one of five single storey buildings that stretched away into the distance. They were brick built with large windows on either side. Inside, despite the windows, the gloom meant that they could hardly see the other end of the building. They followed the boy down the rows of machines. Halfway down, on one side, was a glass sided booth where the supervisor sat. An emaciated old man sat at the desk, poring over a ledger. Edward paused because he could not believe that this was Benjamin Edge, William's old school friend; he looked twenty years older. The man looked at them suspiciously and waved at two chairs.

"Come in; sit down," he said curtly, as if the two of them had just ruined another pair of boots.

"Are you Benjamin Edge?"

"Yes. What do you want?"

"Can I talk to you about the Crossleys?"

Benjamin stood up with alarm written all over his face. "No, sir! You may not. I know of no such people."

"Your reaction suggests to me that you do know them, but do not wish to be reminded of them."

"Very well, you understand. You can leave now."

Clara put a hand up to stop Edward. "Mister Edge, I believe that you were once a friend of William Crossley. He sends his compliments."

"What do you know of William Crossley?"

"We have talked to him about the award of a medal to Robert by the Royal Society. William talked of a warm friendship with you. He said you were best friends at school."

Benjamin had sat down and covered his face with his hands. He seemed not to hear their reason for talking to William, but found comfort in the talk of a warm friendship. "Yes, we were friends once."

"And he told us that you had been kind to his brother, Robert, when you helped him with his Latin lessons."

Benjamin looked up. "Do not mention that foul man," he shouted. "I sinned. I cheated at my lessons. I tried to help him to do the same and he never let me forget it. I will never be forgiven for my sin." He plunged his face into his hands and Clara heard sobs.

"But the Lord has forgiven you. Remember that He died for our sins. You have freely admitted your sin and He has freely forgiven you. It is only you yourself who cannot accept that."

"Then why did Robert take advantage of me," he shouted through his tears, "and just compounded my sins?"

Clara leaned over to him and touched his arm. "Can you tell me what happened?"

"Why are you talking to William?"

"The Royal Society wants to award Robert a medal for services to science. We are gathering information about his early life to help them understand the man," said Edward gently.

"But I don't want my dealings with Robert to come to light. Please, leave me alone."

"Benjamin," said Clara, "my colleague Mister Pennington will not reveal to the Royal Society anything that is confidential. You can believe me."

"But he is a successful man. What would he, or you, care about a man that works in a place like this."

"I am a member of the British Medical Association. I am a practicing doctor. I have taken a vow never to reveal confidential discussions with my patients."

Benjamin stared at her. "You, a Doctor?"

"Yes, one of the first women doctors. There will be many more. I believe that your talking about what happened might help you. Remember also that our Lord can work through strangers to lift burdens."

"I have heard that at church."

Clara nodded.

"When we were at school, I gave him my book of Latin

exclamations that I had got from a boy in the class above me, when I couldn't do it. I gave it to him for nothing, because we were friends. Then, when we had left a few years and his father was teaching him, he sought me out to help him again. By then I had got to like Latin and Greek and was good at it. He seemed to know that. I said no, I wouldn't sin no more. I said that Jesus had told me that it was wrong and I was determined to do right. But then he told me that he would tell the Minister that I had demanded money off him at school for the exclamation book, a lot of money. I prayed and prayed that he would go away, but the Lord held his hand, because He wanted to teach me proper about good and evil. I helped him in the end and now I cannot escape my sin. The Lord won't forgive me, he won't."

He began sobbing again. Clara put her hand on his shoulder. "Being forced to do wrong is not the same as freely doing wrong. Do they tell you that at church?"

"No, I ain't heard that. Sin is sin to them."

"Well, it is true, nevertheless. Robert has forced you to sin and the Lord is ready to forgive you. He has already forgiven you for the first time. He is now willing to forgive you for the second."

They heard a rush of words behind Benjamin's hands that they could not understand. But Clara held onto his shoulder.

When they were outside the gates of the factory, Edward said, "Robert has broken that man. I hope you have undone it."

Clara was less hopeful. "I hope he has someone to tell him again and again that he is forgiven. I have found in many cases that relief from such guilt does not come quickly or completely."

§

Later that evening, Edward and Clara were again with Elijah and Hannah in their small drawing room, listening to William.

"A year after I left school," William said, "the crisis hit Robert. The Master had told him, that afternoon, that Robert would not be entered for the university scholarship examination. Although his marks were good, particularly in the natural sciences and mathematics, his grasp of the classics was, as the old man had said, so shaky and full of holes, that his chances of passing were too small to justify the examination fee.

Robert arrived home and immediately told mother. Without any word of judgment, she comforted him with an embrace. He told me that her ministrations did not quieten his racing heart, for that was what he expected from her. His mind looked forward to the moment when he told father and the anticipation seemed to block out his appreciation of the present. The solution that was finally decided upon, both surprised and frightened him.

Father arrived home and greeted mother. 'Jeremiah,' she said. 'Robert has something to tell you. He is upstairs in his room.'

'Thank you, Rebecca. I already know his news. Samuel told me just before I came away. I will talk to him after dinner. I know what must be done.'

After dinner, my mother remained in the kitchen, to allow father and Robert to talk in the drawing room.

Robert followed father in.

'Robert, I want to talk to you about your future. But

before we do that, perhaps we could share some thoughts about what you do in Elijah's workshop?'

'Yes, sir.' Father had never taken any interest in what we did in the clock shop before. Robert raised his guard.

'Do you enjoy it?' asked father.

Robert was not about to open his heart to his father.

'Yes, sir.'

'Ah. I was hoping that you would tell me what you enjoyed about the work.'

"All of it, sir.'

'I see. And what do you do there?'

'We are..., that is, William and I, are learning how to cut wheels, gears, sir, for clocks.'

'Yes. I know about wheels. And is that all you do?'

Robert did not want to reveal to him his conversations with Mister Dyke, his excitement about the business side of the shop, or the arithmometer project.

'I help Uncle Elijah, sir.'

'Yes. That is good. I am therefore certain that the Crossleys will continue to prosper in Northampton. But I had hoped with William or yourself, that our name would be known beyond this town. For, as you know, I was the only son of my father to go to university. It was that that put me on the road to success. I am now a well-known and respected member of the community and I play my part in educating it and moving it forward in the sciences and mathematics, which to be sure have a very large part to play in the exciting future of our society.'

Robert had heard this broad and expansive philosophy from his father before, at his Society for Scientific Experiment and Mathematics, but he had not heard it at home before.

Robert was surprised and, whilst he remained guarded, he listened expectantly for something that mirrored his own feelings about the future.

Father continued. 'So, Robert, as you might imagine, I am interested in your progress. I have arranged with Doctor Nettleby that after you finish your school career, you will become an Assistant and help me to demonstrate the various experiments that I teach to the top forms. This should be relatively straightforward for you, for I saw that you had a strong capability in these subjects. As we know, it is your capability in the Classics that is lacking. I therefore propose to dispense with the services of your home mathematics tutor and to teach you myself in Greek and Latin sufficient for you to be successful in the entrance examination.'

Any warm feeling that was established by his father's interest in his work at the clock shop was demolished by the announcement of his plans to tutor Robert himself. His heart sank and the anger returned.

'But Mister Graham knows Greek and Latin. He could teach me.'

'Robert, do not raise your voice at me. I did not want to say this, for fear of affecting you and William, but I can ill afford to pay Mister Graham.'

The fact did affect Robert. For now he had confirmation that his father was not the success that he would have people believe. He was not only fallible, but he was poor. The feeling of determination returned. Robert told me that one day he would be successful, he would be rich and he would be known in London and beyond.

He said no more to his father that evening. He bowed

his head to Jeremiah's wishes and retired to his bedroom to stare at the ceiling and contemplate his future."

William's narrative suddenly ceased as his emotions for his brother overcame him. Edward and Clara respected his silence and he soon regained his composure and continued.

"Later that year, Robert started his employment as an Assistant at the Grammar School and Jeremiah started to tutor him in the Classics. Jeremiah no longer beat us. I suppose he remembered my disobedience over going to university. In his tutoring of Robert he was as respectful as he could be, but remained frustrated at Robert's lack of open communication with him.

Robert continued to work with me in Uncle Elijah's shop. He was still involved in the arithmometer project. One Saturday afternoon, we talked as we machined a part. Robert sat and turned the handle whilst I controlled the cutter as it gently shaped the shiny metal disc.

'Robert,' I said, as I peered at the small part rotating at high speed, 'I am glad that we are still doing this together. For it reminds me that we are still brothers.'

'I understand, Will. It is one of the few things that calm me down after a week of battling with father over Latin verbs. How I hate them. Amo, amas, amat... I love, thou lovest, he, she or it loves... How I hate the six ways to say love.'

'Perhaps you should decline to decline love and decline hate instead.' I knew I should not have, but I laughed at my own joke. Robert did not seem to be able to give himself fully to my humour and merely smiled with me.

'But you know,' he went on, 'we will not always be brothers in a clock shop way, Will.'

The mood of careless fun had disappeared.

'Do you recall, Robert,' I said, 'when you found out that I was to join Uncle and Mister Dyke here in the shop. You said a rather strange, but most brotherly, thing. You said that you wished me well with whatever I did in the shop and that I should always remember it.'

'I recall it well. You know, Will, that I am unable to express my inmost feelings at times. I think I was trying to say that although our lives may move apart, we would always be brothers. The brotherhood of the clock shop is one thing, but there is another which I cannot express.'

'Well, there is the brotherhood of our birth, but I am certain that that is not what you refer to, for that relationship is through our father, and I know that you would prefer to banish him from your mind. There is the brotherhood in Christ through our belief in the gospel. But again I do not think that you mean that, for I understand your doubts, which I share.'

'Yes, to both, Will.'

'Robert, you know that Plato said that mathematics is a set of objects which exist outside ourselves and which men discover as they develop the language of mathematics. I believe it, for it is a noble belief. If you believe that too, then we have a shared faith. We are Brothers in Plato.'

It did not occur to us to question whether Plato would have been happy to be thought of as a deity capable of indwelling his adherents. Nor whether Christ would have been happy to share his indwelling with another. We were simply two young men sharing the discoveries that we were making about life and mathematics. Robert looked at me and a broad smile broke across his face. He grasped my hand and shook it gratefully.

'Will, you have the gift of putting into words what other people are too stupid to express. Thank you, brother, for we will always be Brothers in Plato.'

Edward, I believe that these mysterious words brought much solace to Robert, who soldiered on with his job at the School and his Classics with father, until a chance meeting changed his world."

William stopped. A cuckoo clock, somewhere in the clockmaker's house, whistled the quarter.

"William, Clara and I talked to Ben Edge today," said Edward. William came out of his reverie and stared at him. "We believe that you should befriend him again. He might now be in a position to talk to you. And it might help his recovery."

William nodded.

After a pause, Hannah said, "Shall I begin?"

"Thank you, yes," said Edward.

"As William said, it was indeed a chance meeting. I will now tell you how we came to know the Reverend Grey and how our little plan for Robert was conceived."

Hannah began her story.

"I was standing in for Horace behind the counter in the shop, whilst he was visiting the other shops that he had an interest in. A small woman entered. She carried a worn bag from which she produced a handkerchief wrapped around something precious. She placed it gently on the counter and unwrapped it.

'Oh, I do hope you can repair it' she said, in a breathless voice. 'It stopped so long ago.'

I looked briefly at the watch and then the old woman.

'I'm sure we can,' I said and went out to find Elijah. We returned.

'I am Elijah Crossley.' He glanced down at the pocket watch and chain lying on the counter. 'Why! This is French, and rather old.'

'Oh, I am so sorry. Is it too old to mend?'

'On the contrary; I value age more than the modern generation do. I would be honoured to repair it for you.'

'It is not for me. It is for my husband, the Reverend Grey. He is about to retire and his congregation has so kindly offered to have it repaired for him. They are not rich folk, being mostly farm workers, so I cannot pay you much. But Arnold treasures it very greatly, for it was given to him by a French mathematician.'

'But you said your husband was a Reverend?'

'Oh yes, he is Vicar at Upstone. He is to retire next year. We are a little worried about not having enough money, but the church is to give us a little cottage. Because the Vicarage is close to the church, we tell the time by the church clock, which has such a beautiful chime. But next year we will be further away and he is going deaf.'

'Well, as I said, I would be honoured and also very interested to set this timepiece going again. If you would like to leave it, my wife will give you a receipt and I will look at it in the next few days. You should call again in a week.'

'That is very kind of you. Thank you.'

That evening we discussed the Vicar's wife over dinner.

'She was such a dear, Elijah. I long to see the Reverend. I picture him with a long white beard and a stoop from too much reading of fine print Bibles.'

'He sounds like a Vicar of the traditional sort,' said Elijah, meaning to say more.

'Ah,' I interrupted, 'but Robert worries me still. How can he put up with Jeremiah trying to teach him Greek and Latin? I cannot understand it. It is true what they say. Those that are good at something may not be the best to teach it. I think you have to have struggled at something, so you can understand your student's difficulty. Jeremiah finds Classics so easy; how can he understand Robert who does not?'

'You are right, Hannah, but...'

Elijah stared at me, or rather through me.

'What is it?' I asked. 'What is going on in that head of yours, husband?'

'Why, Hannah. It may be a perfect solution. Now, Reverend Grey is worried about money. We are not. Jeremiah cannot teach his son Classics. The Reverend has spent his life amongst poor farm workers, so that he must understand their difficulties in learning anything. For he has to teach them every Sunday.'

'Oh, Elijah: Yes! The Reverend could teach Robert.'

'Yes, yes, indeed. But Jeremiah would not accept our paying on his behalf. He is a proud man.'

'So,' said I, 'we must talk to the Reverend and explain it all to him and get his agreement to tell Jeremiah that he will teach Robert for nothing.'

'But he is a cleric, he will not be able to tell a lie," argued Elijah.

"Yes, my dear,' I replied, 'but he is also a man of the world. For he has spoken to a French mathematician.' "

Silence fell and the storytelling was over. Edward and Clara left the shop and walked out into the Square. When they had walked sufficiently far from the shop not to be heard or seen, Edward turned to Clara in a state of excitement.

"Clara, this is our first clue. A French mathematician! It is all possible now."

"No, I do not think so. The Reverend is an expert at Classics and happens to have met, perhaps at university, a French mathematician. That would have been a very long time ago. Edward, it does not look possible to me."

Edward's face fell and he accepted that Clara was probably right. All the other avenues of investigation of possible authors of the work had seemed to close. Robert's misdemeanors had seemed to escalate. He had disowned his own sister and now he had clearly blackmailed his friend Ben. At the same time, he had entered a mystical, almost religious relationship with his brother. Robert had become a perplexing mixture of the obscene and sublime. "Everything that we discover about Robert suggests that plagiarism is not beyond him. However, we are still no closer to having any proof. Come, let us walk back to the hotel."

Their somber mood meant they did not converse until they got inside. The manager approached them hurriedly with an envelope in his hand. Clara tore it open and read.

"It is from my clinic. One of the patients is seriously ill and I am needed there urgently."

She turned back to the manager. "Can you reply that I will return as soon is humanly possible." The man hurried back to his office. Clara looked apologetically at Edward.

"I will have to go back to London immediately. I hope that this will not impede you. I am so sorry."

Edward feigned a cheerful mood to make parting from Clara less difficult. "Why m'dear. 'Tis the Northampton Steeplechase in a couple o'days. I propose to make the most of the going and hope to come out ahead by a few hundred quid."

Clara turned her eyes skywards and sighed, shaking her head. Then she became serious. She put her hand on his arm and whispered, "Edward, you asked me a question about my marriage. The answer is no."

PART 2

LONDON AND CAMBRIDGE

CHAPTER 9

The Vicar of Upstone

Elijah had repaired the French pocket watch with more pleasure than he had got from any watch before, and charged Elizabeth and the poor parishioners of Upstone a tenth of what he would normally. He and Hannah then visited Arnold in his Vicarage and made their proposal to him. Arnold thanked them, discussed the matter with his wife and then spent a week thinking it over. He had not taught for many a long year and at first doubted his ability to get Robert to the required level. He looked through his books and the previous year's entrance examination paper, which Elijah had obtained from Samuel Nettleby at the Grammar School under conditions of extreme secrecy. Finally, the Vicar prayed it through one weekday morning in front of the altar of his tiny church. He sent a message to Elijah at the clock shop, who alerted Rebecca at the Crossley home, who was also involved in the elaborate plan. Rebecca's part was to have one of her characteristic conversations with Jeremiah, in which she asked questions of him that seeded the very answers that she wanted. Jeremiah had become increasingly disillusioned with his tutoring and seriously doubted that Robert was making any progress at all. Sending Robert to an old Vicar that his brother recommended seemed as good as anything else. His lessons with Robert ceased and he turned his mind fully to the church and to his Scientific Society. Robert, he said with a heavy heart, was now free to find his own way.

§

It was a breezy Sunday afternoon in the May of 1840. The retired Vicar's cottage was in the corner of a field of grass at the end of the village. Robert, now a young man of nineteen, had walked the couple of miles from his home and, to take a moments rest, he leaned on the wide gate watching the horses grazing contentedly. There was a mare and two foals. The sight brought to his mind William and Phoebe. They would marry in due course and have children. There was a discernable feeling of envy somewhere inside him. He knew that his ambitions and the plans to realise them had overwhelmed any of the normal feelings that young men had. He regretted what he had lost, as he imagined himself taking the hand of some young girl and kissing her. He hurriedly shook his head free of the frustration that these thoughts brought to him.

He turned his attention to the cottage. It had a decrepit look about it, for it had been unoccupied for some years before the Greys moved in. It was owned by the Church Commissioners to house the curate but, as the population of the village had dwindled due to migration to the town nearby, the curacy was not maintained. The paintwork of the cottage was peeling and he could see holes in the thatch.

Robert knocked on the door. It opened. and there stood the Reverend Arnold Grey. He was gaunt, for age was beginning to shrink the flesh on his bones. His unkempt white hair fell to his shoulders, giving him a ghostly appearance. But the moment he looked into Robert's face, any apprehension that the young man may have had disappeared. Arnold's twinkling eyes and lively speech immediately made Robert feel at home. Then Arnold went straight to the heart of the matter.

"I understand that you are a gifted young mathematician. I know that we have to study a little Greek and Latin, but we shall have such a marvellous time solving some little mathematical problems that I shall devise especially for you."

The two of them settled into the kitchen parlour at the old table. Arnold looked his new student up and down

"I shall call you Robert and you may call me Arnold. We are old enough to dispense with formality. Please tell me about yourself and start wherever you will."

This struck Robert as too unspecific and he was momentarily dumbfounded. Then he gathered his wits.

"I am Robert, son of Jeremiah and Rebecca Crossley, brother to William, Emily, Patience and Thomas."

The old man thought this introduction was similar enough to a Biblical genealogy to be uncharacteristic of the boy he had expected from Elijah's description. He waited for more.

"I work as an Assistant at the Grammar School and help at my uncle's shop on Saturdays."

"Ah, I know your uncle. Elijah is his name, I think?"

"Yes, sir, I mean Arnold. He is the best watch and clock maker in the town."

"Yes, he is. What do you do there on Saturdays?"

Robert hesitated. He had promised to keep the arithmometer project a secret until they had proved their design. Although he longed to discuss it with someone else, he decided that he had not yet got the measure of this pleasant old man.

"I help to make parts for clocks with my brother, William."

"So, you understand how clocks work, do you?"

"Oh yes, Arnold. From the lever escapement, to the balance spring and the oil wells."

"My word, young man, you are very knowledgeable."

Robert bristled with pride.

"If we go back further than the marvellous inventions you referred to, some men say that the ancient Egyptians invented the clock, based on the flow of water. But the Greeks also demonstrated them and we are interested in the Greeks, are we not? Now, I must confess that I am not mechanically minded. Would you explain to me how a water clock might work?"

Robert took up the pencil that Arnold had provided for their discussion. "It is straightforward. Imagine a receptacle holding a fair amount of water." He drew an open topped box on the paper. "Then, there is a narrow pipe from this receptacle to another below it. Water will flow at a speed determined mainly by the diameter of the pipe. Then, if one measures the height of water in the lower receptacle after a certain time, then the height is proportional to the time elapsed."

"Ah, yes, I see," said the old man. "So, one could say that the flow of the water measures time."

Robert nodded his head enthusiastically.

"Or as the Greeks would say, ὕδατος ροὺς χρόνον μετρεί."

He wrote the words carefully below Robert's drawing, speaking them clearly as he wrote.

"Two of the Greek words should be familiar to you. Chronon, meaning *time*." He pointed to the penultimate word in the phrase he had written, "The word is used in chronograph, a type of watch that is used for measuring intervals accurately. And metrei, the word after, meaning *measures*, gives us the metric system of measurement that England is loath to adopt, because it is what the continentals use."

Robert nodded his head sagely, for he had immediately seen how his tutor proposed to teach him Greek. Yet he sighed, for he also realised the magnitude of the task. Arnold read all of this in Robert's face, and immediately tried to lift his mood.

"Now, Archimedes had something to do with water clocks, but we will leave that for later. Let us look at a mathematical problem."

He placed a clean sheet of paper in front of Robert.

"Draw a circle." He handed Robert a compass. "Now draw a square that just fits outside the circle." Robert did so. "Now convert the square into an octagon." Robert considered this. He knew that an octagon had eight sides of equal length. With a few strokes of the compass he created one by drawing straight lines that cut off the corners of the square. "Notice that, compared to the square, the octagon begins to look like the circle. So, I want you to find an expression for the area of the octagon."

This was easy, thought Robert, who wrote down the expression for the area of the square, which was the length of its side squared. Then he found the area of one of the corner triangles he had cut off when he converted the square to an octagon, multiplied the result by four and took it from the area of the square.

"Very good, Robert. Have you done that before?"

"No."

"Even better, then. For you have just recreated Archimedes' calculation of the area of a circle, which stood as the most accurate method that man knew for many centuries. And, of course, we can use it to find a value for that most mysterious of numbers, *pi*."

Robert looked at him, with a puzzled look on his face. "I understood the calculation," he said, "and I know that the area of the circle is related to the diameter by the number called *pi*. It is very straightforward, and *pi* is but another number. Why do you call it mysterious?"

Arnold smiled at him indulgently and took up the pencil. He drew again the square, and next to it the octagon, both in freehand. Then next to that he sketched, slowly and carefully, a sixteen-sided object and then beside it he began to draw an object that would have twice as many sides again. He stopped.

"I will not complete that, Robert, or we would be here all day. But can you see? As I increase the number of sides it looks smoother and smoother and more like a circle. If I drew an object with an infinite number of sides, it would be a circle. Such is the power of infinity."

"Yes, I see that, but what does it have to do with *pi*?"

"You admit that a circle is a straight sided object with an infinite number of sides. And yet we can see a circle. It would appear that there is nothing mysterious about it. Rather, it is a pleasing object, with a satisfying symmetrical and reassuring shape."

"Yes."

"But if I were to ask you to find an expression for the area of a sixteen sided object, I am sure that you would find it successfully, given a little time. And perhaps also for the thirty-two sided object, which is correspondingly harder. But you would have to repeat that exercise an infinite number of times to find the true area of the circle. And to find the value of *pi*, for the area is determined by *pi* and the diameter, you would need an infinity of calculations. And, of course, infinity can never be reached. Thus you will never know the value of *pi*. That is why it is called irrational. And that was why I said that it was a mysterious number. I do not know it, and I never will."

"And yet we know it exists," exclaimed Robert, "because the circle exists."

At this, Arnold knew that his pupil had followed all that he had taught him and was now stepping beyond his lesson to address problems not yet solved.

"Perhaps, it is a matter of faith," Arnold replied. "It exists, but we cannot describe it completely." He thought it unnecessary to draw the parallel with St Paul's definition of Christian faith.

They continued for another hour or so on more advanced geometrical theorems coupled with some Greek phrases, and then Robert left the cottage feeling breathless and exulted. The horses were still grazing contentedly in the field and the weak sun still shone through the haze. But something had changed inside him. There were moments when he struggled to keep up with the old man's fecund brain. But he knew he had found the one who could help him to realise his dreams. He was renewed in intellectual vigour and determination. He completed his homework for the Vicar with joy. Subsequently, he was successful in most of the exercises that Arnold set him. And on the few occasions when he could not solve the problem, he returned to the cottage with humility and no less determination to find the answer. And whilst the Greek and Latin still caused him problems, Arnold discovered that by coupling it with his interest in mathematics, Robert's tongue was loosened sufficiently to advance his learning towards the entrance examination.

§

The other benefit of Robert's Sunday afternoons with the Reverend was that they helped him to bear the following week of working with his father at the school. If Robert had been working with any other person, his excitement would have spilled out in casual conversation about what he had learned from his tutor. But with his father, his soul was silent and he answered his father's questions with as few words as possible. Robert felt that all men, and especially his father, were his opponents. There were few exceptions. The working classes were not his opponents, because he felt there was no need to interact with them except to order them to do their duty. William was still on his side as a brother, as was his mother, with whom he still had a childlike affection. It was also clear to him, that all other women were neither opponents to his aspirations nor colleagues in their achievement.

His father still could not understand the psychology of his son's character and his lack of reaction to his teaching. He felt that he had failed him at his time of most need, when he had been denied the chance to sit the university entrance examination. Yet, he would have been surprised at how many of his opinions Robert would have agreed with. The inevitability of war in any human society and the need to conform to authority, either to family, town or state was accepted by Robert and was not contrary to his ambitions.

But what troubled Jeremiah most was that his teaching had not been able to penetrate Robert's reserve, whatever tactics he employed. He had been a teacher all his life and believed in his own ability to put his pupils through the local examinations and occasionally the university entrance examinations. He knew that Robert had the ability, but neither his pressure nor his cajoling worked. He shared his disappointment with Rebecca, who was not surprised at the outcome, for she had witnessed Jeremiah's authoritarian rule slowly alienate Robert from him. She tried to mollify him, but was not able to convince her husband that he was not a failure; perhaps he saw through her deception.

Robert had early on developed a determination to outwit his father. In the matter of Jeremiah's self respect as a teacher, he had succeeded.

§

As the seasons passed, and months turned into years, the Sunday afternoon tutoring at Arnold's cottage continued. Slow but steady progress was made in the Classical languages. Eventually, Robert could write his simple geometrical proofs in Latin, which followed the practice of many of the great seventeenth and eighteenth century mathematicians, such a Newton and Euler. This gave him much pleasure because he felt that he had come, at last, into the presence of these masters, and could begin to read their works for himself, rather than hear it second or third hand.

To make his lessons more palatable, Arnold peppered them with personal stories of the mathematicians, for the old man had a love of these people and all their strange ways.

"Isaac Newton never had a relationship with a woman, apart from his mother," Arnold said one day, after a discussion on some aspect of the great man's book, *Principia*.

This news shook Robert to the core, for he was in the same position. He was not sure whether to welcome the similarity with England's greatest mathematician or to worry about the implied criticism of Newton's attitude to carnal relations and, by the same token, his own.

"And the nearest he came to a warm relationship was with a man, Nicolas Fatio de Duillier, a mathematician from Switzerland," Arnold continued enthusiastically, ignorant of Robert's reaction. "It must have been like being in hell to work with him, for he was savagely jealous of those he worked with, Robert Hooke and Gottfied Leibniz. He became President of the Royal Society, and it was said that he helped his friends get prominent positions and university chairs."

Of course, Robert had no way of verifying such tittle-tattle and the thought of questioning it never entered his head. He was, however, surprised both that the Reverend knew and engaged in such talk and also that such great men could be human as Robert was human. All the history he had learned in school had told him nothing like this and it reassured him that if he ever entered this public arena, he would be no different from the rest.

Then Arnold became more serious. "Robert, some of Newton's greatest work concerned infinitesimal calculus. Remember the straight-sided objects, the square, the octagon and so on. Well, as the number of sides becomes very large, the difference between the objects becomes very small. When the number of sides is infinite, then the differences become infinitesimally small. Newton discovered a whole method of analysis based on the examination of such small sections of lines and curves. Unfortunately, Leibniz discovered the same thing at about the same time, which led to a split between the English and continental mathematicians, which held back the subject in this country by a hundred years. This is the area that interests me very much."

Robert looked at his tutor with narrowed eyes and said, "I would also be interested to study that topic."

It was then that Arnold began to teach Robert infinitesimal calculus. It took seven months for Arnold to bring Robert to the point at which he could teach him no more.

"We have reached the frontier of man's knowledge," Arnold had announced one Sunday, looking at a set of equations on the page that lay between them. "Thereafter the page is blank. It is for man to discover what lies on this empty sheet. Whilst these expressions tell the story of whatever is described by a differential equation, the solution is hidden deep within them and can only be extracted through laborious calculations. A means to finding those solutions is now needed."

Robert was surprised and excited. It was gratifying to realise that he understood all that man did, in however specialized a subject. But there was something else, a feeling that took hold of his very soul. For suddenly his head was alive with the possibilities for filling the next page. The old man watched him closely; he knew that Robert was longing to take the first step. The teacher could now stand back. But there was apprehension in his heart. During that seven months, Robert had not been spared his classics, but his enthusiasm was such that Arnold knew that he had reached a standard that would get him through the entrance examination. However, Arnold did not tell him so, for fear that his pupil would leave his tutorship, and he would loose the companionship of the young man that meant so much to him. He shook his head to clear it of these dark thoughts and breathed deeply.

"Well, perhaps I should tell you some more stories of scandal to finish our afternoon together on an amusing note. Have you heard of the Bernoulli family?"

"Yes, sir, I have read about them in one of my father's books."

Robert slipped back into a more formal mode of address without thinking. Perhaps the reference to his father, to whom he would never use his Christian name, had made him do it. Or perhaps the relationship between Robert and Arnold had changed; perhaps they were now no longer the colleagues that Arnold had longed for them to be.

"Well, now. Where to begin..."

Robert barely heard most of it; much of it sounded like the book he had read. But suddenly his attention was wrenched back to the old man.

"... But the most singular part of all of this was that both Johann, the father, and Daniel, his son, were working separately on the mathematics of hydrology, which is the study of fluids. Daniel had become a better mathematician than his father and this caused much resentment to Johann, whose pride was deeply wounded. Daniel wrote a book describing his own work. His father stole some of its content and put it into his own book without mention of Daniel. He therefore committed plagiarism, the worst sin in science."

Robert stared at him.

"To help you remember the word, Robert, it is from the Latin, *plagiarius*, meaning 'kidnapper, seducer or one who steals the child of another'."

CHAPTER 10

The Death of Reverend Grey

It was the Sunday after All Souls in the year 1845 and autumn was creeping towards its end. For a few days the skies had been clear and the nights, pinched with cold, were bearable because the cheery sun in the forenoon followed them. And then a grey sky rolled in from the east and smothered the county. But it did not warm it, for the biting nights persisted and the days had the same hard feeling about them, reminding folk that winter was approaching.

Robert had just completed some extensions to the theory. They had been straightforward and he had almost dismissed them from his mind. Yet he was strangely restless. He had been engrossed during their execution, but when he finished he realised that he had reached the point where all that the old man had asked of him had been done. The work would be complete with the addition of the few pages he was carrying. He was feeling empty, for he thought that there was now almost nothing left to tie him to this man and this cottage. He was now ready for the university entrance examination; it just remained to convince the Head to put him forward.

He stepped over the stile and followed the path over the hills and through the fields without noticing his surroundings; he had done it so often before, at first with apprehension, then with joy and now with this dull ache. He reached the village and suddenly looked about him.

The small church and the houses were the same as ever, but had a flat hue, as if the overcast day had washed away the colour. The rutted street seemed somehow forbidding. He passed the beer house and carefully glanced at the tinkers, poachers and sheep stealers outside. The men were meanly dressed and, in Robert's mind, were thus criminals. He felt intimidated by them. He knew that men like them used their knuckles without much thought. He could see cuts and bruises on their faces and hands. He had heard that they had been fighting with the Northampton Shoemakers, who were a gang of young men bent on drink and trouble. They looked back at him, knowing that he was from the town. But then a wench came out from the house and took their attention away from him. He hurried on, puzzled at such alien lives. What sort of brutes were they, who lived without a thought for any of the things that he considered important. His ambition, his mathematics, his future...

He reached the cottage and, as of habit, leaned on the gate and gazed at the field. The foals had long gone, sold to Lord Wilbraham, for his daughter's trap; only the mare remained. He pulled his jacket around him, for it was getting cold and the nights were drawing in. He noticed a fine chestnut horse tied at the gate to the cottage and wondered who could be visiting. He strode up the path and, as he lifted his arm to knock, the door opened. He looked into a man's face. It was handsome and a little older than his.

"Sir," Robert asked.

"Excuse me. I am a Doctor. I have just treated the Reverend."

"Is the Reverend ill? I am studying with him, for the entrance examination."

"Ah, yes. Come with me and I will tell you." The doctor led him up the path and out onto the road. "It is not good practice to talk about a patient within the hearing of relatives."

Robert nodded his head. The doctor was brief. "Arnold collapsed earlier this morning and is in bed recovering."

The man was about to mount his horse. The Vicar's wife had told him of this student and he had sympathy for those like Robert who came to better themselves.

"Sir, if you please, tarry a moment. Is it a cardiac matter?"

The doctor stared at Robert, his respect slightly stirred.

"He has a cardiac insufficiency; in other words, a weak heart. His temperature is elevated, as is his heart rate. His heartbeat is also irregular, which is a certain sign that his heart is the problem. There is also some congestion or accumulation of fluid in the chest cavity. However, if the congestion passes then there is every sign that he may recover and live for many years more."

"He has been ill before, and has always recovered," replied Robert. "How are you treating him? Hawthorn?"

The doctor raised his eyebrows. He was not used to being questioned thus. However, he forbore to fob off this knowledgeable young man.

"I am treating his heart with hawthorn extract and his congestion with digitalis."

"Are you able to measure the pressure of his blood?" Robert now had the man's attention and continued. "I have heard talk of an instrument, called a sphygmograph, made by a Frenchman, that measures the pressure in the arm. It could perhaps be a useful indicator of condition."

The doctor's shoulders went up. "Yes, I have heard of such things. But even if we had that device, there are not yet any reliable medicines for the control of the pressure."

Robert pursed his lips in frustration that no more could be done for the Reverend.

"I fear that you are right, doctor. Thank you for your time."

"Good day, sir."

Robert was deep in thought as he walked back up to the door of the cottage. He knocked and the Vicar's wife invited him in. She led him straight to the bedside. The old man seemed to be sleeping peacefully. There were two small bottles on the chair next to the bed. The woman explained how much from each her husband was to be given. Robert nodded his head. He moved the bottles to the floor and sat down. He gently took the old man's hand in his own and watched the gentle and rhythmical heaving of his chest. With his elbow on his knee, Robert leaned his head in his other hand and sighed. He had felt strong whilst he had conversed with the doctor, but now a wave of fear passed through him. A tear escaped his eye for all the joy he had had with this wonderful man and for his love of mathematics and of the characters from that world. The Reverend's wife saw the tear and, with a little sorrow mixed with the compassion of a mother, turned away and went downstairs.

Robert sat the night through with Arnold, for he saw how weary his wife was. The candle guttered in the early hours and Robert lit a new one. He checked his patient's breathing and pulse and, because he felt that he had disturbed him, leaned down to the Reverend's face. The old man was mumbling in his sleep. Robert listened and then stood up, transfixed in thought and staring through the window into the starless night. Then he resumed his seat next to the bed and his head began to nod.

He awoke at dawn and looked down at the figure on the bed. All was still. The chest had stopped its regular rise and fall. Robert hurriedly felt for a pulse, but could find none. He ran downstairs and shouted to Arnold's wife, who was asleep on a chair in the parlour.

"I cannot feel his pulse. Where does the doctor live?"

"Tell the boy, yonder. He will ride to the doctor."

She gave him the address and he ran across the lane to another cottage where he banged on the door. A man his own age opened it, wiping the sleep from his eyes.

"I's 'arly! Wha's 'appen'd?"

Robert told him and the man ran off to saddle his horse that was kept in the barn behind the cottage, as he had done the day before, when Arnold had collapsed. Robert trudged despondently back to the house. He went upstairs and found Arnold's wife kneeling at her husband's bed, praying. She looked up at him when he entered.

"He is cold. He is gone. I am just praying for his soul, that it reaches our Lord safely."

Robert was surprised at the woman's self-possession. Perhaps she was just holding back her emotions until a more seemly moment. But he also knew that she firmly believed that her prayers were needed, and that she should look after her man after death, as she had looked after him before it.

An hour later the doctor arrived. Arnold's wife was in the parlour and Robert accompanied him upstairs. They came down some time later and the doctor took the woman's hand.

"Mrs Grey, please allow me to offer to you my sincere condolences at your loss. Your husband died peacefully of natural causes, during the night. I will go now and put the necessary actions in train."

He coughed to clear his throat, looked at Robert and left. Robert walked over to Arnold's wife and embraced her. She began to sob with small convulsions that he could feel. When she had calmed herself, she began to talk. "He was so alive and strong last week. Why he even talked about walking over to town to look up your family. But, of course, he was too old for that. He talked about you, almost without ceasing. How you would pass your examination and go to university. And then the world would be your oyster. Yes, your oyster, he would say."

She buried her head in Robert's chest and sniffed and continued. "Since you have been coming, he has been a new man. He was not sure that he could do it. Teach you, I mean. For he said that he had forgotten all that old Greek and Latin. But when he opened his books again, I could see a twinkle in his eye. It reminded me of when we were first married. He had so much energy and such a sense of humour. And then all those years of battling the falling congregations, knowing that his job was mostly reading the funeral service; it wore him down. But then you came along. He said to me that I treated you like the son that we never had. So, perhaps I did. But we would laugh about it when you went back home on Sunday nights. And now you have seen him off."

§

The funeral was well attended, because Reverend Grey was a respected member of the village. In his long life as their spiritual guardian, he had conducted their services and sat by their bedsides through their darkest hours. His replacement, The Reverend Hardiman, presided over the funeral. They sang Grey's favourite hymn, *Rock of Ages*, and as they sung about their Lord and his life, they all thought of Grey's life of labour and of love. They listened to Hardiman read the whole of 1 Corinthians 13, Grey's favourite chapter, and they pondered on how faith, hope and love had been for each of them.

It was difficult for Hardiman, for he had not known Grey like the villagers had. To give him credit, he had talked to many of them about their dear Reverend, and the congregation were mollified, because their rough but heartfelt words were well translated into pulpit English by him. But the new man was not yet the Reverend Grey, their Reverend Grey. They did not know it, but he would never become that person, because the times were changing, and the village would never again be the centre of life in England.

All of Robert's family attended. His mother held onto his arm to help him through this difficult time, because she knew what the old man had been to her son. William, Emily and the youngsters were keen to see the village and its people that had had this strange and often secretive connection with them through their brother. They looked and they nodded their heads politely, but they did not understand what had taken place. Only William sensed that this was a significant moment, but he sensed it only dimly. He was keen to learn more, for this was the place where his brother, his Brother in Plato, had become a man. During the wake, which was held in the tiny church room, he circulated amongst the villagers. Most were deferential to these town folk, and felt ill at ease with them. But a few opened up with their old memories of the Reverend, and William felt the love and respect that they had for him. He talked to Grey's wife, who saw in William the likeness of Robert and took to him immediately. She held onto his arm and told him all that she had told Robert, as he had held her on that dark morning.

Jeremiah, their father, had not forgotten that this was the place where his own son had had to come to learn the Classics, when his own teaching had not succeeded. He was respectful to all, yet reserved, because he was not a part of it.

Towards the end of the wake, when the villagers were beginning to bid the Reverend Hardiman and his wife farewell, Jeremiah drew Robert aside.

"Robert, forgive me if I seem overly concerned about your future, but do you need further tuition in anything to enable you to pass the entrance examination?"

Jeremiah was not expecting a positive reply, but what Robert said took him by surprise. There was a glow on his son's face as he replied. "No, thank you, father. However, I appreciate your well-meant words. No, I do not need further help, for the Reverend Grey has wrought a new work in me. Soon the world will know me. And then all will be well."

Jeremiah was unable to speak and his son walked out of the School House into the winter sun outside.

§

Several weeks later, a letter arrived from the President of the Royal Society asking Robert to lecture on the new theory.

CHAPTER 11

An Invitation to London

Robert had been expecting the letter since he had posted the paper to the Royal Society two months previously. His rational being told him that it would take time to be sent to the appropriate reviewer and he would need a few weeks to read and understand the seventy-five pages. And, of course, a second opinion might be needed. Yet he had found it hard to contain his excitement. Several times his father had had to remind him of his duties at the school and even in the shop, Elijah noticed that he was not himself.

His mother handed him the letter; she had taken it from the letter carrier at the front door, earlier that day. His father stood next to her. It was the first letter that Robert had ever received, which made it special to him. But this one seemed different. It was contained in a stiff envelope, which had a red one-penny adhesive stamp on the top right hand corner and the crest of the Royal Society on the left, with the name below it. He ran his finger over the crest and felt the embossed three lions rampant. In the middle of the envelope was his name, followed by the abbreviation, *Esq.*, and below it, the address of his family home. He turned it over and gazed at the wax seal with a small imprint of the lions. He tried to control his shaking hand.

"Mother, I need to open this in my room. I will return presently to inform you and father of the content."

His heart was beating uncontrollably as he broke the seal. He opened the single sheet and his eye was drawn to read the first sentence of the second paragraph. He reflected for a moment at his past life, for his new life had just begun.

§

He was standing in the drawing room and looked around him. The familiar furnishings, the china pieces on the polished mahogany sideboard and the painting of a Scottish mountain, brought uncomfortable memories to his mind. The mirror above the fireplace seemed to magnify the intensity of the moment. His father was holding the letter. William stood next to him. His mother was sitting on the settee, with Emily and Patience on each side. Thomas sat on the arm of the settee, next to Patience. His father began to read aloud.

The Royal Society of London for Improving Natural Knowledge
Somerset House
The Strand
London

My dearest Robert,

It was with much pleasure that I received your paper on the Theory of Potentials and Functions for the Solution of Problems in Infinitesimal Calculus. I have had the paper reviewed by several eminent Fellows, which took some time, and was the primary cause for the delay in my reply, for which I am heartily sorry. They have reported that the paper is of particular importance to the field of calculus and lays a significant foundation for subsequent advances in many fields of science.

My desire is that you should come to the Society and honour us with a lecture on your paper. Please let me know when you are available so to do. Let us say a month or so hence; this will give me time to advertise the event and for you to prepare yourself.

I realise that this may be your first such presentation to the Society. To mark its significance to you, I am prepared to subsidise your travelling expenses and those of two guests.

Yours most sincerely,
  Bartholomew Hyde
  President
  February 4ᵗʰ, 1846

Robert's father looked at him and a tear filled his eye. He offered Robert his hand and they shook for a long moment, until his father noticed Robert's discomfort. William patted him on the shoulder and said words of congratulations that Robert could hardly listen to. Patience spoke up boldly.

"Robert, who will you take? Papa, of course. But, who else?"

"I would love to take you, dear sister. Just to see the look on their faces. But it has to be William."

Patience's face turned to mock disappointment. Robert looked at her with a sentiment that surprised him. She would do well, he thought. She was no longer a girl and her lively character and good looks would catch a fine gentleman in a year or two. His father interrupted his thoughts.

"Robert, sit down and tell us how all of this has come about. For it has caught all of us by surprise."

"Why, it was the Reverend Grey."

His face became animated as he remembered and he could not sit still in his seat.

"He was a genius at mathematics and particularly infinitesimal calculus. He led me a wonderful walk, through the history of it all and through the associated theorems. He had an interesting way of catching one's attention. We did classics for an hour by the method of attaching each new phrase and sentence to a mathematical problem or a mechanical marvel. Then, after many months of that, he asked me to write my mathematical descriptions in Greek or Latin. Of course, the mathematics was in the form of equations, which is a beautiful and mysterious language of its own. I say mysterious, for its depth is hidden in apparent simplicity. For example, it is straightforward to find numbers that satisfy the equation, $a + b = c$. $1 + 1 = 2$ is clear to all. In the same way $a^2 + b^2 = c^2$ can be solved without much trouble, and is, of course, the equation that relates to the lengths of the sides of a triangle having a right angle."

Almost everyone in the room understood that.

"So, $a^2 + b^2 = c^2$ contains the beauty of the triangle in an superbly elegant form, and was the reason why I called the language beautiful. But why did I say mysterious? For if one takes another small step and changes the indices to three, giving us, $a^3 + b^3 = c^3$, then it is by no means clear that we can find a solution. Indeed, no solution may exist. If any number, such as 5, or 55, replaces the three, then there is again a mystery about whether there is a solution. This problem was posed by Pierre de Fermat in the seventeenth century and is still unsolved today. Fermat claimed that he had a solution, which was too big to put in the margin of his paper, but no one has ever been found it."

His mother had no need of a solution to this problem, but she was nevertheless radiant with pride as her son lectured them. From his early falling out with words, due to his father's bullying, he had now cultivated a graceful and entertaining way of expressing himself. She glanced around her and saw that her children were also captivated. Jeremiah sat, straight faced, but inwardly struggling to accept that his son had found a much better teacher than he. His struggle went on, for Robert continued.

"When I first wrote the sentences in Latin, to accompany the equations of a mathematical proof, the Reverend made me feel that I was amongst the greats. I had seen some of Bernoulli's theorems in Latin in Samuel's library; Arnold called Latin the lingua franca of mathematics and he, of course, explained the origins of the term amongst the Arabs."

"After an hour of intense language study, he would say let us amuse ourselves. He would pull out a sheet on which he had devised a puzzle for me to solve. They were all based on known mathematics, solutions and theorems from the great names, such as Lagrange, Laplace and Poisson. It was only months later that I even darkly glimpsed where he was leading me. It was like a walk through a magical forest with many partings of the way. At every junction, we would discuss the possible solutions to the equation he presented, suggesting methods for me to try, but leaving me to work through the possibilities. Of course, he was leading me to a point, somewhere beyond the work of Newton, where he wanted me to start off on my own. And when we got there, I immediately saw what was needed, what many scientists required to allow them to apply the mathematics of calculus to the problems of the world, to predict the behaviour of systems that are described by differential equations. And then he left me, alone in the forest."

"We never talked about it for many, many weeks. We did our Greek and Latin, and other minor mathematical puzzles, but he never referred to that problem again. But my mind was on fire. I searched endlessly. Well,..."

Robert broke off and smiled at them, as if the moment was forever clear in his mind, as the birth of a loved child may be to a mother.

"Well, it seemed endless. Until one day, I stumbled, almost without realising it, upon a method to solve the problem. Not a solution, no, not that, but a method. And I told him about it and, to my disappointment, all he said was, "Robert, you are on your own. As are all mathematicians who discover great things." I wanted some reassurance, but he gave me none. I wanted some direction, but he refused. He told me to keep walking through the forest and to trust my instincts to take the right turn. And he said that one day I would reach the edge of the forest and step out into the clear light of Plato's perfect world: the world where I would find the solution. So I did and, yes, I felt my intuition telling me which turn to take and I knew I had the ability to solve each challenge as it occurred. And finally, William," for at this point he was addressing his elder brother, "I reached that place and it was as perfect and as bright, and as right, as Plato said it would be."

William stood up and offered him his hand. Robert smiled at him and stood. They embraced heartily and

William brushed a tear away, as those on the settee clapped and shouted 'Hurrah' and 'Well done, brother.'

His father stood and shook his hand again.

"Robert may I ask you what you have solved?"

Robert looked him in the eye, for perhaps the first time, and said quietly, "Father, I am sorry. Can you wait until I present it in my lecture? I want it to be perfect for the world to see."

§

The town was abuzz with the news, spread by all in the family. A reporter from the Northampton Mercury visited the house and, a day later, they read the article in the newspaper. It began by telling of the honouring of a local man by the prestigious Royal Society in London, which was a glorious first for Northampton, and ended with an affirmation of the town's enlightened and progressive education establishments. The word mathematics may have occurred towards the end of the article, but there was nothing of 'potentials' or 'infinitesimal calculus', much to William's disappointment and Robert's cynical amusement. Rebecca cut out the article and pasted it into her newly opened scrapbook.

A steady train of people came into the school to congratulate Robert. Jeremiah quietly resented the interruption of his classes, whilst Samuel took the opportunity to show the visitors the donor's board. He later said that he had raised more than sixty pounds in the month between the announcement and the lecture.

Both of Robert's uncles visited the house with their

wives. Rebecca and Emily performed the duties of the hosts, and the visits were family reunions with a cause for genuine gladness. Elijah was genuinely happy, but said that he was not surprised, for after a few Saturdays of having Robert in the shop, he knew it would happen. Hannah laughed at him, but agreed. Isaiah was happy but puzzled, for the world of study and Societies was a mysterious one for him. He would have been happier, he said to Robert in a moment of honest regret, if he had understood what all the fuss was about. Robert was reminded that 'separate spheres' applied not only to men and women, but also to men and men.

And the three wives, in their own sphere, discussed how they could celebrate Robert's return from his triumphant day in London. Mary, Isaiah's wife, said that they had a fallow field big enough for them to erect a tent, like the circus had. No, said, Hannah, the celebration must be in the town. Seeing Mary's downcast look, she quickly added that the farm should supply eggs, meat and vegetables, for the greens from your garden are the most succulent in the Market Square. And Rebecca brought them down to earth by suggesting that the town council might arrange a dinner in the chambers, and that, 'you girls should work on your Sunday gowns, for it will be an evening to look your best.'

Throughout these family gatherings, Jeremiah was charming and affable to all. He achieved this difficult state of mind for him, by reminding himself continually of his own mean roots and that Robert was now following in his footsteps of improving himself. But he knew that the knowledge that Robert had penetrated the Royal Society had rankled and allowed him to see a part inside himself that was not attractive. Nevertheless, he hoped to use the success of his son to build bridges amongst the town council and the school trustees, with the hope of righting old wrongs done to him. However, his meeting with Councillor Wilson was not encouraging, for although the Councillor had read of the business in the newspaper and wished Robert well at the lecture, he could not see the gain in it.

§

Robert, William and their father travelled on the London and North Western Line. They changed at Rugby. On the platform, Jeremiah fussed over the luggage and when the direct train to London would arrive. His two sons bore his worries with a smile, as if they had been travelling on trains all their lives.

The wrought iron roof and gas lamps of Euston Station in London took their breath away.

"It is bigger by far than All Saints Church in our humble town," said Jeremiah, temporarily unable to move from the platform. After the bustle of the ladies and gentlemen passing them had subsided, William touched his arm and they made their way to the Great Hall, which was bigger still, with impressive pillars and a coffered ceiling. Their father shook his head slowly and was lost for words. William gave him time to take it all in, but eventually moved him on again.

Their hotel was in a small side street, off to the north of the Strand. Somerset House was to the south, between the main thoroughfare and the Embankment. They had an hour or two before they should be at the Royal Society and, after settling into their rooms, Robert suggested that they promenade along the Thames.

"But do you not need to practice your lecture?" asked Jeremiah.

"Father, I have practiced it so many times already, and the work is imprinted so clearly on my mind, that all shall be well. There is no need to fret."

William found Robert's presence of mind strange. For he was talking as if to a beloved, but aged, relative. William knew that Robert had finally arrived in the place that he had always dreamed of. He himself was impressed beyond expression, but at the same time uncomfortable to be in the world of the gentlemen and businessmen that he saw about him.

They walked along the Strand and turned down Savoy Street, past the small Queen's Chapel, and found themselves on the Embankment, staring at the majestic sweep of the Thames. To their left they could see St Paul's and, to their right, Westminster and the Houses of Parliament. They were all moved to see such power, both temporal and spiritual, gathered into one view. They were silent at the sight and William saw that both his father and his brother were in their own worlds. His father was diminished, but Robert seemed to have grown, his chest puffed out and his head held high as he gazed on his newly assumed purview.

The afternoon was becoming colder as the tide on the river sped eastwards. Somerset House was but a stone's throw from the river, and they were glad to enter its warmth. A solemn secretary greeted them and led them to the President's Suite. They hung their overcoats on the stand in the secretary's office and were ushered through a pair of large and venerable doors.

The room was warm, but more from the decoration and furnishings than any source of heat. Polished wood panelling, inlaid with floral marquetry, lined the walls. A glistening chandelier hung from the high ceiling. An enormous desk was positioned at one end and at the other were a group of armchairs upholstered in red leather. A thick Indian carpet hushed their steps.

For a moment there was silence, for Professor Bartholomew Hyde had not heard them enter. Then the Secretary coughed. Immediately the small figure, who had been bent over a book, leapt up and circled the desk rapidly. His hair was as white as snow, and his suit rather worn. His genial face had the same worn look. Nevertheless his welcome was vigorous, shaking hands and nodding his head. The secretary had introduced them.

"Robert, my dear man, welcome to the Royal Society. We are honoured to have you with us tonight. And, sir," he nodded to Jeremiah, "I congratulate you on your son's singular achievement. And William, I am glad that you were able to bring your brother to us. I trust you all had a pleasant journey."

Robert immediately spoke up.

"Thank you, sir. Yes we did. The train service is now first class, as was our welcome at Euston station, a most impressive building."

"Ah yes, the size of the new Great Hall reflects the confidence that the backers have in the power of travel to give them a return on their money." Robert watched the President's mouth form a conspiratorial smile and his eyes sparkle, as if he was inducting him into the secret world of business.

"Indeed," Robert replied coolly, "there is so much money being spent that some are bound to lose."

The old man's eyebrows rose for a moment at such a skeptical tone in such a young man, and then a look of congeniality spread over his face.

"Ah, you are right, you are right, indeed. Now let us sit down and I will tell you what is to happen tonight."

Robert glanced out of the window that overlooked the river, as they sat down and considered that they were indeed at the place of power in the world of science and mathematics.

"Now, Robert, when I received your paper, I circulated it to several members of the Mathematical Board. They all, to a man, told me how important the results were. They will be in your audience tonight, so you can rest assured that you have a good base of support. I suppose that there will also be those who are not impressed, but that is because they are specialists in other areas, and do not immediately grasp the significance of your work. It will be your job to convince them; that is the prime purpose of such lectures as these: to spread knowledge as widely as we can. On the whole, these are gentlemen and will behave as such. However there is one amongst us who is not, and he will criticise it."

Jeremiah gripped the arm of his chair in alarm and William looked at his brother. The professor continued, "He is just being curmudgeonly and all the members know it; but you should watch out for him tonight, Robert. We are a mixed group here, we are all human and possess all the imperfections that afflict mankind, but we do at least represent the forefront of research in all the sciences."

Robert had studied Hyde's history, but was not impressed by it. For his work had not changed the world and his book was but a collation of existing work by others, with little original synthesis. Its merit lay merely in the clarifying classification; others had since eclipsed the work. From his reading, Robert's cynicism had identified three stages in Hyde's career. The man had progressed through organisation of himself, followed by organisation of others, to procrastination and the maintenance of the status quo for all. He was criticised for running the Royal Society like a well-worn captain, who leads his ship through the doldrums by waiting for something to happen.

§

Robert stood by the podium. To one side was a blackboard on an easel. After a friendly introduction from the President, he began.

"*Mister President, Honourable Fellows and Members, it is with much humility that I accepted your invitation to present to you this new piece of work for, as I stand here for the first time, I see clearly in my mind the many famous and respected scientists that have graced this podium. We all aspire to their greatness as we should, but I know that I am far from that. It is thus with great trepidation that I begin this discussion upon the Theory of Potentials and Functions for the Solution of Problems in Infinitesimal Calculus.*"

The President smiled at this touch of sincerity. He hoped that the rest would be as appealing.

"The theory is based on...."

An hour later applause rang out. Robert was clearly exhausted from his efforts, but knew that he now had to suffer the examination from the floor of the room. A hand was raised and the President accepted the question.

"Mister Crossley, it is no doubt true that mathematicians achieve their best work early, but I congratulate you on your lack of years!"

Laughter broke out.

"But, to get to the point. This is clearly a serious advance in the field of calculus and, although you indicated that electricity and magnetism might be clarified by your work, would you please indicate how this might be?"

Robert had prepared for this question and he replied confidently. *"One such example concerns the Leyden phial experiment."* He drew a cross section of the jar on the blackboard, below the single equation that he had previously written in bold script at the top.

"As you know, the Leyden phial, invented by Kleist, Musschenbroek and Cunaeus, stores electrical charge..."

The question had been elegantly put; Robert's answer was equally gracious and informative. The questioner nodded his head enthusiastically when Robert explained the link between the equation and the theory of the phial, which to that time had been clarified by no one, nor had there previously been any mathematical method to solve it. Clearly, thought the President, this young man has a presence amongst his peers. He wished all the members were like him. There were other questions of detail, which Robert dealt with in a clear and helpful manner that demonstrated his deep knowledge of what he had done and his confidence that what he had done was correct. After half an hour of polite, but firm, thrust and parry, a hand was raised in the front row. The owner of the hand was a portly, balding gentleman whose eyes, though focused on the floor, periodically darted up to Robert. There was some unrest in the audience.

"Sir, you build on the work of Lagrange, Laplace, and Poisson, in deriving your functions. I am struck by the thought that Eldret's theorem might also be useful. It would please me to hear your comments on this possibility."

Robert froze. He was not aware of this speaker's reference. He hesitated and was about to offer to sit down with the questioner and work through the theorem's application with him, when a voice rang out.

"Shame on you, sir. You know that this young man is new to our ways. You should not be using this occasion to exhibit your dirty laundry in public!"

Several of the audience shouted *'hear, hear'* and *'shame'* and the President brought the lecture to a close, before Robert could speak. All went into the antechamber, where drinks were served. The President took Robert by the elbow and whispered to him.

"Well done, sir. That was well done! I have no doubt that the editors of the Proceedings will now accept your essay for publication in a future issue. As the chairman of that board, I am sure that it will be accepted, but the members might want to wait for people working in, let us say, at least a couple of the areas of application you mentioned, to confirm. I assume you would have no objection to that?"

Robert shook his head. Although his heart was still pounding, he listened very carefully to what the President said. The old man continued.

"By the way, Eldret's theorem has been discredited. Not only was it flawed, but also the eponymous questioner had stolen it from a colleague! As I said, we have all sorts here. But you have a friend in the Professor Laidman, who cried shame and defended you. Let me introduce you to him."

Some time later when the last person had congratulated Robert, Jeremiah and William did the same. When they reached the hotel, their father invited them to the bar to toast Robert's success, forgetting in the tumult filling his head that as a Methodist, he abstained from drink. As they each drank a glass of small beer, Robert remembered his father's reaction to his egg collecting, and his own subsequent vow to outwit him. His achievement in causing his father to break his vow of abstinence gave him almost as much pleasure as his introduction to the ways of the Royal Society.

"This has been a most wondrous day for all of us, Robert," said Jeremiah with a smile. "We have so much to tell when we get back home."

"Father," replied Robert, in a serious tone, "I have had invitations from the War Department, from an industrialist and from a London Professor. But most wondrous of all was the Dean of Gonville and Caius College at Cambridge, who wants to offer me a scholarship to take my degree there."

Jeremiah's eyes widened in disbelief. When Robert reassured him, his face shone with the fulfillment of his own dream. But then, in a moment, Robert dampened both his father's and his brother's joy.

"The man in the audience who defended me from Eldret, is the London Professor. His name is Laidmann. He told me that he is about to leave for the continent and that he would like to see me tomorrow. He wishes me to engage in a discussion with him about my work. I must see him. I am therefore sorry that I cannot return home with you tomorrow."

A look of hurt passed across his father's face, but was gone in a moment. "Do not concern yourself about that, my boy. You must do what the good Professor asks. You cannot imagine what might come of it."

Robert said his goodbyes to them at Euston Station, in the Great Hall. All of them felt it was the appropriate place to part. Jeremiah still had a feeling of elation that had stayed with him from the previous day. But an aura of sadness had also descended onto him, for this was a parting of significance. In like way, William was happy for his brother, but he knew that the bonds of their brotherhood were slowly being dissolved away.

CHAPTER 12

The Mathematicians

The dawn chorus had awoken Robert and he was immediately filled with excitement for his new life. A moment later, it was tempered with apprehension when he remembered his forthcoming meeting with Professor Laidmann. He had known nothing of the man until yesterday, nor knew what to expect from the meeting. He was certain that his lecture and the subsequent examination had gone well, for he had prepared himself well enough. But now he was launching out into uncharted waters where he would only have his wits to help him.

He was early for his ten o'clock appointment and had wandered the streets of Bloomsbury for nearly half an hour. He had marvelled at the large houses and watched the nannies push their perambulators around the wooded squares. With immaculate timing, he stepped into the Octagon Building adjacent to Gower Street and was directed up a grand stairway and along a corridor. He noted the names of the Professors on the doors and continued until he found what he was looking for. The name, A. J. Laidmann, Professor of Natural Philosophy, was picked out in gold lettering on a framed board attached to the door. He knocked and a pleasant high-pitched voice answered.

"Come in, come in."

Robert pushed open the door.

"My dear young man. It is so good to see you."

The thin, fair-haired man was a good six inches shorter than Robert. They shook hands and for a moment their eyes locked. Robert saw the kindly gaze of a friend. He drew his eyes away and looked about him, for he was curious to see the man's room. Laidmann noticed.

"I assume that you have not been in the office of a Professor before," he said.

The room was panelled in dark wood and the old desk was piled high with papers in a disorderly fashion, as Robert had expected from the caricatures he had read. But he did not expect the watercolours hanging on the walls. The Professor led him over to one and they gazed together at it in a companionable manner.

"They are by Mary Gilbert-Bowditch, who is the wife of the Reverend John Bowditch. They live in Wiltshire, not far from where my family live."

Robert was taken aback. After a moment he was finally able to talk. "Ah, then your family does not live in London. You must miss them."

Laidmann smiled. "Yes, I do. But I spend five months of the year with them. The country is a quiet place to work, for this office can get busy with the commitments of running the Department of Natural Philosophy."

He looked again at the pictures and spoke wistfully. "See, that is the White Horse at Uffington and that, the fields at Badbury. Mary is a fine artist and I like to support her by purchasing her efforts. Of course, I could not afford to support a famous artist that you might have heard of."

He laughed at his little jest to put Robert at his ease and continued. "You are from Northampton, I understand?"

"Yes, sir. It is a fine town, known for the manufacture of shoes."

"And I should imagine that there are problems with the introduction of machines to help in the production?"

"Indeed, there are. For the workers fear for their livelihoods, as they do in many places. But it cannot be helped, for it is progress. If it did not happen to the shoe factories in Northampton, it might happen elsewhere and put our people out of business."

They had sat down. Robert had given a good account of himself to that point and his confidence increased. The Professor then spent the next half an hour or so explaining the work in his Department. Finally, he said, "Look, Robert, I invited you here for a reason. It is not often that brilliant young men appear. This University does not have the age and bearing of Cambridge or Oxford and we must act with alacrity if we are to attract the best to our ranks. I understand that you have been offered a scholarship to Cambridge for your degree. Unfortunately, I cannot do likewise. And who would turn down the chance to have the word Cambridge associated with his name. But I would like you to consider joining us after you have graduated; of course that is some time in the future and none can tell where we might be then. But please remember the offer. We are but twenty years old as a University, and there were great arguments from both Cambridge and Oxford that the formation of the University of London would be the end of England as we know it. It was nonsense, of course."

They both smiled. Laidmann continued.

"You must understand that Cambridge's adherence to the Thirty Nine Articles as a requirement for matriculation is holding back education in this country, and many fine students are lost because of it."

Robert was suddenly still. His face had turned pale. "But, I have been brought up a Methodist, sir. What am I to do?"

Laidmann smiled at him. "You are a prime example that proves my point. However, let me ask you. Are you a Dissenter, or have you merely been raised as a Dissenter?"

Robert was quick to grasp his point. Memories of his father's churchgoing, and his falling out with the establishment flashed through his head. As did his own vow to cross his father whenever he could. This seemed an ideal means of deviating from his father's wishes.

"I am no Dissenter, sir."

"If that is the case, I should mention nothing about it to them at Cambridge. Unless, that is, you enjoy a debate on the finer points of religious orthodoxy after a couple of glasses of port."

Robert replied rapidly, "I should enjoy a de-bate, but I would enjoy bate-ing a trap for them, even more!"

It was a weak pun, but Robert's first, and he was proud of it. Laidmann took it in good spirit and laughed loudly. He continued. "Excellent, my boy. You should talk to Augustus De Morgan, he has some fine views about religion."

There was a pause. Robert had not expected this cheerful banter. Laidmann was still smiling as he got back to the business in hand. "No, I cannot offer you a scholarship, but I can offer you something else now. I propose to pay for you to visit some of the greatest mathematicians in England. Of course, when you go to Cambridge, you will see Peacock and Whewell, but we have De Morgan here at this university, and Cayley and Sylvester are a stones throw away at Lincoln's Inn. I will write to them, recommending you to them and arranging visits."

"I am overcome with your generosity, sir."

"Well, it is for the benefit of the university, Robert. And if in the end you decide not to join us, the visits will be for the benefit of English mathematics."

Robert shook Laidmann's hand.

"One last thing, for I will not let you off scot free. I will send you papers written by the three of them, so you can prepare yourself for the meetings. You need to widen your appreciation of what is being done by those around you; talk to them about what they think and what they do. De Morgan will tell you without being asked; nevertheless ask him about sound and false paradoxers. Read as much as you are able; for our knowledge progresses through a diffusion from many into each, wherein seeds may germinate as they will."

They were walking down the corridor towards the entrance. With Laidmann's memorable epithet ringing in Robert's ears, they reached the Dome.

"And I may suggest some problems for you to consider. I am interested in the work Cayley has done on octonions. It may be of some use in what I am doing and we could work together. Assuming developments of your own work are not completely engaging you at the moment."

They parted.

Robert walked back to his hotel with his mind awhirl with the Professor and their discussion. His host had been gentlemanly and relaxed with him. But a hard edge lay beneath his charm. His own shock at Cambridge's conformity to Anglican principles amused him now. His naivety would pass, he knew, as he learned of the world and its ways. But above all else in his head was Laidmann's parting remark. Robert was not working on extensions to his theory, for he had no idea what he should be doing, beyond preparing himself to begin his studies at Cambridge. Perhaps the visits that his new friend was arranging for him might light his way forward.

§

Augustus De Morgan was a principled man. That on its own could have been an admirable trait, but he was also a pedant.

Robert knocked upon his door, which was on the same corridor as that of his friend Arthur Laidmann. Laidmann was now, as he promised, visiting a French mathematician of some repute. Robert expected an entirely different meeting to his comfortable encounter with Laidmann. He was not disappointed.

"Come in."

"Good afternoon, Professor De Morgan. I am Robert Crossley. I believe that Professor Laidmann wrote to you concerning..."

"Yes, he did. Sit down. Let me finish this sentence."

Robert had time to look at the man in front of him, as the sentence he was writing was a long one. De Morgan had a full face and his forehead was extending upwards as his hair receded. He was plump and his high, turned-up collar made his neck appear unusually short. He wore wire-rimmed spectacles, which made Robert miss it at first. And then, after a moment, he saw that the man's left eye was closed up. Suddenly, the mathematician looked up and stared at the young man, through his one good eye. Robert looked back, uneasily.

"So, you have a theory."

Robert was about to launch into a description of his work that he had prepared in the train, when De Morgan continued. "I will read it when it is published. Just tell me, in two sentences, what it proposes."

Robert took more than two sentences and he could see the Professor becoming impatient. Suddenly, he was brought to a halt.

"Well, that is just what you might expect. I am surprised that it had not been stated ere now."

Robert had no answer to this, because none was possible. However, what De Morgan had said was his way of accepting and approving of what he had heard. Robert came to realise this on his homeward journey, but at the time his mind was in turmoil. He had forgotten Laidmann's advice about what to ask. But he did not need to, for the famous mathematician burst forth with his well-known tirade.

"Men who profess to be mathematicians are paradoxers, for we all deal in paradoxes, as a fishmonger deals in fish. And like a fishmonger, there are sound paradoxers and false paradoxers. For example, Mister James Smith, of Liverpool, is one such of the latter type. He has written to me without end and has thus made himself famous. He proposes that π = 3 and ⅛. He proves this by showing that all other values are absurd; hence the value is true. And he calls me a snail, hiding in my shell, for not accepting his nonsensical proposal."

Robert stared at him intently, for this strange tale had impressed him greatly. For his staring he received a question from the great man.

"How do you think that I am able to tell a false from a sound paradoxer?"

"By their appreciation of other mathematicians that came before them," Robert replied at once, for he had learned the answer from Laidmann.

De Morgan banged his desk with his palm. "Yes, indeed. Yes, indeed!"

Robert recognised the zealotry of the dissenter in these words and his mind flew back to his Sundays in Gold Street. His reverie was cut short.

"My wife, who discourses with the spirits, has a brother who is a sound paradoxer, yet he persists in doing his mathematics without recourse to negative numbers. He does not believe in them. Of course, his mathematical developments are somewhat hampered as a result."

Where this discussion was leading, Robert could not fathom, nor did he know if the man meant that his wife was dead or whether she was a Spiritualist, of whom Robert had heard. The man had not finished his story yet.

"I mention him, for his abhorrence of one form of number, might lead us into a discussion of double algebra, in which the whole range of numbers, both positive and negative is supplemented by another."

Robert was somewhat relieved that the conversation had turned to mathematics and a mathematics that he had some understanding of. Laidmann had sent him of several papers on this very topic. For what De Morgan referred to was the addition of a number, represented by the letter, a, and another, represented by, $b.\sqrt{(-1)}$. The square root of -1 does not exist; hence it is called an imaginary number. This new double number, $a + b.\sqrt{(-1)}$, had interesting properties that De Morgan was discovering. Their conversation flowered and the strangeness of the man fell away somewhat in Robert's eyes, as they conversed in this other language. The possibilities for the use of these numbers began to form in his mind. After an hour or more, he had recovered from his apprehensions and was overtaken by an excitement, which left him a little breathless.

He pondered his discussion for many days after he returned to Northampton. His future was still not clear. But his misgivings had faded, for previously, in the company of his family and friends, he had occasionally felt that he was unsuited for intercourse with ordinary people. Now, after his time with this unsociable beast, he felt more ordinary and less unsociable himself.

§

Arthur Cayley gave Robert a couple of hours in Lincoln's Inn Fields. Cayley was polite and apologetic, saying that there was work underway on the Stone Building in the Inn and the workmen's noise would make sensible conversation difficult. They walked around the square, which was flanked by fine houses. At points Robert had difficulty either hearing him or understanding him. He was close to the same age as Robert, and had recently come to study at the bar because his Cambridge fellowship had lapsed.

Robert explained to him his own work and Cayley nodded respectfully as he did so. When he had finished Cayley launched into a penetrating discussion. But rather than describe his points using simple examples of practical application, which was the way Robert preferred, he launched immediately into generalisations. Robert struggled to remember them, for he hoped that he might understand them on further study.

When he had finished, Robert asked him about quaternions and octonions. These were similar to De Morgan's double algebra, but were groups of four and eight numbers, respectively, with surprising properties. Again Cayley politely thanked him for his interest and then talked for over three quarters of an hour without pause.

Sadly his labour was in vain, for Robert understood little of what he said. He had read what Laidmann had sent him, but it did little to prepare him for the man himself. He knew that Cayley was an outstanding mathematician, but little of his brilliance was transferred that afternoon in that pleasant London Park. Robert returned home somewhat deflated. What was worse was that Laidmann had chosen octonions as the matter that he wanted to Robert to work on for him. Robert put the papers aside, meaning to take them up at some time later.

He reflected that evening that the Reverend Grey had shown him the delight to be had with mathematics. The meetings that Laidmann had organised for him were showing him that a mathematical brain could be mixed with various sorts of personalities, or even no personality at all.

§

James Joseph Sylvester was less notable for his mathematics than for his hospitality. He was also an amateur poet and the first verse of 'Remonstrance' aptly described his personality.

Oh! Why those narrow rules extol?
These but restrain from ill,
True virtue lies in strength of soul
And energy of will.

Robert and James met at the Athenaeum Club, on Pall Mall, at Sylvester's request. For Robert, everything in London was magnificent, and every visit showed him something new to wonder at. The Athenaeum was no exception. Its pillared portico reminded Robert of All Saints Church in Northampton, but All Saints was humble in comparison to this.

Robert was staring like a gawp on the steps, when a firm hand took hold of arm and propelled him on and up.

"It must be Mister Crossley, if I am not mistaken," said Sylvester, laughing. "For no regular member would act like you are. Robert, I bid you welcome to the city of mathematics and science, and to the future."

This theatrical outburst, so early in the morning, startled Robert profoundly and he mutely did as his new friend bade him. In a moment they were settled in a small waiting room just off the entrance. Sylvester introduced himself, which struck Robert as unnecessary after what had gone before and without further ado the mathematician began to talk.

"My dear young man," he began. Sylvester was only five years older than Robert, but in philosophy and experience more like a father. "You know of course of Plato's allegory of the cave?"

Robert smiled and nodded his head vigorously, for there was nothing he liked better than to talk about the father of it all.

"Good, so I need not remind you of it in detail, but to say that for me mathematics is a real and clear place, whilst what others call the real world is but shadows."

Robert was so entranced by this restatement of the allegory that he opened his heart to this stranger. In return he related the relationship between himself and his brother, William, who considered themselves to be Brothers in Plato, because of their faith in the philosophy. He realised as he spoke that it might appear to be just boyish enthusiasm, but Sylvester's reaction was so violent that a thrill ran through him. For the man grasped his hand and exclaimed, "Bravo, bravo, my friend! Brothers you are and brothers you will remain in a perfect and wonderful place. Let us now stroll around that place and observe some of the objects that we are privy to and dream of some that are not yet revealed to us."

Robert spent the next half an hour explaining his work in the way that pleased him best, through the specific application to various sciences, back to the starting point and then connecting the two together through the concept of potentials, which was the key step in his development. Sylvester appreciated it all and nodded vigorously as Robert talked.

When Robert had finished, Sylvester became uncharacteristically silent as he considered what he had heard and then suddenly told him how significant he believed the work to be. He then began describing his own advances. There were several, but one that impressed Robert most related to optics and a development of Fresnel's theories. Some time later, it occurred to Robert that what seemed to motivate him most was the application of mathematics to physical problems for although he paid lip service to Plato's picture of shadows and clarity, his mind was more comfortable in what most people understood as real.

Their conversation was a true exchange, unlike his meeting with Cayley, which had the characteristic of a lecture. Sylvester looked at his listener with his bright eyes for signs of comprehension as he went. Robert asked many questions and thus learnt much. By the time they finished, he was as excited as his friend, who then surprised him further.

"Robert, this has been a most pleasurable experience! It would be a shame not to extend it and to begin to understand you as a man in addition to a mathematician. I therefore propose to invite you to come to my house in Woolwich this evening."

Then a moment of doubt assailed him. "Am I right to think that you will be in town this evening and unoccupied, and intend to travel back to Northampton tomorrow?"

"Indeed, that is my situation," replied Robert quickly. "I would be honoured to be invited to the hearth of a famous mathematician."

This strange turn of phrase surprised Robert himself, who had just meant to be gracious. However, Sylvester who fed on such quirks, merely said, "Yes, and if the hearth works as it is wont to do, we may see some of Plato's shadows in the smoke."

Sylvester wrote down his address for Robert, shook his hand vigorously and left the club at a run. Robert returned to his hotel and began his notes on their conversation.

§

Sylvester's abode was a tolerably large house in an unprepossessing terrace. The cab dropped Robert at the front door. He had barely approached it when it opened to reveal Sylvester dressed in a finely embroidered smoking jacket, with a woman hanging on his arm.

Robert greeted them. "Thank you so much for your kind invitation, sir. I hope that I have not put your wife to any unaccountable trouble."

The two figures in the doorway looked at each other with wide eyes. Then the woman spoke, in a tone of wonderment.

"Why, James Joseph. I am married so suddenly."

Sylvester looked at her seriously and replied, "And you are married to your cousin, apparently."

The two then turned and looked at Robert. A moment later, in perfect synchronism, they both burst out laughing. An arm from each of them was extended to Robert who was then pulled through the door. Sylvester calmed himself and apologised.

"Robert, my friend, I am so sorry to have embarrassed you thus. This is my cousin, Caroline, to whom, I should make clear, I am not married."

Caroline hooked her arm through Robert's, by way of an apology, and led him into the drawing room. The attention that she paid him was sufficient to mollify him. Indeed, her graceful and enthusiastic interest in all that Robert said, more than mollified him, it enervated him. She sat beside him on the settee. This woman, who was unlike any other he had met, immediately fascinated Robert. She was at once so worldly and yet at the same time made things appear so simple. She immediately introduced him to her Mama, who sat opposite, watching them, as a good chaperone should.

Sylvester had followed them into the drawing room and after the introductions, talked for a few minutes about the Sylvester's houses in Hove and his uncle, who also had a house in London. Then, to Robert's surprise, Sylvester called his cousin an amateur mathematician. Robert quickly turned to her and said, "I am very impressed. But I will be even more so, when you explain the term to me, for it is one I have never heard before."

Her charming laugh beguiled him. "Why, the word amateur means that I do not depend on mathematics for my upkeep. The other word you might have come across before. When the two are put together, they describe a person who occasionally enjoys solving quadratic equations and geometric problems. James Joseph is now teaching me second order equations. As a consequence, I have only limited ability at dressmaking and embroidery, making my skills rather unsuited for married life."

Her description of her mathematical prowess had no tone of conceit, but was done with a gentle self-mocking, which to Robert seemed an admirable trait in a woman. He was so intrigued by her, that he did not realise until some time later, that a domestic mathematical relationship between a man and a woman, subtly undermined his views on the extent of the boundaries of the woman's place in the world. The realisation caused him to redouble his belief in separate spheres and at the same time to make an exception for this remarkable member of the female sex.

Gathered around the small table in the dining room, they enjoyed a workmanlike meal of soup, fowl and pudding. After the last morsel was consumed, the party adjourned. Caroline led Robert back to the drawing room settee and sat next to him with an indecently small gap between them.

"Now we are settled, Robert, you must tell me all about your home and your family."

Whilst Caroline gazed at him intently, hardly hearing what he said, Robert recited their names, saying what each one did, namely, teacher at the Grammar School, mother, Partner in Crossley and Dyke, assisting mother and apprentice at Crossley and Dyke, the last two being what was what Patience and Thomas did. He omitted Emily entirely.

"Oh, how interesting," said Caroline, raising her fine dark eyebrows, whilst Robert closely watched her full mouth and the occasional glint of her perfect teeth. "It appears from what you say that you come from a large family. How do you amuse yourself in the evenings?"

This question momentarily silenced Robert and his description of a Dissenters family evening embarrassed him. "We all study or embroider in the evenings after dinner, then we do our Bible reading and then we are free to read what we will."

"Really! You sound like such a well disciplined family." Caroline decided to drop her polite mask. "I am certain that you will change as you all leave your parents and set up your own home."

Robert breathed again and grinned. Caroline continued. "While Mama and I stay with James Joseph, we are very ill disciplined. Please do not tell Papa, if you meet him. Mama plays the piano and we sing popular songs. Sometimes we even dance."

She giggled and held her hand to her mouth.

"In Northampton there are regular dances at the Corn Exchange. I have been there many times. But when you meet my father you must not tell him, either."

Caroline giggled and a pair of dimples at the sides of her mouth turned her long face, dominated by her strong nose, into a weapon fit to capture Robert's heart.

"My word, I thought that James Joseph was the only mathematician that could dance," she said, looking at her cousin. Then she pleaded with her mother. "Mama, can we dance?"

Having listened to Robert's polite conversation and her nephew's description of Robert before he arrived, her Mother had satisfied herself that this young man was a safe dancing partner for her daughter. Her standards were higher than usual for this was a different matter to the town dances in Hove. The restricted nature of the space available in the drawing room, even with the small table in the centre pushed to one side, meant that some bodily contact between the dancers might take place. She cautiously replied, "Very well my dear, one or two. What would you like me to play?"

Caroline told her what dances she thought were fast enough to allow her to repeatedly cling to her partner as he swung her about, for she had taken an immediate liking to this new friend of James Joseph. They waltzed rapidly to Strauss, Chopin and Brahms. Sylvester clapped his hands in time to the piano and took Robert's place with Caroline, when his Aunt indicated with a curt nod of her head when propriety deemed it appropriate. Unbeknown to Sylvester, she had an unpublished but nevertheless mathematical formula, widely appreciated by mothers, for determining the number of dances that a young lady could have with a young man before unseemly feelings were aroused. Her skill was in performing the calculation in her head whilst playing.

But, of course, the equation was redundant! For both Robert and Caroline had formed a close attachment to each other, primarily at a physical level, but also some time later, at a Platonic one too. It was an attachment that her mother's propriety could not quench and which made some further meetings necessary.

CHAPTER 13

Cambridge University

Despite his being one of the few that had lectured at the Royal Society, Robert entered his college at Cambridge through the Gate of Humility.

His whole family stood patiently around him on the platform at Northampton Station. His mother was weeping and his father was shaking his hand solemnly, as if this was a religious event of significance. His brother William shook his hand in turns and slapped his back; Thomas, now as tall as Robert, did the same. Patience stood next to Emily, in the background, holding her excommunicated sister's hand in sympathy. Emily had sought out purple hyacinth from the meadow by the river that morning and made a posy, meaning to give it to Robert as a plea for forgiveness. But between his father's rapture and his mother's tears, she had not found a moment for the words with him. She now imagined herself lost to him.

A whistle blew. Both the girls waved their handkerchiefs as Robert mounted the carriage. There was much jerking, squeaking and belching of smoke by the train and then he was gone. Although he would be back within eighty days, all of them knew that this leaving marked the end which had been foreshadowed by the journey to London for the lecture: the end of their family life as it had been.

Robert settled into his seat and cogitated upon his family for a moment or two. Then, as St Paul had advised him, he fixed his eyes firmly on the goal. Since his first meeting with the Reverend Grey, his life had progressed in one direction only. His recent meeting with Henry Boyd of the War Department was the most satisfactory sign of his advancement. He had had an hour's genial conversation with Boyd in his office in London, about this and that. Robert had realised that they were not just two gentlemen discussing the weather, but a gentleman conducting an interview of another for a junior position on a Committee of some importance for many men of science in England.

When the hour had ended, Boyd said, "You understand, of course, what the Minister meant when he said that we should bring in new blood to our endeavours. He meant that the committee was over staffed with old men, who had neither earned their places, nor had shown the impartiality necessary in such positions of national importance. We shall pension off some members and bring in new ones. You are an ideal candidate: young and bursting full of energy, and possessing a wide understanding of scientific matters. Your most important credential is, of course, a proven ability in one such area. You will make an ideal advisor and interpreter between the War Department and the foreign language that these scientists speak. If you are willing to accept such a position if it is offered, I will advise the Minister to issue a letter of invitation."

Robert did accept; the invitation letter had duly arrived and an acceptance immediately dispatched. Robert had not told his family, for Boyd had indicated that the existence of the committee should be kept as a confidential matter. Nor had Robert discussed his visit to Birmingham, to the factory of a small arms manufacturer who had attended his lecture as part of his search for an advisor on the science of ballistics and projectiles. The science was of a trivial nature to Robert. The employment by this powerful man was certainly not.

The train rumbled and rocked onwards, taking Robert to his immediate destination, Cambridge. As it did so, his mind continued to toss to and fro the possibilities in both of these consultative arrangements. When a conclusion for action, or an observation simply to be noted, occurred to him, he took up his pocketbook and wrote. He wrote such confidential matters in Greek or Latin, or whichever combination of the two pleased him as most secure at that moment.

§

Robert had ridden from Cambridge station in a Hansom cab, like the gentleman he now was. He descended and stood deferentially in the Porter's Lodge of Gonville and Caius College, beneath the Gate of Humility that all new students pass through. The Porter had ticked Robert's name off his list, informed him that his trunk had already been taken up and began to pronounce on a number of rules that would govern Robert's life for the next three years. He had explained where he should sleep, where he should eat, where he was to be lectured and where he was to meet his private tutor. Finally the Porter, called Black, intoned, "All doors will be locked at twelve o'clock and overnight absences from College will only be permitted with an exeat, which will only be given to you by your tutor in exceptional circumstances."

With that, the Porter ordered his young assistant to accompany Robert to his room. Robert shook the bewhiskered old man's hand firmly and pressed two shillings into it. This was a critical moment. Robert had looked forward to it with trepidation, for crossing this most important of men could ruin one's stay in College. Getting it right could flatten many of life's cobbled backstreets, permitting silent and swift passage from difficulties. The Porter merely said, "Thank'e, sir. Humility indeed. The previous young bugger only offered me sixpence! The rich ones are always tight."

Robert was led to an impressive three story building in Tree Court, through another gate, named the Gate of Necessity. Upon entering his rooms on the upper floor, he found that he was sharing with Charles Benedict Crowley, and that Crowley was the young bugger that Porter Black had referred to. The two students shook hands. Crowley was just eighteen, yet taller than Robert and exceptionally handsome. Little did Black appreciate his own financial perspicacity, for Crowley's father turned out to be the Bishop of Nottingham. Upon hearing this, Robert remarked, "Why, they must have put us together because our home towns are but thirty miles apart."

"You will go far, my foolish friend. It is nothing to do with places. It is because our names have the first three letters in common, which is singular, is it not? In a cohort of one hundred and ten, the chances against that happening are more than five hundred to one."

Robert was not offended by Charles's insulting tone, for he already felt he had the better of his new friend because of the matter of the Porter's tip, which Charles had so badly misjudged, and all the more surprisingly, because of his father's wealth. However, Robert was impressed by Charles's grasp of probability and only questioned afterwards whether he had invented the result or not. It suggested that he might either be a rogue or amongst the top of the cohort and thus was likely to be rated as a Wrangler. He immediately realised that having rooms with a Wrangler would have advantages that he should make the most of, for he himself doubted his own ability to achieve such honour as his talents lay in other directions. He did not reach the conclusion that Charles was both a rogue and a genius until some weeks later.

He was further surprised to learn that Charles's father spoke regularly for the Whigs in the House, in passionate defence of the workers in Nottingham who, unlike those in Northampton, lived in desperate squalor and as a consequence had a hard time of it. It soon became clear to Robert that the Bishop's son had no such sympathies, despite being a staunch churchman.

The following day was Matriculation, during which the new students were duly enrolled, provided that they signed their agreement to the Thirty Nine Articles. Robert signed without compunction. All were given a copy of the Articles, supposedly to govern their behaviour during their time in College. They had returned to their rooms, wearied by the wearing of their gowns during the long ceremony in the Chapel, followed by dinner in Formal Hall, with its unending grace said after the Fellows entered and before the food was brought in.

As they threw themselves into their moth eaten armchairs, Robert remembered De Morgan's suggestion about discussing the Articles over a port. Charles had had a crate delivered with his trunk and had offered Robert a glass. Charles had downed three before his companion had finished one. Robert stretched back in his chair and asked his friend what he thought of the ceremony. Emboldened by the port, Charles answered a different question.

"I declare that I am a staunch believer in the Anglican Church and the Articles of Faith. I will defend them to the end."

In a similar spirit, Robert moved immediately on from the ceremony, to the debate.

"Charles, in the spirit of what a university is and should be, I would like to challenge your beliefs."

"I would be glad to lock horns with you, for I find port loosens my intellect."

Robert doubted that, but did not say so. He began thus. "Articles 2 to 4, include statements that suggest that God took human form in Jesus, who was both fully God and fully man."

Charles nodded his head, in affirmation.

"Let us examine this statement," continued Robert. "God is the embodiment of perfection and thus is not prey to sin. However man, true man, has an inherent tendency to sin. How is this reconciled?"

Charles poured another glass down his throat before beginning. "Let us first establish that Christ did not sin. He thus had that in common with the being of a God. But like man, was prey to temptation, as his forty days and forty nights in the desert indicated. He thus had this in common with man."

Charles paused, believing that his argument was sufficient. Robert clearly did not and commenced his assault. "But we began by establishing that God does not have a tendency to sin, for all that he does is perfect. We see this, for instance, in his righteous anger. Now for man, anger is very often sinful and we are taught to keep control of it. Yet with God, anger is of a righteous nature and thus not a sin. This leads us to the crux of the argument. How can Jesus be fully man, with a tendency to sin, whilst at the same time, be fully God, without a tendency to sin? Or is there some problem in our logic that allows opposite properties to be held at the same time? A piece of coal can perhaps be white at the same time as being black. Or can a snowdrop be black as well as being white?"

"My dear Robert! You miss the very essence of the argument. The properties of Christ are by their very nature, a mystery."

Robert was not to be denied. "If it is thus a mystery, how can we, as mere men, sign our names to it, for we do not understand what we are affirming."

"But the degree that we take is a spiritual exercise."

"That is true, for there will be things in this degree that we will never understand."

Charles began to laugh. Robert smiled at him, satisfied that he had defeated Charles in their first debate. But Charles had other ideas. "Very good, Robert. I think I win that one. Another glass?"

"Ah, I see your game, Charles! A glass, yes, please." He leaned over and the port flowed like blood in a battle.

Robert had his second point ready. "Now, let us turn to Article 17, named Of Predestination and Election. Please explain to me..."

"Robert, Robert! I have had enough of your pedantic theologising. The rebuttal to the attempted loosening of the threads of civilisation in Article 17, that you are about to embark upon, is the same as for Articles 1 to 4. That is to say, mystery. The apparent logical inconsistency between predestination and election is false, as any schoolboy will tell you. The operation of both simultaneously is another of God's mysteries, without which our religion would be inexpressibly dull. Now give me a problem I can get my teeth into. Three dimensional geometry, for example."

This played into Robert's hands, for he and William had until recently kept up their habit of testing each other with geometrical exercises. Robert thought for a moment, and then remembered a problem that he and William had tried, but failed, and had never since seen a solution to. He found a sheet of paper, which just happened to be the back of Articles 29 to 39, and drew two curves that intersected, near to the centre of the page. He marked the word *parabola* next to one. To the left of the intersection he drew a small cross which he labelled *focus*. He showed it to Charles.

"I want you to find the angle between a tangent line on the surface and the parabolic axis in terms of the coordinates of the tangent point."

Charles stared at him, as if a nine year old could solve it. Robert continued.

"The tangent line is twisted by an angle alpha from the plane of the axes."

Charles reacted with a smile. "Ah, yes my friend, a good question. This might take a moment or two."

Charles took the paper and a fresh bottle of port, and seated himself at the table. He began to scribble indecipherably. Robert looked at the clock on the mantelpiece. Eleven thirty. Lectures began on the morrow at eight. He went to his bedroom, undressed and went to bed.

The following morning, he had difficulty in rousing Charles, who refused to join him at breakfast. Robert looked around for the problem that Charles had worked on through the night. He finally saw a corner of the document protruding from beneath Charles's bed. On the reverse of Articles 23 to 28 was a maze of equations and small explanatory figures. However, it was orderly, and Robert could follow it. Charles had completed the problem. When Robert slapped his friend's recumbent figure on the back and thanked him, Charles yawned and asked him what he had done to deserve this praise. He asked him the same question later that day. A surprised Robert realised that Charles had no memory of the work he had done the previous night.

§

The lecture rooms were in Caius Court, which was entered through another gate called the Gate of Virtue. He helped Charles to attend a two-hour lecture from Doctor Lovett and yet got no credit from his friend for putting himself out. The lecture was upon the syllabus for the course, instructions for using the library in the Cockerell Building and an introduction to the history of the College. Lovett was as dry a teacher as Robert had ever experienced and a depressing realisation dawned upon him. A Cambridge degree was what every young man of aspiration desired, but the getting of it was as vexing to the soul as working down a coal mine.

After the lecture and after twenty minutes in which he was able to revive his flagging body and mind with two cups of college coffee, Robert had a meeting with his private tutor. He met Joseph Stannier in one of the many small rooms adjacent to Caius Court, which were set aside for tutoring. The old man smoked a pipe that coloured his white beard brown around his mouth and nose. He wore a dark tweed jacket that looked as if it had been purchased when the man had arrived in Cambridge. Joseph had graduated low in the Wrangler ratings thirty-five years before, but showed enough promise to take him into a career in whatever profession he chose, but had not left Cambridge. He instead had obtained rooms with a giant of a landlady, who ran his life like clockwork. In other words, she led Joseph around the same circles, whether large or small, with a repeatability and precision equalled only by a mechanism from the finest craftsman. However, Joseph was happy with this rather predictable and settled arrangement, for his face wore a perpetual smile.

Robert decided that Stannier was, like the Porter, a man to be treated with respect. Robert believed that he could have proceeded through the first year with only one hourly meeting every week. Stannier insisted on three. Robert agreed and only found out through discussion with Charles that the man was paid by the hour. Stannier insisted on translations, essays and proofs being completed in full, despite Robert having successfully tackled most of the material with the Reverend Grey. Thus Robert's days were filled with much dull writing and uninspiring meetings, unlike Charles, who had a much more lenient tutor and spent much of his time in the various public houses in the town.

Early in the Michaelmas term, Robert showed his letters from Boyd from the War Office and Hardwick from Birmingham, to his tutor.

Stannier scratched his beard. "The letter from the War Department looks genuine and seems to be serious business. The meeting is on the 25th. I will write you an exeat for three days for that one!"

"Thank you, sir!"

"But this other one? Why does he want your advice? He appears to do metalwork!"

"He does do metalwork, sir. But he supplies the War Department with mechanisms that are vital to the defence of the Empire. The two jobs that I am engaged upon are thus intertwined. I could ask him to write you a further letter indicating this fact, but it might be that he is not disposed to advertise his activities too widely. And if this does not suffice to convince you, I could respectfully ask him not to move his donation from this university to the University of Oxford. I understand that he is on friendly terms with the Chancellors of both places of learning."

The imaginary facts concerning donations and Chancellors had come into Robert's mind when he was preparing for this conversation. Stannier hesitated and then made his mind up.

"Of course, there will be no problem with an exeat for that meeting also."

"Thank you again, sir. That is most kind of you. By the way, Mister Hardwick wished me to pass on his kindest regards to my tutor. He also gave me this, to pass on to you, as an expression of gratitude for your understanding concerning my future visits to see him."

Robert slid a ten-shilling note across the table, which was rapidly pocketed by his tutor. Robert did not smoke, drank only moderately, and was in general frugal in his needs. He only spent his money on things that mattered to him.

§

On the 25th, Robert was seated in an elegant committee room in the War Department. He had read the minutes of the previous meeting and done his research in the Cockerell Library. Three of those present at the last meeting were now absent and no doubt pensioned off. Of those remaining, he could recognise none that were scientists or mathematicians. There were representatives from the various parts of the Army, the Navy and War Department. Boyd was the Secretary to the Chairman. It was clear that they knew what they had and what they wanted. What they did not have was an understanding of whether what they wanted was physically possible. There was a discussion of the cost of production of naval chronometers, which Robert followed with keen interest and promised himself to pass onto William when he saw him at Christmas.

Then, to his surprise, a new item was introduced. There was a growing awareness that the inaccuracies in the flight of projectiles from guns and cannons needed to be reduced. The discussion followed similar lines to those that Robert had had with Hardwick in Birmingham, concerning the incorporation of various adjustments to the aiming of weapons. Robert was well able to explain this from a mathematical point of view, but in a form that the gentlemen of the committee could understand. He soon had their heads nodding in satisfaction of their own intellectual capabilities. And in his last sentence, he offered them some hope.

"Gentleman, it is clear that what I have described is mathematically demanding and, although now clearly understood around this table, very much beyond the capabilities of the serviceman under fire. However recent inventions concerning machines that do the necessary calculations suggests that a solution to the problem is possible."

He stopped and left his hook dangling. The Chairman took the bait.

"Well Mister Crossley, that is a most useful contribution and a most interesting suggestion. I think we should ask you to go away and investigate, as much as Caius will let you away from your lectures. By the way, did I tell you that Caius is also my alma mater? The Master was just a Fellow when I was there, but we exchange pleasantries every year when I go up for a drink. Please send my regards if you see him."

Robert noted what he said with a nod of the head and the meeting moved on. He looked about him and, to his surprise, Mister Boyd was glowering at the Chairman, as if he should have been the one to be pensioned off for talking of pleasantries with the Master of a Cambridge college.

He arrived back at the College at fifteen minutes before curfew. When he signed in with Mister Black, the Porter's plaintive tones assailed him. "Now sir, your young Mister Crowley, he's out and about again. If he gets locked out one more time, he's for the Procter. An' it won't surprise me to see him sent down."

Robert could not see the Procter being that hard on a potential Wrangler, but he needed to do all he could for his friend. He fished in his pocket for another two shillings and gave it to the Porter.

"Mister Black, I will go and look for him now. I believe he may be in the Grapes Inn. You would not see one of your students up before the Procter, for trying to rescue his loyal friend. Please give me an extra fifteen minutes beyond curfew to bring him back."

The Porter nodded his head. "Very well, Mister Crossley, sir."

Robert ran as hard as he could for the Grapes, which was ten minutes away. He found Charles with his arm round one of the girls and asked her assistance rather than begging Charles to come home with little chance of success. She helped get him outside, and they stumbled their way back. The Porter slammed the gate shut behind them. At the bottom of the steps, Charles seemed to recover enough to speak.

"Ah, Robert! My dear man, you have come to help me up the stairs. I fear that I might not manage it myself and be found sleeping on the lawn. Remember, my friend, that walking on the lawn is for Fellows only."

They were on the first landing. Charles was still talking. "But wait. The rule says nothing about sleeping, so perhaps that is allowed. By the way, the wench in the Grapes has exceptional breasts. Primo-gropant! Yes, I have been groping her grapes and she mine."

He was quiet as they mounted the second landing and then Charles began singing.

"Fuccamus, fuccatis, fuccant. It is my motto, Robert, my dear, dear friend. Fuccamus, fuccatis, fuccant, for we lay together three times."

"Keep quiet, my friend, or the Proctors will hear. We are nearly there."

Robert unlocked their door and deposited Charles in his armchair. Robert looked at him, partly in despair for his wild ways and partly in admiration for the way he could hold his liquor. Then a thought flashed through his mind. He helped his friend to the table and placed before him the paper on which he had written out the problem that Laidmann had set him on octonions before he came up. He had meant to find a quiet moment to brief Charles on its content. But now his head was bent in close scrutiny of the paper. His voice had lost its intensity, as his mind became engaged.

"Why, Robert, my man, this is a capital problem. Pass that bottle over and I will get on with it."

Robert did as he was bid and the next morning found four sheets in orderly form lying on the table with the solution. The rest was simple. He transcribed the working into his own handwriting and with a brief covering note wishing his collaborator well, sent them to Professor Laidmann.

CHAPTER 14

The Return

Robert had been immediately attracted to Caroline Sylvester and through a series of meetings they got to know each other. These meetings happened during the Christmas holiday and Lent term. At Christmas, he left his family on the day after Boxing Day, saying that he had to go back to Cambridge to study. His father was satisfied with this naive explanation, for his power in keeping discipline in his family was slowly diminishing. In the Lent term his visits to her corresponded to his excursions to sit on the committee in London. By Easter their romance had blossomed and they began to plan a life together.

After the Easter term, Robert visited Caroline's father, Michael Sylvester, in his London house, to discuss a possible betrothal. They sat beneath a large parasol in the garden. The grass had been recently mowed and in the calm of the afternoon the scent enveloped them. His host offered him a cigar and for a moment the business of cutting and lighting occupied them. Michael welcomed him and in a rather abrupt and business like manner explained his daughter's background.

"Caroline married an Arab! She met him here in London and he swept her off her feet. He was a wealthy businessman operating in the Levant. In this one action of accepting him, and in the one word, *yes*, she alienated her family and her race. I told her that she was too impulsive. She still is, God bless her."

A smile came over her father's face. Robert also loved that part of her nature. After a moment Michael continued.

"They had two girls. Her husband died abroad, leaving his fortune to her. All attempts to find her another husband have failed. The Jewish community shuns her because she married an Arab. The Arabs shun her because she is Jewish. And all the English see is a Jewess." He lifted his palms in resignation and then became heated. "I cannot have my two granddaughters growing up without a father. It is bad enough to have tainted blood. But now they will be deprived of a father figure to discipline them. Why, they will grow up like animals."

Robert nodded his head in agreement. "However, sir, there is one further characteristic which makes her unusual. She seems to spurn the normal occupations of a young woman."

Michael stared at him with a puzzled look, and Robert tried to appease him. "Of course, she has the capability to order her house, for I understand that she runs her home in London with care and a loving concern for her daughters."

"Indeed she does, Robert, for there is nothing that concerns her more than the welfare of her children."

"But she does not sew or paint watercolours, or do embroidery. She dances and she is an amateur mathematician! Do you not think that that is unseemly in a woman?"

"Perhaps. I would not know, for unseemly women have surrounded me all my life. To me the woman you describe is seemly." Michael smiled, although he seemed to be concerned with the direction that the conversation was taking.

Robert sensed his mood. "Of course, of course."

Then Michael became serious and said, "I hope that you do not find it distasteful to return to the matter in hand. Do you wish to marry my daughter?"

"Your hospitality has been without fault, sir, and it pains me to say, no, I do not wish to marry her."

Robert's host pulled himself up in his chair and his impatience was clear. "Then why are you here, wasting my time?"

"I hope I am not doing that, sir. I merely wish to make you a proposal. For now that I am in possession of all the facts regarding your daughter and her previous marriage, you might be sensitive to my position."

"Your position?"

Robert was treading a fine course in establishing his position. "You may not be aware, sir, that I sit on an influential committee in the War Department. Whilst this committee is somewhat in the background when it comes to political matters, it would be difficult for me if such a marriage became common knowledge."

In that quiet corner of the garden, Robert's deliberate, slow words hung like the cigar smoke between them. After a pause, he continued. "There is another difficult matter of which I hardly need to remind you. Your daughter and I are from different religions, although our cultural backgrounds are much closer. However, if we were to marry, should it be in the Anglican Church or in the Synagogue? I have no desire to admit to the tenets of a faith without Christ, nor I think is Caroline about to accept Him as her saviour."

Michael watched him without reacting. Nevertheless, Robert felt that he could read his thoughts. He must go carefully now. "Sir, I apologise for having named Him who comes between our religions, but I felt it necessary to be plain."

Michael nodded, but remained silent. Robert continued. "I myself do not have strong views in such matters, for despite Church and State saying otherwise, I feel that it is the relationship between a man and a woman that is the most important in life. And we are talking about life here, sir. The life of your daughter and the lives of your granddaughters."

Michael nodded his head again and raised his eyebrows, but still did not speak.

"I will not swear before you now of my intentions for Caroline, for I would not want to insult you with an inappropriate oath, which would make trivial what I feel for Caroline. Neither should I, for both our religions, warn of such practice."

Michael merely stared at him.

"In the face of all these difficulties and in my desire to do my best for Caroline, my proposal is as follows. That Caroline and I commit ourselves to each other in a marriage partnership, *without* a religious service. Our fortunes need not be thus coupled, for my intentions concern Caroline and her children only, and not her money or her property."

Finally Michael spoke. "Your proposal is to merely live with her?"

"Yes, sir. I will find a house in London suitable for the four of us, or more if she is happy to bear my offspring."

Caroline's father raised his eyebrows and seemed to hesitate. He brought his hands down on the arms of his chair and his shoulders lifted imperceptibly. Robert knew his decision.

"Robert, you claim not to be a politician, but you are persuasive, without a doubt. Have you discussed all of this with Caroline?"

"Not in detail."

"Very well. I will wait until she is happy with this singular arrangement. And if she is, I hope that you will allow us a small celebration in Hove to give the two of you our blessing?"

"That would be much appreciated. However, because of all the difficulties in our union, I would prefer not to involve my family."

"But my dear young man. Not invite your own family. How extraordinary."

"It shames me to tell you that my father has a particular abhorrence, if I might use that unfortunate word, of the Jewish people. My relationship with him is rather difficult and I would not wish to make it more so. You may rest assured that I have no such misplaced scruples."

"I am sure you do not. Robert, you have my sympathy."

"There is one other matter that I would like to discuss with you. I believe that within your circle of friends there are some who own factories that are manufacturing clothing."

"Yes, that is so. You are interested in clothing manufacture?"

"Not as such. The committee that I spoke of earlier is interested in clothing for servicemen, not in purchase, but in ensuring that such clothing is incorporating all the advances that science can bring to bear in such matters."

"Ah, yes, I understand. You wish to talk to such of my friends as may understand the science of clothing?"

"No, sir. I wish to talk to them about how science may help them. I have a wide understanding of the fundamentals of science, and our discussions might throw up new avenues for investigation. Then subsequently, if such clothing has an advantage to the serviceman, then my committee might wish to know about it."

"Yes, yes, I have it. Very well, I will make some enquiries. We should always keep talking to the scientists, Robert."

§

Robert and Caroline, her father and mother, John Joseph and several of their other relatives, for there were many, spent a weekend together at Hove. They toasted the happy couple over dinner after nightfall on Saturday. Michael explained that it was custom to enjoy the Sabbath for being a gift of God and to celebrate marriages and other events on different days.

Early on the following day, the happy couple took a promenade along the front. They had already declared their happiness at their unorthodox betrothal with a kiss, whilst seated in a wooden booth provided for promenaders to watch the sea. Robert gazed at the waves for a moment and asked Caroline why she did not tell him all her background. She was not offended by the question.

"The thought never entered my head that you should become my husband. You know I can be like a silly girl. I rather fell in love with you on that night you came to dinner with my cousin and we danced." He smiled at the recollection. "And then? Well, I did not want anything contentious to come between us. Once I had found you, I could not bear to lose you." He kissed her again and the moment passed.

Later that day the party dispersed to their various homes.

Robert went to Northampton to tell his family that he was moving to London to make it easier to conduct his business affairs when he was not studying in Cambridge. His father asked him what his business was. Robert told him, with no emotion, that he had obtained retainers from several companies to advise them on scientific matters. Jeremiah's reply surprised him.

"You know that your mother loves you deeply. She may not be able to recover from your leaving."

Robert gave him a curious look. Was his father asking him to stay? He remembered his father's admonishment that William and he should tread in his footsteps. How would staying to look after his mother achieve that? He did not answer, but bowed his head to acknowledge that he had heard what his father had said, and left the room.

His last night in his family home was difficult for him. The very rooms themselves filled him with distantly heard echoes of growing up and of his mother's love and his father's discipline. Many of the emotions he experienced were not happy. He felt that the atmosphere was charged with unreality, or a reality without substance like Plato's shadows. Later that evening, when all had retired, he came down to the drawing room and placed his palm on the wall, searching for meaning and tried to listen to the voices within it, to hear all those feint imprints of what the wall had witnessed. He knew that they were but his own memories, manifesting themselves in his head, yet he tried to reach out to understand them. He moved over to the clock that he had stopped, and marvelled that it was still going. Despite the pain of his naivety which cut him still, he knew that time was tempering the steel of his resolve. He knew he would succeed.

He walked into the kitchen and remembered the beating he received for collecting eggs, and wondered at how his mind had been buffeted and bent by his father's behaviour. But he hesitated and reflected, for that boy was another person, and these memories were being presented to him in a book that he could close and set aside. He smiled at the thought; he was writing another book now.

He turned to find that his sister Emily had come into the kitchen and was watching him as he stood lost in his own thoughts.

"Ah, Emily," he said, before she could speak. "You are keen for my forgiveness, for I knew the posy you made was for that."

She was surprised at his reading of her when he left for Cambridge, nearly a year ago.

"I know that you feel bereft, but you should not, for you misinterpret our relationship. You did what I disapproved of. Well, so do many in this world and I cannot maintain active conflict with them all. I merely disapprove of many things. But I will not stop you, for that is not part of my destiny. I know that you will continue to do what you feel you must do, just as I do. You are not my sister still; you are forever to me a stranger. But you now see that I will talk to you, as I would any stranger. Be thankful for that and do whatever you will."

With that he left the room and in the morning he left the house. They did not go to the station to wave him off.

§

Robert moved into Caroline's house. It was large enough for him to have his own bedroom and to make the study his own, whilst leaving enough space for Caroline and her children. They danced often, for Caroline's mother regularly came up from Hove and stayed with them to be near her grandchildren. Robert took delight in dancing with the girls who, at five and six, were old enough to appreciate a male partner. He also continued Caroline's mathematical education, taking over from John Joseph.

He had quickly learned to reciprocate her tactile approach and they developed a bond based on touch as well as words, in which they often communicated through intimacy. He slept in her bed more than his own.

Caroline was relieved to see a close relationship develop between Robert and the girls, who adopted him wholeheartedly as their father. She was quick to explain to them that their new father would be away, studying for his degree at university, for periods in the following two years. Although they accepted this arrangement, they cried when he left for Cambridge in October. To comfort them, he wrote often, describing the Cambridge characters in amusing stories, which went some way to relieving their disappointment at his absence.

The following year, Caroline gave birth to a boy and his domestic bliss was complete. His embrace of this family life soothed his memories of his own harsh upbringing, and he purposely strove to be understanding of his wife who, excepting her interest in mathematics, performed in a model way, never straying out of her separate sphere.

§

Five men sat in the elegant dining room in the house of Michael Sylvester, Caroline's father. Robert sat next to Michael. There were three other guests. One, reminded Robert of his friend Hardwick from Birmingham. Pinchas Abravanel was round and blunt in his speech. He owned a boot and shoe company in London, with shops, warehouses and factories. Not all of these warehouses held footwear, nor did all of his factories make them. Another guest was older and had fine white whiskers. Benjamin Rabinovich and his family also worked in clothing, but his other holdings were less well known. Avraham Shafran was a banker.

Michael, as host, introduced Robert to them as being on a Government committee into the exploitation of scientific discoveries, and also a famous mathematician. To Robert he said, "These gentlemen are my friends and we are also connected by our faith. But we do not advertise the fact."

"Although such facts have been in the news recently," said Shafran.

"Ah, yes, the Don Pacifico affair." Michael turned to Robert and asked, "Robert did you hear about that?"

"Having been until recently locked in Gonville and Caius College, I have missed much that is news." Robert was happy to be companiable. "Please explain it to me."

Shafran took the lead. "David Pacifico, a Jew, was born in Gibraltar and is therefore a British Citizen. However, he has lived in Portugal for many years. He became the Portuguese Ambassador to Greece and had a residence in Athens. He also traded in that area. Recently rioting crowds plundered his home, whilst police looked on. It appears that de Rothschild was visiting Athens at the time to discuss a loan to the Greek Government and, to avoid offending him, they decided to ban the burning of the effigy of Judas, which is an old and venerated Easter tradition in Greece. When the Foreign Secretary, Lord Palmerston, heard of Don Pacifico's loss, he interpreted it as an attack on British sovereignty and sent a squadron into the Aegean to seize shipping to the value lost by Pacifico. They blockaded Piraeus for two months, only leaving after considerable diplomatic frenzy between Britain, France, Russia and Greece."

Abravanel lifted his large shoulders and said, "The Jew did nothing, but it aroused the usual feelings."

Silence fell as they all considered. After a moment, Michael broke it.

"But let us proceed to talk about you, Robert. How did you fare, under lock and key, in Cambridge?"

"I fared well, sir, despite my earlier levity about the place. It is said that a university is but a group of largely like-minded people and it is the characters that one remembers. From the Porter at the gate to the Master, they are all vividly imprinted on my mind like a daguerreotype. It is equally important not to be cheap in tipping the porter, as it is in minding your manners with the Master. I came face to face with the Master, Doctor Benedict Chapman, as he was a friend of the Chairman of my committee and, despite asking me to give the Master my regards when I saw him, he must have communicated my name himself, for the Master invited me to dinner with another couple of undergraduates. We were all in awe, as we should have been, but he had an admirable way of putting people at their ease, as you gentlemen have with me."

The gentlemen smiled at Robert, who by complimenting them was complimenting himself. The art was to do it and then move on quickly, which is what he did. "Doctor Chapman's background was divinity and, of course, he had a sharp mind. I trod my way carefully in describing the advantages that science can bring to mankind, for it is too easy to sound like an enthusiast. But I think he saw my argument. I hope so, for there are other places, such as the University of London, that have a much more enlightened mind. And there is a real danger that Cambridge, for so long the centre of learning in England, will be overtaken by the forces of progress."

Robert privately wondered whether the Master would remember their conversation, for in truth it generally revolved around the admirable duck that they ate and the ancient port that they drank. Students, the Master joked, poor as they are, need to take good food whilst they can.

"But I enjoyed the company of the Fellows most of all. They were the Professors' slaves in the work that they did, for the Professors gave them the problem and the Fellows worked their fingers raw looking for a solution. I advised the slaves sometimes, for I have discovered that advice seems to be my strength. I advised, the Fellows did the work and the Professors got the credit. I have seen several papers in the Proceedings of the Royal Society that bear my unseen imprint."

Shafran, the banker laughed with the rest of them and, as they paused, put up his hand.

"Robert, I could listen to your stories all through the night. But the gentlemen may not have the whole night and I understand there is some advice you wish to impart to us."

"Indeed, sir. Thank you. The British Government has a continual eye on the improvement of its forces, for it fights to defend the Empire in many distant places. To get straight to the point, there is a need to make our weapons more accurate. This requires many things. Firstly, improved manufacture involves a better understanding of metalworking and even of the structure of metal itself. I am sure that you are all aware of this yourself. The design of weapons involves the study of ballistics and how the atmosphere and weather affects flight. Now the universities possess some fine minds in these sciences, but they lack focus and they lack discretion. What I propose is an independent organisation, which employs specialists in all these sciences whose minds are solely concentrated on the improvements that our production requires."

Heads were now nodding and chins were being stroked. Robert continued.

"Such an organisation needs money from a number of sources and the goodwill, or better, the written agreement, of what one might call its members, for it to succeed."

Robert fell silent. The seed was sown. It was now important to keep close to these gentlemen to secure for himself the position that he needed in that organisation when it was formed.

§

After much toil and drudgery, and on the appointed day, Robert graduated, passing out of College in line with his fellows through the Gate of Honour to the ceremony. The choir sang and the speeches wound their weary way. As he sat, he evaluated his feelings. He was not impressed with Cambridge; he had developed a weariness for the university, for Caius and for meaningless study. He felt it to be an anachronistic echo of a world gone by, and not fitted to the modern age. He knew that many people considered the final examinations to be merely tests of memory and speed and that many first Wranglers achieved little of merit as Fellows. His own modest achievement of being safely in the middle of the field meant that he did not attract the notice of the Professors for his outstanding ability, which he knew he never had, or for his dismal performance, which he feared.

Yet he knew that Cambridge had been a necessary step in his ambitions. And, as he reminded himself of this, he realised that he had no concept of where the end point of his ambitions might be. This momentarily unsettled him and he quickly pushed the uncertainty back to the further recesses of his mind, as his hunger to move forward overtook him again.

PART 3

NORTHAMPTON

CHAPTER 15

The Horse Race on Freeman's Common

Freeman's Common in 1859 was a landmark in the town of Northampton. Its name referred to the right of freemen to use it for grazing, but the residents used it as a park in which they could escape the noise and dust of the streets. Regular horse races were held there, and the annual steeplechase was an event not to be missed. The Kingsley Park Hotel lay on the north-eastern point of the Common and had fine views of the course.

Whilst Clara was in London attending to her patients, Edward was standing in the bar of the hotel, discussing the steeplechase, which was to take place the following day. He was a regular race goer, at whichever course took his fancy, up and down the country. Not only did he find horses at speed an energising spectacle, but he also enjoyed pitching his wits with other race goers that liked a wager. He was a student of the turf, which suited his tendencies towards the judging of both horseflesh and human flesh, and his facility with mathematics. When he knew that he was going to Northampton to conduct the investigation around the time of the steeplechase, he had started to study the field to establish his own set of odds for the various horses that he had picked out as contenders.

Edward was drinking a small beer to keep his wits about him. He was generally affable and well spoken, so that conversation came easily to him; he could pass the time with almost anyone, when it suited him. "How is the course looking?" he asked the bartender. The bartender had heard this question enough times before to have an answer ready to dictate. "Well, sir, you should be minded that the course is left handed."

Edward needed to be patient with him, because something useful might come in due course. He took a sip of his beer and shuddered inwardly at the taste.

"Them corners are something sharp," continued the bartender. "There have been a few favoured horses come to grief on 'em. And sometimes, what with people wanderin' all over, lookin' for a better view, the field can be put to confusion tryin' to ride over a dead spectator."

The man glared at Edward, hoping that his dramatic words would evoke a reaction. Edwards tried to look horrified, but not being practiced at it, put up a poor show. However it was enough, for the man continued.

"The hotel stands on a rise, so coming up the town straight and the bend after, the riders have to mount this hill. The best have no trouble with it, but it sorts out the men from the boys, horse-wise that is!"

He grinned childishly.

"How is the going?"

"Well, sir, between you and me, it has rained much in the night over the last couple of weeks and folks ain't noticed it. So, though it looks fair, it's wet underneath."

Edward slipped him a shilling, which was politely accepted, and began to adjust his handicaps in his head as he walked back to town.

On the day of the race, he was again standing in the bar of the Hotel. The view from the large windows was very different. The few workmen that he had seen staking out the course the day before, had been replaced by the large crowds that had taken the half an hour stroll from the centre of town to the Common. There were families with gangs of children streaming out behind them, there were mothers with perambulators pushing doggedly across the deep turf, there were groups of rough-looking men holding jars of drink, there were courting couples and there were dandies wandering aimlessly around. He had already conversed with several of the latter, adopting his affected voice, to create a companionship within which to strike advantageous wagers. He had toured the obvious bookmakers, selecting those that offered him better odds than his own estimates. He had parted with ten pounds over a period of two hours and had come into the bar to quench the thirst created by such intense activity. There was a couple standing next to him in the bar, and he drank. The man, dressed as smartly as Edward, was talking to a most attractive young lady.

"My dear, you shall have that dress that you saw yesterday, when my horse comes in."

Such foolish talk attracted Edward's attention. He turned and addressed the man.

"May I ask which horse you have your shirt on?"

The man burst out laughing, for he had already drunk a little too much.

"Why, sir, Valiant, of course! She is the talk of the town."

"But do you not feel that the odds are too short to make it worth your while?" Edward was speaking to the man, but watching the woman's face. Her eyes showed her tiredness for her companion's boasting.

"Not at all. If you put enough on it, there's plenty to be made."

"But more smaller bets, appropriately spread, will give you less risk. And then your beautiful lady will have her dress."

A cry from outside signalled the start, and all went out to watch the spectacle. The horses rounded the bend close to the hotel and the crowd roared. Edward had positioned himself next to the lady, who gasped as the whips flogged the rumps of the galloping horses. Edward turned his head to her and spoke softly but audibly as the shouting subsided.

"A whip on a rump can, in other circumstances, be a most charming experience."

Her eyes widened momentarily in reply and then became coy. The horses sped into the distance and the moment was gone.

He spent the next half an hour collecting his winnings and paying his debts. At his last collection, the bookie was bent over his bag, packing up his belongings to go. His board showed that he was an Upstone man. Edward presented his paper and asked him if he knew the Upstone Vicar, the old Vicar Grey, his wife and Robert.

"Yes, I do," he replied. "All proper people knew the Vicar and his young student. He were there every Sunday."

The man passed a note and some coins to Edward. He did it with a laugh, for at the annual steeplechase all the bookies made enough to feed their families for six months or more.

"It were a sad day when he passed away. We all went to the funeral, really nice it was. The student brought his family, he were a real gent, he were."

Edward nodded and was turning away, when the man unaccountably continued, as if driven by some deep impulse. "But no one liked the doctor; he were too nice. He had a reputation in the village"

"A reputation? For what?"

"Bless me, I dun' know. Under'and, some'ow. My old mum, she's dead now. She said he were too nice; not like a proper doctor. He would be short with the men and lingering with the womenfolk."

The man finished and bent down again to buckle his bag. Edward turned away. The balance of the day was that his ten pounds had turned into fifty-five, which he considered a good return for a day's racing.

He returned to the bar for a celebratory toast, which he shared with the young lady. Her companion had lost all and had gone off in a temper. Edward took her back to town in his cab, bought her the dress that she so longed for, took her for dinner in his hotel and spent the rest of the night together with her in his bedroom.

§

Four days later, Edward was waiting on the platform for Clara's train to arrive. It steamed in and a hand waved from a First Class compartment.

"Edward, Edward," called Clara. She looked striking in a red striped travelling dress and matching hat. Her face glowed with pleasure that Edward was waiting for her. When he had opened the door for her, she let him assist her, in a quite un-gentlemanly manner, with his hands around her waist.

"Clara, my dear, how are you?"

"I am all the better for seeing you, Edward. I trust you have behaved yourself, whilst I have been away."

"Never expect that. I have attended the races, and had a fascinating day."

As the cab took them up the hill to the George Hotel, he told her about the bookie and his comments about the doctor.

"And how much did you lose? You remember I warned you against the evils of gambling"

"I won forty five pounds. Not as much as I told you I would, but you know how I tend to exaggerate."

Clara stared at him with a newfound respect. "And was that just luck?"

"Luck comes into everything that happens at a racecourse," said Edward with half a mind on his young lady. "But a fair amount of mental arithmetic came into it, as well. The bookies earnings are based on mental arithmetic and I would say that mine is at least as sharp as theirs."

"Well with all that money in your pocket, I am surprised that your pockets were not picked."

"They were not, indeed. However, I usually take extremely serious precautions. The money goes into a very secure pocket inside the top of my jacket sleeve. My wallet, which is loosely placed in my breast pocket contains nothing but this."

He pulled out a fifty-pound note from his wallet and handed it to her. She found it hard to speak.

"I have never held such a note before. I am not sure that I knew they existed."

"Turn it over. The reverse is much more interesting."

To her eternal surprise, the back of the note was blank, save for some lines of doggerel and Edward's signature.

> For two, the bank will pay,
> If you but find the other.
> Look front wards and look back,
> For that way lies my brother.

"The Governor of the Bank of England gave the note to me over dinner one night in London. He gave me several, actually, because they are worthless; but they are just ripe for a jest with a friend or an enemy. The lines took me a couple of minutes to write."

She gazed at him admiringly, as the cab came to a halt outside the hotel. Clara's room had been held for her, courtesy of Edward, and she went directly upstairs. Their conversation resumed over dinner.

"How are your patients, who needed your presence so urgently?"

"There is one that we lost. The others are as well as they might be."

"I am sorry to hear that one has died. It must be always so with a physician!"

"Indeed, it is the way that things are. We treat them, until we can make them better no longer. And then we lose them."

Edward saw the momentary sadness in Clara's eyes, for he knew that she was a conscientious doctor. He tried to shake her out of it.

"Did you attend the theatre?"

"No, but my husband took me to a musical evening, to make up for being away on our anniversary."

Edward found it amusing, to talk with this woman that he was now so close to, about her husband who was not her husband.

"What did you hear?"

"Something of Chopin and something of Schumann."

"Ah. And did you enjoy it?"

"Passingly."

"I am sure that the Chopin was charming, but the Schumann must have been somewhat poignant."

"Why?"

"For Robert Schumann grew up as a prodigy but died not three years ago in an asylum in Endenich."

Clara was silenced by this and stared at Edward, waiting for an explanation.

"As a boy, his compositions were marked by his ability to portray feeling in melody. He read Schiller, Goethe and Byron as well as the Greek tragedies. His inspirational father died when he was sixteen and he ended up studying law in Heidelberg. He struggled to decide between music and law, but eventually began to train as pianist, until a mysterious hand injury made him turn to composition. When his brother and sister-in-law died of cholera, he suffered from a severe depressive episode and attempted to kill himself. He recovered and became engaged to the adopted daughter of a rich noble; when he found out that she would not inherit, he called off the engagement. He pursued instead the fifteen year old Clara Wieck."

Clara raised her eyebrows at the mention of her namesake.

"I am sure that you know the story of their romance and marriage."

"Yes. How did he end up in an asylum?"

"His symptoms were nervous prostration, followed by neurasthenia."

"Ah," Clara explained, "he was reduced to an invalid by overwork or worry or something darker within him."

"Indeed. He recovered, but his critics noted creative decay in his work. He had delusions, seeing angels and devils, and attempted to kill himself two more times, before begging to be committed. There were various rumours of the cause of death. But his was a life full of wonderful music and marital joy, played out to a background of mental instability."

"That is interesting, Edward. However, there are fewer parallels with our case, than I at first imagined."

"Indeed." Edward's brow furrowed. "But, it teaches me to be continually conscious of insane tendencies in those with very great gifts."

They finished their dinner and went to their rooms in sombre mood.

§

Later that night, alone in her room, Clara's mind was in absolute turmoil. She had missed Edward whilst she had been in London; she had known that from the first moment that she had seen him at the station. What was she feeling? It was not that she felt comfortable in his presence, for she also felt that way about her husband. It was that she felt an uncontrollable urge to abandon herself to Edward. Wherever she looked within herself, she could only find one course of action. That she should go to him and lay her feelings before him. And then she hoped for proprietary's sake that he would be sensible and tell her that sleep and work were the best cure for what she was suffering.

She pulled her a dressing gown over her nightdress and knocked on Edward's door. They were in adjoining suites and had a communicating door. Edward soon answered and was not surprised to see her. Clara was intimidated by his poise and thought of drawing back. But her need drove her on. Edward invited her to the settee by the window. There was a lamp lighting the desk that he had been working at, but the rest of the room was dark. The moon illuminated the settee and its glow confirmed her feeling of unreality. Clara was too afraid to speak. Edward sat down next to her and brushed aside the awkwardness that was separating them.

"My dear, I was just reading Swinburne. Have you read him?"

Clara nodded her head. Edward continued. "Do you respect him? I am not sure that I do. I invited him to one of my evenings and we talked metaphysics and other such nonsense, as poets do."

"What were you reading?"

"Anactoria. It is Sappho's lament for her departed lover. She cannot understand the woman's action in leaving her. Sappho says that her lover has lost her chance of immortality, for Sappho would have written of her lover in one of her poems. Is it not gross egotism to assume that one's poems would become immortal? And is Swinburne playing games with us, to write about immortality in such a way, in these very Christian times, when eternal life is only to be had through Our Lord."

"But a poet should be free to write as he wishes," Clara replied quietly, whilst her heart raced.

"Perhaps. And should a mathematician be free to seek what he wishes?"

"Of course."

"So, can I name my new series for the value of *pi* after you?"

"Do not be foolish."

"But I am offering you immortality. For mathematics might stand the test of time better than poetry. At least better than Swinburne's poetry."

She had had enough of talk. She moved herself closer to him and slid her arm beneath Edward's. She could feel the flesh beneath his nightshirt.

"You understand that I am not married to my husband in the fullest way, nor ever will be. But my feelings for you go deeper than those that I have for him. They go very deep. When I returned from London and saw you again at the station, I knew that I would not sleep, for my body was on fire thinking about you. And I knew I must come to you, this night, or forever give up my life as a woman, a woman of flesh and blood and of feelings. For without that, how can I ever know what it fully means to be a woman and to continue to fight for my sex with all my strength?"

"But will it not weaken you, to be taken by a man of flesh and blood?"

"Speak not of taking, my love, for have I not come to you? I am here to join with you, to cleave my flesh to yours, to make us one. For in the flesh, woman has for too long been taken and used and scourged, like our dear Lord. But God did not make women to be taken, but to complete men's creation, as men complete women's"

She stood up and took off her dressing gown. The moonlight silhouetted her womanly shape through her nightdress. She loosed the cords on her shoulders, letting it fall. He placed his hand on her skin and it burned.

Then, as they lay down together, she touched him and knew that the fire burned away the bonds that Alice, his dead first love, had on him. She led his hand to give her pleasure, and she pleased him in return. And as they joined, the fires in them rose to infernos until the dam of their emotions broke and filled them with a shared ecstasy, an ecstasy that they would remember for all of time.

§

The following evening, Edward went alone to talk to William and Elijah, in their Uncle's drawing room above the clock shop. Edward began the conversation rather formally.

"William, we are coming to the end of our investigation. On behalf of the Royal Society, let me thank you for your cooperation and the honest picture that you have painted of your family life. It is clear that Robert had deep gifts that prospered under difficult circumstances and that make his achievements even more worthy."

William nodded his head and waited for Edward to continue. Their visitor adopted a lighter tone. "I am still fascinated by the story of the shop and your part in it. So, it is perhaps for my own interest that I want to hear more."

William glanced at Elijah and his looks told Edward that he was surprised that the commonplace story should interest such an elevated person.

"It will not take long to tell. I got my partnership the year after Robert went up to Cambridge. The business has prospered since then."

"What did you do to prove yourself worthy of a partnership to your Uncle and Mister Dyke?"

"Ah! Now that is a story." He grinned at Elijah, who smiled back at him. "They made me spend time doing each part of the business. For a couple of months, I was behind the counter in the shop. Sometimes I was with Horace and sometimes on my own. It was frightening at first, not knowing all the business, but being expected to try to answer the customers questions."

Elijah interrupted him. "There was that day on which an attractive young woman came in looking for a pocket watch for her mother."

William grinned at him again. Elijah continued. "He had the same foolish look on his face that he has now."

William took up the tale. "She said she could not describe what she wanted, but she would know when she saw it. So I showed her the various types we had and on seeing each, she asked the most obscure questions concerning the various parts of the watch or how the watch should be looked after. Why, it was a more difficult examination than the Local Certificate. And I knew that Elijah had set Phoebe up and he was listening at the door."

Elijah again interrupted him. "And you did not once flirt with the young lady. I was most reassured, because part of her mission was to provoke you. For Mister Dyke would never abide flirting."

William moved onto other things. "When I was working behind the counter, after we had closed, Horace took me over the ledgers, showing me the financial side of the business. When he had taught me, I would complete the daybook and transfer the amount into the master ledger. He was happy enough with my performance. I was fascinated to see the comings and goings of the money. And what I should earn as a partner."

Elijah replenished their teacups and William moved on.

"I went into the workshop for another few months. It was a welcome change from facing the customers, for that was where the fascination lay for me."

"Ah, you have the same inclination as Elijah coupled with the business instincts of Horace," said Edward, by way of compliment.

"Yes, but inferior to them in both respects."

"But sometimes, in partnerships, it can help if there is one who can appreciate the whole of the business."

"Thank you. I did my apprenticeship in watch and clock assembly, but it took me longer than I thought, because it is small and patient work. Then I made new wheels for the clock reserves, as Elijah had in his apprenticeship. I asked Elijah if I could bring my youngest brother Thomas to turn the wheel of the lathe. I had a secret hope that he could himself be apprenticed. To our joy, Thomas turned out to be a bright and helpful boy for odd jobs round the business. He is now serving his time."

"Well done," said Edward. "That must have pleased your mother."

"Indeed it did. To finish my story, finally, after my period of learning, Elijah and I recommenced our calculating machine project. We currently have a machine that can add pounds, shillings and pence. We use it in the shop and we are observing its ruggedness in daily use. Shopkeepers around us have all been in to see it. Some, who are adept at mental arithmetic, scorn it. The rest wonder at it."

CHAPTER 16

The Crossley Academy for Girls

Clara's stride was arrested by a view of the sunset. She was walking from the George Hotel to the Crossley family house to interview Emily. The glorious colours stilled her errant thoughts, which had been musing on the night she had just spent with Edward. Some of her thoughts were entirely carnal, for she had been seduced and then overcome by the power of his body. Others dwelt on his tenderness, as he let her lie with him for hours afterwards and talk of soft, intimate things. Only after these pleasurable reminiscences did she ask herself whether the encounter had fulfilled her need to understand herself fully as a woman and hence to understand all women. Her immediate answer was yes, an undoubted yes.

She walked on and slowly drew her mind back to Emily and the Crossley family. Clara had an interest in her, because she sensed that her delicate feelings could not be protected from the outcome of Edward's investigation; indeed Robert had already assaulted them in the most brutal way. Clara feared for her. William had inner strength and would stand firm whatever happened. Emily was more vulnerable, and all she was trying to achieve might yet be swept away.

Clara reached the house and knocked. The maid answered and showed her into the drawing room, where Emily and her mother were seated. Emily held back, whilst Emily's mother took the lead in welcoming their guest.

"Doctor Cox, we are again honoured to have you in our house. I have treasured your visits, despite the difficult times that we have remembered. Your concern for our wellbeing is clear in your reaction. Thank you. Please sit down."

Both Emily and Clara were surprised by Rebecca's gracious welcome, and Clara's respect for this understated woman grew. Bringing up her children should have been her greatest achievement and she must have been battered and bruised by seeing it happen with such iron discipline.

Clara sat and replied. "Rebecca, please call me Clara. The women of this world have had much suffering. But I hope that, tonight, we can talk about happier things. Emily, I would very much appreciate hearing of your work and life after Robert left."

Her mother nodded at Clara and turned to her daughter, who began.

"You remember, Clara, from our last meeting that I had obtained a job at Miss Cartwright's Academy and Robert had disowned me as his sister?" She paused to collect herself. "Thereafter, I had a settled life for several years, teaching and helping mother around the house. But there were storm clouds gathering, just below the horizon where none of us could see them. I told you of my encounter with the Board of Governors, when I was interviewed for my first post?"

Clara nodded.

"The Chairman was the Reverend Dacre, who was the incumbent at St Giles. The other members were Miss

Cartwright and Mister Wilson. Mister Wilson supported the Academy financially and lived in Cheyne Walk in a large house appropriate to his wealth. Neither Miss Cartwright nor the Reverend knew where his money had come from. Some suggested that it was originally his wife's. However, he had investments in railway projects. All of the construction of tracks and buildings had to be paid for in some way, and it was the likes of him and his money that made it happen. Some of those investors have become very rich and powerful. Some have stayed as they were. And some have fallen into ruin. I wished to the Lord that the supporter of our Academy could have been of the first type, for we did not need much money, but enough to tide us over the ups and downs of numbers of girls or of the feelings of their parents in sending them to us."

Emily paused, as if imagining such a benevolent guardian angel.

"Mister Wilson had his money in a railway company. He was a part owner. How much money he had in it, no one is quite sure of. It might have been much or it might have been very little. Nevertheless he convinced his co-owners to sell shares, offering the purchasers a dividend every six months that was dependent on the success of the company. And successful they were, for after six months the dividends were sent out. He again convinced his fellows to issue more shares. The money rolled in and all were satisfied. But then a clerk at the bank noticed that the capital of the company went down just as the dividend was issued. Of course, what Wilson was doing was paying dividends from the share income, not from the profits that the company was making. For the company was not making a profit, nor it seems was ever likely to do so. The owners had completely misjudged the potential profitability of the company. The clerk told the manager of the bank, but the clerk also told another clerk, who was a friend of Mister Wilson, having been given a gift some time before to cover up another fraudulent activity. The clerk told Wilson, who immediately sold all his interest in the company, just before it was declared bankrupt. The story became widely known through the newspapers, and others who were co-investors with Wilson in various schemes looked very closely at their own books. Mister Wilson was finally left with nothing but his house and his wife's money. He still lives there, but all in the town shun him, and he operates in other places where his reputation has not yet been discovered. During this storm, Wilson had informed the Reverend that it was no longer in his interest to support the Academy. He said that his passion had turned away from education to manufacturing. The Reverend was heartbroken that he could not find another financial guarantor. Miss Cartwright's energy was eventually spent in running a school without money and it closed its doors to new pupils."

"That is a sorry tale indeed," said Clara, "but one that is not uncommon. The world is full of such rogues. What did you do after the Academy closed?"

"I wrote a book. I helped mother at home and I wrote."

"My goodness," replied Clara, surprised by Emily's ambition. "What is the subject of the book?"

"It is a biography of Marie-Sophie Germain."

Clara realised that Emily was somewhat embarrassed to talk more, possibly by the difficulties that she might have had interesting anyone in such a biography. It was her mother that prompted her. Emily continued. "It has not been published. I took it to prominent people in the town, without success. I also sent it to several publishers in London, under a male pseudonym, but found no interest."

"That is very sad, but like Wilson, it is also the way of the world. Please tell me who this woman was, that interested you enough to write a book."

This resolved Emily's hesitancy and the story came out as a flood. "Marie-Sophie was born in Paris in 1776 and had a love of mathematics. She taught herself Latin and Greek in order to read the works of Newton and Euler."

"Emily, I love her already for her ambition and her endurance. Please go on."

"Clara, this biography is very much like your own. You should not find it too unusual."

This gave Clara a moment's thought, for she was surprised at Emily's knowledge of her own life. "How have you come to know about me?"

"William told me your name and that you were a physician. I was intrigued to know how a woman had been appointed to an enquiry of the Royal Society. There is a small library at our Church, and father was a member of the subscription library in the town. They both very kindly let me trace both you and Germain. And the doctor that treated father had also heard of you and your reputation."

Edward's part in her appointment by the Royal Society flashed through Clara's mind and it was her turn to be embarrassed. Now was not the time to share her thoughts. Instead she said, "A reputation, he must have told you, for wanting to do things that men do not want me to do."

The three women smiled at each other, conspirators all. Emily then continued.

"To discover Germain's past, I wrote to many people. Firstly to her nephew, who is still alive and had brought her works together and published them. But to return to her story, her parents tried to discourage her from study of mathematics, feeling that it was not right for a girl. At night they would remove her lamp and extinguish the fire in her bedroom, so that she could not work when they were asleep. But she had a secret supply of candles and would wrap the quilt around her. They found her asleep at her desk one morning, her ink frozen over and her page covered by equations. They relented. Then the Ecole Polytechnique opened. Although women were not allowed to enrol, they were allowed copies of the lecture notes and also allowed to make comments at the end of the course. She sent her comments to Lagrange, a very eminent mathematician, who was a teacher there. She used the name M. Antoine-August Le Blanc, a former student."

Clara exploded. "No!"

"But it mattered not. For Lagrange recognised her work, asked her to visit him and, not being surprised that she was a woman, became her tutor. But thereafter, she never got the education she so wanted. Her best work was on mathematical solutions for resonances in metal plates that were being demonstrated by the German physicist Ernst Chladni. Her equations beautifully described how musical instruments, such as the violin, functioned. However, that work was never fully recognised."

Emily became silent as she lapsed into a contemplation of a life never fulfilled. Her mother brought her back.

"My darling Emily, tell Clara about your academy."

Clara's eyebrows rose and she waited for Emily to speak. "I am sorry," Emily said. "After two years had passed and I had finished my biography, a singular event occurred. It happened in William's shop." She paused and smiled. "I am sorry. I mean Crossley and Dyke. We now think of it as William's. A woman entered looking for a pocket watch for her husband. Horace, Mister Dyke, was behind the counter. Serving customers is not William's forte, although he served out his time at it. The woman was formerly Miss Morrison, who had just started teaching at Miss Cartwright's when I started there. Mister Dyke, who does not normally engage the customers in idle conversation, was taken by her educated manner, for her clothing was rather poor. On being asked what she did, she told him that she had worked in an Academy that had to close for want of a few shillings to keep it going. Then she told him that a niece of Mister Crossley, his partner in the business, had also worked there. It was strange that Uncle had never told him about it, for he and Hannah knew what had happened to me."

"It was strange indeed," said Clara.

"After she left, Horace immediately summonsed Elijah to tell him all he knew about it. He then devised a plan to support the Academy from his own savings, for he knew that his wife would not invest in such a thing. A few days later, he was on our doorstep, eager to talk to me. He knew that Miss Cartwright was now too frail to take up the reigns again, so he proposed that I should run the revived Academy, in the same premises and with the same staff. And he was happy for it to be called the Crossley Academy for Girls. And so it was. The Reverend Dacre is again the Chairman of the

Board of Governors, which now has three members: the Reverend, Mister Dyke and myself. And what a harmonious board it is."

Clara clasped her hands together and said in an excited tone, "I am sure it is. And I am very sure that the Academy is being well run. For it has an energetic and distinguished Head. An authoress and an Academy Head! Well done, Emily."

Emily looked at Clara with embarrassment. Emily's mother looked on her with pride. Then Clara said, "If I may ask you one more question?"

Emily looked puzzled. "Certainly," she replied.

"Do you still have affection for Robert?"

"Affection? I love him. He is still my brother."

CHAPTER 17

Death and a Contract

Clara returned to the hotel in a state of exultation. Her feeling was not due to her interview with Emily. Clara was glad for her and her founding of the Crossley Academy for Girls, and was equally glad for Emily's declaration of an unquenchable love for Robert as her brother. No, her thoughts were with the stars and the moon because of her own love for Edward and the discovery, inside herself, of a girlishness and femininity that she had previously believed was not for her, but only for others.

She sat down to dinner, expecting him to join her, but was disappointed. She ate alone; her attention was focused somewhere other than on the overcooked beef and dry potatoes.

She returned to her room. She read for a while, but then put the book down. She tried to write. She took up a half finished letter to her Aunt, but no suitable words would come, at least none suitable for a maiden Aunt. She thought that some poetry would help her release the wellspring of emotion flooding her mind, but the lines that she read seemed halting and trite. After this seemingly unending litany of pointless activity, the church bell rang eleven. She crept to his door. Her heart was pounding in her chest. She turned the knob soundlessly. The door was locked. Her heart nearly burst. Had Edward locked her out? But no, it must have been the maid that locked it. She knocked softly.

She heard a floorboard creak immediately. The door swung back and there he was.

She took his hand and he led her to the settee next to the window, the settee on which he had seduced her the previous night. Her heart was pounding again. They both sat down.

"Clara. What brings you to me, so late?"

Why should he need to ask, Clara wondered. Then, finding her voice, she replied, "I have just opened a door to the most beautiful garden." Edward was momentarily perplexed. She did not notice.

"Yes, it is for me the Garden of Eden, for in it I feel innocent and blessed by God himself. I feel that I have been given a gift that I must nurture, like a sapling."

Words were flowing from her that were surely not her own. She seemed to be listening to another's voice that was coming from her own mouth. "The sapling has a simple beauty all of its own, that is both for itself and for its future life as a fully grown tree. I feel that our love is young and tender. I feel like a little girl again."

In any company but his, her words would have sounded childish, almost nonsense. She sensed a reserve in him that wasn't there the previous night. She paused and he spoke quietly.

"Clara, be careful not to take too much at once. Love is like a potion that must be taken, a few drops at a time. To drink it all at once can be fatal."

"Oh, Edward, my love. I know that you are experienced. I know that you have had women, even though you have loved none of them. But do not talk to me like that."

"That is not true."

Clara could not tell what he was denying, but continued. "Listen to your own words, Edward. Be careful what you say, for what we have become can be damaged as much by lies as by drinking too liberally."

"How do you know that I have had other women? What does it matter to you? We are not married."

"It matters only that we can be honest. I have opened myself to you. You must be open with me."

"I will be. For you must know that, although I am not married to any woman, I am married to my mathematics. My relation to it is not like the one between you and I; ours is different and very beautiful. But my work has its own beauty, as Plato recognised and as does every mathematician since him. There are times when it cannot be denied. My dear, I am not rejecting you, but the calling is on me. I have begun a problem and my head is alive with possibilities that I must explore or lose forever. I cannot be with you tonight. I will see you tomorrow for lunch."

Clara fell silent, for she knew that she must go, to keep Edward's respect. But the going hurt her, because her heart had told her something last night that she had now found false. She went and lay on her bed, and considered what had happened. Her new understanding of herself and her womanhood had been cruelly undermined. She did not sleep and rose the next morning with an ache in her heart that she could not understand.

§

They took lunch together and talked only of their investigation. She had arranged for William to visit them, in Edward's suite. William arrived as bidden, and they all went upstairs. Clara's confusion was redoubled as Edward gave William the armchair and he sat next to her on the settee next to the window, the settee on which she had given herself to him.

"William, we thank you again for giving us your valuable time. As we agreed, we would be pleased to hear of the events surrounding your father's death and Robert's part in them."

William began. "As the years went by, father grew more tired and his body weakened. You might find it strange, but I felt responsible for his decline. Mother, in her dramatic way, believed that his end started on the day that I defied him."

William was checked by his emotions. He coughed.

"I had to defy him. I had to, for my own and Phoebe's life. How could I not?"

He suddenly stopped and, drawing his handkerchief, buried his face in it. Clara remembered the dramatic way that he begun his narratives to them, with the declaration that they had lived in a home where discipline came before love, for here was love, sitting in front of them. William surely loved Jeremiah, as every son should love his father. But what he had to endure from his own father was beyond belief. And still he loved him. A tear fell from her own eye, as she felt for his anguish.

William lifted his head and continued. "She was right. His decline did begin on that day. It was not perceptible, but it was sure. To begin with, it affected his mind. He became forgetful about things that had been important to him in the past. It seemed that inside he had lost his direction."

William was silent again.

Edward spoke. "He had indeed lost his direction, because he was the most pitiable of all men. He was pitiable, for his grand ambitions were only achievable by exercising control over others. His was the condition that is common with the dictator, whose only ambition is to keep his subjects under his control. And all dictators meet their end, sooner or later."

"These are harsh words, William," said Clara.

"Yes, you are right," he said. "But his children could not be his subjects forever, for the Bible says that a son must leave his father and his mother and cleave himself to another. It is the natural way of things and God will be my witness that I came not against my God, but against my father."

"Amen to that, William. Indeed, no blame rests on your shoulders. You have been a good son, and remain one to this day."

William nodded.

Clara addressed Edward. "Would you ring the bell and ask for tea. And perhaps a brandy for William."

The drink helped the poor man's wits to return. To further ease William's mind, Edward spoke of his enjoyment at attending the steeplechase. "It is a fine tradition that the town has, for it gathers all to it in a celebration, and gives those that toil in the factories a holiday from their labours."

"Unfortunately, the Methodist Church does not hold with horse racing and my family attended a service and a garden party in the nearby park."

"William, I am so sorry. It was crass of me to mention it."

William laughed. "Fear not, for I disapprove of the Church's disapproval. And does not one disapproval cancel out another disapproval, as a negative multiplied by a negative gives a positive."

Edward joined his laughter and agreed with his mathematics. Then, seeing him recovered, asked him to continue. William took a deep breath.

"His bodily health followed the health of his mind. Because he had lost his strength, he was asked to retire from his job at the school. As was the custom, they gave him a little present of money that they had collected. It made him cry with gratitude. The amount did not reflect the long years he had given the school; it reflected the ill feeling they had for him and for his stiff-necked ways. But, thankfully he did not see it that way. Our family were not well off for money, but he tried not see that either. He jested that the gift made us well off. So, my partnership was important, for it allowed the family to live. Phoebe has understood the position and does not complain about the money I give to mother. And Emily also contributes, bless her."

"He passed away in the New Year of 1852. The winter was perishing, but no more that an English winter can be. His body was wasted away. He was nothing but skin and bones. One evening, he complained of a great tiredness and went to bed. Mother sat by him for a couple of hours until his breath rattled and then stopped. I ran to the doctor myself and he came and confirmed what we all knew. I made all the arrangements, talked to our minister, paid for a plot to be opened and a stone to be made. I wrote to Robert. At the funeral, no one would say a word against him, but few praised his life. The minister's sermon talked of duty and discipline and thanked father for his devotion to the job of church treasurer. He had guessed the mood aright."

Clara remembered hearing of Reverend Grey's funeral and knew that the contrast was as stark as the difference between love and discipline.

Edward had waited a long time to put the question that was closest to his interest.

"Tell me about Robert. How did he react to your father's death?"

William seemed to begin this part of his tale with a weariness that Edward had not sensed before.

"Robert came home immediately he received my letter. He did not tell us the train on which he was arriving, so we could not meet him at the station. He just came to the house. Mother welcomed him like a long lost son, which he enjoyed, although one could sense his embarrassment. He seemed to have changed. He was more distant and less conscious of our interests. Now, you might say that his move to London and the taking up of his business full time had filled his head with things other than his family. Well yes, it might have, and gaining his own family would do that to a man, but we did not know that he had a family at the time. But it seemed to be more than a distraction; it was a distaste for the town and its folk. I do not believe that mother felt it, because she was overcome by her loss and her maternal instincts for Robert. Nor did Emily, for she was still struggling with Robert's rejection of her teaching aspirations. Nor did Patience or Thomas. But I felt it."

William stopped for a moment, for his speech had a note of vehemence. He paused until he had calmed and then resumed.

"But he must have noticed my reaction, for his temper immediately changed to affability. I wondered at the speed of the change and his ability to slip off one guise and put on another. He asked me how the arithmometer work was progressing and a little of our previous brotherly warmth returned. We talked wheels and gears and levers."

William's spirit lifted as he described their machine and his conversation about it. He even laughed, when he told them of Robert's account of his activities in London.

"He told us that he still sat on the War Department Committee. Although the meetings took up little of his time, he worked diligently between meetings, researching the things that interested them, from how to make better helmets for soldiers, to devising codes for messages that were harder to break. I think that these were simple examples so that mother could picture his activity in her head. He would go the Reading Room at the British Museum and read about the strength of metal for his helmet example or about the mathematics of codes. He would then report back to the committee about the science and who to talk to further in order to find improvements in the science. He would then be tasked together with the Secretary to visit those people to commission research to make better helmets or codes. He would calculate how many hours or days that he spent on such work and then told the Secretary, who would then arrange for him to be paid. The job meant that he therefore got to know many people working in very different branches of science."

"I asked him about Professor Laidmann at the University of London, with whom he did mathematical work when he was at Cambridge. He told me that the Professor had previously invited him to consider a post in the University when he got his degree, but Robert turned him down. When he saw my surprise, he said that his work for the committee was more important for the country. I have to admit that I did not believe his reason and wondered if some doubt about his own ability still lingered in his mind, a product of his father's attitude to us both. Although for me, my single act of defiance had broken any power he had over me. I suspected that Robert was still trying to outwit him."

Edward nodded at William's perception. It reflected his own conclusion about Robert's present relationship with the memory of his father. But Edward also knew that Robert's position in the rankings of his degree cohort was just below the average. Did the mind that had developed the theory react to the tedium of what he was taught? Or... His train of thought was interrupted as William continued.

"He said that he had his name on at least two contributions to the Proceedings of the Royal Society. Then, I remembered his drinking friend from Cambridge and asked him where he was now. 'Ah, he said, Charles Crowley? Yes, he is living in London, not so far away from my dwelling.' Then he laughed. 'Brother', he went on, 'do not ask me about where I live.' I assumed that he meant that he was living in a rather cheap and dirty boarding house somewhere, that he was too embarrassed to talk about. And yes, he said, Charles and he did go out drinking sometimes. However, he did not drink heavily, not because father forbade it, but because money was too precious to him to waste. This reassured me somewhat, although I thought that he was perhaps just being companionable."

"He told me about his work with inventors. He put an advertisement in The Times once a month offering to help such people realise their dreams. It attracted many strange people to his house. He laughed as he told me that there were those whose dreams must be devised in nightmares. One man told him that he used a number of talking parrots in cages to do work to do with codes, relating to the choice of keywords. Others were more sensible. Some were domestic inventions, such as the man who devised a hand-turned machine that washed garments. Or others had ideas for the military. His job was to judge the idea and to decide whether it would sell. He would then help the inventor to get in touch with patent clerks, whom he paid for himself, then put them in touch with a manufacturer, and finally take a commission. He said that he was still making a small income from the best of the inventions. We were all impressed with Robert's entrepreneurial life. Mother kissed him before she went up to bed. Emily escorted her, for mother was still in somewhat of a shock from father's passing. Patience and Thomas left the two of us to carry on our brotherly conversation."

§

"When we were alone, Robert said, 'William, you remember that I wished you well in all that you did in the shop, when we first went there? I think I foresaw that the shop might be your life, but not mine, and I wanted to wish you well.'

'Yes, I remember,' I said.

'I still feel the same, you know.'

Then I asked him about something else from our past that had been unexplainably disturbing me at the time. 'And are we still Brothers in Plato?'

Robert laughed pleasantly, but I was shocked at his reaction.

'William, I think that was just childish enthusiasm for a philosophy that should be dead and buried. I cannot believe in a place where all mathematics exists and where mathematicians go, like explorers in the jungle with a big gun to shoot their animal. So, we are still brothers, but not in Plato. Perhaps I would call us brothers in business, for I have something that might be useful to you.'

I had recovered myself somewhat and invited him to continue.

'I have convinced the committee that a machine for calculations related to the trajectories of guns would improve our ability to fight.'

I realised what he was implying, but did not react. He continued.

'There is some double-dealing going on in the committee. It was the very thing that the Minister had wanted to stamp out. Another member is promoting a machine from a company, although he tells no one that he owns the company. I also happen to know that the machine is inferior to yours. I privately told the chairman about the situation, but he will not hear of a competition. It is not the way we do things, he said. It wastes time and doesn't work. However, I have managed to turn the situation around, for the good of the committee and of the country.'

It was my first insight into the politics that Robert was now involved with. I did not like it very much. But Robert was determined to tell me the tale."

"'It was one evening late last year', Robert said. 'Although it was only early evening, it seemed prematurely dark and a mist hung over the river. You can judge how chilly it was, for I was wearing my overcoat with a fur collar and a top hat. I was walking on the Embankment near Waterloo Bridge, making towards the Royal Society to listen to a lecture. I paused beneath a street lamp, to light my cigar. I heard footsteps and peered expectantly into the gloom. A figure came into view. To an observer it might appear that we had met by accident, but I knew that it was my colleague from the committee. We exchanged pleasantries for a moment. Then I looked across the river. I could barely make out the lights on the south bank, but I knew where he had come from.

'Arthur, I see that you have just come from your mistress.'

'Nonsense, Robert, I have been to see a friend of my banker.'

'Oh really? I understand that she lives in Coin Street, not ten minutes from the bridge. Number 23, I am told. I should visit her, to see what estate she lives in and whether you support her in the manner she deserves.'

He began to stare at me, with interest mixed with alarm. I gave him some more information. 'Number 23 is next door to an opium den, is it not? It does not suggest a well to do part of town. Perhaps you are not spending enough money on her. But, of course, she is your second mistress. Or is she your third? I have quite lost count.'

He had, by this time, capitulated, for he had his palms up in front of him trying to hush my revelations. Another well-dressed gentleman had just walked past us. I waited until we were quite alone before I continued.

'Arthur. My needs are very simple. I want the best arithmometer to be commissioned by the committee. I want you to withdraw yours from consideration, if another, that is shown to be better, comes along.'

He looked at me suspiciously.

'And do you know of such a machine?'

'Ah, only time will tell.'

He snorted. 'Very well then, but you shall keep your mouth shut about the friend of my banker.'

'Of course, Arthur. Goodbye. Please pass on my best wishes to your wife.'"

Edward was nodding his head thoughtfully. William paused, as if lost in thought and then continued.

"Robert had got quite excited during the telling of this extraordinary episode and took a moment or two to calm himself. Then he added, with a self-congratulatory tone, 'Do you see what this means, William?'

'That you mix with some poor characters, brother.'

He considered. 'Yes, you may be right. But do you see the opportunity?'

'Of course I do!'

'What could you do in three months? For this opportunity will not last for ever.'

'If we had the materials, and the space, and the skilled people, we could complete twelve months work in three,' I said. 'We could change the machine we have, to do something that would satisfy them.'

'Excellent, then proceed with all due speed.'

'I said if we had those things. But that would take money. A lot of money.'

Robert waved his hand. 'I will provide that. Or rather, a friend of mine is a banker, looking for investments of this kind. I can have whatever you need at your bank within a week.'"

§

"I can tell you now, Edward, that it took me by surprise and shock. Of course, I wanted to do it. And I soon convinced Elijah and Horace, for they had the same spirit that I was driven by. Elijah and I saw nothing but a new arithmometer, designed and built especially to help the military aim their big guns. And Horace saw it as a way of expanding his business interests. After a month, we had all of it in place, a new design on paper, a new workshop and men who could do fine work on the lathes we had bought from Coventry. Only when the work was running smoothly, did I have time to reflect on how it had come about. And I admit that I had some sleepless nights, for Robert and his committee accomplices disturbed me and I could only carry on by telling myself that it was nothing but the way of the world in such things."

Edward smiled grimly at him. "Yes, William. If you are not used to it, it can be disturbing. I can assure you that it is the way of the world, but when we can, we must work to make things better."

William breathed deeply, as if his part of the evening was finished. But Edward had another question for him, one that was as close to the core of the mystery as he dare go in plain speech.

"William, what can you tell me about the time that Robert was seeing the Vicar?"

"Close as we were, I knew very little, but that Robert worked very hard during those years, on a mathematical problem that he would share with no one."

CHAPTER 18

Fellow of the Royal Society

"My dear Clara, let me show you some of my mathematics. I wrote them for you last night after I finished my *pi* series."

They were sitting side by side on his settee again. A candle on the low table in front of them lit their faces. The moonlight from the window behind them lit the rest of the room. He laid a sheet of paper on his knee and wrote,

$$P = e \cdot p$$

"The variable, P, represents all that is me. The variables, e and p, represent my names, Edward and Pennington. We could say that, in poetic terms, the equation expresses that our whole is the product of our names."

She smiled, enjoying his embarrassment at trying to match mathematics with life.

"To express the being that is you, I will write another equation."

$$C = c \cdot (1 + \tfrac{1}{2} + \tfrac{1}{4} + \tfrac{1}{8} \ldots)$$

"This is what we call an infinite series, for the fractions go on forever. C represents the whole you. The small c is your name. Your name is multiplied by the series within the brackets. The series is the sum of all the terms, from the largest, that is 1, to the smallest, which is 1 divided by infinity, which is thus infinitely small. You can see that each number in the series is half the values of the one before it."

Clara had seen such things before in her studies and had nodded her head at every statement. Edward continued.

"But what is the solution? What is the sum of all those numbers added together? That is the mystery that is you. I have written a poem to express the mystery."

He took up another sheet and read.

> "To the distant star in the night,
> My heart in love's thrall calls your name.
> The blessed word sighs in its flight
> And echoes your beauty again.
>
> Outwards and back, outwards and back,
> The signals forever must go.
> For the sum of your infinite grace
> Has a depth I will never know."

She asked him to recite the poem again to her. She closed her eyes, imagining his heart in love's thrall, and let her feelings fly where they would.

That very morning she would have resisted him. Tonight she could not. She leaned against him and breathed him in.

§

They breakfasted together and Edward was reminiscing about the Royal Society.

"I was at Robert's lecture all those years ago. It was very well attended, for word had gone around of an important new theory. I cannot remember Robert's face, but gained an impression of a pleasant young man, with an attractive and engaging lecture style. Hmm, wait ... Ah, yes, I remember. I was with the President, Bartholomew Hyde, as he was congratulating Robert. A scoundrel called Eldret had posed an unpleasant question during Robert's examination. Hyde told Robert that the man's theory had been found to be faulty and, what was worse, Eldret had stolen it from a colleague. Robert's face turned white and he had to steady himself. Hyde noticed it also, but all assumed that it was the rigour of the proceedings that had caught up with him. I wonder if..."

Clara put her hand on his arm to stop him. "Yes, of course it could have been an indicator of Robert's guilt, but it is hardly evidence."

Edward nodded. "But what was also memorable was the severe looking man, sitting next to a younger William, watching from the front row. I now realise that the man was Robert's father. He had a look of disapproval that was quite out of place for the father of an invited lecturer."

"What do you remember of last year, when Robert got his Fellowship?" asked Clara.

"Such meetings always have a feeling of celebration about them. Robert was no longer the quaking youth. This time he was a mature gentleman." Clara looked at him askance. "No, he had not got plump and sated," he went on, "it was that he was supremely confidant in whom he was."

"Ah."

Edward smiled indulgently. "His family all supported him. Of course, his father was dead, but his mother was there, dressed rather soberly. Perhaps, being a Methodist, her best weeds were black, both for Sunday services and funerals."

Clara scowled at his unkindness, for she had unsurprisingly developed a sympathy for the female Crossleys.

Edward continued. "They all looked very much out of place, in what is after all a gentleman's club. They sat conspicuously in the front row, a little to one side of the President. He had made some effort to send round a whip, so there was a good crowd present. The President made his usual speech, but tilted it a little more to bringing youth and energy into the Society, as the Government wanted. My god, he really is in the Minister's pocket. Who does he think we are? Senile, crippled geriatrics? That sort of talk causes no end of resentment."

"Do you not believe in cleaning out the societies?" asked Clara. "The BMA is the same, full of physicians with axes to grind concerning their own practices and methods. And as for women,..."

It was Edward's moment to stop Clara. "Of course, I think they should be cleaned out. But neither the President nor the Chairs of the various committees know how to do it. You do it by judging the member's performance in the sphere in which they operate and their work in promoting the science. It is why I spend so much time on my own work. You shall judge them by their actions."

Clara was nodding her head for, in truth, she was like him in her work: dedicated and ambitious, and as frustrated as he was with the institutions. Edward continued.

"But it seems to me as if Robert was tailor-made for that back-biting, politicking crowd. He has his theory and a few papers in the Proceedings, but not much else. I heard that his nomination went forward on the work he was doing in his War Department committee. The Chairman of the committee, helpless to turn it around himself, relied on Robert to make the others give up their interests, as we heard from William yesterday. Robert has obviously learned to fight fire with fire. Always a dangerous occupation."

Clara wondered what he meant by that, but did not interrupt him.

"There was a moment of high drama at the Fellowship meeting, that I only found out about afterwards. Old Jack Butler told me the next day. I had seen the woman, sitting on the front row across the aisle from the President, but took no notice of her. She wore a most elegant dark green dress and had placed her hat on the bench beside her. Later, in the antechamber Robert was with his family, when she approached the group. Jack was in a group next to them and heard everything. She was his wife. The woman in the green dress was his wife. The shock on their faces was palpable. His telling them that she had two children by a previous marriage only compounded it. However, the woman's grace carried the moment, for she smiled and introduced herself, as if they were meeting on a church outing. She is a cousin of James Joseph Sylvester, no less. But, there is a dark undercurrent in all of this. Sylvester and his cousin are Jews. Her previous husband was an Arab and, as Butler said, the two are like oil and water."

"Sylvester's uncle must have had a difficult time finding a new husband for her," suggested Clara.

"Indeed. But there is darker yet. We know that Robert's father had a hatred of the Jews."

"And yet his son marries a Jewish woman." Clara's wide eyes stared into Edward's. "And he does not tell his father. Extraordinary!"

§

The old cottage looked half derelict. Ivy covered the walls and half of the thatched roof. A broken pain of glass was stuffed with rags. The garden was overgrown, although to the side of the building there was cultivation, with cabbages and potatoes growing. The doctor greeted them at the gate.

"I am afraid that you will not get much from her. Her hearing and her memory are failing, although she is bright enough about her childhood."

Edward and Clara were visiting the Reverend Grey's widow. Clara had written to the current incumbent of Upstone Church, who had passed the job on to the doctor. The doctor had agreed to introduce them to the old woman on one of his regular visits.

The doctor greeted them with a smile outside the cottage, a smile that lit up a face that was lined with overwork and worry. "The Reverend and I worked together to tend these people. He was tireless, going out in all weathers to their births and deaths. They respected him, not for his learning or for his oratory, but just for being there. But I got as much anger as thanks. There was often nothing I could do for them. Of course, I could strap up a broken leg, but the man would go out to the field before it was healed, and suffer the rest of his life with it. But when the fever came, creeping silently into their houses, there would be nothing I could do, and it took away both husbands and sons, damn it. All I could do was watch, for I would never prescribe sugared water, as some did."

He led them down the path to the front door, carefully pushing aside the shoulder high nettles as he went. Edward bowed his head to avoid the lintel. Reverend Grey's wife was sitting huddled in a blanket in front of the fire glowing in the simple range. The doctor called to her as they entered, and she got up, the weariness in her emaciated frame slowing her movements. Her face lit up as she stared at her visitors, and her voice was clear and strong.

"I never go without, you know. My neighbour's wife comes in and builds the fire in the morning and her husband tidies my vegetables. They bring me meat and cheese from the market." She laughed. "I live tolerably well, for an old widow. Arnold would be pleased for me."

She bustled about, putting the kettle on the fire and putting cups and saucers on the table for her guests. "They remember Arnold and will not see me go without."

"And I come as often as I can," the doctor added. " She is strong yet. There are worse off than her. And there are those whose mouths deliver nothing but spite about widows," his face distorted as he spoke the word, "and people believe them. And they are left to fend for themselves because of it."

Clara was surprised. "Do you mean that there are widows who have nothing? In this village, so close to a prosperous town?"

"Yes," the doctor's passion was now roused. "There is one that I know of, not in this village but nearby, whose husband died two years ago. The coroner said it was an accident, but folk say she murdered him. It is just the ancient superstitions. Fear and ignorance, stupidity." His mouth creased in anger. "None will speak to her now, nor lift a hand to help the poor woman. She struggles to bring up her five children."

Edward shook his head and Clara looked distressed. "But surely that is uncommon in this day?" she asked.

"No, it happens even in Upstone. There is one..." The doctor hesitated and the two visitors waited. "There is a widow. I treated her husband many years ago when he fell ill with a fever. She gave birth six months later, her first. But there are some who say the child was not his. Tongues wag, whether it is the truth or a lie. I am the only one who visits her now."

"At least she has you, doctor," said Clara. "It is certainly true, that sometimes physicians must do more caring that curing."

They watched the Reverend's widow fill the teapot from the kettle on the range and sit down at the table. Edward pulled up a chair next to her and prepared himself to put a question to her. But her voice rang out again.

"We used to live by the church bell, but then we moved away. My neighbour's wife comes in to wake me at seven o'clock, so she says. I am always awake by then and she knows it. She really comes in to see if I am still in the land of the living. I wake up at daybreak, so I don't need a clock, you see. I awake at daybreak and go to sleep when it gets dark. I live by the rising and the setting of the sun. Well, sometimes I don't sleep, but I don't need to. I listen to the wind in the thatch and the foxes crying and the owls hooting. They talk to me, you know. They tell me about their families and their children. How they work to fill their mouths. How they hurt when their young ones leave the nest. And how they survive when their menfolk are taken from them. Yes, I hear it all. In the night."

She fell silent, but the smile did not leave her lips. And then she began again.

> "The curfew tolls the knell of parting day,
> The lowing herd wind slowly o'er the lea
> The ploughman homeward plods his weary way,
> And leaves the world to darkness and to me.
> To darkness and to me and the owls and the foxes."

"When we were courting, Arnold used to say that he loved me because I could recite poetry. I had five sisters and we could all recite. I wasn't the best. When I needed his attention, I would tell him that he married the wrong sister. Beth would have known more poetry than me. And he would hug me to him and say that I was the right choice for him."

"And he loved The Curfew Tolls, as he called it, and not just because it was written by his namesake. He loved it because it told of the unknown man, buried in the corner of the churchyard. He had a heart for that man and all such in his parish who would live and die unknown, but for Arnold."

"He said the poet's favourite phrase was, 'where ignorance is bliss, 'tis folly to be wise'. He said that I was too learned for him, but he was just being nostalgic for his ignorant youth, the silly old fool. He was learned all right. He knew his Latin and his Greek. He talked to me in Latin sometimes, when he was upset about something. I think he was swearing, but the language saved my ears from his oaths."

She smiled a smile from her youth and they smiled with her. When her reminiscences did not begin again, Edward asked about Arnold's mathematics and Robert.

"Robert, who was Robert?" Edward's heart sank, but she continued. "There was Doctor Mould, his tutor at Cambridge. Arnold was always talking about his beloved Mould. I think he went back to Cambridge, when Mould passed away. He said they sang a mass for him." She looked around the parlour. "Got plenty of mould now. He used to laugh when I said that to him." Clara shivered to see how she was living.

Edward stood up to leave. The old woman struggled to her feet, pushing away his hand that had tried to help her. As they reached the door, she banged her hand on the table. Edward and Clara turned around to look at her.

"This was where he did it. His mathematics." Edward's attention was caught. "Mould did all his mathematics on his little table in his parlour, just like this, as Arnold would say. For he didn't live in the college, he preferred living with the ordinary people outside. That's why Arnold loved him. He was a man after his own heart."

They stared at her, half in expectation that she would reveal something of help to them, yet knowing that she could no longer control her thoughts. They left her still gazing at the table.

CHAPTER 19

The President's Office

It was morning. Edward and Clara were taking a companionable coffee in Edward's suite in the George Hotel. Clara had left his bed, trailing her nightgown, just before the coffee arrived and returned in less than two minutes suitably dressed for a discussion of the case. She sat down upon the settee and set her mind to hear his analysis. He was not yet ready.

"Really, my darling Clara, we are behaving like the working class, or those of the new middle class who have not yet gathered enough capital to possess two bedrooms."

Clara laughed. "Your knowledge of the behaviour of classes other than the aristocracy is increasing by the day. You are right, many couples in England do sleep in the same bed."

"I find it pleasant indeed. Waking to see your face and to feel your body close to mine is such a wonder."

"I find it wonderful too, my love." Clara touched his arm tenderly.

"And what is more wonderful is that my phallus is ready for you again in no time at all."

Clara's forehead furrowed. "Although many wake thus, I believe that few have such conversations as that, except for Lotharios and the romantic poets!"

"Perhaps you should extend that list to include mathematicians. I have a mathematical friend in London who gives me intimate descriptions of his own body and that of the woman he was with the previous night, over breakfast on the morning after. I am careful to order only the strongest coffee and perhaps some toast for such conversations. However, they are usually most instructive."

Clara smiled knowingly and nodded her head. She knew that despite Edward's sharp intellect, he could be as naive as a schoolboy about certain female sensibilities. She watched a smile creep over his face and suddenly realised that it was she who was being naive. She looked down at his lap and then up to his face. "I think that your phallus will do its part in an exemplary manner in providing many in the line to be the 7th Baron."

Edward grinned. "This conversation is getting out of hand. Shall I pour?"

"Thank you, Edward."

She had the cup halfway to her mouth when he began. "The crime, if there was one, would have been committed at Robert's home, for there is no evidence that he had any other places where he could do such difficult work. The question is, did he develop the theory himself or was his work simply to understand his tutor's work? William told us that he worked on something for a long period and that he disclosed it to no one, except the Reverend Grey we must assume. We have no evidence that Robert's work was anything other than developing the theory himself. We have interviewed the family and his clock-making uncle and aunt and that has been enough, for his farmer uncle did not entertain him at the farm for any significant time. We have interviewed, if we can call it that, Grey's widow and his doctor. There is nothing suspicious there, unless the pagan ways of his village patients are that; but I think not. I have slept on all these facts. I have sifted them in my mind and yet nothing has come from them. In the detective's equivalent of Plato's perfect place, where solutions to investigations sit in glorious sunshine waiting to be discovered, I have found nothing. Perhaps I am being dull witted. Perhaps my youth and lack of experience mean that I cannot see the answer."

"Or perhaps you do yourself a disservice, and Robert is innocent of stealing the work."

"Perhaps. What is very clear is that Robert has a character that disposes him to act in a certain way. He now operates in a way that is outside the normal mores of society. The blackmail of a colleague on the War Department Committee indicates that."

"Edward, there is no doubt in my mind that he has the character to commit plagiarism."

"But we have spent most of our time establishing motive and analyzing his character, yet have very little evidence. We know that he did a very difficult piece of work and has not shown the capability to do such work since. This is very weak, as many mathematicians do a brilliant piece of work and then do nothing more thereafter. It is well known."

"I agree," said Clara.

"Nevertheless, we must not forget that many criminal cases are judged on a circumstantial basis. I read recently of a case in which the accomplice of a murderer, who did no more than hide him after the crime, faced the rope with his friend. The judge could find no evidence that he was guilty, only the testimony of another that he held a grudge against the victim. His inference was that he had a motive for the murder and thus inferred that he probably committed it with his friend. This is similar to the mathematical process of induction used by Plato and Euclid. My view is that whilst it may be permissible in mathematics, it is sometimes flawed in law and judgment."

Clara knew the meaning of circumstantial, through her wide reading. Edward finally got to his point. "What is different here is that we can find no evidence that a crime has been committed."

They were both silent for a moment. Edward continued. "If that is the case, it would mean that there are mischief makers at the Royal Society, trying to settle scores or simply trying to turn the spotlight on an intruder who will eventually oust them. Discovering who that might be and what their motive is would make for a fascinating investigation."

"If they ask you to investigate that," replied Clara, "please do not invite me to help you. For reasons I do not need to state, I have not regretted for one moment working with you..." She looked at him with a sentimental smile. "... but I can no longer afford to take such time out of my clinic."

"Do not worry, I would not do it. I have new theorems to pursue and other things call me back to London. I suggest that we finish this diverting interlude and report back to the President."

"Very well. I have a set of notes, which are sufficiently legible to be attached to a summary of our findings. Perhaps you would be so good as to write the summary."

"I am already planning it. I have a structure in my mind. The simple facts, as I have already outlined, will be supplemented by a character assessment of Robert, deduced from the early depredations of his home life and finishing with his subsequent work on the War Department committee."

Clara nodded.

"There is one other thing. We need to talk to Robert's friend at Cambridge. I don't think it will change our minds, but it would lend a more complete feel to our report. I shall look him up when I get back. Are you happy with that?"

"Of course."

"It will take me a week or two to get a meeting with the President. I will let you know the arrangements in good time. And, whilst we are locked up in the railway carriage together, we can discuss how we can continue our other investigations."

§

The visit to Charles Crowley proved inconclusive, for the young man had a hangover and could remember little but that Robert had extricated him from several embarrassing situations, for which he owed him his life and a good part of his fortune. He was making up for the latter by taking Robert drinking with him more than occasionally. Edward added a sentence to his report and sent it to the Royal Society.

A few weeks later, Edward and Clara were ushered into the President's office. Professor Hyde was sitting next to another man at the long table, talking quietly. Hyde rose and shook their hands and asked them to sit opposite. Edward considered whether the adversarial atmosphere produced by the seating arrangement was intended or not.

"Edward, Doctor Cox, this is Mister Steyn, who has been helping me in matters relating to discipline."

The man had his hands folded on his lap and a weary half smile was permanently painted on his face.

"Let me begin by saying that I have read your report with great interest." The President's voice contained neither enthusiasm nor energy. Edward sensed that the meeting was over before it began. The President continued. "I will just remind the meeting why we asked you to investigate this matter."

He spent ten minutes talking about the Minister's rallying call for honesty and integrity in the Society and his valiant attempts to root out corruption. His colleague Steyn nodded fractionally, as if to conserve his energy, when the President paused for breath. Edward had heard the speech before and thus had the freedom to mull over his misgivings about their work. He knew that Robert was guilty.

The President did not even give them the courtesy of summarising their work. He accepted their findings as they stood and praised the Lord that the honour of the Society was not to be besmirched by scandal whilst he was running the ship.

A clock chimed in the distance. The President took out his pocket watch. The hairs on the back of Edward's neck rose.

"I am so sorry, but I have another meeting." The President rose and walked over to his desk to ring the bell. His secretary came in and within five minutes Edward and Clara were standing on the pavement of the Strand with the sharp smell of human excrement and horse dung in their noses, bidding each other goodbye in as modest a fashion as they could.

§

Edward could not concentrate on even the most trivial things of his daily life. He was profoundly disturbed by his failure in the investigation and by the self-serving welcome that the President had given it.

Edward was missing Clara, for her feminine presence had reassured him. In the calm of the railway carriage, with her hand clasped in his, they had formed an agreement that they would meet in no less than two weeks, when she was certain that her clinic was functioning properly and when her husband had reacquired his habit of retiring to his study directly after dinner rather than sitting with her in the drawing room until the small hours, which he did to welcome her home from Northampton. Edward had suggested a small but comfortable hotel near Euston Station for their assignation. Clara had not questioned his knowledge of such useful establishments. The meeting with the President and his assignation with Clara were behind him and the future stretched bleakly out until the next time he would see her.

He did not eat breakfast, for he rose late. His lunches were little more than a few morsels of bread and cheese taken in a tavern and he would push his plate away from him at dinner in the evening, unable to face the effort involved in chewing and swallowing. Only drink quietened his mind, although his friends would remark on his lack of temper, unhappy at their loss of his congeniality, which was occasionally outrageous, but always entertaining. He attended the House and listened, but heard little. Even a pointless and prolonged speech by his archrival, Lord Clapton, did not raise him from his ennui.

In his distraction, Edward took to walking the streets, from bar to public house. The sound of his own footfall mesmerized him and the alcohol blurred his remembrance of the better times with Clara. He met an attractive woman in a hotel bar in Bloomsbury and invited her to join him in the small but comfortable hotel near Euston Station. The excitement of the chase diverted his mind and body for an hour or two. Whilst lying in the woman's arms afterwards, luxuriantly considering his skill in seducing her, he saw not Clara, but the face of Alice looking back at him through glassy eyes. His consternation made him hurry away, leaving the woman sleeping alone. He had believed that his love for Clara had banished the ghosts of his innocent past.

A week later a note, marked on the reverse with the single word 'Steyn', was delivered to Edward's apartment. He tore it open. Steyn, with commendable brevity asked for a meeting the following night, on the south bank of river. The rest of the day was passed in a flurry of meaningless activity, of letters that were written and then thrown away and of books taken up and then five minutes later put back down. For time after time, the face of Steyn passed from the back of his mind to the front, taking in turns the likeness of his saviour and then his tormentor.

§

As the night was cool, Edward wore his greatcoat and walking boots. The mass of thick cloud that had filled the sky from the beginning of the day had disappeared in the evening, leaving only smoke haze obscuring the stars. Edward waited, gazing out over the black water rippling past the moored boats. Laughter reached him from a nearby tavern.

Suddenly, a dark figure was by his side.

"Good evening, Edward. Thank you for agreeing to our meeting."

Edward was surprised by the man's geniality. "Who are you?" he asked.

"You know who I am."

"I know that your name is Steyn and you help the President with discipline."

Steyn nodded his head.

"But I do not know who you are."

"My friend, do not concern yourself with that. I do not know everything concerning you, but that does not prevent my wanting to give you some advice."

"Whom do you work for?"

"The people I work for have the best interests of the Royal Society in their hearts."

"You are not English?"

"No, but I work for those who are. Matters at the national level are not in question here."

Edward stared into the man's face, yet still could not recognise him. Steyn did not appear to be disturbed by Edward's questioning, but continued in an even tone.

"Your infatuation with Madam Cox is preventing you solving this problem."

Edward became angry. "I am not infatuated!" He halted abruptly for he realised that he had reacted like Saint Peter and was ashamed. "How do you know that I care for her?"

"I look. I listen. I use my senses and interpret. This much is clear, that she is clouding your judgment."

Edward was silent. He knew the man was right. Steyn's tone became sympathetic.

"Remember when you are working on your theorems. You need a clear head and solitude. I understand such things, for I have done my own mathematics."

The mist in Edward's mind cleared for a second, until the voice began again.

"What is not clear is where the answer to the investigation lies. That is for you to find."

"So why are you here?"

The man suddenly became angry, but immediately suppressed it. Stepping closer, he laid a gentle hand on Edward's arm

"Edward, your work is not done, for we believe, like you, that Crossley is guilty."

"How do you know that?"

Steyn kept a tight hold on his emotion.

"Because of you. I saw that you sensed something when the President dismissed you at the meeting. Start from there. You will find the answer."

He put the emphasis on the word 'will', as if to give Edward an order.

§

Edward was disturbed beyond endurance. His head throbbed with the accusation that Clara was stopping him finding the answer. He was angry, firstly with Steyn for the suggestion, then with himself and finally with Clara for her mere existence. And his anger with Clara caused him the most anguish, for he loved her dearly. It was she who now populated all his dreams. Yet, despite all this, he knew that Steyn was right. But what was he to do? He could not cut himself off from Clara. That would be a betrayal of all he now was and a terrible unkindness to her. He strode off along the shore, hoping that the act of walking would calm him.

His mind did cool and his thoughts returned to Steyn. Had he seen the man at a mathematical gathering? He had been to two meetings on the continent, one in Paris and one in the Low Countries. From his name it seemed that it must be the second. Edward liked the Dutch, for he felt that they thought without the hindrance of egotism and Empire. And did Steyn work for mathematicians who simply wanted the true author of the theorem to be named? He imagined a sea of faces of those who might feel that way.

But how were they so sure of Robert's guilt? If they knew something, why could they not make it public or even just confront Robert in private? And why should they need to use Steyn? Steyn himself surely had an interest in this matter, beyond that of his masters. It was clear that the man was angry. He was no professional, unencumbered by feeling for those he was pursuing. He felt deeply that a wrong had been done. Perhaps Steyn knew Arnold Grey?

This last thought held his mind for some time as he walked the streets, little knowing where he was going. It was a thought he could pursue, for it offered a solid line that could be followed. He tried to imagine how they could have met and in what circumstances Steyn could be sure that Grey did the work, yet not have any proof. Perhaps Steyn was a previous student of Grey and they discussed the work. Unless Steyn actually saw the derivation of the theorems, it would be his word against Robert's. And Robert was now a formidable opponent with powerful friends in the Society. But Steyn also talked of doing his own mathematics. Perhaps he was the author. Edward's head was beginning to spin with conjecture.

A light from a tavern illuminated his way. He needed relief from his thoughts, and entered. His fellow drinkers accepted him without question, for he had dressed appropriately for the south bank. Yet he became restless after a short time and, like the wanderer that he had become, he stepped out into the murky streets again.

He drank at a number of taverns on his way until, in the early hours, he entered a graveyard and sat on the tomb of one who's home it now was. There was a low wall topped by a railing around the graveyard, but the gate stood open. He put his head in his hands and thought of the President and his French watch. He also had a tenderness for things French, and especially for their women. With sweet reminiscences of mathematics and amorous liaisons, he lay down and allowed sleep to overtake him.

He awoke at first light. After some moments he came to his senses and sat up. Wishing to give mental thanks to he whose death had provided his bed he crawled close to the inscription and read the name. He could make no sense of it. It was in English, yet the name meant nothing to him. He knew that in the morning after much drink, his mind had difficulty in functioning normally. He read the inscription again. A light was slowly lit in his head. This name is of a Frenchman, he thought. But last night I was in London and I cannot have wandered that far. Perhaps I was abducted, robbed and left for dead in a graveyard in France. He checked his pockets, yet his purse and his scented handkerchief were still with him.

He got off his bed of stone and made his way to the gate. There, on a metal plate let into the wall, was an inscription that told him all he needed to know. He had slept in a Huguenot Cemetery, called Mount Nod. He was still in London. He stood back and considered whether this had a bearing on the investigation. Steyn had said that he had had a reaction when he saw the President's pocket watch. He remembered that he reacted to it because it was a French watch, and that Grey had a similar watch. Robert's uncle, Elijah, and his wife, Hannah, had related the visit of the Vicar's wife to the shop to get the watch mended. The mending was to be a present from his congregation upon his retirement. The Vicar's wife had proudly told them that a French mathematician had given the watch to her husband. He and Clara had not forgotten these facts, but they had not considered them to be significant. However, they could be the most significant, if they led to evidence of Robert's guilt.

CHAPTER 20

The Burlington Clinic

Edward dismounted the cab at the corner of the street. A weak afternoon sun lit the scene. Cabs, omnibuses and drays plied the main thoroughfare. A flower seller's display was set against the wall behind him and a newspaper vendor cried out the headlines. Edward walked fifty yards down the quieter side street to number 15. Next to the number was a brass plaque announcing, The Burlington Clinic, Doctor C Cox, Consulting Physician. He was impressed by the surroundings, for he had read the names of several other professionals on the other houses as he passed them.

He pulled the bell and waited only a moment until a woman considerably older than Clara, whose kindly face immediately put him at his ease, opened the door.

"Do you have an appointment?"

"Can you tell Doctor Cox that a Mister Pennington wishes to see her?"

The woman, seeing Edward's immaculate dress, opened the door wider and escorted him to a small room that housed several chairs and the woman's desk. The woman left him and returned a moment later.

"Doctor Cox will see you shortly. Please sit down."

A bell tinkled in a distant room. Edward checked his watch. He had been waiting for twenty minutes.

"Please follow me."

The woman opened a door further down the corridor and bid him enter. Clara was standing behind her desk. She had no welcome for him. She waited until the footsteps in the corridor receded.

"Edward, how *dare* you visit me here! I expressly forbade you."

"I am sorry, Clara."

"I must insist on my privacy. I cannot talk to you."

"But I have solved it! I know what we should do."

"We? The investigation is over. I am no longer your assistant. The interview with the President was the final act. I made that clear in the railway carriage. I can say no more."

Edward misunderstood Clara's meaning and was speechless. He stared at her for a long moment, until he stuttered his reply.

"It is the French watch. I am about to go back to the Reverend's widow to ask her who gave it to him. She must know the identity of the French mathematician. He communicated with Grey and will know whether he or Robert was responsible for the work."

His hurt look softened her.

"I understand. I am sorry," she said. "It is my staff. I cannot allow any loose talk about those who visit me. It would be the ruination of my reputation. Please accept my apologies. Nor can I accompany you, even if such information changes the nature of the case." Clara dropped her voice and said. "We must abide by our arrangements made in the carriage."

"Yes, yes. Thank you. I too am sorry." Edward wrung his hands. "But may I communicate to you what I discover in my further investigations?"

"Of course you may. Please write to me here. And as you leave, please be good enough to tell Mary, who admitted you, who you are and explain the nature of your association with me. Let her know that you may write to me concerning matters relating to the Royal Society. She is party to my working for them, but not of my involvement with you."

"Yes, and thank you again."

Edward left with his mind in turmoil again, but felt that he managed to act sufficiently unaffectedly and official in his discussion with Mary, to dispel any suspicion on her part.

§

The following day found Edward on the train to Northampton, still in a state of pathetic uncertainty. Whilst he had begun to have doubts that the discovery of the identity of the mysterious Frenchman would help his investigation, his primary uncertainty related to his relationship with Clara. He had intruded into her private world, which he knew that she needed to keep private. But her dismissal of him from her office had hurt him, for in their new world of romantic love, they had opened the softest parts of their hearts to each other. He knew that she had said that their arrangement made on the train still applied, but she had said it in a manner that had sown doubts in his mind, like a gust of wind carrying wild seeds into a garden.

A seed germinated and took root as he stood in the reception hall of the George Hotel, dripping from the Northampton rain. He glanced through the glass doors into the bar and saw the back of an attractive lady who seemed familiar and who appeared to be alone. He questioned his senses, for it was the contours of her shoulders and back that were familiar. A vision flashed through his mind of her shoulders and back connected to the rest of her naked anatomy; the vision had been imprinted on his mind during the process of caressing her various parts. It was none other than the glorious Miss Clements, the damsel who was left in the lurch at the steeplechase and whom he had gallantly rescued.

He hurriedly checked into his room and walked into the bar. Miss Clement was idly gazing out of the window whilst holding a glass in her gloved hand.

"My dear Lizzie," called Edward as he approached her. She swung round. Recognition instantly lit up her face.

"Neddy, my darling." She threw her arms around his neck, spraying his jacket with champagne, as she launched herself at him. She was a demonstrative girl, who communicated her feelings in a rather explicit way. It was this characteristic which had left such a mark on Edward's psyche. Their faces were close as he spoke.

"I have just acquired a room. It is unfortunately not the suite I had last time we met, but I am sure it will have the requisite pieces of furniture, namely wardrobe, dressing table, washstand and bed."

"It sounds marvellous. I long to see it."

They kissed, for longer than was appropriate, although by good fortune the bar was deserted. Their lips broke apart and Edward whispered.

"I really need to go and hang up my jacket to dry. Perhaps you would like to join me."

"Indeed. I would love to hang mine next to yours."

No more than five minutes later, Edward's clothes were hanging roughly over the back of a chair, intermingled with hers. She was in her favourite position, namely lying on the bed, unencumbered by clothing. Edward was caressing her back and telling her how he had identified her in the bar by the very memorable shape of her shoulder blades. She rolled over and in a coy tone asked him if he remembered the shapes now before him. His sense of rationality passed into oblivion as he continued to caress her.

His mind and body were soothed for the next few hours, after which she, fully dressed again, gave him a business-like peck on the cheek and left him. He threw himself back onto the bed and considered. He did not feel that his morals were in jeopardy, for he had long since considered that he had none, but there was a nagging doubt that he still owed something to Clara. He might have misread her in the clinic. She might have been unable to speak her feelings and thus the admonishment might have been for the benefit of her employees and her reputation, as much as for him. With a sinking heart he continued to consider these things over dinner and during his subsequent nocturnal wandering through the wide streets and narrow alleyways of the law-abiding town.

§

Edward knocked on the door of a small house next to the Vicarage.

"I'm sorry, but the Doctor is out. Visiting." The old woman in a black dress was obviously the housekeeper.

"I see. Did the Doctor say whom he was visiting?"

The woman's eyebrows rose at Edward's language.

"Mrs Wolcott, the widow," she replied in a haughty tone.

"And where might Mrs Wolcott live?"

She pointed across the road. "Down that track. Two cottages. Further one."

The door closed on him and Edward braved the track. It was passable, although his suede boots were splashed with mud on more than one occasion. He was fifty yards away when he saw them. The Doctor was in his shirtsleeves, throwing a ball to a boy, likely in his mid teens. The boy had some likeness to the Doctor, who recognised Edward as he approached. The Doctor bid the boy go inside and offered his hand to the visitor. His look of worry reminded Edward of his first meeting with him.

"Pardon me, sir. I was just occupying the boy, whilst the widow was attending to some duties. The boy needs a man to direct his energies and his mother has not been well since her husband died. The villagers are scant help."

"Well. I will not occupy you long, Doctor. I wish to ask Mrs Grey a question. I thought it would be better if you were with me."

A look of alarm came and went on the Doctor's face, like the flight of a wren into a hedge.

"It is nothing really. I wish to know the name of the French mathematician who presented the Reverend with his pocket watch."

"Ah, very well. Let me take you to her."

In the silence of their walk to the cottage on the edge of the village, Edward mused on what he knew about inherited characteristics and whether the boy might be a relative of the Doctor.

The Reverend's widow was working in her tiny vegetable garden, bent over, poking at some weeds with a hoe. The Doctor gently guided her back inside. She made them tea and then, sitting around the parlour table, she began where she had left off.

"Doctor Mould used to sit at a table like this. I remembered him, because Arnold asked me about him, not a week since. He was Arnold's tutor and Arnold said that he worshipped him. I told him that the Good Book told us that it was wrong to worship idols and Arnold laughed so much."

She gave a toothless grin to her visitors who, recalling Edward's last visit when she had first remembered the Reverend's tutor at university, had difficulty in fully sharing in the humour. Edward cautiously asked his question. She rubbed her chin and then suddenly, with a sprightliness that surprised them both, jumped up and pulled the watch out of a nearby drawer.

"Yes, I put it in here. Yes. It was the day after he died. I took the watch from the chair at the side of his bed and put it in here. I thought it might be needed at some time or another. I do not need it, of course, because I get up at the sun's rising and go to bed with its setting, just like the psalm said, 'from the rising of the sun unto the going down of the same, the Lord's name is to be praised'."

Edward held out his hand and she placed the watch gently into it. He looked at it. "Who gave it to him?" he asked.

She looked at him with puzzlement. "Well, I think it was a Frenchman."

Edward's heart sank. She did not know his name. He gazed at it lying in his palm. The plain hands were clear on the white face, but they could not speak of its original owner. He turned it over. There was some engraving. He took out his monocle and examined the tiny writing.

To Arnold, a master mathematician, from Claude M

He read the words out.

"Oh, Claude. I thought it was Pierre. I always think of Pierre when I think of Frenchmen. But I try not to think of them, for they are sinners."

Edward did not hear her, for his mind was racing to try to find the man's full name in his memory. He knew many French mathematicians, but he could not locate this one. Yet the woman was still speaking. He suddenly began to listen again.

"Arnold said that he had committed a mortal sin, the seventh sin. He said that a sin is mortal if it is, firstly, sufficiently serious, secondly, reflected on before being committed and, thirdly, committed through free will."

Edward reflected on his dalliance with Miss Clement, as he listened to this definition. He then looked at the Doctor, who did not move.

The woman stared sternly into their faces, but said no more.

§

Clara had left a note for Edward with the concierge of the George Hotel, bidding him to visit her in her room, when he was able. He recognised her handwriting on the envelope when he returned and surprise and joy overcame him. He went straight up to her. They looked at each other across the threshold. Edward saw the compassion and desire in her face that he had not seen in London. She saw his need and drew him into her arms, pushing the door shut behind him.

"I am so sorry, my love," she whispered.

"I should not have come."

"Do you want me now?"

"Yes, but I need to talk first, for I nearly have the answer."

They sat on the chaise and in his excited state he related his visit to the Reverend's widow. By the time he had unburdened himself, he calmed down and said, "She knows very little, but what little she said has puzzled me. Of course I can identify the Frenchman. I can go back to London tomorrow and see two or three of my friends who will tell me who Claude M is. I will then write to him and request an interview, purporting to talk about some mathematical problem. I am certain that the President will pay for another journey, if the truth is to be found."

Clara put her hand gently on his arm. "Edward, I do not think so."

"What do you mean? Am I wrong?"

"Only about the President."

"Ah. It is of no matter. If he will not pay, I will talk to my banker."

Clara smiled at him. "What did the Reverend's widow say that puzzled you?"

"She said that her husband had told her that Claude M had committed a mortal sin: the seventh sin."

"Adultery?"

"Yes," said Edward. "How would Arnold know that? And what bearing does it have on our investigation?"

"I cannot imagine. It may have no bearing at all."

"Perhaps you are right, Clara. However, it seems to be the cause of her dislike of the French as a race."

"There are many with that feeling, including the Ear at the Door." A smile played on her lips, which disturbed Edward's delicate emotions. He took a breath and exhaled noisily. He smiled weakly back at her.

"There was another strange occurrence. I asked the Doctor to accompany me on my visit to the widow. I found him at the house of another widow, a patient. He was outside playing with her son. The resemblance was striking."

"The resemblance to whom?"

"I mean that the boy resembled the Doctor. I searched my mind since for what the philosophers say about inherited traits. Clara, could he be related to the boy?"

"Of course, in a small village many are related. Is he married?"

"I think not."

"His parents, uncles or aunts perhaps."

"Yes. But the resemblance was strong. Will it ever be possible to identify the father by examining the son? What characteristics would one use to do so?"

"My dear Edward, I think not. Indeed there is much confusion in the matter of inherited characteristics. When fossils are considered, Lamarck has said that acquired characteristics are indeed passed through the generations. For example, an organ that is not used in a creature will eventually wither away, such as a wing or a webbed foot. Some more credulous suppose that this can happen in one generation, for they discovered that a man who lost a finger in an accident went on to sire two children, who both were born without the same finger."

"How very singular. The probability of that happening by chance is infinitesimal."

"Indeed so. And there are those who believe that the son will have characteristics that are a blending of those of both parents. But I cannot accept that, for children are born male or female, never an in-between gender. And even with intermarrying over many centuries, the different races are still evident. I therefore accept Lamarck, but without much enthusiasm."

This rather abstract discussion had temporarily defused their lust and they were able to descend to dinner together. However, after returning to their rooms, Clara stole to Edward's, equipped with those items necessary for a night away from her luggage.

"My darling, I am now accustomed to being in love with you," Clara said, as he led her to the bed. "At first it was like a stranger intruding into my life. I examined it, questioning whether this was madness or a wonderful new mode of life. I realised it was the second and have now accepted it."

He fitted a mask around her eyes, telling her that it would heighten the sensation of touch, and stood next to her by the side of the bed. Without a word he began to undress her. Her breathing was shallow and even, as he began. Then, as garment upon garment fell to the floor, her heart began to race and as the final piece fell, her chest was heaving. Then, there was nothing. She stood in a pool of silence, naked and desperate to call out to him to release her. But when her release came, it was not the sight of his smile or a gentle word. It was the feel of his arms sliding around her and pulling her against him, until their flesh met in an embrace both hot with sensuality and cool with the certainty of his love for her. They remained in contact, and she sightless, for the rest of the night, even until that moment when she lay exhausted, half on him and half off and they both fell asleep.

In the morning, the sun crept, inch-by-inch, over them, warming their nakedness. They lay uncovered; her shoulder was nestled in the crook of his arm, her arm across his chest and her leg on his stomach. He woke, but remained motionless, until a smile creased his face as he remembered the way she had given herself to him the evening before, sightless but unafraid. He gently ran his hand from where it rested on her shoulder down over the dip of her waist and onto the soft pink peak of her hip. Then, as the warmth of the sun beckoned her senses into activity, he felt her fingers twitch on his chest. Her head, which rested on his shoulder, twisted fractionally and her eyes restlessly looked from side to side under her eyelids. Small eruptions of her muscles increased in frequency, signalling her increasing consciousness, until suddenly her whole body convulsed.

"Edward, oh ... Edward."

"Yes, my darling."

"I was dreaming."

"Ah. Tell me your dream."

"I was in the Crossley's kitchen. There were two bird's eggs on the table. Their colour is clear in my memory. They were light brown with small dark brown spots."

"They are coots eggs. I used to collect eggs as a boy, as Robert did."

"But how did I know what their colour was? I must have seen them somewhere and then forgotten them."

"Yes... Go on."

"Then I looked again at the table. It had a heart upon it. It was your heart and it was beating, strongly. Then the table reared up like a horse on its hind legs, and galloped away."

"Ah, yes. You slept with your head on my chest and must have been aware of the beating within as you slept. The table galloping away might be a strange feeling that you have about me. It might represent our parting and your resulting distress, or you might simply have remembered my love of horse racing."

Clara shivered at the thought. "There was another scene. Some person, that I could not identify, was lying down. An old man stood above, with long white hair. He held a dagger and his hand was raised, ready to strike, but another hand gripped the wrist and prevented it falling. Then the restraining hand loosened its grip and the knife went down, plunging into the flesh, but no blood flowed from the wound. Then I awoke, filled with fear."

Clara was trembling. "Tell me what it means."

"I cannot, just as no reputable doctor can, although many take money from sensible people to do so."

Clara was disappointed. Edward continued. "The knife might represent death and the old man could be the grim reaper, although he usually is seen with a scythe. An alternative meaning of the knife might be that it represents a phallus, which you have newly experienced and it may thus be active in your mind. I believe that in most cases, dreams are a rather random collection of thoughts and preoccupations. Sometimes they can presage an event, although I am aware of no significant death in our case other than those of Jeremiah Crossley and the Reverend Arnold Grey, neither of which have raised any suspicions."

Clara was about to get up, when Edward suddenly continued. "I suspect Steyn. Of what, I am not yet sure. He claims that those he works for are English. But it is well known in intelligence circles that there are still many continental agitators abroad in the city. It may be that Steyn is working both for the English, in the person of the President, and for those over the channel. Perhaps he means to bring Robert down, for his masters may realise that he is has the capability to change the military balance in small but important ways. I fear that in pursuing him, we may be aiding and abetting our enemies."

CHAPTER 21

Mortal Sin

"Sir, although you are the President of the Royal Society, I would assume that you remain at the foundation of your being, a scientist."

"Indeed I do, Edward."

"Would you therefore agree, that the aim of every scientist is to seek the truth in all things?"

"Yes, that is correct."

"And is it not true that, in some cases, a scientist may have an intuition about the truth, with no evidential basis for his feeling? And, furthermore, is it not true that it is his duty to pursue his intuition, irrespective of the fact that that intuition leads to the truth or not?"

Professor Hyde frowned. "Yes, what you say can describe the seeking of scientific truth in some circumstances."

"You may remember that we, Doctor Cox and myself, presented a report to you, concerning allegations that Robert Crossley had committed plagiarism."

"I remember. You very rightly concluded that the allegation had no basis."

"We now consider that we did not complete the investigation in a satisfactory manner."

The President's eyebrows lifted and he listened with increasing irritation to Edward's description of the French mathematician and his gift to the Reverend Grey of a pocket watch. Finally, he could not contain himself.

"What on earth makes you feel that this person knows anything of value?"

"My intuition, sir."

"Your intuition? Poppycock!"

"But did you not agreed with me that one should always follow one's intuition?"

"Of course I did. But only in science. Your investigation of these most serious allegations is not science. The reputation of one of our most illustrious young Fellows is at stake. I cannot allow you to run about raking up the past on an intuition."

"I was hoping that you would provide expenses for me to visit the man in question. I have written to him, but his son advises a visit, as his mind is somewhat failing him, and a personal interview might bring his old memories back to him."

"If you think that I would ever put such a proposal before the Finance Committee you are more naive than I imagined. His mind is failing. You have an intuition. Why, they would laugh at me! And the result of your investigation went a long way to quieten the misgivings of the Minister about the Society. I have no intention of opening up your inquiry again on such a flimsy basis. Have I made myself clear?"

§

"The President was very understanding of our new feelings about the case. He suggested that we should follow our intuition, as all great scientists should, and pursue the truth to the bitter end."

Clara was surprised. Edward had indicated that the President believed a visit to Paris was needed. Clara was less convinced, and expected him to want to let matters lie as they were. She had suggested that their first conclusions of Robert's innocence were convenient for the President and the Society.

"And what did he say about me?" she asked.

"Ah, he was very firm that you should accompany me. Although he knew that I could converse sufficiently in French, he believed that your fluent language would be important. And, of course, a medical view of the old man's condition would be useful. He said nothing of your being a woman. I was planning to go alone, for I remembered your specific wish not to be further involved due to your commitments. But, he was insistent."

Edward noticed a look of regret pass quickly across her face.

"Well, if the President recommends that I go, I suppose that I must."

Three days later, they took the Post down to Dover and left the quay in a rather smaller ship than Clara would have wished for. However, the weather was well set for their voyage to the continent. Fluffy clouds hurried past them towards the French coast that they had espied from the cliffs above the town. They stood on the deck, watching the paddles rotate and the gulls screaming overhead. Edward who, after his grand tour was now a seasoned sailor, had one hand on the rail and with the other held Clara close against him. Clara was enjoying the challenge of the sea.

"My darling Edward, this is a glorious moment. I have a dream of escaping to a life together with you in another place. Although I know that we must return in a few days, I feel like a young girl, engaged on a secret elopement."

"Let us for a moment pretend that I am taking you off to Venice. We will stay in an apartment overlooking the Grand Canal. After awaking together, late in the morning, we will glide between the walls of palaces in a gondola and let the romance that emanates from the very stones of the buildings fill us with love."

Edward felt her push against him in a silent acknowledgement. They remained there, at the rail, until the ship had cleared the harbour and was beginning to encounter the full force of the English Channel. After an hour of being thrown up and down by the ship, Clara wished to lie down. Edward concurred with her, for the sky was now covered with ominous dark clouds and the sea was rising by the moment. They repaired to their double cabin, secured under assumed names, as a man and his wife. Clara immediately lay down in her full travelling clothes, being unable to stand any longer. Edward pulled up a chair, sat himself down next to her and held her hand.

"Talk to me, Edward. It will take my mind off my stomach."

"Certainly."

He considered for a moment, not because he lacked anything to say, but to select from his immediate memory a yarn that would divert her through its amusement, rather than bore her, which his mathematics would do, or horrify her, which his description of the gallows on Freeman's Common might.

"I was sitting in the lounge of the George, in Northampton, just after the steeplechase," he began, "reading the newspaper with the assistance of my monocle, when this fellow in a business suit hailed me. 'Young man', he said, 'I can see that you are having difficulties reading the fine print. Would it not be wonderful, if our eyes could be cured of this impediment, and the inconvenience of the last two thousand years of the use of shaped pieces of glass placed in front of our eyes was done away with? Of course, the Guild of Optical Practitioners would have something to say about that, but their opprobrium is something that I am willing to bear. I understand your situation, for I too used to have that problem, until I met Swami Gamaskar.'"

"He then went on at great length describing the achievements of various Indian mystics who had the ability to cure ailments as diverse as loss of hair to gout. He had the good sense to say that the fakirs were all fakers, a play on words that would appeal to the cynic in all of us, and thus get even the most unbelieving on his side. The tale of his development of his massage technique and his pills then followed. His eloquence was a wonder to behold. Even Lord Salisbury, who once talked for three hours in the House without stopping, could not outstrip this fellow. He had a charm and an enthusiasm that after a while I came to admire. Of course I did not believe him for a moment, but pondered as he spoke, on the honest yet gullible people that were the bread and butter of this rogue's life of crime. He would spin this pack of lies, all the time watching his prey like the practised fly fisherman will pull his salmon into shore. And all the time he is assessing how much he can demand for his miracle. Too much, and the fish will not pursue the fly. Too little and it does not value it enough to swallow it. My price was thirty pounds.

"Goodness me!"

"But what made me angry and keen to teach him a lesson was when he brought out his letter of recommendation from Lord Berkhampstead. Edward pulled the letter in question out of his pocket. It was written on a thick vellum paper that felt expensive to the touch, and the seal of red wax had impressed into it a heraldic device of lions rampant and scrolls. He placed it on the bed. His tale had made Clara forget her malady. She picked it up and read.

Henry Chappell,
Lord Berkhampstead

To
Whom so ever it might concern,

Doctor Julius Gascoigne-Heart, previously of 9 Turncock Lane, London, and now of 23 Clarendon Square, London, treated the deficiencies of my sight using his patented medicine and his unique massage techniques. I can now confirm, by means of this letter, that due to his admirable treatment, my sight has been completely restored and is now of the same standard as that which I had as a young man. My Head Gamekeeper, who is a sound fellow and has been with my family for over sixty years, has verified this fact. He has sworn, under oath, that my bag for last season included twenty-five immature partridges taken down at a distance of three hundred yards, a feat that I had not performed since I was aged twenty-two!

I understand that Doctor Gascoigne-Heart learned his massage methods under the tutelage of the Fakir Roda Malang of Himachal Pradesh, India, and that he has developed his medicines at the laboratories of the University of London under the direction of Professor J Browning. Professor Browning is available to those of an enquiring mind, to verify the Doctor's developments and to escort visitors around his laboratory.

I can thoroughly recommend Doctor Gascoigne-Heart's miraculous treatment to all who have similar ocular propensities!

Signed
Berkhampstead

"Really, my dear, 'ocular propensities'! Harry Chappell Berkhampstead would not know what ocular propensities were, even if they hit him between the eyes. He was born an idiot and has developed that side of his personality very nicely ever since. Why only last month at our club, he was telling me about his collection of hats. He has over a thousand, from all around the country, and he has had a special dressing room fitted out to contain them, which he calls his *hatarium*. The rogue has read his name in the paper in an article on stupidity and built his ocular world around him."

"So, you see, I went along with him. I pulled out my special wallet and carefully put a fifty-pound note on the table, leaving my hand on it and apologising like an idiot, as Harry might have done, that I did not have a smaller denomination. The sham Doctor must have thought that his dreams had come true, to make thirty pounds with so little effort. He slid twenty across the table. We lifted our hands and transferred them at the same time, each laughing at our good fortune. He was folding my bill into his wallet when he noticed that it was only printed on one side. He read my poetry on the obverse and obviously did not consider it to be up to Byron at his best. His accent changed from medical scientist to costermonger when he discovered his fifty was worthless. Fortunately, there were others in the lounge, so he was unable to attack me as was his dearest wish at that moment"

"'I have admired your very notable skills,' I told him, 'but I have to take exception to the forging of a letter from one of my dearest friends. I will not turn you into the police. I will take the letter and the twenty pounds. Do not bother to massage my head or to deliver the pills. Now please leave, before I change my mind.'"

Clara, rather than applaud him, was now rather more ill than at the beginning of his tale. Her eyes bulged as she sat bolt upright on the bed and retched all over her bedclothes and Edward's letter.

Edward was momentarily nonplussed. But when he realised that his witty tale was not about to get the reaction he expected, he set to and tended to his patient, like a loving spouse should.

§

They spend a couple of days in a draughty Calais hotel recuperating. On the third day Clara declared herself fit to travel and they took the Paris coach. The smell of salt and fish slowly evaporated from their nostrils and was replaced by the fragrance of mown grass from the meadows and horse dung from the road until they reached Paris.

After a morning of asking and seeking, they found Mercier's residence, a large three storey building in a relatively affluent district of the city. An ancient servant led them to a graciously furnished drawing room. Mercier's son rose to welcome them and introduced them to his father.

Claude Mercier was infirm but of very clear mind. Edward greeted him in French. Mercier offered to talk in English for Edward's companion's benefit. He clapped his hands in delight, when Clara said she had studied at the Sorbonne, for no English university would take her, and that French was not a problem for her.

"Did you hear that, Pierre?" he said to his son, with a glint in his eye. "That is how the English treat their women. Madam, I am honoured to be visited by a beacon to your gender." He took Clara's hand and kissed it.

Edward reminded the old man that the purpose of his visit was to know more of the Reverend Arnold Grey, for he had died and the British Royal Society wished to know more about him.

"Do they wish to honour him?"

Edward glanced quickly at Clara to confirm that she had also understood what Mercier had implied. She had.

"Well, sir, that is not clear yet, until his achievements have been established. It will be useful if you would tell us what you know of him."

"Of course. I am happy to tell you what I know, for talking of him fills me with happy memories."

§

"When I was a young and vigorous assistant at the Ecole Polytechnique, my Professor believed that all his young staff should attend a meeting in England at least once in their careers, to find out who was who and what they were doing. We knew that from an English point of view this was absurd, as the English always felt that they did not need the help of the eaters of frogs and snails. However, his mind was broader than theirs and he sent me to a meeting of the Cambridge Philosophical Society.

"I remember as if was yesterday. It was August the 9th, 1830. The meeting was held in Trinity College and the beauty of the buildings and the number of famous mathematicians left me speechless. By talking to them, I soon learnt the history of calculus in England, which is what I suppose was my Professor's reason for sending me there. After Newton and Leibniz first developed calculus in the 17th century, the English were permitted only to use Newton's method of fluxions. England had its own Napoleon."

Mercier paused to smile at his jest and to reassure himself that his visitors had appreciated it. He then resumed.

"For, despite Newton's brilliance, or perhaps because of it, he was a despot. However by the early 19th century, it was clear that it was time to change to the Leibniz notation. The Cambridge mathematicians, lead by Robert Woodhouse and Edward Bromhead, formed what they called the Analytical Society, which later became the Cambridge Philosophical Society. Charles Babbage and John Herschel, as well as George Peacock and William Whelwell, who both taught mathematics at Cambridge, were amongst its members. By the time of the meeting that I attended, the battle was won."

"The meeting was opened by the President of the Royal Society, Davies Gilbert. Gilbert was a star in the English mathematical firmament. He presented his work on the vibrations of heavenly bodies."

He paused and grinned again.

"He was something of an egotist, for in his introduction he spoke of his time as High Sheriff of Cornwall and as Member of Parliament for a town called Helston. He had spoken in Parliament about the ill-advised tendency of teaching the working classes and such an abominable opinion very much upset me. However, his mathematics inspired me, as did that of the other speakers."

He paused again, for his recollection had become serious.

"After having read their work before, it was magnificent to hear them. I met Arnold Grey purely by chance. I had the honour to talk briefly with Gilbert and Babbage. Perhaps I should not have heard their conversation, because it was about the politics of the Royal Society. But at such meetings, these things happen. Gilbert said that he was trying to get more of the members to write and read papers. I was surprised at that, for I assumed that all the members published their work. He said that he was frustrated by amateur mathematicians, like Grey, who would never reveal what they were doing for fear of criticism. This intrigued me, for I sympathised with such a view, as the university professors in France could be very hurtful, in a totally unnecessary way, by criticising the work of others. I introduced myself to Arnold as half amateur and half university mathematician, which immediately obtained his interest. He told me of his work, which impressed me a great deal, and of his poverty as a village priest, which amazed me, for I came from a comfortable middle class family and never imagined such a life. He even told me that he had no pocket watch, for he told the time by the church clock. After two days of listening to the papers together and discussing them animatedly during the breaks, we parted with a promise to write."

"As a leaving present I gave my pocket watch to Arnold, for I had been touched by his humility, honesty and friendship. I had found the English mathematicians a cold group with little interest in me, my work, or my people. Arnold was the only one who listened."

"We wrote often in the few years that followed that meeting. His letters were always so full of wisdom concerning mathematics and life. He had an endearing way of wrapping his wisdom in humour, so that you did not realise the depth until you finished laughing."

"What was he working on?" Edward asked.

"Ah, I am sorry, I have talked about the meeting and not about what you have come for. He derived an expression that links the integral along a closed function to the double integral over the area enclosed. Thus, if the periphery of an irregular area is known, the area is easily found. At its simplest it relates the circumference of a circle to its area. But it is general and can thus be applied to many sciences. When he last wrote to me, he was applying it to electrical and magnetic fields."

Mercier paused and Edward wondered if he was regretting the ending of their relationship. Before he could continue, Edward asked his most important question.

"Do you still have his letters?"

"Mais, oui."

His son interrupted him. "I am sorry, monsieur, but when we got your letter, we looked, but we cannot find them. Papa, I think we must accept that they are gone."

His father frowned at him and did not reply. Edward still hoped.

"Can you remember, sir, when Arnold completed the derivation of the expression?"

"It was in his letter of the 18th of October, 1832. The day was clear and the autumn was turning cold, for the winter was severe that year. The expression matched the clarity of the weather, and I immediately replied, congratulating him on his achievement."

Edward opened his briefcase and pulled out a bound copy of Robert's paper, bearing the date 1845. He opened it at a certain page and showed it to the old man.

"Yes, of course, this is it. How marvellous for it to be published." He turned to the frontispiece and read it. He began to tremble. "How can this be? Who is this Robert Crossley? And the date! It is so long after Arnold completed it."

"Robert Crossley is the name of the man who stole the Reverend Grey's work from him."

Claude had become so enraged, that Pierre had asked them to leave. At the doorstep, Edward had asked Pierre's permission to return, for their only aim was to put right the injury done to Grey.

§

That evening, Edward and Clara discussed what they should do.

"We must get him to sign a letter confirming the dates and contents of the letters," said Edward. "We must take a notary with us to make it legal. It is not what I would wish, for it reduces the thing down to the level of the mountebank offering to restore my eyesight. Letters can be forged, and if we present such a letter to the President, he may not accept it."

"No, my dear, let us fetch the notary later and do things little by little. There are other possibilities to be explored. Perhaps he told of Arnold's work to somebody else. Perhaps he referred to the work in his own publications, that are for all to read."

Edward and Clara returned to the Mercier family home on the following morning. Claude had calmed himself, but was still indignant for his friend.

"How could this man take credit for what was not his?"

"Crossley was Arnold's student in his later years. The young man was eager to make something of his life, but knew his limitations. We will never know exactly how it happened, unless he admits his crime and explains."

"He has taken my dear friend's most wonderful achievement." The Frenchman shook his head in disbelief.

"Sir, please help us in any way you can to right this wrong. Are you sure that the letter was kept."

"Oui," said the old man. "I put them in a wooden trunk."

Suddenly, the son rushed from the room. Edward continued.

"Did you tell anybody else at the time?"

"Of course, I told my dear Angelique. She passed away ten years ago. No one else would listen to the stories of an old man, especially our children."

"Did you publish any reference to his work in your own."

Before he could answer, Pierre ran into the room waving a bundle of letters in his hand.

"Papa, papa, I have found them. They were in the trunk in the attic. Last week, when we searched, I thought you referred to the trunk in your study."

He handed them to his father, whose only word of reply was 'Pah', as he untied them. They were in chronological order. He picked each up in turn and commented. "June 1831, he begins the task. I reply, wishing him well. September of the same year, he encounters a problem that we discuss. I offer some suggestions, or rather, places to look to gain insight. January 1832, he thinks he is making progress. April, progress is slowed. One of his parishioners went over his head to the Bishop and his curate is transferred to the Western Highlands for alleged Calvinistic tendencies." He shook his head. His sympathy for his English friend was clear. "Here it is, 18th of October 1832." A tear fell from his eye, as he handed the letter to his visitor. Edward perused it carefully.

"Yes. Yes. He even writes the expression on the second page. It looks genuine."

"Pardon? What do you mean, genuine?"

"I am sorry. But this letter is the agent that will bring a man's career down. If you permit me to take it back to London as evidence it will undergo much scrutiny. For example, I will need some document from Arnold's home with his signature, to compare it with."

"Ah, I see. I would like it back, of course. But I would like it to be the instrument that establishes that Arnold was the true author, and for the theorem to bear his name. Then I shall be happy."

They took three letters that made the development clear and also had a notary attest that Mercier was in his right mind and the letters belonged to him. As they were leaving, Edward asked the Frenchman whether stealing a man's property was worse than the other of God's commandments, such as the 7th. Mercier merely raised his eyebrows at the apparently academic question.

"What this man did to Arnold was abominable. But our Father put the commandments in the correct order. The 6th comes before the 7th and the 7th before the 8th. Au revoir, mon ami."

CHAPTER 22

Smoke Filled Rooms

Robert got wind of the investigation when Edward and Clara were in Northampton. It may never be clear how he found out. Perhaps a well-meaning member of the family, in their excitement, let slip that questions were being asked in the name of the Royal Society. Perhaps a friend within the Society itself had had a quiet word in his ear. It is possible that someone on the Disciplinary Committee was sympathetic to him, or owed Robert a debt that he wished to clear. It might, of course, be possible that the Disciplinary Committee did not exist at all and that it was merely a convenience of the President to deflect criticism of his action. It this were true, one might ask after the loyalties of the mysterious Mister Steyn, who appeared to be answerable to several masters at the same time. Such conjecture is, however, just conjecture and it is possible that all concerned acted in an honourable manner.

What is clear is that Robert reacted to the information in the same way that he had acted since he had moved to London. To those around him he remained his urbane and genial self. His conversation was both entertaining and, on the later reflection of the recipient, always seemed profitable. His livelihood was not earned through sitting at a desk and labouring with pen and paper, as those employed in large organisations often are. Robert made his way by knowing people, by lunching and dining, and by being interesting, wise, and by listening. His conversation was naturally centred around the human condition. Events occur or decisions are made that affect our lives. Knowledge of them is currency, which can be traded; the ability, apparent or otherwise, to influence them is vastly more valuable. His was a political occupation, which can be directed at improving the lot of either the person thus employed, or the people whom he represents. The politicians that rule us do the first to become secure in themselves and then move on to benefit other people. But there are those who never make that transition and Robert was one of those, although he would never admit it to himself. On the basis of his wealth in knowledge and influence, he gently began to defend his position.

He knew all of those on the Disciplinary Committee, save Mister Steyn, whose motives he could not penetrate. He knew that the committee was not on any document relating to the governance of the Society, but met only when it was convenient to the President. Certain allegations would have been discussed, he had been told, which had been put on the agenda by the President who, naturally for the sake of the Society, wished them to disappear. There were seven members on the committee, including the President himself, and there were two that he could rely upon to support the President. He needed just one more to be sure that the President had his way.

§

"Good evening, Sir Joseph."
Robert was passing a rotund white haired gentleman in a half lit corridor of a gentleman's club.

"Eh, good evening. Do I know ye? Royal Society, perhaps?" The gentleman replied with a distinct Scottish accent.

"Indeed, my name is Robert Crossley and I believe that you will soon discuss some allegations against me in the Disciplinary Committee."

"I understood that the matter has been dealt with, in your favour."

"Some new evidence has been discovered. If you would let me buy you a single malt, I would like to discuss the matter with you?"

"To put your side of the case?"

"Not at all, but I know someone you have been seeking."

"Hmm..., very well."

Sir Joseph McDiarmid was a well-known barrister, who dealt with cases involving financial matters. His reputation was well founded and he was widely known. His second interest was science and his Fellowship of the Royal Society was granted because he was useful in cases of scientific dispute. He regularly advised the President. Robert and the barrister found a quiet corner. They tasted their malts.

"A fine dram, would ye not say?"

"It is fine, indeed. But my experience, unlike yours, does not allow me to say how fine it is."

Sir Joseph smiled at the young man and said, "Why do ye not begin."

"I offer you nothing on whether the allegation of plagiarism is true or not. You are aware of the circumstances from the first hearing. I wish you to explain, to both the Disciplinary Committee and to the subsequent meeting with the investigators, the very wide range of possible interpretations of letters purporting to prove wrongdoing and the various types of relationships between a master and his student."

"That, sir, is nothing more than m' job."

"Then I simply ask you to do your job."

"You mentioned that ye knew somebody that I am seeking." said Sir Joseph.

"You are prosecuting a case involving fraud in a shipping company. The witness that you currently seek is a Jew and he has recently changed his name. He used to be Cohen. He is now Gavrel Abrahams. He can be found close to where you have been looking."

"You are a strange man, Crossley. You ask me to do my job and yet you give me a witness that will bring a man down."

"The matter we are discussing is serious enough to bring me down also. I have done much so far, but I still have much that I wish to do, whiskey tasting included. May I talk to you after the meeting of the Disciplinary Committee? There may be some trading to discuss."

"Over another whiskey, I hope."

"Of course."

§

The night was late and the gas lamps in the President's office threw a theatrical light onto the actors beneath. The President's secretary had made his final check that all was ready. and silently pulled the door shut behind him. Professor Hyde waited until all was quiet. He thanked all for coming and went around the table naming them.

To his left was Mister Steyn. Beyond him were Edward and Clara. To the President's right was Robert. Beyond him were Sir Joseph and his personal assistant; the other Committee members sat opposite. Robert stared at the wall opposite him with a face as cold as stone; he seemed not to be a part of what was happening. It was the first time that Clara had seen him. His face had the same structure as his brother but it seemed to be a mask that had been pulled over a harder and darker interior.

The documents, which had been previously given up by Edward to the President for the meeting of the Disciplinary Committee, lay on the table before him. "I believe that everybody has seen the letters from the Reverend Grey to the Frenchman Mercier, and the notary's attestation, except you Mister Crossley."

Robert did not react. Sir Joseph spoke. "Mister President, I am speaking on Mister Crossley's behalf."

"Ah, very well. Let us begin. I have called this meeting to consider the new evidence relating to the allegations made against Mister Crossley."

Sir Joseph interrupted him. "May I ask, Mister President, who is making these allegations? It is normal to have two sides in a case."

"Why... why it is the Society making them."

"And ye, being the President, represent the Society in this case."

The President looked uncomfortable. "Of course. Now, new evidence has been discovered by Mister Pennington and Doctor Cox, and it appears to indicate that the Reverend Arnold Grey completed the mathematical theory, some time before Mister Crossley became acquainted with him."

"Mister President, I do not think that is the case at all."

Rather than baulking at the interruption, the President looked relieved that Sir Joseph had taken over. "Firstly, let us consider who these allegations are aimed at. Mister Crossley is a pillar of society, and of the Royal Society. He has increased the stature of our august organisation through the presentation and the publication of a revolutionary new mathematical theorem that, even as we speak, is inspiring and enabling scientists and mathematicians around the world to push back the barriers of knowledge. In addition, in his service to the Society and his service beyond its gates, he contributes substantially to employment and to the good name of the Society, extending its influence into the realms of Government by advising on various matters of national security."

"Yes, thank you," the President mumbled.

Sir Joseph continued. "Now let us consider the documents. Has no one considered that the letters from Grey might be forgeries?"

Edward was incensed. "Sir, I obtained them myself from the hands of an eminent mathematician."

"Who is a Frenchman, is he not? Therefore, we must consider the possibility of a plot to bring down the good name of our British Society by the French, using Mister Crossley as a mere pawn in their evil game. Consider, for example, that documents written by Grey could have been obtained. That would enable handwriting to have been copied and signatures to have been forged."

Edward frowned as Sir Joseph went on.

"Furthermore, we cannot accept the letter from the notary, for he is beyond our jurisdiction. And, of course, his letter might also be a forgery. As it stands it has no value in a British court."

All eyes were focused on Sir Joseph, except those of Robert, who still gazed at the wall.

"However, provided that the letters are shown to be genuine, then we must examine their content. Do they categorically prove that Grey completely derived the theorem? Surely the writing of the final expression is insufficient to prove that he did the whole derivation." He lifted his hand to silence Edward, who was about to speak. "The argument I have just given can also be applied to the letters talking of progress on the theorem. The only proof beyond doubt that Grey derived the theorem would be the full paper in his handwriting."

Edward interrupted him again. "But Crossley would have destroyed it after copying it, obviously,"

"No, not obviously, Mister Pennington. We are talking about the law and the law needs proof. We have the full paper in Mister Crossley's hand, but not in Grey's."

The President nodded his head. Sir Joseph had not yet finished. "There is a possibility that Grey started it and was able to write the final expression, but it was the collaboration of Crossley that enabled the two of them to fill in the intermediate parts which, in many cases of mathematics, are the most difficult. And it might also be the case that their collaboration was amicable and that Grey was even grateful to Crossley for solving those parts of the theorem that he was not capable of doing himself. There are many examples in mathematics where two share the work and yet one receives the recognition. In some cases, this may be disputed in private, but there are many where one partner is content for the other to be known as the sole originator of the work."

Edward realised that the difference between the dates of the letter and the paper suggested that such collaboration did not take place. Grey had obviously completed the work well before he had met Robert. But now that McDiarmid had brought the authenticity of the letters into doubt, he did not feel that he could use this as an argument.

"Do not the letters refer to Grey's reluctance to publish the work, which attests to his characteristic of fear of public notoriety, even when that might be praise. The man obviously wanted to remain unknown, and it is entirely plausible that Grey, despite being a collaborator in the development of the theorem, gave the publication rights to Crossley. In conclusion, what I have said has given to you an outline or a mere impression of the difficulty that the evidence poses. It is therefore certainly not clear that a court would find against Mister Crossley."

Edward looked at Robert and said, "What does Mister Crossley say about the matter?"

Robert did not react and Sir Joseph continued. "I have advised Mister Crossley to reserve his position and remain silent. This is his right and from it you can draw no conclusions. What is clear is that the source of the allegations must be exposed and made to withdraw them, or we will be forced to take the person, or the organisation making them, to court."

The President's calm was suddenly disturbed. "Sir Joseph, let us not become litigious, for it would be inappropriate to take the Disciplinary Committee or the Society itself to court. No, we will not let this happen."

"Mister President, may I make a suggestion," replied the lawyer whose calm had never left him. "In view of the delicate balance of the legal arguments and the uncertainty of the outcome, I suggest that we keep this matter within these walls. Mister Crossley says nothing about innocence or guilt, but he will offer his resignation from the Society and he will hand back his Fellowship if that will be acceptable to the Society. The Society can then find some words to announce this in a way that is best for it."

Some members of the Committee were nodding their heads when Edward's fist hit the table. "No, this is not acceptable to the Society. Not only is it important to show to the world that this society will not tolerate deceit and theft, but it is important to put the true author of this work on the paper."

"I am sorry," replied the President, "but the world will know that we still have our standards. And I do not believe that it is appropriate for a new frontispiece to be put in the journal, nor an erratum concerning the author being published, either."

Edward was hurt. "But I promised Mercier that Grey's name would be attached to the theorem. This decision will kill him."

Edward looked at Robert. He was certain that he saw a momentary reaction. The President continued without noticing.

"Sir, it is better for the world to admire the Society, for the lead it takes in moving science forward. The theorem is out there, being used by many. Without Crossley, it may have died with Grey because he would not have published it himself. The Society has done the right thing and will continue so to do. The truth about what has happened, whatever happened, must not leave this room. And as for a promise made to a Frenchman - why, it is worth nothing!"

Edward knew that the outcome had already been determined. "Mister President, you can insult a Frenchman, but you cannot keep what has happened within this room. The newspapers have ways of finding out about such matters. Your possession of the letters themselves will not guarantee secrecy of this meeting. Legally they still belong to Mercier and he has asked me to return them."

Before the President had realised, Edward had swept up the documents into his briefcase. He continued.

"There is the notary in Paris, who can attest to these documents. If nothing happens to put Grey's name on the paper, Mercier may ask him to take action. And if the newspapers should discover what has happened, then the results cannot be calculated."

Sir Joseph put up his hand. "Perhaps I should remind the Baron that his visit to France was specifically forbidden by the President. If the newspapers were to discover what happened in this meeting, then I would expect the Discipline Committee to examine your behaviour and any censure would certainly make publication of your subsequent mathematical work somewhat difficult."

"Do you believe that what I do can compare to what Grey has done? And do you believe that I would not sacrifice my future for Grey's?"

"Brave words Mister Pennington. If I were you, I would not call down such scrutiny upon myself lightly. Are there not things in your life that you would like the public not to know? I repeat, do not call down that scrutiny upon yourself."

Edward remained silent for a moment. Suddenly the President intervened. "Gentlemen, we are agreed. Mister Crossley offers his resignation in writing to me, gives up his Fellowship and we say no more of what has happened."

§

The curtains had been drawn, the gas lamps had been lit and the Crossley-Sylvester family was thrown in upon themselves. The house was filled by their contentment. The fire in the drawing room danced merrily. Robert's son was already asleep. Caroline's eldest daughter was in the playroom upstairs, organising a parallel life to the one downstairs in her dolls house.

Robert sat in his big armchair to one side of the fire, and rather than sit opposite him his wife, Caroline, sat at his feet, with one arm over his knees.

"How was your meeting at the Royal Society, my dear? Did that rogue, the President, play up again?

"No, he was well behaved, my love. The outcome was as I expected."

They were watching Caroline's youngest daughter, stretched out on the rug, practice her sketching.

"Papa, look, the African lion looks sad because he is about to be shot by a hunter."

"That lion is very well portrayed," replied Robert, glad of the diversion. "He should indeed look sad. For he is destined to become a trophy on the wall of some stately home in England."

"Perhaps there is a noble Englishman, brought up in Africa, and friendly to the lions, hiding behind a rock," cried

Caroline. "He will leap forward and take the gun from the hunter and break it over his knee."

"Yes, Mama, yes. I will draw a rock. Look! There it is. Our lion is saved."

"My darling, how I wish we could solve problems that quickly" sighed Robert, and returned her drawing to her. "The world would be so simple."

Caroline rubbed his knee. "Oh, you are solemn tonight. It is getting late and the ladies are off to bed now." She ushered the girl from the room and turned back just before she closed the door. "Come up soon, my darling. I need you to help me get warm."

They smiled at each other. The door shut and Robert turned back to gaze into the dying fire. He contemplated who could have accused him. It was clear that the person, or persons, must have had some knowledge of his relationship with Grey. That, therefore, included the whole of his family. His accusers must also have had a grudge against him. It was not clear who that might be in his family, for his father was dead and he had treated the others with reasonableness. It could be Arthur, whom he blackmailed to get William his arithmometer contract from the Government. It could also be at least three others in London all, who had grievances with him.

He sighed, for his contemplation was getting him nowhere. Names kept going round in his head, as he grew tired. The warmth of the room and the wine he had had with his dinner made him drowsy. He closed his eyes.

Suddenly he was in the kitchen at home. He had just put the eggs down on the table. One egg rolled off, cracked open on the floor, and blood spilled out. His father had gone to get a ruler. He looked at William, who would not look back at him. He shouted, "Why me? Why me? Why not you, as well? Why could I not be like you? Why?" But William would not look at him. He turned away and found himself running down a dark corridor. He did not know why he was running, but his legs would not move fast enough. He ran past a dark figure and said, "Hello Arthur," but the figure disappeared. He ran on. The corridor sloped down and he accelerated. There were doors, poorly made and ill fitting. Behind one he heard the laughter of children, his own children. But, try as he would, the door would not open. Behind another, a voice said, "Robert, I need you to help me get warm." He could not recognise the voice; it was coarse and uneducated. Finally, he stopped running and he found himself at a table, sitting opposite Arthur, and unable to speak. Arthur's voice was deep and resonant. "Robert, you must be punished for what you have done. But no one should know. You must suffer alone. You will not have the your ladies with you, like our Lord. You must suffer alone, alone, alone!"

On the third *alone* he awoke, sweating and shaking. He stood up and grasped the back of the armchair to steady himself. He breathed deeply until he had regained control and stole quietly to his own bedroom, knowing that he could not be with his wife whilst this dream was still real to him. He lay awake and pondered its meaning throughout the night.

He rose early, freshened himself with cold water and dressed for breakfast. He was quiet as they ate and merely told her that he had some clients to see. He had told himself that it was his soul that had spoken to him in the dream, but it need not be obeyed. He should go about the business of earning his living by his wits and by his money, as if nothing had happened.

He had two unusual meetings in the following days and, although he had arranged both, he could not explain his motivation. The first was with the Chairman of the War Office Committee that he advised on. He found the man in his club lunching alone. He passed his table and then turned back as if he had just noticed him.

"Good afternoon, sir."

"Good afternoon to you, Robert. Do you wish to join me for lunch?"

"Unfortunately, I have another meeting in half an hour. There is one thing that I thought you should be aware of. I bumped into someone who knows the bankers in Northampton, who are supporting the Dyke arithmometer contract we have down there. Apparently the bankers are losing confidence in the company's likelihood of completing the machine. I will leave it with you, but you might recall that Arthur's machine was showing some promise, before we changed to the Northampton one. It might be prudent to move our support back to him. Perhaps we could say that Government policy had changed, something like that, so those in Northampton are not embarrassed. "

"Ah, thank you Robert for letting me know. Sometimes it is best to work with those you know."

"Indeed it is, sir."

Two days later, Robert came across Arthur along the Embankment, in much the same place and at the same time that he had met him before.

"Hello, Arthur."

"What! Oh, it is you, Crossley. You startled me."

"Do not worry, Arthur, for this time I am the bringer of good news. It seems that our arithmometer project might be running into some problems. You might get your machine dusted down, for the committee might be asking you for it sometime soon."

Arthur peered at him in the half dark. "Well, who said an old dog will learn no tricks? It is unusually decent of you to let me know, old boy. Is Northampton having difficulties?"

"No, not really, Arthur. I merely thought that it was about time to right old wrongs."

"Really! That is very decent of you. Look, if there is anything that you need in the future, you know where to come."

"I do indeed. I do indeed."

CHAPTER 23

The Letter

William and Phoebe were at breakfast, surrounded by their children and Rebecca.

"Well, are you going to open it? It is from London."

"All in good time, Phoebe, my love. I recognise the handwriting. It is from Henry Boyd, probably asking for a date to visit us and see how the machine is progressing. We will have good news for him this time."

William picked it up, tore it open and read. Suddenly his face lost its colour and his shoulders slumped.

"What ever is the matter, dear? You look like you have seen a ghost."

He swallowed and spoke slowly. "They no longer want the arithmometer. The Government policy has changed. They are cancelling the contract." A hush fell on the occupants of the room. William and his wife stared at each other for a moment. He pushed the letter into his pocket and stood up. "I must go and see Elijah and Horace, immediately."

He pulled on his coat and strode out. He arrived at Horace's house ten minutes later and briefed him in the hall. They then both walked to the shop. They locked themselves into Elijah's drawing room and Horace began.

"Let us establish what this means to us. I will shortly go to my solicitor and have him explain our recourse in the event of cancellation. However, I fear that it will be little, for the War Department are known for their hard contracts. I must then go to the bank, not to tell them the contents of the letter, but to request confirmation of the company accounts. We have a small surplus that will allow us to keep our staff in employment and to pay necessary bills for one or two months. I will then return here to discuss the possibilities. We need at least another twelve months to produce a machine in numbers. To convert the design for the shop and department store market would take us eighteen months. We all know these facts well. We must therefore first estimate how much support we would need from the banks before we could expect a substantial income. Then we should approach the banks to extend the loans we have already taken. It will be difficult but not impossible."

"Horace," said William, with some feeling, "I feel some responsibility for bringing you to this point, after your life of responsible investment. May I be permitted to come with you?"

"Do not feel that way, William, for we all went into the business with our eyes open. We would have regretted not taking our chance when we had it. Do not fear, for it is merely a challenge; it is not the end."

Within two hours, they were back with Elijah. The solicitor and the bank clerk confirmed Horace's estimates of their financial position. They had indeed enough for two months. The contract would pay them a severance payment that would keep them running for a further two months. To continue to profit, they would need support for over a year. Horace converted this into a number which, though they all knew approximately, to see it in pounds, shillings and pence, gave them grave concern. Elijah tried to cheer them. "At least our two companies are separate, and even if the arithmometer company is to be no more, the clock making business will carry on."

"Yes, Elijah, thank you for reminding us of that comfort," said Horace. They knew that each would feel the impact differently. For Horace it would be no more than an inconvenience, for through his careful investment of his wife's money he was a relatively wealthy man. Elijah and Hannah were both at an age when their bones told them that it was time that they should retire. They had put by enough to live as comfortably as they did now. William would take Elijah's place in the shop and would thus be modestly secure. But he would have lost in his own esteem and in those that he worked with. He was ambitious for his family and their future, and a loss like this would hurt him.

"I shall go away and plan a description of the business and its potential," said William taking the initiative. "I will then come back and we will combine it with your financial assessment."

Horace nodded his head, happy to see William thus engaged with a dogged enthusiasm. "Yes, let us do that."

§

"You have all seen Crossley's proposal and the letter from the War Department. Thomas, what do you think?"

Four men sat in a panelled room above the hallowed portal of Abrahams' Bank. The afternoon sun spilling in through the narrow windows lit up the Chairman, Jacob Abraham. Michael Abraham, his son, and the two partners, Thomas Crichton and Archibald Amberley sat opposite him.

Jacob had inherited the bank from his father, and he from his father before him. Jacob watched his son like a hawk.

Whilst Michael was a bright enough young man, mused Jacob, and he had been with him at the bank for nearly twenty years, he was still learning. Thomas and Archibald were his mainstays.

Thomas thought for a moment and then answered Jacob's question. "The letter must have shocked them. It was a damned strange thing. It seems that the Committee have been paying them and had commissioned work of an experimental nature. Even if the machine was not performing as they might have expected, surely they would have seen it through to the end, or got them to change it?"

"Sounds like the War Department, Tom," said Jacob. "All back to front. At least they could have thrown the infernal machines at the enemy. Might have helped in the Crimea if they had."

The absurdity of some of the tactics that had been used in that war still rankled and they all nodded. Thomas continued.

"And I heard a rumour that William's younger brother, Robert, is on the committee."

"What, the Royal Society brother?"

"Yes, that one."

"My god. Little good it did them then," snorted the Chairman.

"But it comes as something of a blow, Jacob," said Amberley, "The Crossley account has been good for us, as it has for them,"

"I know that Archibald," Jacob agreed, "but they are asking for a lot. Michael, what do you think of the commercial prospects for these machines?"

The middle aged man straightened. "Well now, to tell you the truth, I could not fully understand the military application but in stores and shops, I can. How often have you gone in to buy some cartridges for your shotgun or two yards of muslin with your wife?" The others smiled at his little joke, "And the young thing behind the counter could not tell you how much they cost, without getting sir from behind a door. I have seen the machines that the Crossleys are making. They are big, but they could make them the size of a suitcase. They would sit nicely on the counter of any respectable store. We could even reduce the staff numbers here at the bank with such machines."

"He has a point, Jacob," said Crichton. "Even if we do not want them, if our competitors have them, then so must we."

Jacob nodded his head sternly. "You are all of you right. We are staring the future in the face, even if we do not like it." He looked around as if to indicate than he was about to conclude the discussion. "Now, we took Crossley's money when it was offered. But I will not give him any of ours when he asks for it, for the man is the son of that old bugger Jeremiah Crossley. Like father, like son, I say. He will not have a penny of mine!"

§

Horace Dyke was a Northampton man. His parents owned a prosperous clothing shop in a fashionable little street, just off the Market Square, catering for the well off section of the town. He was a bright boy, who got a scholarship to Magdalene College at Oxford. At a College Ball, he met Violet Mary Spinney and they got on well enough, although theirs was never an overstated relationship. They respected each other's conservative views of life. To him, her money was a means of preserving his middle class way of life. To her, he was learned, cultured and was sensible enough not to squander her inheritance on drink, gambling or other forms of licentious activity, too disgusting to give respect by naming them. Her parents were sufficiently impressed with his manners and his degree to overlook his background in trade, for their daughter was endowed with neither looks nor vivacity sufficient to attract a catch from the upper classes, which would have been their preference

Violet Dyke's conservative inclinations could be deduced from her belief in the superiority of the British and of the British Empire. She did not believe in the education of workers, nor in church schools, or in the proliferation of Academies in the town. She was vaguely aware of the publication of *The Origin of Species*, but believed that the subsequent discussion was somewhat absurd.

She was not overtly political. Her views had been formed by the slow osmosis of philosophy from family, friends, and church. She could not easily say why she believed such things as she did, but when they were expressed to her she knew they were right. She did not care to read philosophy, as her husband did, nor the newspapers, for they contained too much politics and crime. She found Austen and other such progressive women novelists not to her taste. She would occasionally read Walter Scott, preferring an adventure story of knights and castles, where romance and social aspirations were kept in their proper places. She had as little consciousness of the rights of man, as she had of women's suffrage. The principle that the woman had the money and the man the energy to use it, was a sufficient meaning of life for her. And, of course, the incessant demands of the All Saints Church Ladies Society allowed her little time for entertainment. For her life was a busy one, which both exhausted her, but also insulated her from the dangerous and changing world outside her small circle.

When the bank turned down William Crossley's proposal for a loan, Horace went to his wife, as a last resort. For the first time in their married life, she refused him. Four months later, The Crossley and Dyke Arithmometer Company closed it doors.

§

Rebecca took the letter and the closure badly. Over the autumn, she lost her fighting spirit and would sit in a chair in the kitchen and brood silently. She was aware of some evil that was at work in her family that was beyond the normal activity of Beelzebub, whose operation she kept in check by long and fervent prayers asking Her Father in Heaven to cast the shield of His Spirit around them. Thoughts of the iron rod of discipline that her husband had used to rule the family perturbed her still; her meekness in allowing him to rule them with such a lack of compassion was a regret that she had carried ever since she had challenged him over Emily's request to attend Sunday School. Emily had become her dearest friend, but since her Academy had become her life she saw her less often. Sunday lunch was a family gathering, but sometimes her work drew her back to her school, despite the invocations of the Minister that

Sunday was a day of rest. She thought much about the visits of the two from London, the mathematician and the doctor. They were a strange pair; there was a connection between them that went beyond the similarity of their professional lives. They listened to the stories of the family with an attention that belied the knowledge necessary to give Robert an award. It seemed that they were seeking something else, some piece of knowledge about Robert and the Reverend Grey. There was no outcome, for there was no award and no explanation of their visits.

She sighed, and thought of her Robert. William would succeed, it was clear, but Robert had a fragility about him that had brought her closer to him in her concerns than her other children. He had a fear of what the world might do to him that he had covered up with his bravado. He so wanted to please his father by his mathematics and by his science, but he could never in the end do so. And yet the Reverend Grey had touched him. She could see the pleasure in his face when he returned from Upstone on a Sunday evening. And there was a long period, when he was struggling with something important. Two or three times she had seen the incomprehensible papers that her son was pouring over, written in the Reverend's hand she had assumed, and the other papers with the copying and the workings, in Robert's own hand. It was another language to her, and not just the equations and the Latin. There was a striving in his face, a joy that was mixed with an apprehension. And the joy when he announced his achievement to his father was alloyed with a fear that she could read, but Jeremiah could not.

The strange way that the Government contract had been obtained had puzzled her. She could not understand what

Robert did in London, although it was he who had seemed to bring it to William, as a gift or, perhaps, as a token for their previous closeness that was now a wide divide. And the manner of the ending of the contract had a mystery about it that bode ill. Robert was bound up in it, without doubt, and his father before him, living on in his son's head.

She could make nothing of these broodings, but they had their effect on her; for as winter came she took to her bed. She slowly lost her appetite and her will. In January, as a gentle fall of snow painted the town white to the delight of the children, she slipped away.

§

When Clara had interviewed Emily as part of their investigation for the Royal Society, the two had bonded and had been corresponding regularly for about half a year. Emily needed someone to share her frustrations with, whilst Clara had developed sympathies more akin to a second mother. It was therefore natural that Emily should write to Clara of the news of the death of her mother, for now Emily felt bereft and in need of a compassionate reader to whom she could open her heart. Clara naturally wanted to visit her and to attend the funeral. She immediately packed and found the times of trains the following morning. In that way she would arrive the day before the service and interment. She also sent a note around to Edward's club to let him know that she was going.

Edward met her on the platform.

"Why did you not ask me to join you on this journey?" Edward asked in an annoyed tone.

"I naturally assumed that as the investigation was over, you might have other more pressing matters to attend to. You have not communicated with me for over a month."

"I assumed that you did not wish to see me. I am here now because I want to go one last time to the place that has taken up so much of my thoughts."

"So I see."

Edward opened the carriage door and helped her in. After placing their luggage in the rack he sat down opposite her. He remembered the first journey they made to Northampton, when he sat opposite so he could admire her and explore her variety of expressions. This time he sat opposite her because he could not bear to sit close to her. She took up her book and he his newspaper and this is how they remained for a large portion of the journey.

Suddenly he threw his newspaper down. She looked up from her book.

"You are very quiet Edward. You have hardly uttered three words the whole journey."

"I have a mathematical problem that I cannot solve. You know that mathematics is my life and when I cannot do it, I feel like an imbecile, like a babe in arms who smiles sweetly at his mother, but who cannot even control his bowel movements."

"The picture you paint is enchanting. But I do not believe you."

"Damn it, Clara! How do you always know when I am lying? The annoyance of men is one of the triumphs of your gender. A plague on you all!"

"You are an insensitive brute and a bigot. I will have no more to do with you."

He glanced at her to confirm that she was merely playing with him. He saw something in the turn of her head that confirmed the fact. He was all the more infuriated. She was right that mathematics was not his problem; love was. He found their relationship deeply frustrating. He wanted her presence continually. He felt incomplete without her next to him. He knew that he could not have her, for her career and her husband who was not her husband continued to stand between them. He has spent the previous month trying not to think of her. He had mourned the death of his love for her, but he had not been able to lay it to rest. However he could not tell her. He said, "I am still angry with the President for dismissing our evidence."

Clara accepted this train of thought; talking about the Crossleys would take his mind off what ailed him and the time might pass in stimulating speculation. She said, "He did not dismiss it, for the meeting merely heard how difficult it might be to deduce that Robert plagiarised, when the evidence was clear. He merely made a judgment. He was offered Robert's Fellowship, and took it with both hands."

"Yet I feel a failure for not knowing what he would do."

"You did what was right. The responsibility lies with the President."

"But I know there is something more. There is something staring me in the face."

"The 7th sin?"

"Yes and no. Perhaps there is nothing in it. Perhaps Grey's wife was just confused. Mercier had no reaction to my question about it."

Clara nodded. "Indeed, there was nothing there."

"I am puzzled by the doctor. He seems out of place at Upstone. It is so poor; he could be earning much more in a town. He is not from the village, or these parts, by his accent. Why would he come to such a practice?"

"But why are you concerned with the doctor. What part does he play?"

"I do not know. It is as if part of my mind guides me through my conscious existence and another part is a maelstrom of thoughts that I have no control over. The past, yes, that other part of my mind is full of that, but also the present and the future, and some imagined things that I cannot make any sense of. It is like your dream that came from the same place within you. The doctor has come from that place. I have not dreamt about him, but I need to find out if he has a part in this mystery."

The tension between them had been broken. They were conversing without rancour. Edward told her of his plan to go to Upstone directly after the funeral and then talk to people in the town.

"Will you come?" he asked her.

"I am sorry, my dear. I hope to spend some time with Emily. She is so much looking forward to our time together."

"Very well. It is good that you are consoling her. It must be difficult for her to be at home when Robert is there."

The train pulled slowly into the station. Edward stepped down and was about to help Clara, when a young woman hurried up to him, calling his name at the top of her voice.

"Edward, Edward, my love, is it you?"

It was Lizzie Clements. She put her arms around his neck and kissed him.

"Lizzie, let me introduce you to Doctor Clara Cox. Clara is assisting me with my business in Northampton."

The two women stiffly exchanged pleasantries. Miss Clements said she must be somewhere else, apologised and hurried away. Clara dismounted from the train herself and did not exchange another word with Edward that evening.

CHAPTER 24

The Doctor's Secret

The morning of the funeral was cold and blustery, and the rain stung their faces as they walked from the hotel. The Methodist Church on Gold Street had a listless look that reflected their feelings. Edward and Clara entered and sat near the back. A quiet hymn tune came from the organ set discreetly to their left. The coffin, supported by two trestles, was in the aisle just in front of the platform. A small display of flowers lay on top. Occasional sobs could be heard. The five children sat on the front row, all now in their middle age. The uncles and aunts, with Mister and Mrs Dyke, were across the aisle. The congregation was drawn from the church, which had been the family's social life. Everyone stood up as the Minister entered. He led the service with little sympathy, as if he saw Rebecca through the lens of her husband. In his short sermon, he simply reminded those gathered of Rebecca's difficult life and her now glorious joining with her Redeemer.

At the end of the service, Clara sought out Emily, and the two of them disappeared through a door at the side of the church to make their arrangements for the afternoon. Edward did not intend to be present at the interment at the Wesleyan Burial Ground nor at the wake at the Crossley family house. He realised that his presence would be difficult for Robert and he did not want to increase the family's sorrow further.

The family was waiting at the door of the church to thank those who had braved the weather to give their last respects to Rebecca. Edward shook hands with Robert. There was a moment of silence in which they regarded each other coldly.

"Robert, let me offer my heart-felt condolences at your loss," said Edward.

"Thank you," replied Robert with an expressionless face. "She was a wonderful mother and a great support to me."

"Indeed. When do you travel back to London?" Edward knew that it was a strange question, for it had an unpleasant and unspoken suffix that said, tell me and I will avoid travelling at that time. But Edward had asked because he knew that there was unfinished work to be done with the gentleman in front of him.

"I leave the day after tomorrow. There are affairs that I must attend to with William."

Edward had that afternoon and the next day to complete his investigations. He nodded his head, turned and strode off to his first interview.

§

Edward watched the Reverend Cantwell leave the Vicarage, walk along the edge of the rutted road and turn into the small churchyard. He leaned down to uproot some weeds obscuring the few words on a gravestone. His hat fell off beside the stone revealing a tonsure of coarse grey hair.

Edward told his driver to wait as he stepped down from the carriage that he had hired to get him the few miles to Upstone. He walked across the road and entered the church.

St Thomas had but a single aisle with a table covered by a plain cross on a linen cloth at one end and a dozen pews on either side. The Reverend was taking a prayer book from his satchel and preparing to read the daily office. At the scrape of the door, he looked up, surmised that the well-dressed man was his visitor and hurried to meet him.

"Oh my dear, I am so sorry. I completely forgot that you were coming. My goodness, my, my."

"Reverend Cantwell, I am Edward Pennington. I wrote to you a few days ago."

They shook hands and Edward felt the calluses. This was no scholar. He probably helped the tenant farmers gather in the harvest and herd the sheep.

"Yes, I got your letter. But I know little of the things of which you spoke."

"I did not expect you to, Reverend."

"Of course, but I know of John Hardiman, who followed Reverend Grey as Vicar. John is one of my flock now. He lives in the same cottage that Arnold Grey and his wife occupied when he retired. Of course, one never retires and John helps me with visiting and the occasional service. He is a wonderful friend and colleague. But of course, he also knows nothing of the coming of the doctor. Arnold arranged all that. It must be nearly twenty years since the doctor arrived. As you rightly assumed, the Church Wardens are the only remaining link back to that time. Both are still alive, hale and hearty. Job said that he would wait for us at Tom's cottage. We can go there now."

Tom Heazell's cottage was at the other end of the village, right on the edge of the road. There were splashes of mud on the front wall thrown up by the passing carthorses. The village was on the busy road from the mills to the south and the town to the north. The door was at the back, and Edward had to push the overgrowth back to follow the Reverend down the side of the house.

Seeing Edward's clothes, the two old men tugged their forelocks when Edward entered. The Reverend noticed and spoke to them with a laugh. "This is Mister Pennington. He wants to pay his respects to you and to ask you about the doctor's appointment."

Tom Heazell sat in a chair with his leg propped up on a stool. He spoke slowly, as if putting the words in order was difficult for him. "I carn't get 'bout like I used to, but m' mind is still passable clear. I remember the Reverend Grey tellin' Job an' me that he were lookin' for a replacement when old Samuel Hobson passed away. The Reverend looked right put about over it."

Tom hesitated and looked at Job for inspiration. Job's face was half hidden behind enormous whiskers, but his voice was still strong. "Thas right. He said he was writin' to the doctors in town for names. Didn' get none for a long while. Good job it were summer; not so many gettin' ill. Then all of a sudden like, Doctor Packwood appears, and that's that. Reverend didn' says n' more about it."

"Did he say which doctors he wrote to? I have some names." He pulled his notebook from his pocket and read from it. "Poultney? Mawby? Vinnicombe? Drage?"

The two old men screwed their eyes up whilst they thought and shook their heads. Tom answered for them. "It were like Job says. The Reverend didn' tell us nothin' 'bout it at all."

It was getting dark when Edward reached town and the George Hotel. He met Clara in the lounge before dinner and sat with her as they ate. Few words were passed between them, just those sufficient to relay Edward's lack of progress and Clara's agreeable afternoon with Emily.

§

He did not meet her at breakfast, but read the note that she had left at the reception desk. She was going to accompany Emily to the Academy and would be there all day. He would see again her at dinner that evening.

Edward had appointments to see the doctors on his list that morning. Directly he had eaten, he hurried out and took a cab to St Giles Street. He could have walked from the hotel in five minutes, but used the cab to save him searching out the address. Doctor Daniel Poultney's practice occupied the ground floor of an elegant Georgian house. Edward assumed that the doctor and his family lived in the three floors above. He pulled the bell next to the polished brass nameplate and an elderly valet answered the door. As Edward entered he was reminded of his own house in London, but at the same time a feeling that he was in the wrong place overcame him; Packwood did not come from here. He was shown into a waiting room furnished with such chairs and a settee that the wealthy clientele might find comfortable. Five minutes later he was sitting opposite the doctor himself. He briefly explained his investigation.

"I understand." Poultney nodded his head with a tolerant air. "However, as you can tell from what you see about you, I only treat those who can afford my advice. I know Upstone thankfully just by its name. I do not remember any letter from the Vicar of that place and if I had received it,

I would have been unable to recommend any colleague of mine for such a position."

The doctor finished the sentence with emphasis and thence stared at Edward, silently telling him that the interview was at its end. Edward left the place, musing on the insolence that money and position breeds in a man, and pitied the doctor for his lack of humanity.

His mind slowly cleared as the cabbie drove him to the north of the town, to an area close to the army barracks and the boot factories. Doctor George Mawby's small clinic was on Grafton Street, nearly opposite St Andrew's Church. The sign outside had no pretensions and the front door was propped open. The waiting room was lined with benches; on one sat a poorly clothed mother with a small boy whose persistent cough made Edward feel uneasy, despite his sympathies for the working class. A moment later the doctor entered. Edward opened his mouth to address him, but the man turned to the woman. He led her and the boy through a door and in the space of two minutes the child's coughing had stopped and he skipped back out of the door sucking a sweet, followed by his mother. Edward heard his name called and opened the door. Like Doctor Poultney's consulting room, the walls were lined with shelves. Rather than expensive volumes of medical journals, the bare planks supported miscellaneous piles of papers, cardboard boxes and bottles of coloured water. The doctor's bowler hat and his umbrella were the only articles on the shelf behind the desk. Doctor Mawby sprang to his feet and shook Edward's hand with a smile on his face.

"Please excuse me for treating the boy before you, sir. There is nothing wrong with him, save for his aversion to attending school. However, to his credit he has developed a canny skill at acting, which might serve him well, if he can but find the right stage for it."

Edward introduced himself and recited the same reason for his visit that he had given to Doctor Poultney.

"Yes, that was a strange business indeed." Mawby had become serious. "I was just qualified and was working under Doctor Ebenezer Steadman at the Infirmary. I grew up in the town and both my family and Steadman's attended the Church in Gold Street. It was he who inspired me to become a doctor. I did not have the money at that time to set up my own practice, but that was not a difficulty, for I wanted to work amongst the poor. And the Infirmary was full of those. It was excellent experience, for I came face to face with all the diseases and injuries that plague the poor and I learned quickly. Dear Ebenezer said that I could make a career in the Infirmary, for I was as quick to see how to organise the treatments as I was to administer them. But that was not for me."

Edward's interest was aroused by the mention of Gold Street. "Did you know the Crossleys at the Methodist Church?"

"Oh, everyone knew them. Old Jeremiah became the Treasurer. I talked much to him, because the church helped me to buy this property for my clinic. He was rather serious and very precise with the money. But he had a wonderful family. The two eldest boys, William and Robert, were as good as Jeremiah was at mathematics. It is strange, is it not, that a proficiency in mathematics can be passed down from father to son. And now Robert has achieved great fame in London."

Edward had not told the Doctor that he was investigating Robert, but that he had been sent by the Church Commissioners to learn the background of Reverend Grey for a study that they were doing into ministry in the poorer villages. It was clear that Robert's loss of his fellowship had not become common knowledge, and respect for the Crossleys was still high.

"Returning to the Reverend Grey..."

"Ah, yes. Steadman received the letter from Grey and showed it to me. Although it would have involved a reduction in my salary, I was keen to live and work amongst the poor and I told Steadman so. Steadman heard nothing back from Grey for several weeks, so he suggested that I go out to Upstone and seek out the Reverend myself. I did so, and discovered that Grey had never received Steadman's letter. Whether Steadman forgot to send it or whether it was lost on its way, we will never know. When I told the Reverend of my experience in the Infirmary and of my desire to work in such a country practice, he seemed heartbroken. He shook my hand, hard and long, and told me that the position had already been offered and accepted by another. I asked him what brought on his sadness, but he would say no more."

"I am certain that you would have been well fitted for the position," replied Edward. "But you have a thriving clinic here, serving those that you have a heart for."

"Indeed I do, sir." Mawby laughed and looked at the shelf behind him. "But I am still wearing the same hat that I bought when I qualified. I am fortunate that my head has not grown since."

Edward's sympathy was so aroused by Mawby and his work that he promised himself that he would send Mawby an anonymous letter containing a donation to his clinic. Yet, Mawby had told him nothing that contributed directly to the mystery of the Upstone doctor, but only deepened it. Nevertheless, Edward left with the feeling that his instinct about the case was right.

§

Northampton Infirmary was a fine three-storied building. Edward entered the large porch and a board on the wall listing the donors and the staff arrested his gaze. There were three physicians, namely Steadman, Vinnicombe and Drage. Edward asked for the second of these and was directed down a corridor. The odour of carbolic acid and vomit assailed his nose.

Henry Vinnicombe was heavy jowled and rubicund. Edward imagined that he was partial to port or other drinks that dulled the mind to this environment. Unlike Doctor Mawby, he remained seated as Edward leaned over his desk to shake his hand. Nevertheless, Vinnicombe was pleasant enough. He listened to Edward's introduction, accepted his reasons for being there and then began his story.

"I got Grey's letter and thought nothing of it. Then, a day or two later, by a strange coincidence, my brother Charles wrote to me. His assistant had a desire to move to a new practice. I therefore wrote directly to Grey telling him of the man. Grey wrote to Charles, accepting his offer and all was arranged. I think the young man was called Packwood and he is still there, in Upstone."

Edward knew immediately that this was the witness he was looking for, but was not satisfied with his brief telling of what happened.

"It would help the study I am engaged upon, if you could fill in some of the background. For example, what was the reason that Packwood gave for wanting to move?"

"I did not speak to him."

"But did your brother suggest a reason in his letter to you?"

Vinnicombe paused and glanced out of the window. "The matter concerns a fellow physician. I feel an unease in the telling."

Edward replied in a reassuring tone. "My report will be confidential to the Commissioners. We are simply trying to understand the difficulties that a country parson faces. I hope the outcome will benefit all that work in those remote parishes."

"I understood that Grey was in a difficult position. Such medical positions are hard to fill, because young physicians can earn higher salaries in the towns. It would be seen as a backward step for any aspiring man. Grey obviously realised this, for his letter was written with a sense of fear and despondency; I could feel it in the words he used."

Edward nodded his head. "And Packwood?" he prompted.

"Packwood needed to leave my brother quickly, for he had become involved with a young lady, the wife of one of his patients."

"And was there any offspring?"

"One was imminent, according to Charles's letter."

"That is most unfortunate, for all concerned, including your brother."

Vinnicombe shrugged his shoulders. "Packwood moved very quickly and any unpleasantness for Charles was avoided. And Grey found his man, sooner than he could have imagined."

"Did Grey know about Packwood's liaison?"

"After Packwood arrived, Grey wrote to Charles for a testimonial. Charles felt obliged to tell him."

Having learned enough, Edward wanted to draw the conversation away from the doctor's misdemeanours. "The life of a country parson is indeed troubled. They lack money, they lack support and all the troubles of their parishioners are heaped upon their shoulders. Doctor, your information has been invaluable, as an illustration of what they face. I hope the Commissioners can find some way to ease their burdens."

Vinnicombe agreed. "Grey was a good man. He was almost too good to be caught in the middle of all of that trouble. I understand that his parishioners loved him."

"Yes, I think they did."

§

Edward had no need to visit the remaining names on his list, for he had the information that he was seeking. He took a cab to the Academy, shouting at the cab driver for haste as they went. The door was open and he ran in, opening doors and disturbing the classes until he found Clara in Emily's office on the second floor.

"Clara, I have it. You must come with me now. I have found the key to the whole mystery." He looked at Emily, who was staring at him with a look of surprise covering her despondency.

Clara rose and confronted him. "Can you not see that I am engaged in important discussions with Miss Crossley. How can you be so insensitive, with your crass behaviour."

In his excitement, Edward had forgotten their encounter with Miss Clements. "Ah. Forgive me, please, Miss Crossley and let me give you my sincerest condolences. However, it is of overwhelming importance that Doctor Cox and I complete our service to the Royal Society by visiting a person of much significance in Upstone." He walked over to Clara, put his hand under her elbow. "There is no time to be lost."

Emily picked up her handkerchief and pressed it to her mouth and nose as Edward and Clara left. They mounted the waiting cab and Edward shouted, "Upstone, as fast as you can!"

As they shot along the paved roads out of the town, Edward turned to Clara.

"My dear, I most sincerely apologise for many things. I am sorry for dallying with Miss Clements, when I should have been true to you. I am sorry for barging in on your most kindly support of Emily in her time of need. And I am sorry for taking you off in a cab with such primitive springs over some of the worse roads in England. By the time we pass Queen's Cross we will be hanging on for our lives."

Clara appraised him coolly and the look on her face suggested to Edward that she was considering whether she could forgive him for such a long list of indiscretions.

As she was about to forgive him for the poorly sprung cab, Edward continued. "Do not speak yet. Let me tell you what I have discovered and what we must do when we get to the village."

Clara was shaking as Edward gallantly helped her down from the cab outside the doctor's house. She sighed as her boots and the bottom of her dress immediately became covered in mud. Edward banged on the door and continued to do so, but there was no reply.

"Perhaps he is out treating a patient," said Clara. "He could be anywhere."

"No, not anywhere, my dear. I think I might know where he is."

They crossed the road and turned down a small track. The mud was awkward to avoid and Edward had to hold her hand at various points. She neither smiled at him nor thanked him. They reached the pair of cottages and Edward again knocked on the door. A woman with red cheeks and untidy hair eventually answered.

"I need to talk to the doctor," Edward said with a distracted air.

"The doctor is not here," the woman replied firmly.

"The vicar has been taken ill. I am a friend of his and was visiting him when he had a seizure. It is most urgent."

The woman stared at him and was silent for a moment. She then turned back into the cottage and mounted the stairs. Edward and Clara were left at the door for a minute or two. Finally the doctor descended, saying, "I was treating Mrs Wolcott. Now, what is this about?"

A strange look crossed his face as he recognised his visitor and Edward swore to himself that he saw the doctor's chin tremble.

"Please let us return to my house," the doctor stuttered, "where we can talk in a civilised manner."

They entered a small consulting room that also seemed to be his living room. There was a desk against the wall, two armchairs and a small circular table covered by a cheap linen cloth with embroidered edges. They sat around the table and were silent for a moment.

"I wish to talk to you about the death of Reverend Grey," said Edward.

"Come now, sir. That was a long time ago. I can barely remember what happened." The doctor's voice had a rather strained note about it.

"Let me help you remember," said Edward reasonably. "Before you came to Upstone, you were working as a young doctor under Charles Vinnicombe, a sterling man by all accounts. I have talked to his brother, Henry, who works in the Infirmary. You had a good position and a good career ahead of you."

The doctor was becoming uneasy. He loosened his collar. Edward continued.

"Now, what is interesting to me as part of the puzzle of the Reverend's death is why would you sacrifice such good prospects to take a position like this."

"I wanted experience of deprivation. I wanted a chance to help those who could not help themselves. I had a heart for the poor."

"I heard such words recently from a doctor in the town," replied Edward, "and I believed him. But I do not believe you, Doctor Packwood. The Reverend Grey knew why you came, because Charles Vinnicombe told him your circumstances in a letter of recommendation. And Henry Vinnicombe knew and he told me. Why can you not admit it? I think that you do have a heart for your patients and there are some that you love more than others. Why everyone in the village knows your partialities."

The doctor stared at the tablecloth and a silence fell upon them. Eventually his breathing slowed, for he had made his decision.

"The thought of my other child, so far away, still pains me. At least here I can see my boy regularly, although I can never declare him my own. My haste in moving was to save myself, yes, but also to help to preserve the good name of Charles, for I respected him greatly. And, yes, Mrs Wolcott's boy is my son." A smile escaped him as he said the words. "The need to hide all of this has weighed heavily on my shoulders all these years and blighted my life." His smile turned to a grimace

Edward had little sympathy for him. "No, it did not just blight your life, it had an effect on many about you. It is of this that we must now talk. Did Robert Crossley kill Reverend Grey?"

Clara's eyes widened and she put her hand to her mouth. The doctor was still.

"Yes," he said quietly. "He had some knowledge of medicine, of treatments and of new apparatus. I told him of the treatments that I was administering to the Reverend on the afternoon before he died. I think it was a Sunday, the day that the young man visited for his lesson. On the Monday morning, I was awoken very early by the news that Grey had died. I hurried to attend. Crossley took me upstairs and I examined the now cold body and the two vials of medicine next to the bed. One was empty. I stood up. He had come close and he whispered in my ear." The doctor shook his head as he remembered. "His voice was detached, as if it was coming from a distance, not from the man next to me. I will never forget it. He knew of my adultery, I know not how, but he threatened to expose me unless I destroyed the medicine and declared death by natural causes. I took fright and did as he said."

Edward laid his hand on the doctor's arm.

"You have done well," he said, "for the truth is a precious thing."

Packwood nodded weakly.

"But," Edward continued, "although we can never put right this wrong, we can bring the real culprit to justice. You must take your story to the police."

A look of fear flared in the doctor's face.

"It must be done, doctor, it must be done. We will accompany you there, now, for I wish to speak to the Inspector myself."

CHAPTER 25

The Confession

Edward and Clara remounted the cab when Packwood had procured a horse from his neighbour for the ride to town.

A little while on, Clara whispered to Edward, "Are you sure he will follow us?"

"Yes, my dear, I am sure, for he can do no other and, anyway, to refuse would not serve him well, with the two of us as witnesses to his own confession."

By the time they had arrived at the Police Station the sky had darkened. Edward bid Packwood wait outside whilst he talked to the Inspector. He and Clara entered the Inspector's stark office and related all they knew. The man was tall and gaunt, and listened attentively with his penetrating eyes firmly on Edward, assessing him. After a minute or two he began to nod his head in satisfaction. A moment later he called in the Sargeant and instructed him to bring the doctor in and interview him in another room.

After the Inspector had listened to the doctor for a few minutes, he understood the seriousness of what he had heard and wanted to arrest Robert as soon as possible. It took Edward no little cajoling to persuade him to allow the family to hear the evidence and Robert's explanation, before an arrest was made.

"Very well, Mister Pennington. I will give you no more than an hour in the house with the accused. I will be outside in my carriage. I will have men posted in the front and the back, in case he bolts. If he escapes, I will hold you responsible."

"Thank you, Inspector."

"But if you can get him to confess, sir, so much the better."

§

It was dark by the time that they arrived at the house. William opened the door to them. Inside was still decorated with black crepe and it reinforced Edward's foreboding. William led them into the drawing room. Robert was sitting next to the fire, but jumped to his feet when he saw Edward.

"Why are you here, Pennington?" snapped Robert. "We are still mourning the passing of our mother."

Robert was facing Edward as if readying himself to strike him.

"I wish to talk to you about the Reverend Grey," Edward replied firmly.

"What new falsehoods have you brought with you this time?" Robert stared at his accuser. "You were defeated at the Royal Society when Sir Joseph exposed the gross errors in your interpretation of those damned letters. Whatever it is now, you will be defeated, and our family will continue without a word against it."

Edward had no need to be defensive. "I think it was you who lost. You lost your Fellowship, if you remember."

William looked quizzically at Edward, for he had not yet heard this piece of news.

"Your innuendoes forced me to resign it, damn you."

"The Fellowship was a matter between you and the President."

Robert fell silent for a moment and appeared to accept his loss. But he was still defensive.

"Let us move on," he said. "I repeat, why are you here, Pennington?"

"Very well. May we sit down?"

William beckoned for Edward and Clara to take the settee, whilst he sat opposite Robert. Edward turned to William and began.

"Let me explain to you, William, for Robert is aware of what I am about to tell you. I have recently had discussions, witnessed by Doctor Cox, with Doctor Thomas Packwood, whom I think you may have met at the Reverend Grey's funeral some years ago. During these discussions, I learned the following facts about the Reverend's death. The doctor was treating him with two medicines: hawthorn extract for his heart and digitalis for his congestion. The two bottles holding these medicines were placed on the chair beside the patient's bed when the doctor left him on the afternoon of his death. Both were approximately three quarters full. When the doctor was called to examine the body the next morning he found that the bottle of digitalis was empty. Robert's own evidence indicates that he was the only person to attend to the Reverend that evening and night, as the wife was downstairs overcome by her fatigue. The implication is clear. Robert administered the digitalis to the old man, who did not survive."

Robert's face had become rigid. William was agitated, for he feared the worst. "But did not the doctor testify that the Reverend had died from natural causes?"

"Indeed he did," said Edward, his voice became louder, for he could no longer conceal his anger. "But at some point during the night, Grey, in his fevered state, had inadvertently spoken about the doctor's adultery with a patient's wife, which the doctor had previously admitted to the priest in the confessional. Grey also knew of a case of adultery that had caused the doctor to leave his previous practice and apply for the job in Upstone. When Robert realised that he could silence the doctor, he administered the whole of the bottle of digitalis to Grey. In the morning he blackmailed the doctor with the knowledge of his adultery. He had murdered his teacher and covered his crime."

William was speechless. Robert then began his defence.

"Edward, you have no direct evidence of such action on my part. The bottle could have been knocked over accidentally by myself or by the wife, or the wife could have poured it away by mistake. Arnold, bless him, could have died as the doctor said, by natural causes."

Robert's cool demeanour seemed to enrage Edward.

"If that were so, why did you blackmail the doctor, as he himself testifies?"

"Edward," said Robert raising his palms as if to placate his foe. "The doctor was emotionally unstable because of his secret. He could have said anything about the accident. I blackmailed him to protect myself from the possible outburst of his fevered mind."

"Damn you, Robert," shouted Edward. "That is nonsense and you know it. The lure of the Royal Society and a career based on your fame as a mathematician was too inviting to resist, even at the expense of the Reverend Grey."

After a moments silence, William finally found his voice. "Robert, Arnold was your teacher and your friend. He was more of a father to you than our father ever was. I envied you."

Robert considered this for a moment. "But he was old. He was nearly dead. He had nothing left to give the world, except his last few months. It was nothing compared to what I could do."

Edward was quiet, for the two brothers were brothers again, but for the last time. "You sacrificed your love for him, Robert. You did love him, did you not?"

"Yes, I loved him. Brother, you do not realise how much that decision cost me." He hesitated. "I murdered the man who had been the father I never had, the father that turned me from a boy into a man." Robert's voice, which had sounded repentant and sorrowful, became hurt and angry. "The man who taught me how to speak, after my own voice had been crushed out of me by the man who called himself my father."

With trembling, he said, "Yes. I poisoned him and stole his work."

§

A terrible silence filled the room. When he was ready, Edward rose and walked to the window, where he pulled back the curtain and looked out at the street.

"Robert, the Police Inspector is waiting in his carriage outside. I have asked him to wait until we have finished our conversations."

"Do not fear Edward, I will give myself to him when you tell me."

Edward considered his reply for a moment. He was astonished at Robert's composure, for his admission was the end of his dreams and, ultimately, of his life. Edward believed him, but still needed to understand him. He would invite him to explain himself to the family. He asked himself for whom was he doing such a thing: perhaps for the family, or for the President, or perhaps just for himself.

"William, would you ask the rest of the family to come in. Robert is about to explain himself and his actions."

William was incredulous, but did as he was bid. In a minute all had come in, Emily leading Patience by the hand, with Thomas following them. Phoebe came last and closed the door behind her. Fear was written on their faces. William had told them nothing, but they had read his face.

Edward resumed his seat and nodded at Robert to begin.

Robert was still engaged in his conversation with his brother. "William," he said, "we were so close, almost like we were twins. All those theorems we solved together at school. All the things we found together, like the coot's eggs. If you could not see them, I saw, and vice versa. Little did father know that we were working together, by exchanging a word, a phrase, the least little sign."

William's heart was being wrung dry, but Robert could not see it. He continued. "But then we drifted apart. Perhaps it was merely growing up. Perhaps it was just a natural process? But I needed something to fill the gap, the hole in me produced by not having you close to me. So, I found the Reverend and his work to fill that hole, and so maintained my upward progress."

Robert looked at William for agreement but, finding none, continued nonetheless.

"Why did I steal the theory from him? I did it because he was about to take it to his grave. By his prevarications, he had lost the energy to present it. Why, it would have put the course of mathematics back by who knows how long? Twenty years, a generation, two generations? Did not Newton delay English mathematics by a hundred years by his insistence on the pre-eminence of his own work over that of Leibniz, which is now adopted? So, in lecturing at the Royal Society, I have maintained the forward momentum of English mathematics, and perhaps the forward momentum all of mathematics all over the world. How have I done wrong there?"

"But you killed him," said William.

"Yes. I killed him," Robert replied as if it meant nothing. He then leaned forward in his chair as if to describe a mathematical theorem. "William, imagine that moment, if you will. I had endured years of struggling, of being beaten both physically and emotionally, the like of which would have broken many people. It was as if I was standing at a crossroads. The way ahead was straight, but would lead through years of further struggle, with no guarantee that I could ever achieve my destination. And remember how many times father had told us that we must go to university, so that we could lift our heads high amongst our fellow men. I saw before me a way to do that very thing. Arnold had told me in his sleep, of the doctor's adultery and of his child born out of wedlock, the seventh sin, as he called it. And there lay my future before me. A quiet, painless way of allowing the old man to meet his maker and a way of silencing the only one who would recognise what I had done. It would allow me realise all my ambitions. I had but a few hours to make the decision, after I realised the importance of what Arnold had told me in his sleep. Should I take my chance while it was available, or wait until he died naturally, with the possibility that, for whatever reason, I might be further thwarted? They were difficult hours. You know what I chose."

Emily shuddered and let out a stifled gasp. Robert continued his reasoning. "No, no, whatever you think, it was the right choice, because it was successful. It was the most successful thing you could ever imagine. People respected me and listened to me. I was able to do wonderful things for the family and for England."

Robert's eyes were lit with a zealous light that dazzled them for a moment, until it flared and went out as he looked around him. He looked grimly at Edward. "Until Pennington, that muck spreader, came here talking to you and exposing our family secrets." He shrugged. "Was it my fault that my father turned me into what I am?"

William nodded his head almost imperceptibly. Edward was not sure whether it was in agreement with Robert or the opposite.

Robert paused. "Our father did not love us," he said.

This time, William nodded clearly, and Edward knew that there was still some vestige of their brotherhood that remained.

"I think that he loved no one, not even himself," Robert continued. "You might think that all people love themselves, for selfishness is in all of us and is the sin that leads on to many others. But he did not and that fitted him ill for his life with those around him."

He paused again and then slowly said, "Rather he hated both himself and us. There were many times that he demonstrated his hatred for us and, by way of excuse, he called it discipline. But after a time I came to see that I could outwit him. Even in the matter of the coot's eggs, I found him wanting. When he tried to tutor me, I demonstrated that he could not teach. When we celebrated my lecture at the Royal Society, I induced him to break his vow of abstinence, the fool. And even in my choice of wife, I succeeded. I married a Jewess, for I knew that he abhorred them. It was I, only I, of all his children, who finally overcame him."

His face wore a mask of superiority as he considered what he had done. "And did I not do good, in getting our advanced machine into production, over the inferior one that my so-called colleague on the Ministry Committee was making? Was I not working for the good of the country and the Empire? Such men as him, with his secretive and dishonest dealings, need to be found out and defeated. The Chairman was helpless before them. I knew that the only way to deal with them was by their own methods. Where is the immorality in that, for did not right prevail in the end?"

Edward opened his mouth to talk about morality in public life, but Robert threw his arms wide and shouted, "I did it for you! I did it for our family. Why, for a while we were the most famous family in the town. Yes, and in all of England!"

The Inspector was called from his vigil outside and, apologising to the ladies, clapped his handcuffs on Robert's wrists and escorted the prisoner away.

§

The room was filled with weeping.

The women cried openly. Phoebe, Emily and Patience sobbed into their handkerchiefs. And Clara stared at Edward, tears rolling down her cheeks. Thomas stared passively, unable to look at his brother, shaking his head slowly as the anger filled him.

William's face was frozen, drained of all emotion. He was trying to understand what all of this meant. He knew that he wept inside for it would be the last time he would see Robert. He could not speak, because he was filled with the horror of what his brother had done. And yet, this horror was shot through with pathos, because once they were close. *'You were my brother,'* he said to himself, *'you were my Brother in Plato. Now it is as if you are my enemy.'* He suddenly felt a hole inside and his tears flowed. But, he knew that his brother was like a gangrenous limb that must be amputated from the family. He wept for his brother's lies, and for his calumny in trying to put the blame onto his father and the family's shoulders. He remembered his brother's words. *'I did it for you.'* William silently cursed his brother and then realised that his curse was but foolishness. Somehow he and the family would carry on.

§

Robert was sitting opposite the Inspector in his office. A constable was taking down his confession. Robert had described in intricate detail what he had done, even down to the effect of digitalis when taken in small doses and when taken in large amounts. He had welcomed the chance to have all of his actions committed to a document, which he assumed could help both the police and society in the future.

However, he did not stop talking when he had described the stealing of the theorem and the murder of the Reverend.

And what he said then made no sense to the constable and precious little to the Inspector.

"What I have done is to uncover one of Plato's forms, a mathematical object that exists in its own right, but not in the world as we know it, until it is brought across. Plato described the world in his Allegory of the Cave. Most of mankind dwells in the cave and see but shadows of real life. Outside is the true world, where perfection exists, illuminated by the glory of the sun. And if a cave dweller escaped to the real world and ventured back inside to release those captives, they would not believe him and, what is worse, they would kill him. I have journeyed outside the cave when I found the mathematical theory. What I did to escape the cave has very little significance compared to what I discovered in that perfect place. My stealing and my poisoning matter little; what is important is that I brought this theorem into the world for all to wonder at and for mathematicians to work with and climb to greater heights."

"Mathematics is not of my or any man's invention. All mathematics exists, even that which will be discovered in the future. It is waiting there in Plato's perfect place for men to discover, as I have done. And, in the bringing of it into the world, I have wrapped myself in transcendence for eternity. What I now have to suffer can never change that."

The following day, the Inspector sent copies of the confessions of both the doctor and Robert to the Treasury Solicitor's Department, for prosecution of the case against Robert. He thence remained in detention until the Assize Court was convened. It was the beginning of the end for Robert Crossley.

CHAPTER 26

Northampton Borough Gaol

Edward and Clara returned to the hotel and talked long into the night in his room. Both needed to calm themselves: Edward from the exultation of apprehending a murderer and Clara from the emotions she had spent in watching a family being destroyed. When they had exhausted what was in their hearts about the events of the day and a tired silence had fallen on them, Edward jumped up.

"I must send a letter to Edmonds. Although I will travel back tomorrow, my love, I should write it now and give it to the night porter to get it on the early train to London."

He sat at the desk and began to write. A moment later he sealed the letter and went downstairs to the reception to arrange for its delivery. Without knowing what she was doing, Clara rose and moved across the room. Her fingers touched the velvet of the seat back and she dreamed of Edward's back pressing against the velvet. Her feelings about him had been suspended on this tumultuous day and she knew not whether she loved him or hated him. Her memories of him, his boyish naivety and his tenderness, pulled her one way, whilst the vision of Miss Clements pulled her violently in the opposite direction. Perhaps the memory of that hated girl would fade, as the tide of time washed all things away.

She looked to the desk and remembered the letter he had just written. She had not recognised the name of Edmonds and let her eyes roam over the desk for a clue to his identity. She pulled a sheet from beneath a small pile and began reading. Her initial curiosity slowly turned to horror.

Who creeps at night and makes curtains twitch?
The old, the bold, the Professor Pox!
He makes his way to brothels dark, which
Will fete and sate. The wily old fox!

Now, the Ear is not the type of dandy who would frequent the bawdy houses of East London. No, the Ear is more enamoured of quiet evenings beside the fire, with a friend or two, possibly of the artistic persuasion, discussing the merits of the latest volume of poetry or a portrait of the great and good. It came, therefore, with some surprise, to find that the piece of doggerel printed above is circulating amongst the more prurient members of polite society. As a piece of serious poetry, it has some flaws and the obscure metre is barely kept intact. There is a coarseness that tells of dark alleys and danger, rather than the refined emotion of writers that have become our national treasures. However, the message in the lines is clear. Gentlemen who have been called upon by the esteemed Government to investigate public morals, and thus, to suggest legislation that will protect the weaker members of society, should not be tempted to combine pleasure with business!

She could hear Edward bounding up the staircase and hastily replaced the paper. She was beside the bed, hurriedly gathering her hat and coat when he entered.

"Ah, you are going. Parting is such sweet sorrow." He began to caress her shoulders. She pushed his hands away.

"I am sorry, Edward, I must go now. I must return tomorrow to the Crossleys to comfort them in their devastation. I will see you in London, perhaps."

With that ambiguous farewell she disappeared through their adjoining door. Edward heard the key turn. Clara ran to her bed, buried her head in the pillows and began to sob.

Clara had known that Edward was *The Ear at the Door* for some time. After Edward had read to her the Ear's column in the train on their first visit to Northampton, she had become acquainted with the wife of the Editor of the very same newspaper. They had gossiped about the Ear's identity at a meeting in a teashop on the Strand, and the wife had shown her a letter with an original draft of a column. They pretended to analyse the handwriting, although neither had any competence. However, the flourishes were unusual, as were the number sevens, for they were struck through with a small line midway down the upright, which the French did to avoid confusion with the number one, which they always wrote with an exaggerated serif at the top. Clara had re-examined Edward's letter of invitation to join his investigation, to find flourishes and the French seven.

Is life always like this? Clara asked herself in her turmoil. I have seen the hand of people working against me throughout my life, but I thought our love would make this small corner of my life different. I thought he cared for me as a kindred spirit and would not take advantage of me. And now I find this. How could he?

She changed into her nightdress and as sleep slowly overcame her, she resolved to take control of their relationship, as she had in all other aspects of her life.

§

It was with a heavy heart that the following morning Clara pulled the bell at the Crossley family home. She asked to see William, but was told by the maid that he had gone to work in the shop and that only the mistress was in. Clara reproved herself for such an elementary mistake. She asked to see Phoebe, who took her hand in hers and welcomed her in. They sat together in the drawing room as the morning sun streamed in warming the air between them. Clara offered her condolences and, fast on the death of William's mother, it immediately felt as if she was presuming the same fate for Robert. Again she was angry with herself for her clumsiness. Phoebe hardly noticed.

"I felt like a helpless bystander throughout the whole episode. It was a terrible, terrible story that unfolded last night, almost too terrible to contemplate. Of course, I knew that all was not well between William and his brother, and their father. William told me what had gone on; the beatings and the cruelty that was poured out on their emotions. And yet William always seemed to be able to rise above it, because he had an inner strength. But I never realised that Robert had been so broken and twisted by it all that he never truly became himself."

She paused, as if possessed by a mother's unfathomable love for an errant child. Clara wanted her to talk it out, so she said nothing.

"Perhaps Robert was just being himself when he did those terrible things. I do not know; nor will I ever know. Only The Lord himself knows and will judge him rightly."

"You did well in supporting William and the family."

"That may be; thank you. But I fear for them, for we have not heard the last of this matter."

Clara stared at her and was taken aback to realise what she should have realised herself. She turned the conversation back from terrors to come, to the past, for she could think of nothing more. "Did William ever suspect his brother?"

"They were brothers, were they not?" Phoebe spoke sharply and then regretted it. "I am sorry, Clara. I meant that they had a bond, a very close bond. You will say that such closeness would mean that the one would know what the other was doing. But William did not. I believed him when he said so. Robert deceived him during those days when William thought he was working on the theory. Of course Robert was just studying it, line by line so he could be questioned on it. Thereafter he was dazzled by the Royal Society and by the influence that he gathered about him."

Phoebe was calmer now and looked at her friend with frankness and acceptance. "And no one but the doctor knew of Robert's evil that night. William could never have imagined such a thing of his brother. But now he must face it. It will be hard for him, because he finds himself helping Robert to shoulder the responsibility."

Clara shook her head violently. "No, most certainly no! He should not do that."

Phoebe was unmoved. "It is not of his choosing. They are brothers and such bonds cannot be so easily broken. I hope that I can lessen his burden by being a support to him, so that the feelings he takes to his own grave are not too heavy."

This sombre picture of William's psyche sent a chill through Clara. She was lost for words. Phoebe continued.

"For myself, I gird myself by remembering William as he was, during our courtship and our marriage since. He is a fine man, Clara, honest and upstanding. Or rather, he *was* fine, but he is now like a bruised reed. However, he will be strong again when the emotions are blunted and the memories have faded. I pray for it every night, Clara, and the Lord will deliver to us those things that are needful."

Phoebe's visitor could say no more, for her mind had been filled with a pathos that overpowered all her reason. And Phoebe's last words could not be gainsaid.

With the words of this strong and faithful wife echoing in her ears, Clara made her way towards the Market Square and to Crossley and Dyke, Clock and Watchmakers. She had not noticed those she had passed along the way, or the dark clouds that were now covering the sky. Those around her saw an elegantly dressed woman, but little realised the errand of mercy that she was engaged upon.

Mister Dyke called William to the shop. He then disappeared discreetly through the door to the workshop. William had told his senior partner of the previous evening's events. Horace was still considering the implications for the shop.

"Thank you, Doctor Cox, for talking to Phoebe. This morning I was so overcome with it all, that I was unable to listen to her concern for me. I hardly said a word to her before I left, and I regret that most sincerely."

"William, you can put any regrets out of your mind, for she is a strong woman who well appreciates the difficulties you face in coming to terms with this."

"Yes, you are right. So she is. But I am not sure that I ever will." William was halted by his own grief and a tear filled his eye. At that moment Hannah appeared.

"Elijah has asked me to take over the shop. You may sit in our front room, where you will not be disturbed."

They went upstairs. Clara sat quietly whilst William composed himself.

"Doctor Cox, you know all of our history. I need add no more. There will be more for Robert, for the law must take its course, and I fear the worst. But we will carry on; beneath our sorrow today is a strength that will carry us on tomorrow. The factory is closing soon..."

"Is there nothing to be done?" Clara interrupted him.

"No. Our chance has gone. The Ministry contract has been withdrawn and the bank will not support us any longer. It would take too much money for us to change the design to meet the needs of shops in the town squares of England."

Clara shook her head. "It seems that it has been taken from you so quickly."

"I think that that is the way such business is. To succeed, you must move quickly and when you fail, everyone deserts you as fast as they can. But we are not downhearted." He smiled a brave smile at her. "There is still the shop, which is still the finest watch and clockmaker in the town. There is still the Society that my father founded, which still has a good attendance. And Emily still runs a fine Academy for Young Ladies. As a family we have much to be thankful for."

Clara smiled back at his courage. She knew that he would nevertheless have moments of fear and continued self-questioning to endure, before peace descended on his heart.

§

Some time later, back in London, Edward picked up the newspapers that had been sent to him by Henry Grieves from Northampton and turned, in the first, to the page indicated by a scribbled note above the paper's crest.

Northampton Mercury
29th September 1859

ADMISSION OF MURDER
A Northampton man has given himself up to the Police for a murder that he has claimed to have committed twelve years ago. In this extraordinary case, we are led to understand that Robert Crossley has admitted to the murder of the Reverend Arnold Grey. The Reverend Grey was the Vicar of the Parish of Upstone and at the time of his death was tutoring Mister Crossley for the Cambridge Entrance Examination. The doctor treating the Reverend believed that death was due to natural causes. However, in an interview with the Police, he has noted that the administration of a large dose of digitalis, with which he was treating consumption and a weak heart, would have produced the same fatal symptoms. Crossley delivered himself to the Police two days ago and

*has since been remanded in the Northampton Borough
Gaol, awaiting the next Quarterly Session of the Assizes. It
is also understood that the doctor attached to the gaol has
examined Mister Crossley. After his examination, Dr. D.
Drage declared that the prisoner is physically hale, but had
an unbalanced mind. The accused continues to vigorously
proclaim his guilt.*

Edward noted with some satisfaction that Grey's doctor
had not been drawn into the mire. His discussion with the
Police Inspector on this point had obviously been acted
upon. He then read the following:-

Northampton Mercury
8th November 1859

TRIAL OF A MURDERER
*The trial of Mister Robert Crossley has taken place at the
County Assizes this week. Due to the interest that the case
has aroused, the Court and the adjoining Avenues have been
crowded. Mister Crossley is accused of the wilful murder,
for material gain, of the Rev. A. Grey, Vicar of Upstone,
on the night of the 8th of June 1845. **Mister James Lewis**,
for the Prosecution, described Crossley as a deceitful and
accomplished thief and liar, in that he stole a mathematical
proof that the Vicar had been working on for many years. He
passed the proof off as his own, and by such means gained
admission to a Fellowship of the Royal Society, a prestigious
London society for the promotion of science. His admission
allowed him to develop a career as an advisor on scientific
matters to Her Majesty's Government and many other*

*companies. His motives were thus avaricious and clearly marked him down as a murderer and danger to society. In mitigation, his defence counsel, **Mister Talbot Blake,** reminded the Court of the assessment given by the Prison Doctor of the defendant's state of mind, and, although the court could not ignore his assertion of his own guilt, this assertion was based on his mental unbalance. After due process, which was the shortest that our Court reporter had experienced in his long career, the Jury found the defendant guilty of murder. The court was witness to a demonstration of the accused's mentality when, upon being invited by **Judge Jasper Creighton** to make a final declaration before sentence was passed, Mister Crossley spoke for twenty five minutes on the philosophy of Plato and on his discovery of the proof (which he stole from the Vicar) in Plato's perfect place. The arguments that were made need not be repeated here, as it was clear that they were not material to those legal arguments put forward by the Learned Counsel. Furthermore, our Court reporter does not doubt that those present understood little of what Crossley said, but probably came to the conclusion that the Prison Doctor was right in declaring that the defendant was not in his right mind. The Judge was not moved by the declaration of the defendant for, after donning his black cap, sentenced him to be hung by the neck until he was dead for his most heinous crime. Amidst angry cries agreeing with the judge from some Upstone villagers that knew the Reverend, the prisoner was led away to await his sentence at Northampton Borough Gaol.*

Another paper was folded in with that of the 8th of November and Edward now turned to it.

Northampton Mercury
22ⁿᵈ November 1859

MURDERER HANGED

Yesterday, in the courtyard at Northampton Borough Gaol, the sentence of hanging was carried out upon Mister Robert Crossley, who had been found guilty of the murder of the Reverend Arnold Grey on the night of the 8th of June 1845. Our Court reporter was amongst a small group of townspeople who had been invited to be present at the hanging. The moment was swift and uneventful, due to the fine skill exercised by the Southern Counties hangman.

Although it has been discussed previously, it bears being said again, for letters may well be written on this matter. Public hangings are not beneficial to the spiritual health of society and, whilst all due ceremony and respect must be observed in the act, it is right that it takes place within the compass of Her Majesty's Prison. Those amongst us old enough to have witnessed the last public hanging on Northampton Town Racecourse, not thirty years ago, will remember the furore that was generated by the crowds eager to witness the spectacle. It was by no means the solemn and serious event that was witnessed by our reporter yesterday.

Edward pursed his lips and sighed. The death of this man, he pondered, whatever he had done, was indeed a serious moment for all.

§

Horace Dyke could not convince his wife otherwise. They sat, after a solemn and subdued dinner, in their drawing room, in front of the fire. They were talking about what many other wives and husbands were talking about: whether it was respectable for them to have any association with the name of Crossley.

"My dear Horace, the ladies hold no grudge or ill-feeling against the family. Indeed, it is not personal, for it is understood that it was Robert alone who thus conspired and acted, and he is no more. No, it is a matter of principle."

She did not say what principle was involved and Horace knew better than to ask her. All he saw was their profitable investment on the shop slipping through his hands and the end to his agreeable and undemanding occupation therein.

"Violet, perhaps we could rename the shop *Dyke's Watch and Clockmaker*?"

"No, my dear!" Since her refusal to lend money to support the factory when the Ministry contract was terminated, her attitudes about many things had hardened. This last, awful event had vindicated her and she would brook no argument. She knew that they could live perfectly well without the income from the shop in the Square. They had other income and Horace could find her some other investments, which would be more agreeable to her.

With a sad heart, Horace told firstly Elijah and then William, of his wife's decision. Elijah's face could not conceal the sadness that he felt and, although he shrugged his shoulders and said that it was time he retired, he felt for William and his family who depended on the business for their future. William heard Horace out without question or protest, for Horace could see that the death of his brother had silenced something inside him. When Horace had finished, William took him by the hand.

"Horace, you have become a good friend to Phoebe and I. Do not feel downhearted for we will succeed whatever happens. We both saw that our time in the town was coming to an end." He shook his head and a rueful smile crossed his face. "The town where we were both born and grew up, and met and got married. But we still have each other and our children, bless them. No, we have talked about what to do, Horace." William took a breath and straightened his bent back. "We will take ourselves and find a new place for us all in London or Birmingham, where my skills can be put to good work. You wait, Horace. Why, in six months, or a year at most, we will be well settled again."

With a tear in his eye, Horace smiled at the young man in front of him and clapped him on the shoulder.

"Yes, I believe you, William. Let me write to some of our suppliers for you. I think that between the two of us we can find you a go-ahead place that would welcome your energy."

It did not take Horace long to find him a position and, in a couple of months, William and his family were gone.

Before he went, William could find no one to take on the Society for Scientific Experiment and Mathematics that his father had started with the help of Gold Street Methodist Church, and it had to close its doors just before Christmas.

Emily worked on at the Academy. But one by one, as word spread about the Crossley name, parents withdrew their children. The following summer the Academy too, closed its doors and Emily retreated to the family home. She was not too old to find a husband to support her, she said to herself, for she knew that she would never leave the town and employment was no longer open to her. Patience had married and moved out of the house. Emily knew that her sister was glad to change her name, and to begin a new life as a Johnson. Thomas remained with Emily and helped her keep her sanity. After his apprenticeship in the shop had ceased, he had got a lowly job in a shoe factory. He got some jibes about his brother, but his thick skin enabled him to smile, to shrug his shoulders and to carry on.

§

"Clara, I have come to see you to pass on the news that Robert has been executed. His Counsel lodged no appeal, so his sentence was carried out with unusual speed. It was as if those concerned wished to wash their hands of the matter as soon as they could."

They were sitting in Clara's consulting room. Edward had written to her requesting a meeting to discuss the outcome of their work in the town. Clara had consented, for she wanted the formal setting to tell him that she intended to finish their relationship. But she was finding the words would not come easily to her, for from his pallor and his dark eye sockets, it was clear that he was not well.

"I know, Edward, for Emily has been writing to me regularly. Much misfortune has fallen on all of them as a result of Robert. William and Phoebe have had to move away to Birmingham, and Emily has had to close her Academy. It seems that the good people of Northampton no longer wish to speak their name."

"I had another meeting with Steyn," said Edward.

A look of alarm came over Clara's face, for the name filled her with dread.

"It was out of character, because he congratulated me. I did not appreciate his praise. He also seemed to have some sympathy for Caroline, Robert's wife. He told me that he had attended Robert's trial and seen her there. Robert did not see her, for his mind was elsewhere, but she stared at him for long periods imagining, as Steyn supposed, how fate had taken two husbands from her. It appears that she loved Robert."

Edward fell momentarily into a trance searching for some truth. At last he exclaimed, "Ah, yes. I have it. Steyn must also be a Jew and thus through Semitic ties, he has a concern for Caroline. He knew that Robert had initiated the formation of an organisation to foster military research through a group of Jewish businessmen, which contained Caroline's father. Steyn took great personal pride in persuading the group to turn their financial strength to other directions. The organisation was stillborn. The feeling that this whole matter has benefitted the Continental powers is growing within me and it gives me no comfort."

Clara shook her head. "Edward, these are deep matters that I would prefer not to dwell on. As is your work as the Ear at the Door."

Edward did not react, but gazed at her with a soulful look on his face. "Ah, you know that, do you? I am indeed the Ear. But you are wrong in assuming that I may wish to comment on Robert in my column. The Ear only comments on matters of morals."

Clara drew herself up. "And is my husband a matter of morals?"

Edward looked baffled for a moment. "Why do you say that?"

"I know you wrote a piece on him."

"Oh, that. I burnt it the very night that I wrote it. I thought it might come between us. I am heartily sorry that you saw it. It was crass and insensitive of me even to consider it." An infinite sadness seemed to invade him at that moment, for he felt that all his mistakes had lost him this dear woman. "I have given up writing the column. I intend to retire to my home to look after my estate and perhaps do a little more mathematics."

Clara was shocked. "You mean that you will leave London?"

"No, I will keep my house on, but I won't be in it very often. And whilst we are talking of mathematics, I noticed that the President has had an erratum printed in the Proceedings of the Royal Society. The erratum says that the work described in Robert's paper was incorrectly attributed, due to a printer's error. The President requests that all recipients of that issue return their copy, so that they can be sent a revised one. Of course not all will be returned, so Robert's name will remain forever associated with the work for some readers. The newspapers considered that the reason given for making the change was, shall we say, inaccurate and they made a meal of it. I admit to helping them with their insight, for the sake of our friend, Claude Mercier, although I knew it might further discomfort the Crossleys a little. I now hear that the President intends to stand down over the matter."

"Claude will be pleased that Greys's name will finally be on the work," said Clara.

Edward sighed. "Unfortunately, Claude died a few weeks before my letter reached him."

"Oh, no..." Clara put her hand over her mouth and bowed her head.

"Clara, the whole business has brought me low, as low as I was when Alice died. I cannot come to terms with what has happened. Not just to Claude, but to everyone. I have brought to light the stealing of one man's work by another. There is no value that can easily be placed on that, and hence no just punishment that can be measured out. I never imagined that I would bring into the harsh light of society's notice the taking of a man's life, nor that another's life would be taken in retribution. Is there no mitigation, no means of bringing the criminal back into the pail? The man whose life was taken was old; he had done what his Lord had commanded of him, with skill and good humour. There was not much left to take. But Robert had half his life ahead of him and that was taken from him. William's job has also been taken from him. If we are to believe Robert himself, England will have an inferior arithmometer for its armies. And Emily, dear woman, has lost her Academy. How are the scales of justice balanced by all of that?"

Clara stood up and, without understanding what was driving her, walked around the desk. She stood in front of him and, taking him by the wrists, pulled him up out of his chair and into her arms.

"Do not let the injustices of life perturb you." She whispered.

He looked into her eyes, seeking that which she could not give him. "And am I to lose you, as well, Clara?"

"No, I love you too much for that, Edward, my dear. But I have a husband. We can meet, but it will be when I allow it, and it must not come between my husband or my work, and I. Can you bear that?"

Author's Note

This book was inspired by the work of George Green, (1793-1841), a miller and mathematician who lived in Nottingham. His 'Essay on the Application of Mathematical Analysis to the Theories of Electricity and Magnetism' was published privately at his own expense in 1828 because he thought it would be presumptuous for an uneducated person to submit such a paper to a learned journal. After Green's death, the essay was rediscovered and brought to the notice of mathematicians and scientists by Lord Kelvin.

Despite his feelings of inadequacy in Latin and Greek, Green applied and was admitted, in 1832, to Gonville and Caius College Cambridge. He graduated in 1838 as 4th Wrangler (4th top of the cohort) after James Joseph Sylvester (1814-1897), who came 2nd. Whilst Sylvester's family is imagined, Augustus De Morgan (1806–1871) and Arthur Cayley (1821–1895) were famous mathematicians, working in London in the period in which the book is set. George Peacock (1791–1858) and William Whewell (1794–1866) were well known teachers of mathematics at Cambridge. Professor Laidmann and the characters in the Royal Society are imagined.

Doctor Clara Cox was inspired by Elizabeth Garrett Anderson (1836-1917), a much revered pioneer of women's rights, whose curriculum vitae is in many ways more incredible than Clara's.

The Northampton Town and County Grammar School was endowed by the town mayor, Thomas Chipsy, in 1541 and was located on West Street, on the site of the ruined Church of St Gregory, as described in the book. Whilst the current school has moved to an extensive site elsewhere, there are two wonderful examples of schools of the era preserved in the centre of the town, which served to inspire me further.

The Society for Experimental Science and Mathematics was inspired by numerous like-named local societies around the country. In the location of the book, the Northampton Philosophical Society was formed around 1743 and the Northamptonshire Natural History Society in 1876.

www.ingramcontent.com/pod-product-compliance
Lightning Source LLC
Chambersburg PA
CBHW032131190626
46814CB00005BA/1652